SOMETHING GLORIOUS

To Peter and Louis Carlino
with fond memories of good times.

Whit

By William W. Whitson

THE CHINESE HIGH COMMAND,
A HISTORY OF COMMUNIST MILITARY POLITICS, 1927-71

DOING BUSINESS WITH CHINA: AMERICA TRADE OPPORTUNITIES IN THE 1970'S

THE MILITARY AND POLITICAL POWER IN CHINA IN THE 1970'S

SOMETHING GLORIOUS

BOOK ONE

1894-1905

BORN FOR FLIGHT

WILLIAM. W. WHITSON

Cogent Publishing

Putnam Valley, New York

Cogent Publishing, a division of The Whitson Group, Inc.

3 Miller Road

Putnam Valley, NY 10579

Email: Cogent@aol.com

Published by Cogent Publishing, a Division of The Whitson Group, Inc., 3 Miller Road, Putnam Valley, NY 10579.

Manufactured in the United States of America

Library of Congress Cataloging-in-Publication Data is available on request

ISBN 0-925776-01-7

10 9 8 7 6 5 4 3 2 1

This book is dedicated to my father,
Colonel Wallace E. Whitson, USAF

"Love is the way we walk in gratitude."

Acknowledgments

For evaluations of different aspects of the story I challenged the patience of many friends. I am grateful to Dr. Marshall Heyman for his examination of character behavior for consistency; to Dr. Leonard Duhl for a different view; to Dr. Theresa Abrams for her scrutiny of David's precocious development; to Dr. Deborah Porter for her wisdom about both children and China; to Drs. David and Rebecca Grudermeyer for their professional assessment of John and Maggie Harrison as parents; to Dr. Marcia Greenleaf for her meticulous critique of the whole story; to Patrick Miller for his detailed reactions to both the story line and its rhythm; to Doug Latimer for his early editing; and to Colonel James Barnett for his fierce defense of technical details about aircraft engineering when others argued for ruthless cutting.

I owe a special debt to Veronica Whitson for her skillful editing of successive versions.

Above all, I am indebted to my muse, my wife, Judith Skutch Whitson, for her unfailing good humor and her focus on relationships as the novel matured.

Needless to say, none of those friends should be held accountable for the final version of the story.

Author's Note

So much of this story seems stranger than fiction that readers might wonder if I have stretched credulity beyond all reason. Perhaps most startling are the many similarities between our own decade of the nineties and the same decade a hundred years ago. It was also a time of high tech, including the Manly-Balzer radial engine and the competition for first flight; sensational press articles about UFO sightings across the entire country; small wars; fierce commercial expansion and competition; a popular passion for extra-sensory perception, competing with new and old religions, and a spirit of growing feminism challenging a male-dominated society.

For a detailed coverage of the whole era from 1895 to 1905, I drew on Dan Rather's superb version of Mark Sullivan's *Our Times* (1996, Scribner), Page Smith's scholarly *America Enters The World* (1985, McGraw Hill) and Walter Lord's *The Good Years* (1960, Harper). For a probing comparison of the two end-of-century decades, I used Brad Steiger's *A Road map of Time* (1975, Prentice-Hall), which makes a persuasive case for a hundred-year cycle subdivided into four twenty-five year "seasons."

For details on the general aviation scene, Sherwood Harris' *The First to Fly* (1991, McGraw-Hill) and Jack Carpenter's *Pendulum* (1992, Arsdalen, Bosch) are excellent. For more data on the Manly-Balzer engine, nothing is better than Robert B. Meyer Jr's definitive *Langley's Aero Engine of 1903* (1971, Smithsonian Air and Space Museum)

Most students of early aviation have put to rest the controversy between Gustave Whitehead and the Wright brothers. But the real possibility that Whitehead actually flew first reminds us that our era of industrial creativity, espionage and sabotage is not unique. For two persuasive studies of Gustave Whitehead, see Stella Randolph's *Before The Wrights Flew* (1966, G.P. Putnam's Sons) and *Lost Flights of Gustave Whitehead* (1937, Places, Inc.). For a fascinating insight into the

Wright brothers' inventive process, nothing is better than Peter L. Jakab's *Visions Of a Flying Machine* (1990, Smithsonian Institution Press).

As for the sighting of mythic airships over San Francisco and the rest of the country in 1896, see Daniel Cohen's excellent *The Great Airship Mystery* (1981, Dodd, Mead & Co.). In the current context of UFO's and aliens, I leave it to the reader to decide if they were fact or fiction.

Some people may be offended at David Harrison's precocity and psychism. In my own defense, I can only say that I have drawn all of David's strange experiences from the lives of either personal friends or historic figures like Eileen Garrett, whose two memoirs have guided me: *Adventures in the Supernormal* (1969) and *Many Voices; The Autobiography of a Medium* (1968, G.P. Putnam's Sons). In addition to the contemporary Proceedings of the British Society for Psychical Research and *Borderlands, Volumes I & II, 1894-95* (1894-5, edited by W.T. Stead in London), I used the past twenty years of records of the Institute of Noetic Sciences, the 16 definitive volumes edited by Rhea A. White called *Exceptional Human Experience* (published by the Exceptional Human Experience Network) and Dean Radin's superb overview of the entire field, *The Conscious Universe* (1997, Harper).

PRINCIPAL CHARACTERS

(In alphabetical order)

FICTIONAL

EDWARD AMBLER, M.D.	PHYSICIAN IN CARMEL; CLASS OF 1882, HARVARD
GERALD ASHLEY	ASSISTANT TO J.P. MORGAN IN NEW YORK CITY
RAMON CISNEROS	FOREMAN OF THE HARRISON RANCH IN CARMEL, CA
JAIME CISNEROS	RAMON'S OLDER SON
JUAN CISNEROS	RAMON'S YOUNGEST SON
MICHAEL COYLE	A TAMMANY "CHIEFTAIN" IN NEW YORK CITY
EZEKIAL "ZEKE" HARNER	PETTY CROOK AND ENTREPRENEUR
JOHN HARRISON	ENGINEER, CLASS OF 1894, BERKELEY
MAGGIE HARRISON	MUSICIAN, CLASS OF 1894, MILLS COLLEGE
DAVID HARRISON	BORN 1895, SON OF JOHN AND MAGGIE
LIN T'AI-CHI	CH'I-GUNG MASTER FROM SHANGHAI
LIN MEI-YIN	LIN T'AI-CHI'S NIECE; BORN 1895
JULIE SIMMONS	SCHOOL TEACHER IN CARMEL, CA
LILY WANG	PHILOSOPHER, CLASS OF 1894, MILLS COLLEGE
LARRY WANG	SHANGHAI BUSINESSMAN; LILY'S FATHER

HISTORICAL

IVY BALDWIN	BALLOONIST
TOM BALDWIN	BALLOONIST
STEPHEN BALZER	NEW YORK ENGINE DESIGNER
GLENN CURTISS	BICYCLE MANUFACTURER IN HAMMONDSPORT, NY
"MONK" EASTMAN	NEW YORK CRIMINAL
PAUL KELLY	NEW YORK CRIMINAL
SAMUEL LANGLEY	DIRECTOR, SMITHSONIAN INSTITUTION
CHARLES MANLY	ASSISTANT TO LANGLEY
THEODORE ROOSEVELT	ASST. SECRETARY OF THE NAVY; PRESIDENT
GUSTAVE WHITEHEAD	AIRCRAFT DESIGNER IN BRIDGEPORT, CONNECTICUT
ORVILLE & WILBUR WRIGHT	BICYCLE MANUFACTURERS IN DAYTON, OHIO

PROLOGUE

POINT LOBOS
NEW YEAR'S DAY, 1900

Four-year old Davey Harrison could not have explained how it happened.

At one moment, pleased with his new, blue denim cowboy outfit, he was on the ground, safely enclosed by his father's legs in scuffed leather riding boots. Standing nearby, his mother, Maggie, was a reassuring image of grace, her hair gleaming like burnished copper, her tall, slender figure willowy in a simple white shirtwaist tucked into an ankle-length, gray wool riding skirt. From his position at the edge of a cliff, high above Cypress Cove, Davey could see Monterey cypresses dancing in the soft westerlies. He closed his eyes to let his other senses drown in the mystical beauty of his familiar world: the soothing balm of noonday sunlight on his face; astringent air with its heady aroma of ocean brine and eucalyptus; the call of sea-lions; the whisper of wind through scented pines and the crash of ocean surf against the rocks far below. He felt that ineffable peace reserved for children who do not know that they are separate from all nature. When he opened his eyes, he saw a huge eagle soaring on an updraft. The eagle's effortless grace inspired a sense of wonder and envy. *How I'd like to see what he sees. I wonder if he would give me a ride?*

And then it happened. Suddenly, like a camera that has switched to wide-angle, his awareness abruptly expanded far beyond the familiar. With a joyous smile on his face, he instantly surrendered to a game that he loved more than any other: the Becoming Game.

For the rest of his life, Davey would never know whether he had taught the Becoming Game to himself or had learned it from his mother. But he would always associate it with his mother's compassion and love. When he was barely two years old, he had first tried "becoming" flowers and had been delighted to hear them sing, "We love you too!" Now, nearly five years old, he could communicate with trees, his dog Poochie, his pony, Su-Su, cattle and horses and other flora and fauna on his parents' Carmel Valley ranch. His had become a world of warm, personal friends, bonded by a feeling that defied easy description. "Oceanic" was what his mother called his illusion of identity with nature.

Whatever that meant....

But never before had he tried to become a splendid bird like this eagle. He had simply watched the eagle circling upward. For only an instant, the lense of his mind had turned inward, searching for communion with the bird. And then he felt once again the exalted thrill he loved the most—a kind of waking dream of flying. It was his favorite form of play and entertainment. Fantasy or not, from the first time he had taught his mind to empathize with small birds, he enjoyed a sense of actual flight. It was so realistic that he felt transported out of his body: suspended at the scene but not in it. Now, he eagerly waited for the unfolding of his inner motion picture. The process was a familiar one; only its direction held him in quivering anticipation. In such a state, he had discovered that he didn't have to make hard decisions. He must simply wait for a benign force of overwhelming authority to guide him through a swirling mist of disorientation to some new adventure of the mind.

As focus gradually emerged from his confusion, sight was the first sense to become fully functional. Hearing, touch, taste and smell remained dormant. But that didn't perturb him. The momentary absence of normal sensory signals was a familiar introduction to the Game. He knew he would soon feel the wind in his face, the caress of cool air. He would then experience flight high above the distant Monterey Peninsula to the north.

And there it was! He quickly discerned the ridge line of the Aguajito and the single dirt road that connected Monterey to Carmel. He seemed to be flying about a hundred feet above Jack's Peak. Two people were waving to him. Why, it was Poppa and Doctor Ambler! How had Poppa shifted five miles from Point Lobos to Jack's Peak so quickly? Although the angle of the sun was still at a noontime high, what had been a clear sky had become canyons of towering cumulus clouds.

With the return of his tactile sense, Davey suddenly felt pressure against his stomach, a sensation that forced him to shift his focus from the distance to his immediate surroundings. A glance to the right shocked him to an awareness that he was lying down on a machine, a wing over his head. But how could an eagle turn into a machine? Could this be one of those airships from stories his mother had read to him in *Frank Reade, Jr, and His Airship?* Momma had said those airships weren't real; they were just stories. But maybe she was wrong. Doc Ambler *must* know more than Momma 'cause Doc was a *Doctor*. Doc Ambler had said that thousands of people had seen cigar-shaped airships across the whole country three years ago.

But further scrutiny persuaded Davey that this machine couldn't look like a cigar. It reminded him more of a kite, bobbing on the wind. The unfamiliar word, "biplane," formed in his mind as he examined its bottom and top wings. Their filmy covering was so thin that he could see through them. About eight feet in front of him was a projection of two smaller wings. How did he know that he could use a lever to change their angle and direct the nose of the machine up or down? And how did he know that he could use his feet to make the machine bank right or left? What fun! He practiced minute adjustments until the strangest feeling began to grow in his mind. He no longer felt separate from the machine. Was the machine part of him? Or had the machine taken possession of him? Nothing suggested a clear answer; but he liked the feeling very much. Unlike his earlier flying dreams, when he moved naturally but never knew how, now he understood the mechanism with which he could control his flight.

Suddenly he felt a puff of wind that lifted the right wings skyward and sent the left side earthward. With all his strength, he tried to regain level flight; but some force restrained his ability to lower the right wings or raise the nose. Helplessly he felt the machine lose altitude and aim itself directly at an oak tree a hundred yards ahead.

"Davey! Davey! Wake up! It's all right.... You're safe! It's only a dream." Maggie Harrison rushed to Davey's side and wrapped her arms around his small body lest he squirm free from John's embrace and fall off the cliff. While Davey had watched the eagle, she had noted the vigilant expression on her son's face. When it changed to an immobile, almost lifeless stare, she knew instantly that he was absorbed in fantasy. She had learned from past experience that his wooden demeanor was a symptom of a "Davey Dream."

Davey could see his mother's anxious face hovering above him as well as the eagle that had triggered his fantasy. Its flight path seemed to be an effortless ascent on a helix of updrafts from the ocean far below. Frustrated and fully awakened from his dream, David released a flood of hysterical tears, his sobs interspersed with gasps for air. "I was flying...! But I was about to hit a tree. I couldn't make the machine go up."

Maggie gently wiped his brow. "How did it feel, Davey?"

For a long moment, Davey stared at her, his eyes turned inward to recapture the experience. Before Maggie could shake him to prevent such a return, Davey suddenly smiled brightly. "It was a daisy, Momma! It was the best I've ever had. I loved it!"

"Madre de Dios, Maggie!" John Harrison exploded. "What's he talkin' about? I thought we'd settled that nonsense." John's "California southern" accent, the heritage of Virginia forebears, converted "I" into "Ah."

Maggie bristled. She had been struggling with John's disapproval of Davey's "inner listening" ever since he had returned from his year-long absence. How much longer could she tolerate John's fears about Davey's rich inner life? For the past six months, she had restrained her desire to shout, "Oh for God's sake, John, give Davey some time to grow up!" She had lost count of the times that a tearful Davey had asked her why Poppa seemed so angry all the time. She wiped Davey's eyes and held him gently. How could she answer her husband? "He fell asleep and just had a bad dream. Are you all right now, Davey?"

"That eagle's hungry, Momma," Davey murmured to his mother.

"How can you tell?" Maggie thought she already knew the answer. But she wanted her son to acknowledge his feelings.

"I heered him, Momma."

John Harrison refused to credit that reply. He looked up and watched the bird. "Of course he's hungry! Eagles are scavengers; they're coyotes of the sky. He'll find his next victim pretty soon."

Davey smiled at his father. "Poppa, I know you'll call it one of my..." He searched for John's favorite word. "...fantasies; but the eagle can sing to me; he wants us to feed him."

Maggie's heart swelled with pride in Davey's sense of the eagle's "song." "John, take some of our salmon to the edge of the cliff. Then come back and we'll wait to see what he does."

"That's silly!" John objected. "A wild eagle won't eat cooked salmon."

"Maybe this one is a gourmand," Maggie replied.

John tried to show amusement at this repetition of a game grown familiar, a game of Maggie's pretense that Davey could "hear" the soundless songs of trees and animals. During the past six months, he had struggled with a sense of exclusion, a festering resentment and a gnawing fear. Until today, he had consoled himself with the hope that his pragmatism must finally have driven away the demons in Davey's mind. Now he wasn't so sure. He kneeled over the picnic basket and pulled out what was left of the large salmon that Ah Ying had prepared for this New Year's Day outing. He thought, *I must be crazy to indulge them in this fantasy. But it's Davey's day, the first day of the new century and anything goes! The eagle wouldn't dare come near us anyway.* He quickly placed the salmon at the edge of the cliff; then he returned to Maggie and Davey.

They watched the eagle with interest; it seemed to hesitate, to drift toward the Pacific. John glanced at Davey, fearing that his son would be disappointed at failure. To his astonishment, Davey's face was suffused with joyous expectation.

Smiling, Davey closed his eyes again. "I'm coming! I'm coming!" he cried.

John thought, *What the hell does he mean by that?*

With a heart-stirring rush of wings, the eagle swooped past the trio, executed a perfect stall, and gently dropped to earth beside the salmon, which he quickly devoured. Speechless, the three Harrisons watched the great bird spread its wings to catch an updraft in a near vertical takeoff.

Maggie hugged Davey fiercely while he squirmed and bubbled. "That was one hungry eagle! He was sooo glad for that fish. Thank you, Poppa, for playing the game with Momma and me. Isn't it a wonderful game?"

John tried to smile but the experience brought the shocking realization that the game had gone beyond his capacity to accept or understand. Frowning, he stood and walked moodily to the horses while Maggie packed up the picnic.

Maggie realized she could no longer pretend that John was the same adoring, indulgent, confident man she had married. Although he frequently wore a frown with troubled eyes, she had believed that he had finally come to terms with Davey's psychic gifts. Was he just scared of the Wright brothers? A sudden premonition of catastrophe brought tears to her eyes. *How could we have tied our marriage into such a knot?* Her mind took her back six years earlier to San Francisco.

PART I

MARRIAGE

"After marriage arrives a reaction, sometimes a big, sometimes a little one; but it comes sooner or later, and must be tidied over by both parties if they desire the rest of their lives to go with the current."

RUDYARD KIPLING, PLAIN TALES

CHAPTER ONE

SAN FRANCISCO
OCTOBER, 1893

For an hour, Lily Wang listened to Maggie Andrews' mystical rendition of Chopin's etudes. Her teacher, the popular, gregarious Leander Sherman, showered Maggie with compliments for her deft mastery of rubato, her left hand keeping accurate time while her right hand teased dreamy rhythms out of the melody. After Sherman suddenly hurried away to another engagement, the two women moved to their favorite cozy nook, a tiny room that looked down on the two-story parlor of Sherman House on Green Street. The time had come for Lily to dissect the tumults of Maggie's heart.

"Are you in love with him?" Lily Wang poured mild Soochow tea into both cups, then scrutinized Maggie's face for evidence of apprehension.

"I don't know." Frowning with confusion, Maggie used the soft four-toned rhythms of Mandarin, the language of her childhood in China. "Since he loomed out of the fog last summer on that dreadful road to Carmel from Monterey, he's pursued me like... like a ghost."

"I thought you liked attention." Lily had barely tolerated Maggie's yearning for public acclaim during their teens together in Shanghai. To a well-educated young Chinese woman, to whom modest anonymity was the banner of feminine virtue, Maggie's behavior had seemed notorious. But Maggie's missionary father had always treated her like his first-born son. If she wanted his attention and respect, she had been forced to behave like a tom-boy. Five inches short of six feet, Maggie wore a white, high-collared shirt-waist, maroon ankle-length skirt and black leather boots. She was a prototypical Mills College senior, almost ready to face the world, presumably as a pianist in Sherman's famous musical emporium. Thanks to his sponsorship and success as an impresario, she had met sev-

eral of the greatest performers of the age. Surely, after her coming graduation from Mills in June, 1894, her own stage career would be meteoric.
Unfortunately for her sense of destiny, not to mention her peace of mind,
she had recently met John Harrison. "You know me too well. I suppose you
think I deserve all this discomfort."

"I would *never* wish discomfort for you, Maggie." Lily wore a white
poplin dress over an underskirt of green and white sateen. Under her high
collar, she wore a lace choker. A straw skimmer with a green band around it
added a few inches to her five foot-two inch height. Despite her diminu-
tive size, she could focus the power of her whole being on anyone when it
suited her. Now her eyes smoldered with luminous intensity as she gave
her full attention to Maggie. "I think people generally get what they ask
for—if not what they deserve. Now, let's look at the evidence. How often
have you seen him?"

"Well…, after that first time in Carmel, I didn't see him until school
started again last month. You must remember? He tracked me down, insisted that I come out of class." Maggie giggled at the memory. "He said
he was a relative with urgent, sad news. I was embarrassed."

"So he's a liar and a dramatist. I don't recall that you minded so much."

"Maybe not; but now I can't get him out of my mind." Maggie shook
her head and looked forlorn. "Oh, Lily, he's so… vulnerable. I seem to
want to take care of him. Is that love?"

"Perhaps; but that's the wrong question. The issue is *should* you be in
love with him? How often have you seen him since then?"

"Ten times, I suppose. Once, maybe twice every weekend."

"He deserves no credit for that. Isn't he a student at the new University of California at Berkeley? A walk to Mills College shouldn't tire him
much."

"Are you kidding? He *never* gets tired. He thinks nothing of walking
miles for fun. We've walked around piles of whalebones on the piers; we've
walked around every mansion on Nob Hill; we've looked at every flower in
Mister Lick's conservatory in Golden Gate Park. My feet have been so sore
that I envied the bathers at the Sutro baths."

Lily frowned. She thought a man's leisure interests spoke volumes
about his sense of *decency*, an all-important goal that she believed to be under siege from the barbarism of American culture. "So how else did he en-

tertain you?"

"We've laughed and cried at several of Mister Morosco's melodramas at the Grand Opera House. He took me to see building preparations for next year's Midwinter Exposition. And he's dragged me to the kinetoscope parlor in the Chronicle building three times."

"You actually *enjoyed* those peep shows?"

"Well...." Maggie suddenly felt defensive. "They're a wonder, of course; but if it weren't for the magic of the motion, I wouldn't be very interested in wrestling or blacksmiths or trained bears." For an instant, her mouth opened slightly and her eyes became misty. "He's so muscular and tall; and those dark brown eyes...; I could just drown in them; and.... Oh *chih kuo ying chu*! (Fruit thrown at him by *women* would fill a coach) and...."

"I know he's handsome," Lily interrupted coldly. "As far as I'm concerned, that's a strike against him. Most handsome men his age think the world is a theatrical production for their benefit. What about his family?" Lily still couldn't understand the American passion for personal independence. In her view, too many young Americans translated the idea of liberty into license, a selfish search for personal satisfaction without regard to filial duties and obligations. She insisted that family must always come first.

"I know all about his family," Maggie replied with enthusiasm. "Do you really want to hear the details?"

"Of course. Before your infatuation with that cowboy goes any further, we must examine his credentials." For emphasis, she added in English, "Would you buy a poke from a pig?" In protest against Maggie's misuse of Chinese aphorisms, *ch'eng-yu*, Lily massacred colloquial English, often deliberately.

Maggie rewarded Lily's fractured slang with a delighted smile.

"Of course not," Lily continued with triumphant logic. "We're talking about your whole future, not just pokey pigs. Why should a dashing, irresponsible cowpoke...," Lily paused in mid-stride and asked, "Is that the same poke that pigs use? How does it relate to a slow-poke? What a miserable language...," then resumed, "Why should he be suitable for the exquisite daughter of Presbyterian missionaries? Also, remember Lin T'ai-chi's prediction."

The mere mention of Lin T'ai-chi chilled Maggie, whose sudden pallor evoked a glance of tender compassion from Lily. Both remembered their brief encounter in Shanghai with the famous Black Hat Tantric Buddhist lama in the spring of 1890. Lin's mastery of *feng-shui* and the mysteries of *ch'i* had rewarded him with wealth, devoted followers and a vision of the harmonious relationship among God, nature and humanity. A week before their departure for San Francisco, Lin's forecast had cast a pall over the trip.

"You are only seventeen, my beauty," he had said to Maggie. "But you will soon spread your wings. You have only four years of childhood left before you take flight. Use those years like money in the bank. Near the end of that time, you will meet the father of your son, your *only* son. The father will bring you much grief. The son will be an eagle and the joy of your life."

"Why will my husband bring me so much grief?" she had asked.

"Because he will lose control of the fire element in his nature. At first, the coals of his anger and passion will burn low. Then ambition will almost consume him and everyone around him."

Resentfully, Maggie had stamped her foot. "Can't my fate be averted? I've had *enough* grief from men!"

"Each of us has a destiny: spiritual lessons to be learned," Lin had replied with calm tenderness. "For the sake of your son's destiny, you may not deny your own, which will lead you into a world far beyond your imagination."

Despite her pragmatic approach to life, Lily had no doubts about the accuracy of Lin's predictions. Only by heeding his esoteric prescriptions could one hope to ease the burden of destiny. Lily had been stunned when Lin offered Maggie no such prescription. Now the least she could do was try to mitigate Maggie's predestined anguish. At least if the devil were rich, it might be easier for her to bear suffering. "Is John Harrison likely to bring you so much grief? Now be good enough to help me find the answer."

"Very well," Maggie sighed. "I think his greatest loyalty is to his family and the family name."

"That's a good start," murmured Lily.

"He comes from the James River Harrisons. He..."

"His people live on a river?"

"No, silly. The James River is a great river in Virginia. His first ancestor in America was a man named Richard Harrison. Three hundred years ago, he was the first mate of a ship, the *Bartholomew Gilberti*."

Lily shook her head. She thought, *Worse and worse. Everyone knows that sailors are the dregs of humanity—no roots, no past, no future, just their miserable existential lives aboard some dirty scow. What will I do with her?*

"Richard was the first white man to be killed by Indians on the Eastern Shore of Virginia." Maggie felt strangely reassured by John's roots. "In 1637 his son, Benjamin, received a royal grant of six hundred acres."

"That's promising," said Lily. "Does your cowboy still own the land? Or do you plan to spend your life at sea, literally as well as figuratively?"

"Oh Lily! *Fu kuei fou yün!* (Wealth and position are like floating clouds). Weren't we taught to renounce all worldly ambitions?"

"Don't hurl *ch'eng-yu* at me!" Feeling personally responsible for Maggie's fate, Lily tried to calm her nerves. "I have warned you repeatedly that our aphorisms are sloppy substitutes for thought. But you persist in memorizing them as if to validate your spurious Chinese identity."

Maggie pouted. At the age of sixteen, after her parents were murdered by Boxers, she had joined Lily's household as a sister. Hungry for family, she had cloaked herself with aphorisms, social customs and Confucian rules of relationships. Finally, to liberate her from her staged Chinese identity, Lily's father had shipped them off to San Francisco for their college education. "I don't care what you say. *Ch'eng-yu* are the distilled folk wisdom of China."

"Nonsense!" Lily replied as she stood up and turned away to conceal her extreme irritation. Trembling slightly, her small fists clenched, she turned back to Maggie, sat down and lifted her teacup. "We expect such stupidity from our peasants and foreigners, especially Americans who have no culture and little heritage. You should know better; don't lavish your jewels on a pig."

"You mean 'throw pearls before swine,'" Maggie corrected absently while she poured tea into Lily's cup. "Why should I agree to your class-conscious prejudices? Who made you such an authority on your own culture?"

Lily gently grasped Maggie's hands. "I may not know everything about China. But I understand *you* almost better than myself. You are much too tolerant and... indiscriminate. To you, the myth and whimsy of the Kitchen God are just as significant as the profound wisdom of Confucius."

In a discussion like this one, Maggie always felt handicapped. Lily's focus in college was philosophy. She had stuffed her brain full of pattern sentences from Plato and Lao Tzu to Kant. "Don't you think all those things are just diverse expressions of the Chinese soul?" Maggie asked.

"Perhaps." Lily shook her head with impatience. She was normally amused by Maggie's tangled anthropology. "The problem is that you fervently believe they *are* the culture of China. That's like describing the noble heritage of my family by the color and thickness of the paint on our house in Shanghai."

"I'm sorry, Lily." Maggie knew better than to punctuate her ideas with aphorisms, especially around Lily, who could always see through her. She stared disconsolately out the window at a passing carriage. "You think I'm a failure as a Chinese woman?"

"*Hua she t'ien tzu*. (You're a parody of a Chinese). You know a lot *about* China. But you're *not* Chinese; and you never *will be*, no matter how hard you try." Lily resolved to discipline her impatience with Maggie's relentless caricature of China's ineffable wisdom. "Be who and what you are, Maggie. Come out of your floating clouds and help me understand your problem."

"Oh very well…. My cowboy, as you call him, no longer owns *Brandon*, their great estate in Virginia."

"Why not? Did his family gamble it away?" Lily decided to throw obstacles in the way of Maggie's liaison with her hot-headed young man.

"You must correct your thinking, Lily. John comes from an important family. Why, one of his ancestors, Robert Henry, was wagonmaster for General Nathaniel Greene, who commanded all American revolutionary troops in the South a hundred years ago."

"A heritage of rebellion!" Lily could barely contain her dismay. If she were not a student of the *Yi Ching*, the Book of Changes, she would have despaired. But, like all Chinese, she knew that impoverished peasants could become emperors and vice versa. "I suppose his ancestors also fought for the South in your Civil War? Is that how they lost all their property?"

"John's father, Nate… Nathaniel, *did* fight for the South."

"Next you'll tell me he was in the cavalry. They are always the worst—intrepid violators of women and the land, our two greatest treasures. It was only by Kuan Yin's grace that my ancestors escaped from the harsh brutality of *our* famous cavalryman, Genghis Khan.”

“John’s father didn’t have to fight. He was well established in the cattle business here. Why, years before the war, he bought a great Carmel ranch called the *Rancho Cañada de Segundo*. He paid Lazar Soto five hundred dollars for four thousand acres.”

Four thousand acres? Lily had some sense of the value of land now in the Carmel Valley; her father owned a house high on Jack’s Peak in Monterey.

“In 1860, he bought the Portreo de San Carlos to bring his total ranch to nearly nine thousand acres.”

“So why did he leave such responsibilities to fight someone else’s war?” Lily was beginning to think the family might be afflicted with some genetic flaw. Was this a warrior family, all descended from the mythic Kuan Kung or, heaven forbid, the evil Ts’ao Ts’ao?

“Out of his deep sense of loyalty to family, he went east and enlisted under a cavalry General named Jeb Stuart. He was in several great battles. Doesn’t that testify to the family’s sense of commitment?”

Lily considered the question. She searched her mental file for precedents from her personal guide to ethical behavior: *The Romances of the Three Kingdoms*. As a child, her education had started with tales of triumph and betrayal from that great epic. Like millions of her countrymen, in the book and in the operas that had flowed from its pages, she had discovered appropriate role-models for her own choices at periods of crisis. Grudgingly, she admitted, “A truly American family. So where is the father now that his son needs guidance?”

“The war ruined the family in Virginia and damaged Nate’s health. He died in his sleep four years ago.”

“And the mother?”

“She died one month after her husband.”

Lily nodded as if a great light had turned on in her mind. “So this cowboy is actually a great landowner whose roots lie deep in the history of the country. But why is his complexion so dark?”

“Lily, he met us at the end of a great cattle roundup after weeks in the sun.

“Does he have no breeding? I agree with your proverb, ‘Better unborn than unbred.’ He should have a Mexican overseer for such hard work.”

“He *does* have an overseer: Ramon Cisneros. But Ramon could not guarantee the respect of over a hundred Mexican horsemen after his parents died. When he was only seventeen, John had to spend long days in the saddle."

Lily's expression softened. The fact of John's wealth meant possible approval of the match. "He sounds like a man of the soil. I respect that. But do you?"

"Why?" The question caught Maggie by surprise. "Why shouldn't I?"

Lily fixed her gaze on Maggie as if to read her very soul. "You are an impractical musician, Maggie. With your fascination with astrology and mythology, you think you need only change your perception to change the world. You...." Lily pursed her mouth in self-reproach for being so candid. "You're an artist; you respect moral courage and scholarship. He's certainly no scholar. He's just a practical engineer whose life has taught him to value physical courage. I suspect he prefers order. You have always preferred the creative joys of a rich disorder. Half the time, your companions are spirits."

What could Maggie say? She shook her head in silent protest.

"Don't you dare shake your head in disagreement!" Lily exclaimed. "You're like a beam of light, dancing through life on impulse and enthusiasm. You love dramatic surprises; you've designed your life to attract them, or create them. You see spiritual—no, *miraculous*—significance in your every chance meeting with a flower, an animal, even another human. You think nothing is accidental. You revel in ambiguity and whimsy. Does he?"

"No," Maggie admitted dolefully. "He loves physics and mathematics and linkages and gears. Abstract ideas turn to stones in his mind."

"And in his mouth, I dare say. Is he kind?"

"With me he is—invariably. Anyone who loves horses and his vaqueros like John does *must* be the soul of kindness."

Lily brooded. "How about music? Does he like your music?"

That question gave Maggie pause. Music was her life. She had learned to speak its language through hours of study and listening and practice. She had worked hard enough that she might become a fine concert pianist. Her voice, though yet untrained, could reach high-C. "I love anything by Mozart and Beethoven and Chopin and Gabriel Faure's *Requiem* and Cesar Franck's *Symphony in D-minor* and Ravel's *Pavanne for A Dead Princess* and...."

"Enough! Everyone knows you're a hopeless romantic. What does he like?"

"Oh, Lily, he plays the guitar like an angel—in the Spanish style with lots of fingering. And he sings beautifully: haunting Scottish and Irish ballads like *Shenandoah* and *Greensleeves* and *The Minstrel Boy* and...."

"Common trash for common people, I'm sure," Lily complained. "Frankly, you and John come from different classes. You're a middle class princess; he's a rich, working class peasant. You have almost nothing in common."

Maggie tossed her auburn hair petulantly. "What's your evidence?"

"Your own testimony. For God's sake, Maggie, look at the facts. Your life is theater and music. You love real opera; he loves Morosco's melodramas. You love the classics; he loves popular music...."

"I like popular, too," Maggie said defensively. "I just love that new Negro composer, Scott Joplin. Why, I play his rags all the time...."

Lily shook her head impatiently. "You must not delude yourself. Is there poetry in his soul?" Lily pleaded for something that might mitigate what seemed to be a confrontation destined for Maggie and John.

"I don't know. But he is the most *masculine* human I have ever met. Maybe that's why I like to... perform for him. He makes me feel... alive!"

Lily smiled. "And you are one of the most *feminine* humans I have ever met, despite your confusion about your power as a woman. In that sense, you *are* Chinese because you believe that relationships can solve all problems."

"That's true." Maggie frowned at an insight. "But I didn't have to learn that from the Chinese."

Lily nodded. "How does John approach problems?"

"Like an engineer, of course. Systems and procedures and...."

"...gears and linkages," Lily finished for her. "How do you feel about him?"

"*Kan ch'ai lieh huo* (dried firewood and a roaring fire)!" Maggie said with a sparkle in her eyes.

"Oh, Maggie, that's pure lust! You know very well that will fade. With his cattle and his horses and land and money, his essence is the earth. He's certainly a materialist." Lily squinted her eyes as if to see a distant object. "And there's something else in him. Hidden. Something... threatening beneath his lost little boy vulnerability."

"You don't think he cares for me?"

"He adores you! But such feelings always fade; marriage transforms them into something else. I think the demon of ambition drives John Harrison too much. Hasn't he said that he must do something glorious?"

"Well, yes." Maggie nervously twirled a strand of her hair into a curl. She wanted Lily's blessing, not this litany of criticism and doom. "But isn't that just a manner of speaking?"

"Perhaps. Things might be different if you knew more clearly what you want from life, from marriage. And I would be happier about your infatuation with this cowboy if you were more fully conscious of your own hunger for control and… power."

CHAPTER TWO

SAN FRANCISCO AND MONTEREY
JULY, 1894

"Oh God, what have I done?" Maggie asked Lily at ten minutes before ten o'clock on the morning of June 30, 1894, only three weeks after Maggie, Lily and John Harrison had graduated from college.

"Nothing much...." Lily fussed with Maggie's floor length, white satin wedding gown to make final, unnecessary adjustments of the long tulle veil held precariously by a cluster of orange blossoms. "You've just persuaded yourself to marry the most eligible land owner in the Carmel Valley."

"And you *do* approve?" Maggie's voice betrayed her anxiety.

"If I disapproved, would I have spent John's money and my valuable time just to make a party?" Lily pretended a frown of stern rebuke. "Would I have examined the dim sum so carefully? Would I have demanded the best string quartet that Leander Sherman could find? What's the matter with you?"

"I'm just... not sure," Maggie whimpered. "I...feel like I'm abandoning a career for a cloudy future. I'm... gambling!"

"Of course you are!" Lily cooed. "But all your friends from school and John's friends from Berkeley and Carmel and many of Leander's friend's are waiting for you. You can't turn back now; so pull yourself together."

For the next twenty minutes, oblivious of flowers and friends in courtly dress, Maggie's mind darted like a tennis ball back and forth from the ritual phrases of the ceremony to gloomy thoughts about her future.

"Do you, John, take Margaret Andrews to have and to hold from this day forward...?"

Faint suddenly from a sickening wave of panic, Maggie felt stifled by the thought of John's masculine presence. What would it be like tonight?

Would he be brutal? He seemed so vigorous and strong and...eager!

"Do you, Margaret, take John Harrison to have and to hold from this day forward... 'til death do you part?"

How long until death? Can I really commit the rest of my life to this man? I don't even know him! Have I lost my mind? Maybe if I fainted, we could postpone this stupid ritual. Twenty minutes later, Maggie Andrews had changed her name to Maggie Harrison, witnessed by well-wishing friends, some already tipsy with bubbly champagne or Budweiser draft beer.

But all the alcohol in California could not have lifted the spirits of many of the hundred guests. The country floundered in bitter depression and no one, not even tall, handsome impresario Sherman, felt immune from its cruel whimsy.

Their fear was an emotional sounding board for Maggie's own doubts. Bits of conversations barely pierced her consciousness as she and John circulated. A guest asked, "John, are you related to our former President, Ben Harrison?"

"Why, I s'pose I am, Josh. He's a James River Harrison too. Why?"

"Gallopin' inflation was all his fault," blustered Josh, florid with heat and champagne. "That damn—beggin' your pardon, ma'am—Sherman Silver Purchase Act just shovelled money into everyone's pockets. The dollar wasn't worth a plugged nickel last year; came damn close to devaluation."

"Now, Josh, don't blow a gasket," remonstrated John's rotund banker and friend, Fred Mackie, "just 'cause the Fifty-first Congress spent over a billion dollars buying and minting silver...."

"I thought Grover Cleveland persuaded Congress to cancel the Sherman Act last year," John protested. The worried expression on his face caught Maggie's attention. Could he be facing financial problems?

"Pardon us for this unseemly dissection of our economy, Mizz Harrison." Fred nodded deferentially as if the subject might exceed her mental capacity. "Boys, the fact is the President din't stop at canceling the silver give-away to ever small b'inessman and his dog. He also promised to pay off all Civil War bonds and American Silver Certificates with gold. For nearly a year now, European investors have been savaging our gold reserves."

Josh had no idea what Fred meant. "Is that bad, Fred?"

"If the gold in our Treasury drops below a hundred million, Cleveland may have to appeal to Wall Street for money."

Josh grabbed a glass of champagne from a passing tray and downed it in two long swigs. "Sounds reasonable; I bet J.P. Morgan, Carnegie and Rockefeller have more cash than the guvmint. I swear, Fred; I'm confused. I don't know which is worse: easy money and inflation or tight money and depression."

"That's a tough one, Josh. Two years ago, wages couldn't keep up with the inflation and we had over thirteen hundred strikes in a single year. Since Cleveland took office last year, and started his tight-money policy, twenty percent of our railroads have filed for bankruptcy. In this year alone, over five hundred banks and sixteen thousand businesses have failed."

Their attitude irritated Maggie, who couldn't abide fools. "Gentlemen, at Mills College economists taught me that inflation destroys a whole society; depression merely destroys the poor. The lesson from the last two years seems as clear as the nose on Mr. Mackie's face."

"And what's that, Mizz..., uh, Harrison?" Fred asked with a patronizing tone he normally reserved for children and idiots.

"Money changers, not Presidents, make the choice for depression or inflation because they dominate the economy of our country," she persisted. Coupled with her general dislike for ritual, Maggie's discomfort with the wedding cried out for a scapegoat. Maggie's teachers had influenced her to hate bankers, especially central banks. Pompous Fred Mackie seemed to personify their awesome greed; so she enjoyed focusing her anger on him. She knew her antagonism toward Fred Mackie wasn't rational. But his prominent snout and porcine eyes reminded her of the bully who had murdered her parents.

"Money changers? Do you mean bankers, my dear?"

"Of course. The European money trust, especially the Rothschilds, dominate banking philosophy in this country as they do in all of Europe. They're all vicious predators."

Mackie wanted to be kind but this beautiful young creature was provoking him. "Oh, that old chestnut."

"Chestnut?" Grateful for a target for her untimely wrath, Maggie plunged ahead. "Bankers have deliberately contracted the money supply in this country ever since Abraham Lincoln financed the Civil War with Treasury Notes, so-called greenbacks."

"Inflationary irresponsibility, worse than Andrew Jackson," Mackie asserted.

What kind of woman would turn her wedding into a diatribe against banks?

"You call greenbacks 'irresponsible,'" Maggie retorted, "because Lincoln hated the national bank idea as much as Andrew Jackson and Napoleon and von Bismarck. Lincoln wouldn't borrow from a privately-owned central bank and mortgage the American people's future. European moneychangers were so desperate to retrieve their criminal control of the currency that they hired John Wilkes Booth to assassinate the President."

The silence that followed that bombshell spread to other polite conversations, sensitive to the slightest hint of sullied marital bliss. One by one, people joined the group around Maggie, who seemed to be making a speech.

"After Lincoln's death in 1865, the National Banking Act of 1863 gave those blood-sucking vandals another chance to bankrupt the country. Slowly, they began to contract the currency."

"Why... Mizz... Harrison, I believe you're addled," Mackie said with deceptive calm. "Do you have evidence that bankers deliberately contracted currency in circulation?"

"Why do you pretend ignorance of the infamous Contraction Act of 1866 to retire greenbacks?" Maggie challenged. "When they first set out to seize control, nearly two billion dollars were in circulation; that was $50.46 for every man, woman and child in the country. It was enough to match supply with demand at reasonable prices. After just one year of their manipulations, there were only 1.3 billion dollars in circulation, or $44 per capita."

Under her breath, Lily frantically murmured, "For God's sake, Margaret, shut up! This is not the time to reveal your power to memorize everything you've ever read."

Sensing an opportunity, Mackie delivered his favorite bromide. "You must understand... uh... Miz Harrison, what's good for b'iness is good for the country." Fred Mackie delivered that non sequitur with a sonorous tone, the mixture of unction and pompous authority that he always practiced to great advantage on most people to whom he denied loans.

"Oh, I see," Maggie interrupted breezily. "You mean like the rights of George Pullman this very moment to mobilize government lackeys to destroy his worker's lives and shut down the nation's railroads in the name of profit?

In a dreamy stupor, "Poor John" was largely oblivious to the confrontation between his new wife and Fred Mackie. He simply couldn't believe that the vision of loveliness beside him had agreed to marry him. In his mind, Maggie could do no wrong. He loved her willowy figure, her slender ballerina form and her adamant refusal to bend to the rage for smallness: tight kid gloves, shoes a size too small and tight-laced corsets to achieve a wasp waist. Her choice of clothes that gave her lithe body maximum freedom had convinced him that she must be a true western woman. Her high forehead, grey-green eyes, wide, generous mouth and shining auburn hair exuded a vivacity and a joy in life that had captured John from the moment he had first found her in the fog, her buggy broken down. She was so transparently generous that John felt fiercely protective, as if to shield her innocence from harsh reality. She seemed to have no guile, almost no mask, no hint of ulterior motives. Her fight with Fred Mackie was so out of character that he assumed Fred had somehow provoked her. Now he gently guided her away from the fuming Mackie. "Maggie, allow me to introduce my best friend, Ned Ambler. He's our family doctor."

Maggie found herself facing a slender man, only an inch or two taller than herself. His startling blue eyes echoed the joy in his smile. He nodded a deeply tanned, balding head and reached for Maggie's hand. His cool touch had a strangely calming effect on her nervous state of mind. *A true gentle man*, she thought. *Must be in his mid-thirties. Why do I feel safe near him?*

"It's a great pleasure to finally associate your face with such a familiar name," Ned said in a rich, deep voice.

"Familiar?" Maggie asked while Ned released her hand.

"For the past nine months, John hasn't been able to utter a sentence without your name." He withdrew while other well-wishers advanced to shake hands and offer congratulations. From a vantage point near the piano, he discovered that he couldn't take his eyes off of her.

"She's certainly a beautiful bride, isn't she?"

The question forced Ned to attend to a young Chinese woman, the

Maid of Honor, whom he had met briefly the day before. "I'm entranced!" Ned said with a smile. "You must be her best friend?"

"I am," Lily replied. "After her little contretemps with Fred Mackie, I may be her *only* friend."

"Excluding her husband, of course."

Lily pondered that remark. "I like John well enough but I'm not sure yet that they *will* be friends. Do you know him well?"

"Almost from the moment I began my practice in Carmel thirteen years ago. I was his family doctor from the time he was eight. I guess I know him better than anyone else at the party. Does something in him bother you?"

"Not as an individual. I have even cooperated with his courtship. In my advice to Maggie, I heeded Plato's admonition."

"Plato? What was that?"

"He is supposed to have said, 'By all means, marry. If it succeeds, you will be the happiest of humans. If it fails, you can become a philosopher.'"

Ned warmed to Lily's wisdom and elfin beauty. He noted that there was no wedding band on her finger. "It appears that you've reversed the process: philosopher first, marriage next. You have doubts about this match?"

"I'm still not sure the two of them belong together. He strikes me as a simple, decent man. She's very complex. Her sense of reality is so much... *richer* than his that he may...." Lily suddenly felt that it was improper for her to confide in this stranger. Yet she felt curiously at ease with him, as if she had known him for years. She disciplined herself and finished lamely, "may find her too flighty for his taste. Does John like to take charge of things?"

"Not really. He just wants to do something glorious, as he puts it."

"You mean he just wants attention?"

"It may be as simple as that...." Ned stared at Lily with interest. Could John's passion for great causes be that simple? "According to my old mentor, William James, we generally lead lives that try to compensate or maybe atone for childhood illusions. John didn't get much attention as a child. I think now he wants to impress people—favorably, if possible."

Lily groped for an elusive insight to share with this warm and gentle man. "Maggie needs attention, too; but she likes to run things her way."

"Her way?"

"Yes, she hates anyone else's dictatorial behavior. Is John ever dictatorial?"

Ned searched his memory. "Hardly ever. He might be pushed to ruthlessness against anyone who threatened his family or his ranch. Otherwise, he has a sweet personality, even indulgent. His principal flaw is that he's a romantic, wants to pour himself into some great cause."

"I wonder how he got that way?"

Ned sipped his champagne before answering. "At an early age, he came to believe in King Arthur, the Roundtable and especially Lancelot. Tell Maggie to read about Lancelot. Courage: that's John's god. John's father underlined all his romantic illusions with tales of courage from the Civil War."

Lily frowned. "I suppose we mustn't worry about them. As long as they love each other, maybe they won't fight."

Then Ned said something that filled Lily's heart with hope. "All marriages run into crises. I'll watch over them, try to help them over the rough spots."

"Then you are married, yourself? You have some experience?"

"I've been married for twelve years; have two children. Thank goodness my wife and I have worked out most of *our* differences. Will you come down to Carmel occasionally so that we can compare notes?"

Smiling, Lily felt a strangely buoyant confidence in Ned. "Here's my hand on it. I look forward to it. But look, she's going upstairs to change. I'd better go help. Nice to meet you, Doctor."

Tearfully, Maggie said goodbye to Lily when the bridal couple boarded the noon train to Monterey. A cattle roundup would not permit the honeymoon that Maggie deserved. But John didn't want her to think that life must be all ranch work and no elegance. To reassure her, he had arranged their wedding night at the magnificent new Del Monte Lodge on the edge of Monterey.

CHAPTER THREE

CARMEL VALLEY
JULY, 1894

Maggie spent the first hour of the trip to Monterey staring sightlessly at the passing landscape, her mind a tumult of questions. Could that terrible Fred Mackie be one of John's better educated friends? Or were they all peasants? Had she forsaken music and a career and culture for cows and mud and manure? Would there be any young women? Or just rough cowboys? Had she just made the biggest mistake of her life?

John ascribed Maggie's withdrawn silence to fatigue. "Why don't you close your eyes and take a nap, sweetheart?"

Soon, Maggie's head nodded as she surrendered her anxiety to the hypnotic repetition of clickety-clack, clickety-clack. She leaned her head against John's shoulder, placed a hand in his and fell into a deep sleep.

Late in the afternoon, she awakened to the sound of a shrill whistle and a series of jerks as the train came to a stop in Monterey. John seated her in a colorful tallyho, then barked commands at Mexican laborers who loaded her worldly possessions on board. When they first spied the sprawling new Lodge, John said with forgivable civic pride, "Just look at it, honey. It burned down seven years ago. The railroad barons rebuilt it from ashes a year later. The dinin' room seats seven hundred guests at one sittin'. Ain't it grand?"

Maggie was less impressed by the building and its gingerbread architecture than she was by the crowds of women in wide hats and diaphanous summer gowns. It seemed that every woman carried a colorful parasol. In the light breeze, Maggie thought they resembled galleons under full sail with bustled sterns and wide-brimmed top-gallants adorned with birds and flowers. The men looked like peppermint candy sticks in their striped cotton suits and straw boaters. Everything seemed to be in motion: pine branches dancing on the wind; several unicycles and perhaps fifty bicycles moving along the cinder paths; ten people playing croquet and tallyho's laden with laughing guests entering and departing the grounds.

"Where does the Lodge get all its food?" Maggie asked.

"I suspected you had a b'iness brain under all those curls!" John replied with a grin. "They need a ton of beef, poultry and vegetables ever' day. So I sell 'em a lot of beef and dairy products, especially my 'Jack' cheese."

Maggie nodded absently. Although her rest on the train had banished some of her anxieties, they returned while she and John followed a bellhop to their room on the ground floor. She wondered if a soldier felt such tingling apprehension before a battle. She entered a large suite of rooms with pastel blue walls, white drapes and white furniture. Under other circumstances, she might have felt warmly welcomed by the decor and the view across Monterey Bay. But the sight of the large double bed made her stomach growl. And that made her angry at herself. She reminded herself that John was a gentleman, a caring, indulgent man who would surely be a gentle lover. But such self-reassurance failed to quiet her nerves or lift a pall of tension that made their conversation sound like a poorly memorized dialogue between strangers. "Lovely room isn't it?" she asked.

"Yeah. I'm sorry the trip was so tiring."

"I... I don't remember. Where are we?" Maggie's stab at humor fell flat.

"Why, honey, we're in Monterey!" John blushed at his stupidity and tried to divert himself by uncorking a cold bottle of champagne. While he twisted the cork, he could think of nothing to say. Although he could not imagine loving any other woman, he was so obsessed by the coming test of his performance in bed that his brain felt like mush. Prostitutes and vaqueros had taught him the basic moves. But he had no idea how he should treat a nice girl. "Do you feel like a little supper?"

"Why I... I'm starved!" Maggie gratefully grasped anything that would postpone the inevitable. "I suppose I should dress?"

"They generally wear clothes in the dinin' room, I think." This time, John's blush was so deep and so prolonged that he wanted to sink through the floor into hell. Anything would be better than this.

Maggie stared at John. His misery was so evident that she couldn't bear to look at him. Seized by her perverse sense of humor, she choked down a guffaw, rushed into the bathroom and tried to muffle uncontrollable laughter until tears streamed down her face. She imagined different conversations when she appeared in a world of nudists.

"Madam," the maitre d' says stiffly, "we generally do not dress for dinner." "Why," Maggie says, "my husband told me that I *should* wear something for meals." "My dear woman, any clothes at all would be overdressed. Only staff wear clothes to hide their ugly bodies." "Should I undress now? Or is it appropriate to wait for the main course?"

The sounds in the bathroom were like spears in John's heart. Were they groans of pain? Up to this point, he thought he had played his role fairly well. He had wanted to seem calm and worldly wise. All he wanted was Maggie's trust and respect. But that one remark had stripped away his thin pretense of sophistication. He felt like an awkward schoolboy, altogether unworthy of his new responsibilities. Wondering if the marriage was over before it had ever had a chance to get started, he sat on the bed and disconsolately downed a glass of champagne in one long gulp. He poured himself another glass to keep himself company while Maggie continued to stifle giggles behind the door.

"Johnnie," she said when she finally emerged, "I'm afraid to go to dinner. The moment I see the headwaiter, I'll remember what you said. I'll walk in and imagine everyone without clothes on. I just know I'll die of laughter. And everyone will think I'm demented."

"You… you're not mad at me?" he asked with a forlorn look of defeat. "You don't think I'm just a big country hick?"

"If you are, so am I." In the bathroom, the absurdity of the situation had captured Maggie's love of whimsy. "Now let's get ready for dinner. But first, kiss me and tell me you love me. And then give me a glass of champagne."

Later, giddy with champagne, marvelous food and a sense that everything was hilariously amusing, she welcomed him into her arms with an open heart. His lack of experience was both reassuring and a little disappointing. By midnight, both of them were emotionally and physically depleted. They finally surrendered to exhaustion and drifted into sleep.

Late next morning, Maggie awakened with mixed reactions to her first night with sex. On the one hand, some moments had certainly been physically pleasurable and not as humiliating as a few American novels would have had her believe. On the other hand, she had felt a singular absence of passion. That bothered her because she had tried hard to open her mind and body to his loving. For the moment, she explained it away as inexperience. Indeed, she had to admit that part of herself she called "the Watcher" had perhaps diverted her own potential for lust by seeking correlation between the sex act and musical rhythm. Even as John was reaching for one of his climaxes that night, she had thought idly that Wagner's *Liebestod* might be a suitable accompaniment. She would have been surprised to hear John's review of their wedding night.

He had suffered inner conflicts so tormenting that he preferred to hide them from his memory. His desire to possess and consume Maggie had awakened something so deep, so primitive that he had felt his self-control slipping into oblivion. At a moment when he was ready to surrender himself to his lust, he would repeatedly hear his father's voice, sternly cautioning him against self-indulgence, against enslavement by feminine wiles and, conversely, against misusing a good woman as if she were a whore. And so he had wrestled with his appetites and had treated each climax as if it were at least an assault on Maggie's sensibilities if not a betrayal of his filial obligations. Before he had finally sunk into sleep, he wondered despairingly how he might ever balance his raging desire with his sense of duty to his father and his wife.

After their first night together, there were still butterflies of apprehension in Maggie's stomach. While they shared a late breakfast she came to the daunting realization that she really knew very little about him. Could Lily have been right? Had he behaved like an uncultured peasant last night? Must love-making be so much grunting and moaning and sweating? Had she thrown away her career away for that? Would she like the ranch? The house? The people? Would she find a friend, perhaps that nice doctor, Ned Ambler?

Late in the afternoon, seated in a buggy under Ramon Cisneros' firm control, she forced herself to suppress such doubts. She tried to like Monterey as they made their way down narrow streets. The prospect of living nearby suddenly made everything seem worthy of her attention.

The blissful cool of the fog stimulated a mood of expectancy that seized her mind almost from the moment the buggy plunged into the heavy mist. The mood was enhanced by an aroma, a pungent blend of eucalyptus and Monterey pine and the salt breeze from the ocean. Along the rough road from Monterey south to Carmel, ice plant welcomed her with a riot of color.

While John chattered about the ranch in Spanish with Ramon, Maggie began to feel the heat of the day. In the Carmel Valley, when they emerged from the last tendrils of fog, the temperature was a shocking 85. Maggie glanced longingly at the Carmel River on her right. She wondered if a swim before supper might be permissible.

Then they rounded a turn, rolled to the crest of a hill and stopped. There across wide fenced and cross-fenced pastures stood the single-story ranch house, surmounting a gentle hillock and sheltered by old oaks and eucalyptus. Designed like an H, the east-west bar joined two north-south wings. John said the bar was a huge, comfortable living room with a large stone fireplace at either end. A red-tiled roof shaded a broad veranda that enclosed the west, south and east sides of the house. In the late afternoon light, its serenity eased any doubts that still lingered in Maggie's mind. As their carriage rolled up the drive, Maggie liked the way broad fields of wild flowers flanked the drive northward from the river road to the house.

John helped her down and escorted her across a wide patio with borders of flowers and a bubbling fountain at its center. As they entered through a pair of large carved doors at the center of the H south wall, John eagerly seized Maggie in his strong arms and carried her across the threshold. Almost from the instant her feet touched the floor, she felt that she belonged.

John proudly called Maggie's attention to a celadon 100-knot Chinese carpet which stretched the full forty-foot length of the room. "The day after I first met you on the road to Monterey, I ordered this rug from Fetti through Larry Wang's agents in Tientsin."

"You're joking! How could you know then that you wanted to marry me?

"You were the most beautiful creature I had ever seen. I couldn't just moon over you. I'm not built like that. I had to act. So I decided to decorate this house as if you would live in it some day."

"But how did you know my favorite color is celadon?"

"Why, honey, you told me so on that foggy day last year."

Maggie shook her head and marveled. The company had captured the color so well that the rug seemed to be a strip of spring lawn bridging the two fireplaces. She turned to the north and caught her breath. Through a floor-to-ceiling wall of glass, she saw a large, tiled patio. Twenty feet from the house, flowering bougainvillea adorned an eight-foot high fieldstone wall. Across the base of the wall, gray-green lamb's ears seemed to be an extension of the carpet and boasted tiny purple flowers. Beyond the wall, the glory of a scarlet sky echoed the flaming red and purple bracts of the vine and forecast sunset.

"When did this happen, John? You never mentioned the patio, that beautiful field-stone wall or the wall of glass. In fact, you told me this wall was thick adobe with tiny barred windows."

"You frowned when I described it. So I talked to an architect at Stanford. He said he could remove it and put in glass if we used steel posts to anchor the main beam. I'm right pleased with the whole effect." Sunlight bathed the wall and the bougainvillea and the lamb's ears in color. "The north light is steady all day on this rug and makes the room light and airy. I hope you like it."

"I love it!" She walked to the east fireplace and saw that two long couches faced each other across a dark rosewood Chinese coffee table, covered with copies of *Harper's Weekly*, *Century Magazine*, *The National Geographic*, the *Atlantic Monthly*, *Vogue*, *McClure's* and of course *The Ladies' Home Journal*, the source of all wisdom for homemakers. "Truth time, John. Did you buy these just for me?"

John grinned sheepishly. "I asked Lily what you might like the most. She seemed right pleased at my question. I wanted you to feel welcome. I grew up in this house and love it... well, almost as much as I love you. I wanted you to feel the same way."

Maggie gave John a fierce hug. "What about those empty shelves around the fireplace? Are you waiting for books?"

"No. I figured you might want to put some of your things there. Lily told me your father collected porcelain. Maybe they would look good there."

So this is why Lily changed her opinion of John during our final academic year.

She was conspiring with him! Maggie felt a flash of jealousy at the thought that Lily might have stood in this room, might even have captured John's heart while they discussed interior decoration. But she banished that idea as unworthy of either John or Lily. He was right; her father's Ming porcelains would add a delicate touch to the room. Then she saw a grand piano behind a couch. When she saw sheet music by Stephen Foster and Scott Joplin, she felt deeply moved by her husband's thoughtful sensitivity.

Hand in hand, they inspected the east wing, which contained a large master bedroom at the northeast corner and two guest bedrooms. The west wing held a kitchen at the southwest corner. A substantial dining room extended the east-west living room and separated the kitchen from a large library at the northwest corner. From the massive dining room table to the desk and tables in the library, the furniture was solid oak, the heavy Spanish motif that promised to outlast its owners. To her surprise, Maggie liked it. Like the rest of the house, it embraced Maggie without fanfare. Unashamedly utilitarian, it said to her, "Use me; carve on me; polish me. I'll grow old with you without pretense." But the library absolutely captured her soul. It seemed fifteen degrees cooler than the outside temperature. John explained that it was well insulated by a west wall of double-thickness adobe-brick, lined with walnut shelves of books: a triple shield against the afternoon sun. Against the south wall, also lined with books, a large fireplace served both the library and the adjacent dining room. The north wall was a huge floor-to-ceiling wall of glass that offered a view of the distant Cañada Segunda mountains. Through the east wall of glass, she could see the patio and its wall of bougainvillea.

Maggie began to glow with a sense of belonging, a feeling that had eluded her in China and at Mills College for too many years. In some deep part of her being, she felt that this was a spiritual homecoming, a resolution of many levels of fear that had assailed her after the death of her parents. She fought to control tears as her mind embraced the house and gardens and river. *Thank you, John; thank you, God. I'm home!*

CHAPTER FOUR

CARMEL
JULY–SEPTEMBER, 1894

For the next two months, Maggie could not have asked for a more attentive husband. John treated her like a princess—on horseback. He taught
her to ride in the Mexican manner, seated well back in the western saddle.
At first, her training on an English saddle in Shanghai confused her. But
before long, she could steer a cutting horse almost as well as any of the
vaqueros, whose approval only confirmed their faith in the patron's good
sense. Through the rest of June, while the newlyweds searched for stray
horses, cows and calves, they explored John's favorite places: a bea-
ver-built dam holding a willow-shaded pool where they swam in the nude;
an eagle's nest on a wind-swept cliff from which they could see westward
to the Pacific Ocean; a field so thick with wild flowers that it was a blanket
of yellow and scarlet.

From these trips, Maggie began to glimpse John's abiding love of nature. At first, he was as tongue-tied as he had been on their dates in San
Francisco. But her curiosity soon breached his defenses and the words
poured out. When he talked about the land and his childhood, his eyes
sparkled and his face shone with sweet memories. Here was the home of
his heart. Here he had proved himself in that terrible summer of 1890 after
his father had died and he had to behave like a leader. Here rain and
storms and the land had toughened his mind and his body and here he had
brought his soul's bride.

Days of riding and nights of loving nurtured a glow of self-discovery in
Maggie. For most of her life, especially during her childhood in China, she
had crafted her behavior and her self-evaluation for someone else's approval: her parents, who had been fearful of judgment by the Chinese or
God; her Chinese playmates, who had laughed at her foreign manners;

even Lily and her father, who had criticized her pretensions of being Chinese. In her zeal to respond to so many cautionary authorities, like a chameleon she had taught herself to adapt her coloration, her surface personality, to any situation. But she had never felt confident of any one of her many masks. Indeed, Chinese of all classes had revealed such a diversity of self-deception that she believed no one should ever be accepted at face value. She had concluded that the only safety must be some inner harmony that she must discover and impose on all doctrines of heaven and earth. And so she had selected music as her mediator, her sorcery for reconciling life's contradictions.

That first month on the ranch changed everything. Around John's tolerant, earthy style, she was sometimes giddy with happiness at the joyous novelty of her own flowering. A good listener, he urged her to explore her imagination without fear of criticism or misunderstanding. As she settled into her new sense of belonging—and authority, she sparkled with nesting projects. One day at breakfast in early July, she said, "Johnnie, why don't we have running water in the house? The outhouse is… disgusting."

A wave of guilt washed over John. He had intended to install modern plumbing before Maggie arrived. "I'm sorry, honey. I reckon things *are* a trifle primitive here. I'll put plumbin' in a bathroom and the kitchen in a week. Anythin' else?"

"Please run pipes to my future gardens. And will you agree to a telephone?"

"A telephone? What for? I cherish my privacy. You git a telephone and, next thing you know, strangers will be tryin' to sell you somethin'. What's the matter? You feelin' lonely already?"

"No…." Maggie lifted a cup of coffee to her lips and reflected. "It's just that I would like to talk to Lily once in a while. And if we had an emergency and needed help…."

"Like a fire in the barn? We're so far out that it would have burned down by the time help could get here. We've always handled our own problems. But it's a good idea. I might as well run pipes to the barn, too. And, honey, if you want a phone, I'll have one installed. It may take a while 'cause we'll have to string the line for miles. What else?"

"Well…, now that you ask." Maggie smiled with teasing eyes. "I like Maria and Carmen well enough. But I'd like to hire a Chinese woman for the kitchen. Lily has recommended someone."

"A Chinese on this ranch?" John's face became thoughtful, his mouth a thin line of disapproval. "I don't care much for the Chinese, you know."

"I know; but my Spanish is just passable. And even if it were fluent, these two Mexican girls don't have a brain in their heads. They say, 'Si, senora' to everything I say, then scurry off to giggle at each other. And now that you're getting ready for the round-up, I guess we won't be able to take many rides. And even when you're here, you aren't much interested in my ideas for decorating the house. And I miss the sound of Mandarin. And Lily says the woman is a superb cook. And...."

John chuckled. "Enough! I surrender. What's her name?"

"Ah-ying Chou," Maggie replied. "She's waiting in Monterey. I'll need a buggy and driver today to go get her."

Waiting in Monterey? She must think I'm a pushover. But John couldn't resist her challenging eyes and audacious charm. He shook his head in tolerant admiration and grinned. "I swear, Maggie; do you have a master plan? Or do these things just occur to you when you wake up ever' mornin'?"

Maggie stood up, squeezed herself between John and the table and sat on his lap. "Ask me no questions and I'll tell you no lies," she whispered, hugging him and rewarding him with a long kiss on the mouth. She could hear Carmen and Maria giggling nervously in the pantry.

With Ah-ying's arrival that afternoon, Mandarin became the language of the house. The elderly Chinese woman encouraged Maggie's unerring sense of style to transform John's run-down California ranch house into a gracious environment adorned with books, carpets, linens, porcelains, sterling silver and wall hangings. Bubbling fountains were built where future wild flower gardens would soon become a perimeter of color around the house. Until late August, the delights of nesting consumed Maggie's energies. By then, the brutal heat deterred her from venturing out of the cool house with its new self-sufficiency: plumbing.

And then, little things began to dramatize the contrast between her house and the rest of the ranch, fueling her resentment of ranching as a dirty, dawn-to-dark business. On rare occasions when she ventured out and caught glimpses of vaqueros or John at work, she was not impressed by the muscular violence of horse-breaking and calf-branding, from which John returned sweat-stained, smelly and exhausted most afternoons.

Her protest began with the house. She didn't approve of house-proud women; but neither could she tolerate any thoughtless invasion of her world, a world of serene cleanliness and order that she had worked hard to carve out of what she began to see as a primitive wilderness. First she begged John to take off his mud-stained boots before he entered what she came to think of as *her* living room. Next, she insisted on a strong post-and-rail fence around the entire house to deter cattle, deer and other animals from devouring her coming crop of flowers and vegetables. As the days passed, she awakened each morning with some new idea for reinforcing her defenses against her primary enemy: not just the ranch but the vaquero mind-set of slovenly machismo that seemed to threaten her thin hold on civilization.

As August drew to a close, she noticed that John had become quiet and withdrawn. Something was worrying him. Was it her fault? Had she pushed too hard for change? She dismissed that idea with the consoling thought that he would have said something surely. Another woman perhaps? Nonsense. She just knew there couldn't be another woman worth John's attention within a hundred miles. She didn't want to appear too nosy; but neither did she want to be treated like an innocent, self-indulgent child, excluded from adult discussion and decision. One day she asked Ramon Cisneros if something unusual had happened that might be troubling the patrón at the ranch.

Ramon looked puzzled. He had come to admire her for her verve and her compassion for tenant families on the ranch, especially the way modern plumbing was finding its way to every family's cottage. "No señora," he said frankly. "In fact, after the round-up next week, we'll be able to relax." Then he remembered that John had recently paid several visits to Monterey. Could they have marital problems already? *Carajo*! Was the patrón straying from the fold so soon? What could he say to her especially since he didn't know what John was up to?

Maggie found it increasingly difficult to ignore the expression of concern on John's face. Finally, after supper on the night of August 31, she could stand the suspense no longer. Next day, he was to leave with thirty vaqueros and a large *remuda* of extra horses for a month-long roundup. She gently removed the newspaper from his hands and sat down next to him. "Johnnie, for the past month, you've worn a worried look. You have avoided my questions. I can't stand your silences much longer. Talk to me!"

"You're just imaginin' things, honey. Aside from gettin' ready for the round-up, nothin' is troublin' me." He quickly changed the subject. "I swear, the feelin' in this house is a tribute to your genius, honey."

Her mind a turmoil of doubts and suspicions, Maggie wearily turned off the living room lamps, went to bed and waited for John. Perhaps seduction would succeed where confrontation had failed. That night, she gave herself to him as if she might never see him again. For the first time, he was able to banish all Puritanical doubts about his lust. The joining of their bodies felt like they had blended their spirits. She was so deeply moved by the storm of his hunger that she completely forgot about her earlier motives. Long after he had drifted into sleep, she remained alert and thoughtful.

When she awakened the next morning, she was sorry to see that John had left before dawn, as he had warned. The silence from the barnyard and the chow line warned her that only a handful of cowboys had remained behind. The rest had ridden forth to find and brand strays in the hundreds of narrow valleys in the mountains east of Carmel. Then they would drive the herd to the railroad in the Central Valley. It would be an exhausting ordeal quite beyond her imagination.

For the next two weeks she tried to occupy herself with music and reading and good works among the women of the ranch. But time soon began to hang heavy on her mind. The nights were especially hard to bear, John's absence accentuating her sense of remote isolation. Even Ah-ying's jokes with Chinese aphorisms failed to lift Maggie's mood of growing resentment. She fought its dark menace with questions. Was she feeling this way because she felt abandoned? Or did she merely need someone intelligent to talk to? Or perhaps she felt imprisoned by routine, a repetition of hours and days of relentless boredom? By the third week of September, she convinced herself that her unfamiliar mood was John's fault, particularly his stubborn silence. If he didn't see fit to confide in her, she would investigate for herself.

The next morning, she made her decision. She selected her finest day-time "battle dress," as she called it. Much as she disdained the corset, she put one on to achieve the image of fashionable maturity, the popular bell-shaped, "pouter-pigeon" effect, a forward thrust of the bosom with a corresponding fullness to the rear. Then she put on a handkerchief-linen blouse with a pleated front, a high choker collar and a large bow at the neck. She wrapped a long, gray linen skirt around her waist. Over the blouse, she wore a short, sky-blue Shantung silk jacket with leg-o'-mutton shoulders. From her only hat box she gently withdrew a sky-blue velvet hat, trimmed with a silk ribbon and ostrich plumes. Finally, she drew on gray gloves and surveyed the general effect in the mirror with satisfaction. Charles Dana Gibson couldn't have done any better, even if she wasn't a Gibson Girl. She found Ramon Cisneros in the kitchen, sipping a cup of coffee and flirting with Ah Ying. "Ramon," she said with a confidence that she didn't feel, "Please have someone bring the buggy. I'm going to Monterey."

Wringing his hands, Ramon was abruptly terrified. "Señora, the patrón has ordered all hands to make sure you do nothing that might… cause an accident. He doesn't want you to go anywhere, especially on that bumpy road."

"Ramon, I'm not a prisoner. If you don't arrange a buggy for me *right now*, I'll saddle my own horse and ride into Monterey alone!" Maggie glared at him until he nodded forlornly and yelled for Antonio and Jaime to do her bidding, and to disappear across the border if she didn't come back safely.

They made the one-hour trip to Monterey in silence. Maggie had to ask for directions twice before she found her way to Mackie's bank on Alvarado.

A breakfast argument with his wife about his irresponsible tiddling had started Fred Mackie's day with a bang. A vicious headache was piercing his brain when he heard Maggie Harrison's voice outside his office. With no escape possible, he hastily buttoned his checkered blue vest and shouldered into a black frock coat, which he thought went well with his gray silk tie and gray wool trousers. While he smoothed his thinning hair, he tried to rearrange his face into his banker's mask, an expression of impassive non-commitment. Then nodding to a grinning teller, he managed a wan smile as he welcomed Maggie into his office. "What an unexpected pleasure, Mizz Harrison," he simpered.

"I'll come straight to the point, Mr. Mackie," Maggie said imperiously. "Is my husband in some kind of financial trouble?"

"Well now, Mizz Harrison…. I ah… that is to say… uh, why do you ask?"

"That's none of your business, sir. Please just tell me 'yes' or 'no.' Is that too much to ask of a small-town banker?

Suddenly something snapped in Fred Mackie's mind. That "small-town banker" bit pushed him over the edge. "I'm sorry, Mizz Harrison," Fred replied with quiet authority, a mildly shocked expression on his face. "We have promised total confidentiality on our accounts."

"But I'm his wife," Maggie cried. "Anyway, I don't want to see his account. Can't you tell me if he's in trouble?"

What the hell; everyone knows that answer anyway, Fred thought. *She could have asked the barber for a faster opinion than I'm giving her. Maybe a quick answer will get rid of her. John shouldn't mind; it would violate no confidence.* "His trust fund is healthy; he's in fine shape—*financially.*"

"Trust fund?"

"That's right. Old Nate made me the trustee of his considerable fortune until John reaches the age of thirty."

Maggie gasped. John must feel humiliated to have to come to an idiot like Fred Mackie for money. What could Nate Harrison have been thinking? "Have you ever approved of special withdrawals?"

"Yep. Just a month ago, I gave him an advance to cover the cost of the round-up. As you know, this depression has driven beef prices way down."

A light suddenly turned on in Maggie's mind. Ranching was more than the back-breaking routine that exhausted everyone involved. It was a business! How could she have been so blind? No wonder John looked so preoccupied all the time. But why didn't he want to talk about it? Was he embarrassed about his trust? Did he think she wouldn't be interested? Her resentment jumped a notch at the thought that she had been lavishing money on house decorating while John worried about paying his vaqueros. "You mean he may be in financial trouble after the round-up?"

"Well." Fred had to think about that proposition while his head pounded mercilessly. "Not really. Even if he fails to make a profit this year, he doesn't owe the bank any money. I just loaned him his own money out of his trust."

"Thank you, Mr. Mackie. You have been more help than you can know. I'll tell John that you can keep a confidence, just like you promised. Forgive me for prying but do you have a headache?"

"Why yes. Does it show?"

"You've been pressing your temples with both hands ever since I walked in the room. Frankly, you look miserable."

"Frankly, I feel miserable."

"Did you feel... loggy, confused, maybe with a headache when you woke up this morning?"

Fred nodded. "Can you recommend something for a hangover?"

Maggie smiled. She couldn't imagine making friends with Fred Mackie; but it wouldn't hurt for the local banker to speak well of her. "You may have forgotten this old remedy. Mix a glass of tomato juice with a dollop of Lea and Perrins Worcestershire Sauce and a few shakes of ground pepper. Drink it down. In half an hour, you should begin to feel human again."

"I tried that recipe," Fred said miserably. "It just made me feel worse."

"Hmm, maybe you need a healing touch. May I touch you?"

"Why... I think I'd be happier if you shot me."

Maggie moved behind Fred and placed both thumbs on acupuncture points beneath his ears while her palms pressed against his temples. She applied pressure with her palms for about thirty seconds. "There now," she said. "You should feel some relief now. And thank you again for your help."

Fred had been astonished first at Maggie's cool touch. It made him think of his mother, who had once cupped his head in loving hands. Then, wonder of wonders, he felt a marked reduction of pressure in his head. His eyes no longer felt like they were about to explode. Strangest of all, he could taste mint. He thought, *I'm damned. I wouldn't have thought wisdom could come in such a beautiful package... even if she is a damned Populist. When she walked in, I wanted to throw her out. Now suddenly, she's my doctor.* He bowed his head in gratitude, escorted her through the door and assisted her into her buggy.

On her way back to the ranch, Maggie's temper almost boiled over. Now she had the evidence that John had tried to protect her..., no, *exclude* her from his own crisis. Had Lily been right? Was it possible that he thought of her as a Victorian child-bride like Dora in *David Copperfield*? The more she thought about his patronizing behavior, the more she felt diminished. When she calmed down, she realized that he had done what any self-respecting man would do. It was business. Women weren't supposed to get involved in business. So he felt that he must wrestle with his problem alone. That conclusion led her to the further insight that the ranch was the source of this misunderstanding. John was imprisoned by it just as much as she was. She resolved to confront him when he returned from round-up. Ranching was really beneath him. He must give greater purpose to his life and she must help him discover that purpose.

CHAPTER FIVE

CARMEL
OCTOBER, 1894

"So you barely broke even after a whole year's work?" Maggie's tone mixed disbelief with disdain. A part of her wanted to reach out and comfort John, whose hardship on the drive had etched furrows of worry across his haggard face, bronzed almost black by a month in searing sun. But her compassion could not overcome her sense that John was wasting his talent on a losing business. Lily had been right. It wasn't rational for someone with money and education to torture himself when there were plenty of Mexicans around who thought the work was romantic. "I'm not impressed, Johnnie. Why did you struggle through four years of college? Why did you to get a degree in mechanical engineering if you intended to squander your education on horses and bronco busting and cattle drives?"

"Now wait just a minute, Maggie." John was bone tired. All he wanted was a hot bath and a kiss and twelve hours of sleep. He had been home less than an hour and the shock of her welcome was the last thing he had expected. He knew something had provoked her to snipe at him now. But emotionally he was so depleted that he could only hear the passion in Maggie's voice. "If you'll just slow down for a minute, maybe I can figure out what you're sayin'. Let's see…. You want me to give up ranchin'?"

"Yes. Look at you! You've aged ten years in a month. You look like you can barely stand up, like you've been tortured to the break point. If you get pleasure out of such torture, you must be a masochist."

"Honey, ranchin' has its special ups and downs 'cause it can't get away from mother nature. But it's just a b'iness."

"I thought a good business was the one that gets the most money for the least effort. Ranching seems to yield the least money for the most effort. Why can't you do something… intelligent?"

John shook his head wearily. His brain seemed to have lost the power of thought. "Maybe at supper tonight we can try to agree on what you mean by that word. Until then, I'd appreciate a little quiet around this house." He turned from her and trudged into their bedroom where he blessed her for insisting on hot and cold running water. His bath felt so luxurious that he almost fell asleep in the tub.

After dressing leisurely in a wool shirt and gray wool trousers over clean, highly polished boots, he walked across the living room to a sideboard where he poured a glass of claret. Then he moved to the sound of women's voices in the kitchen where the aroma of his favorite dish, beef stroganoff, set his taste buds tingling. Pleased that the dining room table was set with candles, he nodded to Ah-ying and put a free arm around Maggie's waist. "Now I'm home, mostly. There may still be a piece of me about ten miles east of here. But I'm not goin' out there tonight to hunt for it."

Maggie smiled a warm greeting. "Come sit down and let us serve you. And forgive me for greeting you this afternoon with my frustrations. Maybe I can present my case with a little less heat now."

"I've been thinkin' about what you said." John took a sip of claret while Ah-ying offered platters of beef and noodles. "I don't think you're really concerned about my misuse of my education."

"That's not true!" Maggie protested, feeling her temperature rising again. "But I...."

"Doesn't matter," John interrupted. "I heard the excitement in your voice. That was a lot more important than all the reasons you could think of. If you want to talk about reasons, I'll listen." What he couldn't tell her was that he had awakened with the shocking realization that he cared more for her approval and respect than he did for money or prestige or "something glorious," however it might be defined. Now he felt moved to reveal himself. "I've always thought of ranchers and cowboys as romantic figures, kinda like knights."

"Medieval knights?" Maggie couldn't conceal her astonishment.

"Well, yeah, sort of. They've just traded their coats of mail for leather chaps and slickers. But their function has never changed. They must still face constant danger from man and beast and weather to carry out a sacred trust: keepin' the peace in the kingdom. I think of my ranch as a kingdom."

As she listened, Maggie began to understand that John must live each day in a kind of waking dream, filled with challenges to his faith, courage and strength. If true, then his principal reward for a cattle drive was not money but satisfaction and a reaffirmation of his right to be the trustee of his kingdom. "Did you think of your father as King Arthur?"

John nodded, a self-deprecating smile on his face. "I guess so. But if I look at it all through your eyes, it must look like a silly pretense. The funny thing is that I've been thinkin' like you. I've been wonderin' what I could do to use my education to better effect. If I'm gonna have a family some day, I can't keep on tiltin' windmills like ole Don Quixote."

Maggie was suspicious. She had expected much more resistance. "Who could run the ranch if you started some new business?"

"Ramon. He makes most of the decisions anyway. No, the real problem is what to do with my engineerin' and my love of nature. Any ideas?"

Maggie did have some ideas. But she wasn't like John, whose notion of an idea's value was how to make something work better. Even a practical idea satisfied her search for meaning only if she could find its proper place in a wider context of abstract principles. She was a natural philosopher. "Do you believe in the survival of the fittest, Johnnie?"

"I swear, Maggie, how you do go on." John looked slightly discomfited, a familiar reaction whenever Maggie tried to draw him into a philosophical discussion. "I haven't thought about it one way or the other. I s'pose wild animals find life is a struggle to survive. Why do you ask?"

"Because your answer influences your notion of your role in society. And that bounds your choices of what to do next. Do you think we're victims of fate? Is our future inevitable?"

"Oh, I see what you're sayin'." John thought it was a long way around the subject. But he decided to give the question its due. "I think you have to have the courage to fight against givin' up. I *don't* think we're victims. At least, I don't think our future is inevitable." He grinned. "And Lancelot sure wouldn't think so, either."

"Good for you—and Lancelot too!" Maggie exclaimed. "I don't believe that we are helpless before a "natural" struggle for survival. While you were gone I read Mr. Ward's fine book, *Dynamic Sociology*. He says society is an organism. Our institutions are adaptive mechanisms to keep it healthy."

John was impatient to hear Maggie's definition of an "intelligent" business. "So how does that help me select a good b'iness?"

"We must not be passive, like a rancher waiting for the weather," Maggie asserted. "Our salvation isn't just a matter of standing by and smugly waiting for natural evolution to save us. We must be inventive to help the weak escape from their grinding poverty."

While Maggie tried to draw John into her enthusiasm for the common man, he devoured his food and gulped down several glasses of wine. He loved to hear her talk, no matter what the subject. While she spoke, her complexion changed to a rosy hue as if to reflect the heat and power of her ideas. She used words and phrases like "plight of the masses," "equity," "equality before the law," "liberation," "capitalist greed," "people's democracy," "insensitive trusts," "government indifference," "corruption," "socialism" and "one man-one vote." Social equity seemed to be her passion. As he listened, John slowly began to understand that she was defining a broad social purpose that she could admire, regardless of the specific role he might play. At the heart of her political spirit seemed to be a plea for justice and courage to act.

Finally, after swallowing half a glass of wine in one long draught, she concluded, "I want our children to understand that salvation must come from our personal efforts. We must apply scientific findings to social issues as well as nature. It's time for social reform. We've got to be more efficient." Maggie flushed. "I must sound like a Social Gospeler."

"What's a Social Gospeler?"

"A person who seeks salvation through compassion and good works in society, not through hypocritical, Sunday-go-to-meeting piety and fire-and-brimstone sermonizing."

"You mean you don't like Billy Sunday?"

"I think he's one of the worst hypocrites. He's just a tool of businessmen and politicians. He uses his religion to justify their rapacious exploitation of the common man.

"I'm not sure where you're goin' with this, Maggie," John said, his eyes slightly unfocused from too much wine and too rich a conversation. "But I sure admire people like the Weyerhaeuser and James Hill in the North-west; or Harriman who now controls most of the railroads into Southern California; or J.P. Morgan on Wall Street. They're prime examples of the wealth and power a man can amass in this great country if he only works hard."

John's footnotes plainly agitated Maggie. "John, I'm sorry you see those capitalists as heroes. In my view, they are the worst products of our flawed social and economic systems. All they can think of is money and power and lording it over everyone else."

John thought she was extraordinarily beautiful. Her hair glinted like bright copper in the candlelight. Her eyes flashed with the sincerity of her convictions: Saint Joan at the head of her legions of peasants. "So you don't want me to be a hero like them?"

"In my opinion, none of them is a hero!" Maggie cried. "They've sacrificed everything that's gentle and kind and beautiful to financial combat. Just think, a hundred and thirty families in Pittsburgh and New York have an aggregate wealth of over three hundred million dollars!"

John had had a taste of these views at their wedding. They hadn't mattered to him then. But now he was searching for the key to Maggie's respect. So far, it was eluding him. "Are you opposed to makin' money?"

"No. I oppose *how* they made it. I think the American capitalist doesn't care a whit about law. They've exploited the immigrant, the wage laborer and the tenant farmer so ruthlessly that they live in near slavery. It's not simply a national disgrace. It's a scandal before God!"

Suddenly, John was struck by the intuition that Maggie wanted to apply some of her Populist ideas to the ranch. "Do you think I exploit our ranch hands?"

"Exploit is too strong a word. But I think it would be more equitable if they could own stock and receive benefits. Every ranch hand should own his own house on land we have deeded to him. We should guarantee their employment through good times and bad. We should provide all health services without charge. We should assist their children in their education. We should not abandon them when they grow old or when they most need our help."

John couldn't believe what he was hearing. Was she a goddam socialist? Did she mean to incorporate the ranch and give away ownership? He

could feel his mouth tightening with disapproval. Benefits maybe; ownership? Never.

"I believe these rancheros have ambitions for their kids just as noble
and prayerful as ours will be for our children," Maggie continued. "That's
why we must work out some practical ways to bring equity to ranch families. I'll draw up a plan for you."

"Well, sweetheart, I'm glad I've had more than my share of claret tonight. Otherwise, I might be too shocked to speak. Do you think we really
ought to start a revolution? Is this your idea of somethin' glorious?"

Maggie flashed him a luminous smile. "It certainly is. This country
won't amount to a hill of beans unless it draws on the creative energies of
the common citizen—not just the scientist or the robber baron or the Wall
Street investment banker. I think we're witnessing a dawning, a great watershed in human history."

"What kind of watershed, Maggie?" John asked.

"Liberation of the common man from commercial and royal elites."

"Elites?"

"Yes. Those nabobs who learned nothing from the French revolution
and still twist all rules of equity and justice for their own benefit."

"And where do you think this liberation will lead us?"

"I think the new century will bring a very radical redistribution of
wealth here and in Europe." Maggie lifted her chin. She hoped John had
followed a fraction of her plea for equity. "If that doesn't happen, there
will certainly be a revolution! And I'll be at the front of it."

John stared morosely into the fire. What did all this have to do with
him, he wondered. "I'm still baffled about a b'iness to use my dubious talents."

Now was the time to reveal her brilliant idea. "I think it's primitive to
make ordinary people walk to work. I've been reading about the bicycle
craze back east. Why don't you make bicycles?"

"Bicycles?" John made the word sound dirty.

"What's wrong with bicycles? They're efficient. They're good exercise. They save time and allow people to find a little leisure in their lives.
They encourage men and women to get out and see the countryside. And
they're fashionable. In New York, the papers say Lillian Russell rides one
every day with Diamond Jim Brady in Central Park."

"Is that so?" John had a sinking feeling that bicycle manufacturing would be a sad ending for his medieval knighthood. "Well, not everyone approves. Tom Reed, the Speaker of the House of the Fifty-fourth Congress, was asked what he thought was the greatest problem for Americans. He said, 'How to dodge bicycles.'"

Maggie pouted. "I'm serious, John. No one is making them in Monterey yet. I bet you could design a dandy bicycle. Pretty soon, your name would be on everyone's lips."

"I'll think on it, Maggie. Would you really like me to spend my days in Monterey instead of hanging around the ranch?"

"It's not a matter of how I feel, John. I don't want to push you into anything that might make you unhappy. I just think you're cut out for something better than herding cattle. Will you think about it?"

"I said I would. Now would you like to hear some strange stories about the cattle drive?"

"Of course." Maggie had eaten little while she dominated the conversation. Listening to John's stories, she sipped her coffee with a sense of pleasure in the hope that her pleas had changed his vision in ways that would ultimately benefit everyone.

CHAPTER SIX

CARMEL
OCTOBER–DECEMBER, 1894

For the next three months, Maggie investigated the life of ranch families. She wanted plenty of background information to validate her proposal to John for a reasonable package of benefits. At first she thought of handing out a brief questionnaire. But Ana Cisneros, Ramon's cheerfully wise wife, reminded Maggie that most of the women couldn't read. She suggested a more intimate approach. "Invite a few of the women into your kitchen every morning and let them make little dolls from pipe cleaners. Let each doll represent one of the women or a member of her family. While they make the doll, you can ask them about their family." The project captured the wit and imagination of all the women, who dressed the tiny figures in cowboy boots and wide Mexican sombreros or flaring skirts and mantillas. Their attention to detail astonished Maggie, whose innocent little game reaped unexpected benefits.

At a practical level, their description of each figure—who it represented, his or her personality, quirks, private dreams and reputation on the ranch—gave Maggie an insight into every soul on the ranch, almost two hundred people. After she had spent part of each day with one or two ranch women, they would go home to tell their friends more about the patron's wife. Each evening after inspecting several figures, she wrote down the names and stories about each personality to be sure that she didn't forget. Those pages of biographical sketches soon filled two large boxes and inspired the idea that she should incorporate them into a book of stories about the ranch. She decided she would give John a leather-bound copy entitled "The Kingdom of Harrison" for Christmas.

At a more subtle level, the gaiety and shrewd wisdom of the ranch women reinforced Maggie's passion for the underdog. They reminded her of Chinese women who had also endured multiple challenges to their peace of mind, especially male authority. In China, she had seen enough injustice, especially toward women, to last her a lifetime. Whether bound by the cruelties of their social system or binding around their feet, most Chinese women were doomed to a life of servitude. The woes of peasant women had convinced her that China's rural culture and social system nurtured a rigid hierarchy of self-serving masculine exploitation, sanctified by precedent and the autocratic authority of the Emperor. She still burned with resentment at three Confucian laws: when a woman is young, she must obey her father or older brother; when she marries, she must heed her husband; when her husband dies, she must obey her own son. She wondered if the Catholic Church had the same effect on ranch women that Confucius had on Chinese women: mandating women's subservience to man.

Maggie's friendship with the women prompted her to expand her inventory of music. Sometimes she would play the piano while they taught her their favorite ballads. As the days flew by, everyone soon understood that her curiosity about their lives was her way of showing her compassion. As an expression of their respect and welcome, a few women began to bring personal problems to her: a husband who was drinking too much; a husband who was spending too much time at Mama Rosa's cantina in Monterey; a sick child who needed the same healing wisdom that Maggie had given, without charge, to the Señor Mackie, who had spread the legend of Maggie's beauty and healing skills across the Peninsula. When the older women compared Maggie favorably with John's mother, all the ranch women began to call her Doña Margarita. By mid-November, Maggie was so busily involved with life on the ranch that she stopped thinking of it as a primitive backwater, unworthy of her attention. Day by day, she was beginning to think of it as her kingdom too.

Watching her invest herself in the ranch, John decided to experiment with the bicycle business. By mid-November, he had hired two assistants, had assembled machinery and had designed his first bicycle. The process of starting a small business challenged everything he had learned in college and filled his mind with exciting ideas. With the long ride to and from

Monterey, the installation of machinery and wheels and tires and other materials, the days were long. But the fatigue that John felt each day when he returned to the ranch was pleasant, the feeling of using his mind and body for a good purpose.

One cold, rainy evening after supper, they watched a fire in the living room and talked about their day. "I want to thank you for your idea about the bicycle b'iness, honey," John said. "I think I'll sell lots of bicycles for Christmas. At first, I wasn't too enthusiastic. But it's more complicated than it might look. And I meet lots of interestin' people who want a bike."

"I'm so glad, Johnnie." Maggie was genuinely thrilled that her suggestion had panned out so well. More to the point of her prior dissatisfaction, she thought their new roles at the ranch and in the town would be more likely to sustain their marriage. "I'm learning a lot about life on the ranch, too."

"Not feelin' so lonely any more?"

"Heavens no! I seem to be busy from dawn to dark."

"I'm mighty pleased. Maybe we can plan on a campin' trip to the Rockies next summer. How'd you like that?"

"Why, I think the three of us should have a grand time!" Maggie exclaimed.

"Three of us?" John asked.

"Yes, Johnnie; sometime next June, you're going to be a father."

John's initial reply was disturbing. He stared at her with a question in his eyes. Then he looked into the fire and searched for the many implications of her announcement. His strange reaction to the news troubled Maggie. But she was soon reassured when he grinned ruefully and took her in his arms. "It's hard to believe, honey."

Maggie nuzzled his neck. "You want a child, don't you?"

"Of course! It's just that... well, I reckon I din't expect the responsibility so soon. We'll have to mend our ways. Have to stop ridin' all over hell's half acre. Can't have you runnin' the risk of an accident now."

From that day forward, Maggie detected a worrisome shift in John's attitude. On the one hand, he went out of his way to accommodate her every whim. On the other hand, he behaved as if she were suffering from a terrible disease. He insisted on absolute quiet around the house when Maggie napped. He excused himself from frequent love-making. He refused to let her get near a horse; no more rides into the countryside.

While she planned a Christmas celebration, Maggie's fertile brain conceived of alternative explanations for the emotional distance which slowly separated her from her husband. She thought, *He's simply inexperienced. It's just another example of his consummate thoughtfulness. He'll relax soon and everything will be fine again.* By mid-December, it was painfully clear to her that that rationale was an illusion. Something was bothering him so much that he couldn't bring himself to speak of it. She liked to bring her problems out in the open. John seemed to prefer to chew on them until they were chewing on him. She prayed that the spirit of Christmas might resolve her doubts.

Christmas morning started well. John was obviously deeply moved by her gift, the stories of ranch families. He cherished it so much that he read it periodically throughout the day. His eyes misting after glancing at a page or two, he would suddenly get lost in the story and forget where he was. Maggie had not imagined that he would be so emotional. He also liked a new saddle, presented by Ramon Cisneros on behalf of all the vaqueros.

Maggie was genuinely surprised at John's first gift: a new phonograph with twenty cylinders of music, including the popular "After The Ball," "Daisy Bell," the United States Marine Corps Band, a whistler, a coronet soloist, several Irish songs and several opera singers. The quality of sound was terrible, scratchy and ragged; but she was touched by his thoughtfulness. She also accepted a three-wheeled contraption—a tricycle of which he was very proud. A small buggy-seat, enclosed by a fringed top, rested on springs between two rear wheels. The top could be collapsed like an accordion on the back of the seat. It reminded Maggie of Shanghai rickshaws.

At eleven o'clock, he insisted that she climb onto the tricycle. With some misgivings, she acquiesced and soon found herself on a trip to each home on the ranch, John pedaling and shouting his glee. "*Hola, Miguel, venga, venga a ver la señora en su tricicleta! Felices Pascuas y prospero Año Nuevo.*"

John's delight was contagious. Soon, screaming for a ride, several small children were running beside the tricycle. "John," Maggie cried, "why don't you let one of the young vaqueros pedal while the children ride?"

"Are you kiddin', honey? Take all the kids you want; but no one else can drive you around. I wouldn't trust a vaquero to get near you; you're too valuable now. Just tell me when to stop for a fare. Tell 'em each kid has to give you a kiss on the cheek." John began to feel tired after an hour of pedaling on narrow dirt roads from one red-tiled cottage to the next. But he felt satisfied with Maggie's response to his gift. When she finally returned to the warmth of their living room, she was exhilarated from the outpouring of love. In two hours, nearly every person on the ranch, including the children, had greeted her and wished her a Merry Christmas and Happy New Year.

Her brain was buzzing with the joy of the day when Ah Ying announced Christmas lunch. Maggie had planned it carefully to reflect the eclectic culture of the ranch: a first course of egg-drop soup accompanied by platters of Chinese shrimp toast and spring rolls; a second course of boned trout almondine with broccoli; a third course of venison, cooked in the Mexican fashion over an oak fire, with mashed potatoes and Szechuan stringbeans, hot with chopped pepper; and a final course of cool flan, the Mexican custard, served with tiny warm, crisp Chinese honeycakes. Over coffee and port, she tried to explore what she considered John's excessively protective attitude. "Why wouldn't you let Ramon or Antonio ride the tricycle today, Johnnie? Do you honestly think I'm so frail?"

John peeled the wrapper off a cigar while he looked thoughtfully at Maggie. Should he tell her why her pregnancy had so terrified him? He looked wistfully at the flowerless bougainvillea in the courtyard and thought, *If she can't forgive me at Christmas, she never will.* "Somethin' terrible happened a long time ago, Maggie. I believe I would die if it happened again."

Apprehensive, Maggie tried to remain calm. "Tell me about it."

"When I was five years old, Poppa gave me a Shetland pony. He told me that I must never ride it unless he or Ramon was there. But I disobeyed him. One day I saddled the pony and started to ride him around the ring." John's expression was grim; he clipped the fire-end of the cigar, inserted the other end in his mouth and struck a match. "I reckon nuthin' would have happened if the pony hadn't shied from a garden snake. He reared and I lost one of the stirrups."

Maggie wondered how such an accident could lead to tragedy. While John puffed at his cigar, she poured a second cup of coffee for herself and watched John's eyes turn inward, back to that scene at the corral seventeen years ago.

"Momma happened to come out of the house at that moment. She saw me tryin' to hang on while the pony ran faster and faster around the ring. I s'pose she was afraid I'd fall off or maybe be dragged if she didn't stop him." John's eyes misted with the memory; he took a sip of coffee to gain control of his emotions. "Anyway, she raced out and screamed for help. When nobody responded, she jes opened the gate and ran in front of the pony to slow him down. The damned animal ran right over her; knocked her down."

"Oh, Johnnie, that must have been terribly painful. Was she hurt seriously?"

"Everthin' would have been fine, Maggie, except for one thing. Momma was five months pregnant."

Maggie held a fist to her mouth in apprehension. For a moment, she couldn't breathe. She just knew what was coming next.

"About that time, Poppa and Ramon arrived. They carried her into the bedroom. Ramon rode away for a doctor while Ana came in to try to help Momma. I knew somethin' was wrong; but no one would tell me anythin'. So I huddled in a corner in the hallway outside Momma's bedroom, our bedroom now, and waited. Lots of people came and went; but they ignored me as if I was some kind of criminal." John looked at the ash on his cigar, flicked it into an ashtray and took a sip of port.

Maggie couldn't bear the agony in John's eyes. Tears clouded her vision as she clenched and unclenched her fists and shook her head in sympathy.

"After about three hours, I suddenly heard a scream..., lots of screams. That's when the doctor arrived. And then Poppa came out. His face was black with the worst fury I've ever seen. He came over to me and lifted me by the shoulders and said, 'You little devil; you've killed him. You've killed your brother and you damn near killed your mother. Get out of my sight before I kill you.' He shook me 'til my teeth rattled. Then he said, 'I 'spec you'll bear the brand of a murderer the rest of your life.'"

Maggie wiped her eyes with a napkin, stood up and put her arms around John's shoulders. "Sweetheart, that's not going to happen to me! I'm not going to try to stop any wild horses."

"Maggie, I know that. I couldn't stand it if you did somethin' foolish. This child means more to me than most kids. It's a kind of... symbol, I guess. If we have a healthy, happy child, I'll feel like they... like my parents have forgiven me. Then maybe I can finally forget what happened."

"I understand. Very well; I'll just stay at home. But, Johnny, you don't have to treat me like I'll break at the drop of a hat. I'm stronger than you think."

John shifted so he could seat Maggie on his lap. He held her while, unable to speak, he closed his eyes to dam up his own emotion. Disgusted with himself, he wiped a few tears away with his napkin and asked, "Do you see now why I have to do somethin' glorious with my life?"

"But it wasn't your fault, Johnnie!" Maggie cried. "You're being much too hard on yourself."

"One part of me knows that; but buried mighty deep there's another part that sneers at me. You must think I'm a terrible weaklin' to give in to this."

"You, a weakling?" Maggie stared at him in dismay. "Never! But thank you for telling me." *So he has demons too!* In a rush of sympathy, she said, "I had a terrible shock too when I was young."

"You never told me, honey. What happened?"

"It happened when I was sixteen. Maybe you've heard of the Society of Righteous Fists. They're called the Boxers. They hate foreigners."

As Maggie talked, John watched her eyes turn inward. She seemed to withdraw into herself as if she were going back to that time.

"My father and mother were very busy then. So I was often on my own. But I loved the villagers, especially Li-Wei, our cook. From the time I was ten, whenever I was in trouble or sad or curious about things, she was always ready to stop what she was doing and comfort me or explain things. I... I loved her very much."

"So what happened, honey?"

"One day the Boxers descended on our sweet little village like wolves." Maggie's eyes flashed with anger and her jaw hardened. "Fortunately for me, a villager warned of their coming and hid me in our attic. So I saw everything that happened in our house."

John forced himself to stay silent while Maggie gathered her inner resources to endure something that she had wanted to banish from her memory.

"A big, ugly thug who looked like Mr. Mackie at the bank ran into our house. My father shouted at him in Chinese to get out. That fat brute roared some oath, swung his big sword through the air and.... Maggie's eyes brimmed and her lips quivered. "He... he beheaded my father. I... I saw his head just... roll across the floor."

"My God, sweetheart." John stared at her.

"Then my mother came in, screamed and tried to attack that monster. He just... threw her down and raped her. He called in other Boxers who raped her over and over and... over."

John marveled at Maggie's voice which had turned cold with hatred. *So that's why she confronted poor old Fred Mackie. Let the wrong man get in her way and she'll treat him like that damned Boxer.*

"She screamed and screamed." Maggie involuntarily covered her ears with her hands. "They... used her and used her and then... they strangled her."

John wanted to take her in his arms, but she was oblivious of him, of their home, of everything except those few minutes that had changed her life.

"Then Li-Wei arrived. She was hysterical and yelled at the Boxers." Maggie shook her head as tears began to stream down her cheeks. "Poor sweet Li-Wei. They stabbed her and stabbed her until her body turned red with her own blood." Maggie covered her eyes as if to shut out the image, still haunting her after five years. "The threw her body in the street and warned the other villagers that she deserved to die because she had worked for foreigners."

John tried to hold her in his arms then. But she refused to be comforted. The memory seemed to have seized control of her, transforming her into a rigid, bristling pillar of resentment. Finally she turned to him and said simply, "So you see, John, I have my demons too."

CHAPTER SEVEN

CARMEL VALLEY
JANUARY–JUNE, 1895

On New Year's Day, Ana Cisneros and Ah Ying assured Maggie that her first four months of pregnancy had been extraordinarily easy. Several young mothers on the ranch told of their suffering from nausea and dizziness, their cravings for bizarre food, and of their nasty dispositions. Maggie was so healthy that she began to feel a perverse kind of guilt as if she were not bearing her share of trouble before her child was born. She listened eagerly as they all gave her sage advice. But she kept asking herself questions for which their earthy good sense could provide no easy answers. How could she best guide her baby's mental and physical development? Should she just let nature take its course? Or should she try to exert more direct influence over her mind and spirit? And if she could shape her development, who should the baby become? It did not occur to her that her child might be a boy.

One evening after supper in early January, she chanced to pick up a book of poetry. For the first time she read the immortal lines from Wordsworth's *Intimations of Immortality from Recollections of Early Childhood*:

> *Our birth is but a sleep and a forgetting:*
> *The Soul that rises with us, our life's Star,*
> *Hath had elsewhere its setting,*
> *And cometh from afar;*
> *Not in entire forgetfulness*
> *And not in utter nakedness,*
> *But trailing clouds of glory do we come*
> *From God, who is our home.*
> *Heaven lies about us in our infancy.*

As if hypnotized by divine revelation, she stared at the print, thinking, *Kuan Yin and God have pointed my way*! Two questions replaced all the others that had hounded her for several months: "Will my baby be able to talk to God?" and "If so, how can I keep her from losing such a divine connection?" Answers to those questions must shape her plans for her baby's future.

When she told John about her exciting discovery, he grinned and shrugged with bemused bafflement. He had not been indifferent to her questions; he just thought her anguish was the price she must pay for an overheated imagination, or her inexperience, or her curious world of abstractions, or all three summed up under the title of "vapors." Surely, child rearing would soon banish her morbid brooding. In any case, the problems of beef prices and his bicycle business seemed much more pressing. "Maggie, I swear! I never knew a young mother could worry so much about philosophical questions. I'm bound to say it all seems very simple to me. I say set a good example; keep a tad clean on the outside and full on the inside and he'll turn out well enough. What more do you want?"

Horror-struck at his smug complacency, Maggie felt so outraged that she couldn't bring herself to speak. It didn't occur to her that the focal point of her own personality had been shifting. The prospect of a child had forced her to think responsibly, to assess ends and means and to plan. She raced to the library and collapsed on a couch in tears of frustration.

John followed and, kneeling beside her, tried to comfort her. "Look, honey, why don't you talk to Lily about these ideas? Didn't she study philosophy at college?"

"Yes," she whimpered. "But she lives in San Francisco. I'm just driving myself crazy with questions. I need to talk to someone every day."

John believed he loved Maggie in every way a man could love a woman. He would do anything for her. Should he take up the study of philosophy with her? Should he try to cultivate an interest in all the books that his father had collected on religion and the so-called classics? He glanced at the walls of books and shuddered. A practical problem-solver, he felt that most of them were jammed with nonsense. Then a brilliant solution came to mind. "Why don't you talk to Ned Ambler? You liked him well enough when he dropped by to check on your progress."

"B...b...but, what does he know about a child's development?" she whimpered.

"I don't know. All I can tell you is that he studied natural philosophy at Harvard. Besides, he's our family doctor; maybe he can tell you how to be a good mother."

Ned received John's call for help as he finished breakfast and was preparing to visit some patients in the Valley. He readily agreed to join Maggie for a preliminary discussion of her problem. He had not seen her since Christmas day. He could therefore rationalize this visit on professional grounds, but his nervousness warned him that he must be very vigilant. His fascination with Maggie far transcended her medical condition. He wouldn't, *couldn't* admit that he had fallen in love with her; but he had to face the fact that the very thought of her set his pulse racing. Over a pleasant lunch, he studied her carefully. She had expressed a desire to study works by the philosophers. "Are you sure you want to do this? Most great thinkers will bore you to death."

"Perhaps. But Lily once accused me of being a beam of light, dancing through life on impulse and enthusiasm. Well, now that I'm going to be responsible for another soul, I think it's time to focus my beam of light. Fortunately, the library is stuffed with good books."

"But Maggie, I don't think philosophy has answers to your questions about your child's development. You should consult an alienist like William James."

"No," she answered stubbornly. "I'm just as smart as Lily. And my father respected those early pioneers. Let's start with them."

"Very well." Ned wondered if her real purpose was to impress her father and Lily. "Maybe we can short-cut those ponderous tomes. Do you believe there is an unbridgeable duality between God and man?"

"I don't want to debate religion, Ned. I listened to enough of that around my parents in China. How does that question concern my baby's development?"

"You said you're wondering if a child can talk to God. That must mean you think God will be separate from your baby."

Maggie quickly thought of a list of popular dualities: optimism/ pessimism; masculine/feminine; doing/being; logic/intuition; physical/ metaphysical; objectivity/subjectivity; pragmatism/aestheticism; and so forth. "No. I think dualities are fictitious. God's love must be like *ch'i*. It's the pervasive breath of life in all its forms."

Just the way I feel! Ned thought, entranced by the play of light on her lustrous auburn hair and her animated face. "So there's a good start. God and your baby will be one and the same." Quite unreasonably, his mind leaped to assumptions about Maggie's world view, suddenly in total agreement with his own. He had to discipline an insane urge to confess his love. Instead, he calmed himself and considered how best to guide her through the jungle of two thousand years of philosophy. His mind raced. *Like me, her whole nature screams for esoteric harmony.... I should help her* validate *her nature—not challenge it.* "Very well. It may help you to understand that much of philosophy focuses on that first question."

While they roamed through the library, Ned captured Maggie's imagination as he pulled selected texts from the neat rows and briefly summarized their themes. Her nearness, the faint whisper of her perfume, a smile playing across her lips, her eyes darting from a book title to his face, all seemed to energize him. He found himself riding on a crest of unfamiliar intellectual and emotional vivacity. Philosophy had never seemed so romantic, so laden with double meaning. Time disappeared. At four o'clock, he suddenly gasped, "My God, Maggie! I must go or I'll miss a promised appointment with a patient. Shall we get together every Wednesday to review your ideas?"

"I would like that."

Never willing to do things by half, Maggie soon plunged into a dialogue with Plato. From Ned, she enthusiastically adopted a theme of critical importance for herself and her child's future education. He argued that the search for God was an "ascending" path, the path of wisdom; God's love was a "descending" path, the path of compassion. One must experience *both* paths to find the harmony of spiritual wholeness. By the end of her second trimester in February, Plato—and Ned Ambler—had persuaded her that God's descending Love, like *ch'i*, is ever-present and sustains the flowering of nature, what he called "a visible, sensible God." Ned soon reinforced that first principle with Plotinus' idea that the visible world is a manifestation of compassionate Spirit. Her own biases having been bolstered by those sages, they moved on to the second century and

Origen's echo of Plato.

Each Wednesday became both a torture and a glory for Ned Ambler, who squirmed uncomfortably under his relentless self-reminders that there could be no sensible future except friendship for the two of them. He was already married and had two children. His practice and his livelihood depended on his reputation for integrity. He respected Maggie—and John. A hundred times a day, he drew on those facts to banish his fantasies to a dark cave in his mind. But to little avail. Without even trying, Maggie's growing dependence, quick receptive mind and captivating beauty enslaved his good sense.

Maggie was not oblivious of Ned's agonies. Nor did she want to exploit his affection. In the first place, she loved John. She had married him, hadn't she? So she *must* love him. But when she tried to share an abstract idea with him, his disinterest was apparent. One morning when they had barely awakened, she asked, "Do you think a child can talk to God all day?"

He replied drowsily, "Does it really matter, Maggie?"

Her answer set the tone of their growing intellectual alienation. "Of course it matters. How can our baby become a whole person if she can't talk to God?"

After that, John despaired of conducting a sensible conversation with Maggie. His apparent indifference rewarded Ned with Maggie's confidence, friendship and even affection. The interweaving of great ideas with their flowering personal relationship satisfied all kinds of yearnings in her soul. In Lily's absence, Ned became her only real friend, willing to meet her at every level of her being. He became more than her navigator through the history of ideas. His incredible storehouse of knowledge and wit and... yes, affection offered her a balanced judgment, a stabilizing perspective toward every imaginable issue. Every Wednesday, he made her feel wanted, appreciated... loved. She couldn't imagine continuing her intellectual journey without her mentor and guide. And so she pretended that her relationship with Ned was harmless.

As they read companionably in front of the library fire one afternoon in early March, she touched Ned's hand lightly. "I wonder when the descending path finally became fashionable?"

Ned wanted to answer, "When the first man discovered a woman's body." Seated close to her on the couch, he had to dig his nails deep into his palm to keep from taking her in his arms. "You might take a look at Leonardo da Vinci for an answer in history. His passion for detail in nature started a great countervailing trend against the mythology of the Christian Church."

"Isn't the descending path simply divine Love, extended without conditions?"

"That's a reasonable definition," Ned replied.

"Then I'll bet the first mother knew that when she looked at her child."

By early April, Maggie spent each morning in the library where, for at least three hours, she consorted with great men who had tortured themselves with riddles of life and death. After fifteen sessions with Ned, she had reached the philosophers of the 16th Century.

At breakfast on a beautiful spring morning when the air was redolent with flowers, she offered John her great discovery from the day before. "Johnnie, did you know Galileo invented physics in the sixteenth century?"

John grunted and stared out the window. Deeply troubled by the Del Monte Lodge's order for bicycles, he was in no mood for Galileo or profound philosophical insights, especially when he preferred coffee and a moment of quiet before facing the day's trials.

"But I can't stand that wretched Locke. I bet you believe in his 'British empirical' thesis."

John wondered how some dead philosopher named Locke could have anything to do with a child's development? "Honey, if Locke's thesis is empirical, I'd probably agree with it. What is it?"

"He thinks our experience in the world *causes* our perception of it," she said accusingly as if the very idea were plainly absurd.

"Sounds reasonable to me." John pushed his chair away from the table. His impatience to get on with his Del Monte problem offered no time for more speculation. "I can't imagine another explanation. Can you?"

"Of course! Ned thinks human consciousness may project a scene before it's actually perceived."

Eyes wide with disbelief, John wondered how much longer he would have to endure Maggie's constant reference to Ned Ambler as the source of all wisdom. When he had first urged her to listen to Ned, he had not expected his wife to become such a devoted student. Now he felt increasingly alienated and even jealous. On Wednesdays, his imagination would frequently divert his attention on a bicycle design to visions of Maggie and Ned sharing their affection in front of a fire. He felt jealousy was beneath his dignity, especially since he had initiated the situation. It still bothered him to think that he had encouraged his wife to turn for consolation to another man, even someone as well-educated as Ned Ambler. "You mean to say he thinks we invent the world out of our imagination?" He had hardly asked the question when his own suspicious imaginings provided an answer. Snorting his exasperation, he fled to the barn for his horse.

Maggie felt wounded as she watched John's retreat. She had never imagined that her quest for guidance might antagonize him so much. But she saw no easy escape since Ned's companionship and advice had become a weekly refuge from her own fears and confusion. Her consolation came one morning in mid-May from a 17th Century philosopher. Triumphantly, she shouted her joy when she read Bishop Berkeley's argument that perception is a complex synthesis of information from *all* sources, the most important being God.

On the strength of that single idea, Maggie decided to share her insights with her unborn child as if he could understand her every word. "Listen to this, honey. Berkeley thinks the mind is a treasure house of information. Did you know the conscious mind is only the tip of an iceberg of knowledge?" When she asked herself why she couldn't enjoy what she believed to be the mind's rich awareness of life in all its many levels, it came to her that her education and its guiding Cartesian premise of dualism had victimized her. She vowed to vitalize her daughter's life with esoteric wholism. Her life *must not* be a sleep and a forgetting.

Two weeks later at nine o'clock at night, John Harrison endured a consuming attack of guilt while he waited in the east wing hallway and overheard the torture of childbirth for Maggie. Her screams and moans made him wonder if something was dreadfully wrong. As he paced back and forth, he worked himself into a fury of self-condemnation. He cursed himself for a long litany of flaws in his character that loomed with stark clarity in his mind's eye: his thoughtlessness, his selfishness, the death of his sibling, his obsession with machinery and his neglect of Maggie while Ned Ambler comforted her through her pregnancy. Suddenly, it dawned on him that this was a replay of the trauma he had suffered seventeen years earlier. Once again, he waited alone and ignored outside his mother's bedroom as people busily came in and out of the room for hot water, towels and more towels. Once again, he waited in an agony of doubt. Something terrible was happening and he was to blame. In front of the liquor cabinet in the living room, he hesitated. Then, his hands shaking, he opened a bottle of twenty-year old brandy and filled a small snifter. He gulped it all down like medicine and filled it again. He stared bleakly across the north patio at the wall of bougainvillea and saw windblown purple and scarlet bracts become rivers of blood. He blinked, quickly drank another snifter of brandy and poured a third.

Momma, Poppa, he vowed, *so help me God, bring me a healthy child and I'll pledge my life to his upbringing. I'll prepare him to tackle life like a great war; I'll teach him everything I know to win his battles. Just give me the son that I killed, your son, Momma, and I'll make you proud of me.*

John's fantasy of his future role with his son diverted his mind from the struggle in the bedroom. After another gulp of brandy, he began to build on a mythic father-son relationship. It didn't occur to him that the baby might be a girl. He must be a son, the hero of John's vision of hunting, fishing, riding, shooting, bicycle building, story-telling beside campfires, singing…. The vision framed a bright promise if only Maggie and Ned Ambler would do their job. *Maggie!* He owed her a lot!

Suddenly he heard an infant's first loud protests at life. David Andrews Harrison entered the world at the stroke of midnight on June 1, 1895. Snifter in one hand, the bottle in the other, John raced to the bedroom in time to see Ned Ambler emerge with his sleeves still rolled up.

"Congratulations, John!" Ned smiled as he rolled down his sleeves. "Jesus, man; you look like hell. You been fighting?" Ambler took the brandy snifter from John's hands. "This is the best stuff I've tasted in years. Just for another shot of this ambrosia, I pray I'll be here next year for a repeat performance."

"Is she all right? Was it… difficult… painful?"

"John, there's no such thing as painless childbirth. No man can even *imagine* the pain."

"Sounded like she was dyin'. Worried the hell out of me."

"Well, Maggie is a marvel… pure grit. She just pushed through the pain and the noise. Remarkable self-control for a first time. I think that youngster was anxious to join the world."

"Is he all right, Doc?" John asked. "All parts present and accounted for?"

"He's a strong, healthy nine-pound boy, John. The most powerful set of lungs I've heard in years; could win a hog-calling contest now without any practice. I'd keep him if I were you."

John offered Ned a wan smile, escorted him to his buggy, thanked him and paid him in gold. Then he quickly washed his face, combed his hair and tiptoed to Maggie's bedside.

"Where is my baby, John?" she asked, sleepy-eyed. "I want to see him. I want to be sure he's perfect, just the way you promised."

While a mantra of gratitude repeated itself in his mind (*Thank you, Maggie; thank you, thank you…*), John smoothed her hair and moistened her lips with a fingertip of brandy. When Ana brought Davey to Maggie, he promptly fell asleep on her breast.

PART II

DAVEY

"For unto us a son is given."

HANDEL, THE MESSIAH

CHAPTER EIGHT

CARMEL VALLEY
JUNE, 1895–APRIL, 1896

For the first month of David Harrison's life, Maggie's mood vacillated between joyous fascination with her son and brooding depression. Through the final three months of her pregnancy, she had felt like a beached whale. Even her Wednesday afternoons with Ned Ambler had been a mixed blessing. Ned's insights and subtle flirtation had reassured her. But many 16th century notions about man's relationship to God had confused or angered her. Then suddenly, all the weight of a dependent being had disappeared. In the next month, she supposed her body was still adjusting slowly; but attacks of disorientation frequently intruded on a dreamy state in which her only anchor seemed to be the unexpected—a son. At first she felt a whisper of disappointment. But soon she began to watch him for hours, awake or asleep, and ponder the miracle of birth. She found an abiding pleasure from simply staring at his miniature perfection.

By the end of a month of discussions with Ah Ying, Ana Cisneros and especially Ned Ambler, she had designed a strategy for preserving Davey's perfection. First, she must surround him with love. Ned told her that each sense must have its own memory. Therefore, she must teach Davey's senses to remember love in every imaginable form. Second, after Ned convinced her that fear was the common enemy of all philosophers, she resolved to keep fear away from Davey's consciousness. She believed she must encourage his *ch'i*, his fundamental life force, to be a daring spiritual warrior. Third, rebelling against the disciplined strictures of her own Presbyterian upbringing, she saw a sense of play as the most abiding mark of God's love. Nothing should be so serious that laughter could not heal it. Finally, something Ned had said convinced her that adult conversation would foster Davey's brainpower.

John had never experienced a mother's obsession with her newborn babe. At first, he was amused at Maggie's long silences while she studied Davey's every move as if he were a laboratory specimen. But by the end of the summer, John was increasingly annoyed at two people: his baby and his best friend.

John's annoying sense of competition with Davey for Maggie's attention confused him about his role and even his authority. He could barely hide his dismay at Maggie's interest in only two subjects at meals: the baby's latest smile or frown and Ned Ambler's opinion about the baby or philosophy. He blamed her preoccupation with philosophy for making Davey's development a tempest in a teapot. Surely, the growth of a child was a natural process, like a weed. Given that viewpoint, he approached his vow to oversee Davey's rearing from the mistaken belief that Davey would learn nothing of much importance in his first two or three years. And anyway, wasn't the messy first year of a child's life "woman's work?" His big job would come later when the boy could learn some skills.

John could tolerate Maggie's temporary insanity with the baby. That would surely pass. But "Ned says" became a phrase that taunted him with his own inadequacies as either a husband or father. To avoid self accusations on either count, he adopted a strategy of silence, unless something had happened on the ranch or in the shop that might conceivably divert Maggie's attention from her son and mentor.

One night at supper, John listened to yet another repetition of Maggie's four principles of child rearing with skepticism. Her focus on Davey's needs, Davey's sleep and Davey's entertainment had made him feel as if he were a guest in his own house. It had reached a point where, even after a wearing day in Monterey, within fifty feet of the house he felt he must walk on tiptoe lest he break one of Maggie's rules. "And how will you implement those principles?" he asked.

"I want to banish fear from the whole house. It should be a place that fosters my baby's health and happiness."

It was obvious to John that Davey's well-being had empowered Maggie to seize control of the house and its environs. He had already noted the authoritative way she had commandeered a guest room for the baby. Indeed, he had been astonished at how she had converted the room into a stage set of colorful paper birds and flowers.

"Ned says the sense of smell is the most powerful stimulus of memory. So I'll surround Davey with some fragrance that he'll encounter naturally throughout his life: flowers. That's why I told Ah Ying to fill his bedroom with fresh roses through the summer. When it comes time for hay-cutting, I'll throw open his windows to be sure he catches the aroma of new-mown grass. And during the day, I'll keep him in the kitchen so normal kitchen smells can remind him of love for the rest of his life."

To be polite, John nodded. "And the other senses?"

"Ned says everyone should touch him and massage him, which is what a grandma or elder sister would do if Davey weren't deprived."

John said nothing; it couldn't hurt much. And maybe, just as the women had come to respect Maggie like one of themselves, so the vaqueros might soon accept his son as a mascot.

"As for hearing, Ned says everybody, even the vaqueros, should talk like he can understand bicycles and politics and everything. I want Ah Ying to talk to him in adult Chinese; I want Ana to talk only Spanish. While I read in the library, I'll talk to him about my ideas as if he can understand every word. And I want him close to our normal conversations at meals. No baby talk!"

As John listened, a seed of suspicion nudged at him. "Won't Davey be confused by the babble of foreign languages?"

"No; Ned says the babble will excite his brain cells."

John thought adult conversation wouldn't help Davey much to become a good engineer; but it probably wouldn't hurt him either. Why argue the case now? "How do you plan to tie all those stimuli together?"

"With music, of course. Ned says, if Davey is like most babies, he believes he is the whole world. So I want the world to seem melodious across a wide range, from my piano renditions to the folk songs you sing him every night."

For several weeks, Davey's development seemed to validate Maggie's strategy. But as time passed, a demon named "Normal Progress" began to seize control of her mind. Was Davey growing fast enough? Were all his faculties superior or merely adequate? From his relentless passivity, she could only infer answers. Why was he so quiet? And why could he accept affection only from Ah Ying, Maggie and John? If Maggie handed him to a stranger, he would whimper or cry miserably. She had to conclude that her desire for everyone to touch him wouldn't work.

Nevertheless, Maggie often reminded John—and herself, "He's such a good baby! Why, look how he entertains himself quietly without any need for adult attention. The only time he seems to *welcome* a doting adult is when he's hungry. And even then, he only wants me to feed him." She had mixed reactions to that behavior: a sense of proprietary right to protect her son against all outsiders and a growing sense of some subtle pathology at work in her son's psyche. Despite Davey's passive good spirits and good health, she turned to Ned Ambler increasingly for advice and consolation.

By the end of the summer, when they spent Wednesday afternoons together, they thought nothing of friendly gestures of affection: a light touch on the shoulder, the hand, even the cheek. Ned savored her trust like an addict does wine. He didn't mind that their conversations intermixed philosophy with child rearing and music and politics. That gave him hope for prolonging his instruction. By September, he had become so besotted with her that he would willingly have done anything to claim her smile.

By the week before Christmas, she prayed that the philosophers of the 18th century might help her understand her baby's long silences. In January, Kant's notion that transcendental idealism is a totally independent reality of which we couldn't be conscious offered no help. She asked Davey, "Is that true?" She persuaded herself that he answered, "No Momma, I'm playing with *all* realities!" Then she took heart when she read Kant's belief that the "self" belongs to both worlds.

In February, she talked excitedly to Davey about Hegel. By then, she had crammed her notebooks with excerpts from every philosopher who agreed with her emerging vision of harmony as a natural state. She joyfully adopted Hegel's belief that all separateness and all intellectual subdivisions of the human being are illusions. She was convinced that a passion for God must power one's search for ever deeper levels of coherence and unity.

In April, with disgust, she worked her way through Schopenhauer's pre-Freud suggestion of sexual motives in human behavior. What she considered wasted time with him was redeemed in May, 1896, by her discovery of Helmholtz' experiments with reaction time and neural transmission. In exultation one Wednesday night, she tried to share her findings with John. "Remember that Ned said last year that we may imagine a situation before we actually see it?"

"Vaguely." Tight-lipped, John stared at her. He wasn't sure he could stand another supper of praise for Ned Ambler. "Why?"

"Well, we studied Helmholtz today. He's so fascinating. He has proved that the unconscious process in the brain *precedes* conscious experience."

John stared at her with weary tolerance. "And you figure *that* insight is important for our son's development?"

"That *must* be what's happening to Davey. He must be about eighty percent unconscious and only twenty percent conscious. That would explain why he's so quiet all the time. Ned says he must be processing inner and outer rhythms at his own speed. He'll verbalize them when he's ready. Until then, we should let him entertain himself with his fantasy world."

"Let him do something without guidance from the eminent Doctor Ambler?" John gulped down a snifter of brandy and felt the liquid fire burn its way down his throat. "Why, you astound me, Madam. I didn't know you could take a step without Ned's approval."

She bristled at John's sarcasm. "At least he shows *some* interest in Davey. Do you ever think of him at all? Or are your toys in Monterey and this miserable ranch so important that our son is beneath your contempt?"

"Is that the way you feel about my bicycles? Just toys? For God's sake, woman, you suggested the b'iness. Or is it impossible for anyone to measure up to our family doctor? Spit it out, Maggie. Are you in love with Ned?"

"Why, I… I never heard of such a thing. How could you even suggest that?"

"How could you even suggest that?" John mimicked with scorn. "You must think I'm blind. Ever'one sees the way you two moon over each other. It's sickening!" John gulped down another snifter of liquid courage.

"Have you gone to bed with him yet?"

Maggie turned pale with shock. "Take that back, John Harrison. Don't you dare accuse me of such a thing. Your mind is a... a sewer!"

"Oh, Maggie, at least admit you've thought of it. He's so damned perfect for you: fillin' you with all that nonsense about God."

Maggie struggled to control herself. "Don't you believe in God, John?"

"I believe there is a God; yes." John looked away from Maggie in distaste. "I just don't see much point in talkin' about Him day in and day out. Such talk doesn't interest me. In fact, it bores me to death."

"So what does interest you?"

"My family, my ranch and my bicycles. All very local and very simple. You must regret being tied down to a simple rancher who has no interest in great issues of life and death."

"Don't you even care about politics? About what's going on in this country?"

"Like what?"

"Well, like the relationship of science to religion. Don't you care that traditional Christianity is facing a major challenge from science?"

"Not much. I wouldn't mind if we wiped out every preacher in the world. They're mostly lazy ne'er-do-wells with the gift of gab, out to take advantage of the gullible and the uneducated. The Bible's good enough for me."

"It's... it's primitive to accept the Bible as God's revealed law. Charles Darwin has forced us to re-examine our whole religious tradition."

John shrugged and tried to contain his discomfort at Maggie's obsession with God: what He was, what He wasn't, or how to reach Him.

Maggie continued stubbornly. "Ned says the concept of survival of the fittest attacks the belief that the Bible provides an absolute moral code of behavior."

"Don't *you* believe in the Bible?"

"Absolutely not! My *parents* did, of course. Their childish confidence in the revealed word of the Bible was the bedrock of their romantic evangelism. But I don't think I ever believed in it as much more than an overwritten novel. Certainly not now!"

"What's changed, Maggie?"

"Everything is changing. Now many natural and social scientists challenge all the old fashioned ideas about religion and society. That's why this time is so exciting. Some Darwinian scientists believe the individual actually has no control over his destiny. They think the Bible is mostly myth and the focus on personal salvation through strict self-discipline and moral behavior is an illusion. For them there is no escape from natural selection."

"Do you believe that? Is that what you want our son to believe?"

"Of course not! That's too cut and dried. I believe in free will."

"Get to the practical point, Maggie. What's this all about?"

"It's about our covenant with God and the best path to political reform."

"So we're really talkin' about *political* reform? Like free benefits for my lazy vaqueros? You think maybe Davey will be an underdog like them?"

"You sound like Billy Sunday if you think poverty is the result of laziness," Maggie said scornfully. "His answer to unemployment is work harder. You know the times are very violent with strikes and killing and exploitation of labor. We better change things, beginning with this ranch, or we may face a real revolution."

"That's another thing. I hear from Ramon that you've been stirring up the women to demand their rights and benefits. Have you decided that you're supposed to run this ranch?"

"No; but it wouldn't be hard to improve things around here. You said I could propose a plan to you."

"I didn't mean you could hold political meetings with the women behind my back. Is that why you sent me off to make bicycles? So you could start your own little revolution here?"

Maggie could see this was more than alcohol talking. Maybe she had gone too far, too fast with her inquiries about life on the ranch. Now he was suspicious of both her relationship with Ned and her ambitions for equity on the ranch. Remorse suddenly assailed her confidence. "I apologize if you think I went behind your back. I won't hold any more meetings without informing you. I don't want to fight with you, Johnnie."

"I accept your apology. I swear, Maggie, I don't want to come home after a long day of work and an hour's ride just to argue about religion and politics. Why can't we find somethin' that interests both of us?"

Maggie nodded. "I don't know. You don't care about God or philosophy. And you don't think I can understand your practical problems at the shop. But…." Maggie's chin quivered with rage and some small measure of guilt for caring so much for Ned. "But you shouldn't accuse me or Ned of misbehaving. I'm loyal to you and to our marriage. And so is Ned to Amy and their children."

John apologized for accusing her since he knew she was speaking the truth. He trusted Ned Ambler like a brother. Indeed, Ned had been his best friend for several years, playing the role of a father figure after Nate had died. But John needed someone to blame for his doubts about his qualifications as a husband or a father. In the heat of his argument, Ned was convenient.

After supper, when they separated to bind up their emotional wounds, John thought the most important insight from the argument was Maggie's respect for neither bicycles nor the ranch. He wondered if they could ever share any interest aside from their son. Then it occurred to him that he might use her interest in ranch families to build a broader, deeper foundation for their marriage. The very process of finding a compromise with her might give them something to talk about. He resolved to involve Maggie more deeply in the intricacies of ranching as a business.

CHAPTER NINE

CARMEL VALLEY
APRIL, 1896—SEPTEMBER, 1897

While ranch hands worked through the summer towards another roundup, the women and Maggie crafted a proposal for a benefits package that consumed Maggie's interest almost as much as Davey. John congratulated himself on his shrewd choice of the ranch as a topic for conversation. Maggie had not given up her Wednesdays with Ned; nor had she abandoned philosophy. But her meals with John were no longer boring. Through their debates about the practical meaning of equity on the ranch, they discovered a common interest in politics, which yielded an astonishing document on the first of September, a kind of declaration of independence for all ranch families. John signed the document and Ramon Cisneros co-signed on behalf of ranch employees. Thanks to the hours of discussion, each ranch family could buy their house with a mortgage extended by John. A fund was established to provide health and educational benefits. Perhaps the most revolutionary idea was the principle of profit sharing. When John and Ramon explained all the ideas to assembled ranch employees at a party that evening, gratitude and pride shone in everyone's eyes. And Maggie was the heroine of the hour.

Next day, Davey gave his mother and father another cause for celebration. Soon after her arrival, Ah Ying had surprised Maggie with her own wide-ranging collection of Chinese aphorisms, *ch'eng-yu*. While Davey lay in his crib, they peppered their conversations with that folk wisdom. They often flung *ch'eng-yu* at each other like tennis balls, rewarding a particularly incisive *bon mot* with shrieks of laughter. So Maggie shouldn't have been so astonished when Davey held up his arms to Ah Ying and said, "*Fei!*"

"I just don't believe it!" John said when he came home from Monterey that evening. "He's supposed to say 'Momma' or 'Poppa' or 'Dada'. Where did he learn 'fly,' even if it is in Chinese?"

Maggie stared at him in amazement. "You've been telling him to fly ever since you first threw him into the air!"

"I guess that's right. But you're the one who wants to make him darin'."

Maggie grimaced with impatience. "I don't mean *physically* daring. I mean *morally* daring. Your hero in King Arthur is Launcelot. Frankly, I think he was a dreamy, romantic fool. My hero and the one I'd like Davey to emulate is Merlin."

Thereafter, although Davey learned speech slowly, his prolonged passivity continued to trouble Maggie. Ranch women couldn't understand Maggie's concerns about her son's mental-emotional growth. Of course, none of them had the luxury of spare time for reading, introspection and worry. Only Ned could mollify her with reassurances that he was doing fine. She finally settled down to a busy autumn that very soon turned into the Christmas season.

Davey's second Christmas Eve! So much to celebrate. Maggie surveyed the living room with satisfaction. She tilted her head to assess the bold statement made by tall red candles in beds of pine boughs on both fireplace mantles. Humming snatches from Handel's *Messiah*, she smiled at the glory of a huge twelve-foot Christmas tree at the center of the room. She admired its clever decorations: over a hundred tiny figures that she and the women of the ranch had made once again from pipe cleaners. Besides their pleasure from sharing ranch gossip with Maggie, the women made money. Demand for the tiny dolls from other ranches had nurtured a budding cottage industry.

On New Year's Eve, Maggie happily told herself that her twenty-six months of study with Ned and her daily lectures on harmony to her infant son had finally rewarded her. For a moment, she could luxuriate in a glow of gratitude for her harmonious relations with John, Ned and her world on the ranch. Although she believed her differences with John had not disappeared, she thought the September agreement had sealed an uneasy truce between them. She hoped they could maintain a cautious balance between pain and pleasure by confining their conversations to the ranch and national politics, avoiding religion, and treating Ned and Davey as sensitive subjects.

One night in early April, John had just finished singing "Streets Of Laredo" to Davey when the boy suddenly hummed an accurate echo of the ballad.

"He has perfect pitch," John cried. "Why, he might be a musician some day!"

As John and Maggie tiptoed out of Davey's bedroom into the living room, Ramon entered from the kitchen in a high state of excitement. "*Que tal, Ramon?*" John was surprised at his unusual appearance at nine o'clock.

"*En el cielo, Patrón.* In the sky, an airship! Come and see."

"Impossible!" John exclaimed. "Scientifically impossible, Ramon. You must have fallen for this newspaper hoax about airships."

"What hoax, Johnnie?" Maggie asked.

"It's amazing what an irresponsible press can do with mass hysteria just to sell newspapers."

"Quick, Johnnie," Maggie cried, grabbing her fleece-lined jacket. "Let's go see."

They raced into the yard where Ramon pointed to the brightly moonlit sky to the north. John moved behind Maggie and took her in his arms.

"Oh, John, look at it. It has two..., no, three lights. They... aren't they under a long, cigar-shape? And how long do you think that tail of light is?"

John blinked his eyes against the cold and the fuzziness of the apparition. "It must be several hundred feet long... *if* it's real."

"Of course it's real! We're seeing it aren't we?" Maggie shuddered from a nameless fear. "I feel... strange. Have you ever *heard* of such a thing?"

"Of course. Haven't you been readin' the newspapers, honey?"

"No," Maggie admitted guiltily. "I guess I've had my nose in philosophy and the women's problems too much. Doesn't that thing... scare you?"

"Why, no." John tried to summarize his feelings about the airship. "I guess I've been some disturbed only because I *think* I see it; but I don't *believe* what I see. I feel a bit like a fella who's lost a leg but still feels an itch. I guess I don't trust my brain."

"Tell me what you know about the airship."

"It all started last November in Sacramento, where folks first saw an airship move across the night sky. The San Francisco *Call* made it a big sensation, called for explanations from scientists... and preachers, of course"

"But isn't that wonderful!" Maggie squirmed in his arms. "Aren't you excited? First electricity; the telegraph; the telephone; the phonograph. Now we've conquered the sky! Where will all these inventions take us next?"

"Trouble is, Maggie, no one has invented a motor powerful or light enough to move a balloon so fast. It's way beyond our scientific knowledge now." *Or is it?* His heart raced at the prospect of building such an engine.

"You think it has a motor?" she asked apprehensively.

"Look at it; it's movin' *against* the wind."

"Why do you call such a thing 'impossible?'" She shivered under the warm jacket and moved closer to John. "Jules Verne's novels tell all about such a machine. Don't you remember? You loved *Robur The Conqueror*. And you read *Clipper of the Clouds* out loud to Davey. Surely his stories are based on scientific fact...."

"All fiction, Maggie. The whole country has gone crazy over the prospect of flight. Look, it's gone now." John was troubled at the speed of the thing.

"Oh, Johnnie! Do you suppose they're Martians?"

John frowned as he led Maggie back into the house. That theory was the only one that seemed remotely plausible to him. "Could be. Some folks think those canals prove that the planet was once inhabited. But I think most sightin's have been hoaxes; too many people, especially newspapers, tryin' to squeeze a dollar from the gullible."

"Are the canals hoaxes, too?"

"No. Professor Lowell saw them through his new telescope at the observatory in Arizona three years ago. He thinks Martians failed to manage their planet properly, says they must have wasted their water. I wonder if that could ever happen to this planet?"

"You said 'sightings'. Have many other people seen them?"

"For the past four months, newspapers across the country have reported the same story. Airships have appeared to thousands of folks in eighteen states."

"Why, Johnnie, I...." Maggie wondered why hadn't he mentioned this sensation to her? Had she deluded herself about their uneasy truce? Was his silence a protest against the vaqueros' benefits agreement? Or did he think she simply wasn't smart enough to understand technical theories about aeronautics? "I feel as if I've missed something really important."

"I doubt it, honey. Frankly, the press has handled the whole thing like another swindle. Look at Hearst. His *Examiner* has been havin' a circulation war with the *Call*. So the *Examiner* accuses the *Call* of naïve support of the airship craze. But Hearst's *New York Journal* gives sensational attention to airships. I think it's all fiction—typical newspaper irresponsibility."

"But Johnnie, we just saw it; that was no hoax. Besides, if it's not a scientific possibility, how could they get away with such a hoax?" She could feel her apprehension turning to anger at the press and herself for her stupidity.

"Most people are desperate for anythin' that relieves the boredom of daily life. Some farmers in Kansas reported that cattle have been mutilated and even carried into an airship; other people claimed they invented the airships. In Aurora, Texas, some local profiteers say an airship crashed and dead aliens are buried there; some people lookin' for notoriety swear they were abducted by airships; others swear they met some of the crew."

Maggie was speechless. "What do scientists say about the airships?"

John put on his face of practical engineer. If not in child rearing, at least in this field he could claim some authority. Perhaps he could show Maggie how *she* sounded when she pretended she had mastered philosophy. He knew that several people were working on small motors. But those efforts were still mere promises. "They offer all kinds of theories: refracted light; meteors; fireballs; the planet Venus; even lighted balloons; all nonsense."

"But surely it's worth discussing?"

"Why bother? Ever' scientist knows a powered airship is *technically* not possible now."

Science certainly didn't have all the answers. What was it that Ned had told her about William James's opinion of science: a closed system of ideas? "Well," she said huffily, "maybe you ought to show those nay-sayers how smart you are. I'll bet you could fly before anyone if you put your mind to it."

The mix of challenge and pride in her voice pierced John's imagination with a jolt. *Now that would be truly something glorious*, he thought. *I wonder if I could do it? Maybe I ought to start small… with a light engine.* "It's a mighty complicated problem," he replied wistfully. "Anyway, as things stand now, all sightings are probably hoaxes. It's pointless to discuss them."

For the next four months, Maggie couldn't dismiss her fascination with the sightings. She wanted to encourage John; but she didn't know how. One morning in August she stumbled on an article that seemed to point the way. It was so stunning a victory for her that she scarcely knew how to use it to tease him. After they had put Davey to bed that evening, she asked idly, "Didn't you tell me last April that powered flight is an impossibility?"

"That's right," John answered, his nose in a magazine about hunting. "Why do you ask?"

"Oh, nothing important; I just wondered if you had heard of Samuel Langley at the Smithsonian Institute?"

"Sure. He's an astronomer; heads up the Institute."

"Then you would consider him a qualified scientist?" Maggie restrained a giggle while she set her trap.

John set his magazine aside and stared at Maggie. "What's got into you, Maggie? He's one of the greatest scientists alive."

"Well, I was about to call him a liar; I thought I might even write him a letter to tell him my husband thinks he's a fool."

John flushed. "All right; you've got somethin' up your sleeve. You have that smug, cat-that-licked-the-cream look on your face. Let's have it."

Maggie's eyes flashed with triumph. "In the library today, I found an article by Alexander Graham Bell. According to him, Langley set out to prove that flight *is* possible."

"You can't mean it! What did Langley do?"

"He wrote an article in 1891 in a book called *Experiments in Aerodynamics*. He said that flight should happen before the end of the century."

"Big words! What has he done to prove his prediction?"

Maggie consulted her notes. She was so delighted to disprove John's smug, self-satisfied attitude toward flight that she had taken down the details with great care. "He built models. He flew the first one in March, 1891, from the Pittsburgh Observatory. According to Bell, he flew models even after he went to the Smithsonian."

"Were they really flights? Or just little hops?"

"Model Number 5 had a..." she had to check the unusual word. "a wingspan of thirteen feet and it flew a hundred and twenty-three feet. Then in May last year, with a small steam engine, it flew over half a mile. Mister Bell witnessed it and wrote the article."

"I swear, honey, models are one thing. But has Mister Langley promised to build a man-carrying machine?"

Maggie hastily scanned her notes, her triumph suddenly fading. "No. In fact, he said he just wanted to prove that flight is scientifically possible."

John retrieved his magazine. "Just as I figured. He's not serious; anyway, where would he get any money? Who would invest in such a fool scheme." His apparent disdain belied the stirring of interest in his stomach. *Wouldn't that be something glorious if he invented the first man-carrying aeroplane in history?* How would *that* stack up against the great Doctor Ned Ambler?

CHAPTER TEN

THE ROCKY MOUNTAINS
SEPTEMBER, 1897

John Harrison looked back to see if Doc Ambler had fallen behind. Every time he went on a hunting trip with Doc, he swore it was the last time. Doc really wasn't interested in hunting. He preferred to examine high-country flowers and trees with his camera. He got more excited about a hidden valley or a sunset than he did about killing a mountain lion or a big buck. But John reckoned it was always good insurance to have a doctor along. More than once, Doc had proved to be a cool customer in a crisis.

It wasn't that John could not appreciate the glories of a Rocky Mountain early autumn. In fact, he thought the Colorado Arapahoe country was as beautiful as any he had ever seen. From the railroad town of Granby, where they had outfitted, the vast panorama of Lake Granby, snow-capped Longs Peak to the east and Clark Peak to the west must inspire any man—unless his soul was dead. But their impact on John was not primarily aesthetic. Instead, it fostered a kind of clarity in his sense of himself. The hunting only validated his self-image, giving it visible shape and texture. His body felt lean and hard. Two weeks of wandering in brisk mountain air had blown away a cloudy mist from his mind. On his red sorrel, he felt on top of the world, confidently at home in this place, at this time. He was so happy that he grinned at nothing, just enormously glad to be alive.

Under his tall, rangy body, the stock saddle creaked and groaned, suffering the pounding pressures of a hundred and ninety pound cowboy against the unyielding back of a sweating horse. Unlike his vaqueros, who loved silver wherever they could put it, John wore down-at-the heel boots that reached almost to his knees. He disdained rowelled spurs as too brutal and preferred the simple cavalry pair that his father had worn with Jeb Stuart. Over gray Levi's tucked into the boots, he had belted a pair of leather shotgun chaps. Around his waist, he carried a belt of pistol ammunition, a caliber .44 Colt at his right hip and a Bowie knife on his left. Soft leather gloves, a red flannel shirt, a knotted yellow scarf around his neck and a wide black Stetson on his head completed the uniform of the typical working cowboy. A Winchester repeating rifle protruded butt forward from a leather case strapped to the left side of his saddle. A rawhide riata coiled around the pommel of the saddle, behind which he had strapped his slicker. A superb horseman and crack shot with pistol and rifle, John was fully equipped to survive in the wilderness.

When he spied a creek bubbling out of the mountains into a familiar valley, he decided to stop and make camp. It had been a hard day but it had also been rewarding. A sway-backed, buckskin pack horse bore the deer that he had killed five miles back. The other pack horse, a roan with a sweet disposition, carried a tent, sleeping bags, Doc's camera and the rest of their grub. Astride a beautiful palomino, Doc brought up the rear. They set up camp under a grove of aspen, bright gold in the late afternoon sun. After they unloaded, hobbled and fed the horses, John skinned the deer. Doc pitched the tent, hung up a Coleman lantern and went off for dry wood. The way he fell into a kind of trance before the awesome glory of a mountain sunset amused John, who knew it would be pointless to remind him that a fire would be useful *before* night descended. By now, he reflected, Doc should know that night doesn't arrive slowly in the mountains. It happens suddenly. One instant, the light is adequate; suddenly, it's so black even the horses are blind. It wouldn't be helpful to have Doc stumbling around in search of wood after that, even if he did have a Coleman lantern.

But everything worked out fine. Their two weeks together had taught them an efficient routine. Soon, they were enjoying venison cooked in onions, sliced potatoes and hot coffee. After they cleaned their gear in the stream, they settled down to talk. John went through the ritual of preparing a cigar while Doc took out a pipe and tamped his favorite tobacco into place.

"John, I must say that you look better today than I've seen you in a coon's age. Must be the mountain air."

"I feel liberated, Doc. It's the only way to describe it."

"Why, if I didn't know you better, I'd say matrimony is pinching a bit. Surely Maggie is a loving wife?"

John sighed. For the first time in months, he felt he could trust Ned Ambler—and himself. "She's a remarkable woman; but maybe she's too loving, Doc."

Ned chuckled neutrally before responding with caution. What most couples called love during the final year of courtship had almost no resemblance to their feelings for each other a year after the wedding. He sucked on his pipe and wondered what "too loving" might mean. "I don't get your drift, John."

"I can't explain it too clearly, so you'll have to bear with me." John stared at the fire and blew a smoke ring into the darkness. "When we were first married, it was wonderful. We did all kinds of things together, things I love to do. And I still had some sense of control over my life."

"And later?"

"When I learned she was goin' to have a baby, we started driftin' apart."

Ned nodded. A baby could separate or unite a couple.

"It wasn't Maggie's fault, of course. We just had to stop sashayin' around the country; you know, t'give the youngun a chance. I mean...."

"You don't have to explain, John. I advised Maggie to cut down on her riding and vigorous physical activity when she first came to see me."

"Well, there you have it. But what was I supposed to do?" John examined the glowing embers at the tip of his cigar and flicked ash into the fire. "That's when I decided to try out her idea about bicycles. Maybe I spent too much time in my new shop.... Anyway, I began to feel out of the picture ever' time I came home. Maggie spent ever' mornin' in the library stuffin' herself with great thoughts. While she waited for the baby, she spent most afternoons talkin' Chinese to the cook or Spanish to the other women."

"Was Maggie ever really interested in the bicycles?"

"No. Frankly, that kinda peeved me 'cause I got into the game to impress her. But hell, Doc; bicycles aren't a very entertainin' subject after ten minutes. So when I came home at night, we ran out of things to talk about."

"Wasn't she interested in the ranch?"

"That's a funny thing. When she first saw the ranch, she seemed to love it. Then I reckon she got bored. Unless you're involved in workin' the cattle, a ranch isn't very excitin'. But then she began workin' with the women and the problems they brought to her."

"So she changed her mind about her life on the ranch?"

"Yeah. Then, well maybe I should blame you for what happened next."

"Blame me?" Ned felt genuinely surprised. "What did I do?"

John stared disconsolately into the fire and remembered his jealousy of Ned. "She began to think of ways to apply all that philosophy to what she calls 'equity' on the ranch. So we argued a lot. Then…; I swear, I can't believe it was deliberate…." John stared at the fire with a frown, his mind caught by a new idea.

"What might have been deliberate?"

"They way Maggie slowly found her way into ranch management."

"Didn't you want her to get more involved with ranch life?"

"I'll admit the ranch kinda bored me. I was captured by the bicycle b'iness and thought Ramon could handle ranch routine. Anyway, last year, just to have somethin' to talk about at supper, I began to teach her about ranch management. Pretty soon, Maggie's concerns went from the women to their husbands and boyfriends. It just became natural for ever'one to seek her advice about personal problems."

"Sounds like a loving woman to me, John. You should be proud."

"Yeah." He chuckled. "It's really kinda silly. When I was gone all day, Ramon began to ask her for advice about the ranch. Little things at first. But I was shocked one night at supper to discover that she knew more than I did about grain and beef production, crop rotation and so forth."

"That bothered you?"

"It made me feel guilty…; as if I had neglected my duties."

"So what did you do?"

"I wasn't sure what to do. Now I ask you. Do I seem to be tongue-tied when we talk?"

"Not at all, John. Why?"

"Well, around Maggie, my tongue seems to get twisted in knots. She always wins any argument 'cause she thinks twice as fast as I can and talks about ten times faster. She makes me feel stupid. Don't that beat all?"

"What did Maggie say to you?"

"Said somethin' about her essence bein' water. Said she can't help it if her curiosity just flows into other people's lives. Said the power of love is infinite and irrepressible. I swear, how could I answer that line? I'm not sure I even understand what she meant."

"Did you talk to Ramon about the situation?"

"Yeah. I finally told him to work out any small problems with Maggie. I told him to rely on her good sense 'cause she really does have a good b'iness brain. But I warned him to come to me about any arguments with her."

"So you really turned over your authority to Maggie?"

"I reckon. I taught her so well that, the next thing I knew, I was signin' that big agreement with the ranch families a year ago. Now I don't feel like I have any control over my house or the ranch anymore."

This is serious, Ned thought. *This is a power game. Lily was right; Maggie loves power, probably plays the game the way she breathes, inspired by love and fueled by her need to be needed. How can a poor amateur like John stand up to an act of nature?* Ned wanted to be reassuring. "The situation isn't entirely unusual, John. The first years of any marriage involve a lot of compromises. It's often damned tough, especially those months after the first child."

"That's what I told myself. But after Davey was born, I felt even more isolated. Maggie doesn't deliberately keep me out of her world. But aside from playin' with the boy now and then, I feel about as useless as a four-card flush. When I get home ever' day, I feel like a guest."

"That must be a strange feeling. Do you reckon why?"

"Well, as I said, Maggie has taken complete control. About a year ago, she moved all the furniture around to protect Davey. I sometimes think she's usin' my own son as a kind of weapon against me—maybe not deliberately."

"Aw, that's hard to believe, John. Surely she didn't select that bronze you're so proud of?"

"Remington's *Bronco Buster*? Naw; I saw a picture of it in the October, '95 issue of *Harper's Weekly*. Had to have it! I think Owen Wister and Fred Remington say it all in their writings and paintings. And now Remington's bronzes just capture everthin' I feel about the power of a man and a horse, fightin' out who's in control. I wish Remington would do a bronze of me and Maggie. Maybe he could figure out what's goin' on."

"Is Maggie arrogant with her authority?"

"No. She's very sweet. Ever'one loves her. It's just that the women, Ah Ying and Ramon's wife, Ana, even the young vaqueros look to her for orders." John struggled to find the key to his feelings. "I jest feel like a stranger and I hate the feeling. Back there, I don't know who I am anymore. Out here, I have no doubts... about anythin'. That's the way I used to feel before I married Maggie."

"But surely you two talk about the baby?"

"We talk; but I'm not sure we communicate." John stared forlornly into the fire. "Maggie thinks the boy isn't growin' fast enough."

Ned chuckled. "She's complained about that several times. What speed would make her feel happier?"

"How the hell would I know? She acted like it was my fault that his first word was 'fly'—in Chinese for God's sake. Then she was afraid he wasn't talkin' enough. She seems to think he's takin' too long to enter the world."

"Enter the world?"

"Yeah; it never occurred to me that he was somewhere else. He looks mostly there whenever I see him."

Ned grinned at John's stab at humor. "What is she reading these days?"

"It beats all. Two years ago, right after Davey was born, I found her readin' a fella named Plotinus and another one named Origen."

Ned nodded. "I selected those books, John—at your urging, if you recall."

"Yeah; I remember. But she's been at it ever since. Now she's readin' Darwin." John chewed on his cigar and finally threw it into the fire. "I asked her why she was readin' that stuff."

"What did she say?"

"Said she wanted to guide Davey home to God."

"I thought she wants Davey to enter the world?"

"Confusin', isn't it? Her spiritual zeal seems to depend on the week's routine cycle of work. It all starts on Wednesday, sewin' day. Generally, Ah-ying does that while you teach philosophy to Maggie. On Thursday, which she calls 'mid-week rest,' she's on the warpath for God. Friday is cleanin' day. That brings her back down to earth 'cause she likes to pitch in with Ah-ying and a couple of ranch girls dustin', sweepin' carpets, scrubbin' floors and polishin' the stove. She says the work's good for her soul. By the end of bake day on Saturday, she feels so virtuous that she's usually too tired to bother with God. That's when she tackles me for not doin' *my* job with Davey. Then Monday is wash day. She often helps Ah-ying and the girls hang out laundry to dry. That sure takes the starch out of 'em. On Tuesday, they iron all that stuff. Then it starts all over when you come on Wednesday."

Ned felt stricken with guilt. *Have I fostered this rift in their marriage?* "It occurs to me, John, that you two are flirting with an argument about the nature of God. Do you talk to her about that idea?"

"Not much," John replied ruefully. "I don't see the point. I don't have the brains or the vocabulary anyway. Isn't God beyond description? Why, it would be like tryin' to describe love. Even the best poets miss the mark."

Ned sympathized with that viewpoint. After all the millions of words about what God is or isn't or how to find Him, you either found faith or you didn't. "That has always been a dilemma for poets and philosophers and ministers and students who try to 'eff' the ineffable. Life and death and God are pretty serious subjects."

"Sometimes, I wish I had burned that damned library. She spends half her life there, talkin' to great thinkers and lecturin' Davey about their ideas. Why can't she just rear Davey and try to live life without a road map?"

"But John, why does her interest in philosophy threaten you?"

"To tell the truth, Doc, I don't think I'm good enough for her. By nature I'm a simple man. But I get the bad feelin' that I try to be someone else just to get her approval. Except out here, I don't know who I am."

"Let's stick to religion for a moment. What does God mean to you?" Ned examined his pipe idly as if to minimize the importance of John's views.

John took his time. He savored several puffs on his cigar before answering. "To tell the truth, Ned, I rarely think about God. But since you ask, I believe God is all around us, right now. I think God is the Love that gives life to you and me and everthin'. My son is just another expression of God."

"Do you ever feel God's presence?"

"All the time; all day long; right now! Listen to the wind. Look up there at those billions of stars. Feel the night all around us, Ned. But what are you drivin' at? Do you think Maggie has a different idea?"

"I think Maggie feels the same way." Ned inhaled deeply from his pipe and looked up at the stars. "You think God is all around us. So does she; so do I."

"I don't think God is our problem, Ned. I think it's Davey. I think she may want him to go one way; I want another. I would hate to have to fight her over that."

"It wouldn't be the first time parents quarrel over a child's future. To me the only persuasive proof of God's existence is a child's survival of childhood in spite of all the damage parents can do. Of course, most fathers leave a child's early training up to the mother."

"Well, I'm feelin'... guilty about the whole thing. I made a vow to my parents to watch over Davey's upbringin'. I fear I'm lettin' him down."

"If you have bad feelings about this, you better have this out with Maggie soon. Otherwise it could get pretty nasty." Ned stretched and yawned. "Now, let me change the subject. I've arranged a little surprise for you. If we ride hard tomorrow, there's a little valley where a classmate of mine from Harvard will be hunting. I want you to meet him."

"Aw, Ned. I kinda hoped we could avoid people. Is he someone special?"

"Depends on your viewpoint. His clothes are sometimes a trifle... bizarre. His boots are custom-made from alligator skin; his knife scabbard is custom-mounted in silver; he wears custom-tailored buckskin suits and shirts; his belt buckle and spurs are pure silver; the barrel of his Colt is engraved in gold and silver; and the handles are pure ivory with an embossed buffalo on one side and his initials on the other. What's my friend's name?"

"Dunno. But he sounds right interestin'. Tell me more."

"He runs five thousand head on his ranch in the Badlands. His own hands call him 'four-eyes.' But they respect him. Once in a Montana saloon, a drunken cowboy tried to make fun of him. He knocked the cowboy down with a single punch. Come on, what's his name?"

"Teddy Roosevelt! Why didn't you say so in the first place? I wouldn't miss meetin' him for the world."

CHAPTER ELEVEN

THE ROCKY MOUNTAINS
SEPTEMBER, 1897

"Do you reckon he ever sleeps, Ned?"

John Harrison slouched on his sorrel and brought up the rear with Ned Ambler. The Assistant Secretary of the Navy led a long column of hunters, guides and packers north along the foothills of the Laramie Mountains. Far to the west, they could sometimes glimpse the Laramie River twisting its way north. Beyond the river, the sun was just about to dip below the Medicine Bow Range. It had been a hard four days with slim rewards for all their effort. They had glimpsed bighorn sheep, fleet-footed pronghorn antelope, bear and bobcat. But ever since John and Ned had joined Teddy Roosevelt's noisy party, the animals had simply vanished. At the end of his fourth day with Roosevelt, John was as discouraged as Roosevelt's friends were tired. It wasn't just the poor hunting. What bothered John was Roosevelt's helter-skelter, impulsive style. "Why is he in such a rush?" John muttered to Ned.

"Why, John; that's the way he lives life—with his hands on its throat. He was very sickly as a child. Had bronchial asthma that damn near killed him. So he *has* to live each day as if it's a bonus. He thinks personal values are a myth if you don't do *something* to demonstrate them. He once told me the worst of all fears is the fear of living."

"But how the hell does he expect to *find* anythin'? He's too damned impatient. He's pushin' too hard." Even John was weary. In his superb condition, if that was true, most of the others must be exhausted.

"I agree." Ned worried that his surprise meeting with Roosevelt might have ruined the whole trip for John. "He rides too long and walks too little. He's going to need a base camp if he wants to shoot any big animals."

At that instant, John saw something that drove all fatigue from his mind. As Roosevelt rode under a cliff, directly above him a mountain lion, a puma, crouched on an overhanging oak. *Why hasn't that cat skedaddled?* John wondered. *He must be spooked or hurt.* As the lion prepared to spring, John was already pulling his new Winchester '96 out of its long holster. He got off two shots before the lion struck Roosevelt's saddle and fell to the ground, dead. Chaos ensued. Mules brayed and kicked, two horses threw their riders and ran away and everyone shouted conflicting orders. John trotted forward to inspect the lion, lying on the trail. It was a magnificent animal: six feet long with another three feet of black-tipped tail. As he had suspected, the cat was a cripple; a fore-paw was crushed, perhaps from a boulder. One shot had pierced the puma's left eye; the second shot had entered behind its left ear. It must have died instantly.

"Bully! Just swell!" Roosevelt's expression showed wonder, shock and gratitude. "That's the best shooting I've ever seen. Why, you probably saved my life, Harrison."

"Pure luck, sir," John said. "If he'd been gray, I wouldn't have seen him."

"I'm surprised he attacked; a puma usually avoids people," Roosevelt said.

"Maybe we surprised her; she probably felt trapped," Ned suggested. "Or maybe she has some kittens nearby."

"Ned, get out your camera." Roosevelt was in high spirits. "I'll stand next to Harrison and you can capture all three of us."

"Three of you?" Ned asked.

"Absolutely: Harrison, me and the puma. I'll keep the picture on my desk for the rest of my life just to remind me of an obligation—and of how life is a hostage to accident, fate, karma, destiny; whatever you want to call it. From the moment of his spring, how long would it have taken the puma to get me?"

"I don't rightly know, sir," one of the guides answered. "A few seconds."

"Bully!" Roosevelt's enthusiasm was explosive. He seemed ecstatic that he had escaped harm by such a slender thread of chance. "By godfrey, this little affair makes the whole trip worth while. I was afraid I'd have to go back to Washington tomorrow with nothing to tell for my trouble."

Several guides galloped off to retrieve the runaways. While Ned took several pictures, every hunter had to dismount and examine the puma. A few kicked it; two with political ambitions struck heroic poses and asked Ned to take their pictures also. It was a young 200-pound female with a small round head, a black spot over each eye and black stripes between the eyes.

Suddenly quiet, Teddy Roosevelt said, "Mr. Harrison, I would be grateful if you and Ned Ambler would join me for a little chat after supper. I need your help on something.

That night, perhaps because of the puma incident, Roosevelt was bubbling with good humor. Behind his tiny pince-nez glasses, his eyes darted from Ned to John and back again. "I've about made a decision about my political future, boys. But first, I want your views about the state of our country today. Do you have an opinion, Mr. Harrison?"

"Please call me John, sir." Roosevelt's relentless formality made John uncomfortable. He smiled inwardly at the story of one of Roosevelt's early commands to start a cattle drive: "Hasten quickly there!" he had said. "I'm an engineer, sir. I never have paid much attention to politics. I wouldn't know how to form an opinion about the whole country." In fact, John was relatively indifferent to national politics. Through his observation of political corruption in San Francisco, he had acquired an amused tolerance of human vices. Like the weather, they must be expected and endured.

"But surely you have some sense of the *muscle* of this country?" Roosevelt's insistent demand for an opinion was intimidating. At John's silence, he lost his patience. "Here are the facts. We've about recovered from the depression of '93. Our industry produces nearly a third of the world's steel, about a third of its coal and a third of its iron."

"What about the cost we've paid for that progress, TR?" Ned wasn't impressed with such figures. His travels through California and Nevada and Wyoming had opened his eyes to the plight of miners and tenant farmers.

Roosevelt nodded vigorously. "I was going to get to that. Our rate of progress has severely stressed our social structure. I think the strikes of the nineties were just a prelude to what's coming. A great battle has been joined between financial interests and the middle class."

Ned pointed his pipe at Roosevelt. "I thought you believed in Darwin's philosophy of the survival of the fittest?"

"On the mark, Ned. I do believe the natural order of things must finally push the best to the top. You have to break a few eggs to make an omelet."

"Listen to him, John," Ned advised. "If you haven't figured it out yet, *we're* the omelet. The way the system works now, I don't think the middle class can win against the life insurance companies, the railroads or the oil companies."

John grinned. "I never thought about it much. But Maggie, my wife, is all for the underdog."

"Your wife's opinion interests me, John." Roosevelt puffed thoughtfully on his cigar. "What does she want from government?"

John reflected for a moment, suddenly conscious of his woefully shallow grasp of Maggie's political philosophy. Feeling increasingly uncomfortable, he could only stare at the fire.

Ned took over. "I've been studying philosophy with her. I think she wants a square deal for the common citizen. She thinks government and the trusts conspire against working people everywhere. She thinks government ought to tax the rich and the trusts to pay for better education and easier money for everyone. She was outraged last year when McKinley beat Bryan."

"She sounds like a Populist," Roosevelt suggested. "How did she feel about William Jennings Bryan?"

"His speeches inspired her," Ned said. "Thought he really was the 'Great Commoner' like the newspapers called him. But she finally concluded that his policies didn't make any sense; he's just an enemy of property."

John flicked his cigar ash into the fire and smiled at Roosevelt. "I recall that she was pleased with your idea to take ten or twelve Democratic leaders out and shoot them."

"We shouldn't sell Bryan short," Roosevelt said. "He broke all precedent in American politics by traveling eighteen thousand miles to get the support of ranchers and farmers and workers all across the plains states."

"What's so unprecedented about that?" Ned asked.

"No other Presidential candidate had ever traveled so far or worked so hard to get out the vote. That man is a phenomenon with a silver tongue. He made strong men weep with his eloquence. And remember; he lost by only six hundred thousand votes. He taught men—and women—that they had a right to be resentful. Now, the resentment is explosive. Aren't you a rancher also, John? Are you satisfied with cattle prices? The condition of your vaqueros? Their housing? Their education? Their spirit?"

John flushed at what he took as a mild rebuke. "My ranch is another matter, sir. I try to provide a proper home for every vaquero and his family. I pay for their medical bills; their schoolin'." Suddenly he turned his complaints about Maggie into a small boast. "Why, my kitchen is full of their women all day long, talkin' with my wife about their kids, their husbands and their problems. I've loaned 'em money to buy their houses from the ranch."

Roosevelt beamed. "What else do you do besides shoot like a demon and make a good life for your employees, John? What are you doing with your engineering?"

"I make bicycles; they're the comin' thing."

"That's the ticket!" Roosevelt cried as he extricated himself from his fringed buckskin shirt. Despite the forty-five-degree cold outside, the small fire had turned the tent into an oven. Now he seemed comfortable in his long johns. "But mark my words. You better find a good motor for your bicycles. You could call one with a motor a moto-cycle."

John stared at Roosevelt. The idea of a small motor had been on his mind ever since he had bullied Maggie about the airship hoax in April. "I think a moto-cycle is the way to go. Why a single tire for a motorcar costs forty dollars now! A cheap moto-cycle is bound to be more popular. When I get the chance, I'll go to Europe and talk to DeDion."

"Who's De Dion?" Roosevelt asked.

"He's a Frenchman who came out two years ago with a small engine that's air cooled, hits eighteen hundred revs per minute and uses electrical ignition."

Roosevelt warmed to John, who seemed to personify an American spirit of the age, pushing back the frontier of knowledge, searching for a better way.

"What's so special about electrical ignition?" Roosevelt settled himself on the woolly softness of a lambskin.

"DeDion's engine uses a cam system to make and break electrical sparks in each cylinder. That means that, for the first time, we can time those sparks. And maybe make a motor even smaller than the two-cylinder engine the Duryea brothers put on a four-wheel buggy two years ago."

"I remember that news." Roosevelt's eyes flashed with excitement. "Didn't they win the first big road race in this country?"

"Yessir. Their motorcar hit seven miles per hour on the fifty-four mile course from Chicago to Waukegan."

"If you go see DeDion, you better stay away from Spain." Roosevelt's expression turned grim.

"You think there'll be war, TR?" Ned asked.

"There *must* be war! Innocent women and children in concentration camps have died by the hundreds from starvation and disease. So I've been trying to bring the navy to a war footing all summer."

Ned knew that Roosevelt's bellicose speeches had embarrassed the Secretary of the Navy for months. "But why is the condition of Cubans suddenly our responsibility, TR? Why should we lift a finger for them?"

"First, because it's our destiny. Read John Fiske's *Manifest Destiny*. He has all the right arguments. Or better yet, read Mahan's latest book: *The Interest of America in Sea Power*. If we're going to make the Monroe Doctrine stick, we must attack Cuba."

Ned knew Roosevelt had allied himself with expansionists in Washington like Senator Henry Cabot Lodge. But he still saw no domestic political reason why Roosevelt should beat the drum for a war against Spain. "What's in it for the common citizen, TR?"

"Ned, the near election of Bryan proves the spirit of reform is explosive in this country today. How many employers do you know who treat their employees like John does? The common laborer, the common citizen, the tenant farmer, the miner, the logger, the steelworker, the seamstress; they're getting a raw deal. What's more, they know it."

"But..." Ned took his pipe out of his mouth and stared at Roosevelt. "How does their resentment at their treatment in this country relate to the Cubans?"

"Don't you get it, Ned? To a lot of Americans, the Cubans are symbols of their own misery. They think big business, the robber barons and city bosses are just like the Spanish: greedy, brutal, corrupt."

"I s'pose the guvmint gets its share of hard knocks, too," John said.

"That's a shrewd observation, John. A war with Spain could bail the government out of a tight spot. All those people who supported Bryan in '94 are tired of city, state and federal government connivance with venal trusts."

In Roosevelt's class at Harvard, Ned had heard him tease similar insights from his studies of philosophy and psychology under William James and political economy under Charles Dunbar. James had said publicly that Roosevelt seemed to be in a state of permanent adolescence, praising war as an ideal social condition because of its demand for manly strenuousness. "So you think saving the Cubans could also save American politicians' skins?"

Roosevelt grinned. "Your choice of language leaves something to be desired, Ned. But foreign adventures have often diverted the attention of a dissatisfied electorate from a country's domestic political problems."

"Would you resign from the guvmint if we have a war?" John asked.

"I would certainly resign if only to avoid a bleeding ulcer." At his guests' expressions of concern, Teddy offered his engaging grin. "Oh I'm not sick; but if I had to have many more meetings with that collection of misfits and incompetents called the War Department, I'd certainly get an ulcer."

"If you resigned, what would you do, sir?" John asked.

Roosevelt stared into the fire as if he were looking with clear vision at the future. "Every generation should have its war. This may be the only war that comes our way for at least another generation. This is my last chance; I'm thirty-nine now. I couldn't stand by and watch others carry our banners. I'd have to be in the thick of it. That's why I need your help."

"What could I do, sir?" John couldn't imagine how he might help the Assistant Secretary of the Navy.

"Earlier this month, the President endorsed my idea of a volunteer regiment of cavalry. When the war starts, I'll lead that regiment to Cuba."

"Would that be good for your political career?" Ned thought Teddy would lose valuable political momentum if he dashed off to war.

"Anyone who gains a little fame in this war can take it to a political bank. If we can do the job without too many casualties, I may be able to cash a check on that bank in the 1900 elections. If we win a war, the American people will almost certainly re-elect President McKinley."

Suddenly, Roosevelt's genius for joining his own talents and fortunes to the historical moment became clear to John and Ned. Ned felt a little depressed by the workings of Teddy's shrewd political brain. But John felt inspired. Here might be *his* only chance to emulate his forebears who had done something glorious for their country. Convinced that this one conversation paid for the whole hunting trip, he had a final question before he said his goodbyes. "If you form that regiment, would I have a chance to join it?"

That was precisely the offer of help that Roosevelt had wanted. He thought of his repeated childhood nightmare about a werewolf springing on him from the foot of his bed. He owed this young man a lot; maybe even final liberation from that werewolf. He stood up and reached for John's hand. "That's one promise I'll be glad to keep."

CHAPTER TWELVE

CARMEL VALLEY
DECEMBER, 1897

Through the months after their hunting trip, Ned pondered John's marriage as if he were diagnosing a favorite patient's serious illness. He soon realized that his own conflict of interest was part of the problem. Intertwined with his assessment of the strengths and flaws of John's marriage were such nagging questions as "If Maggie were divorced, could I divorce Amy?" "Would Maggie marry a simple minded country doctor, fifteen years her senior?" "Could I live with a woman like Maggie Harrison?" By late December, he had convinced himself that his infatuation with Maggie was a childish fantasy. If not always exciting, his wife was at least predictable and comfortable. Liberated from the burden of his romantic illusions, he could finally mobilize theory and fact to clarify John's marriage. Ned listed what seemed to be their shared and conflicting goals. A half-hour before his luncheon with John on the last day of the year, he finally discerned a plausible path for healing.

At noon, he greeted John in a private room in the Del Monte Lodge. The heat of a cheery fire ten feet from their table reminded them that December in Monterey could be raw and cold. Warmed further by a dry sherry for Ned and a Mexican beer for John, they inspected the menu in silence. Finally, they both ordered a fish chowder. The waiter's departure was a signal for Ned to begin. "Your father once talked about the fog of war as the greatest threat to sane decisions, John."

"You think Maggie and I are at war?" John asked wistfully.

"Call it what you like but I think your relationship is suffering from more than its share of fog." Ned started a familiar ritual of stoking his pipe while he organized a sequence of thoughts. "Please allow me to inventory some of your strengths and vulnerabilities."

"The way things are goin', it's hard to remember any strengths."

"Understood; you feel that way 'cause they don't seem to be working for you with Maggie. Your greatest virtue is your selflessness. As long as I can remember, you've put yourself in second place after the people you love."

John took a cigar from a leather case and began his own smoking ritual. He clipped and sucked on the weed mechanically while he listened.

"Curiously, that virtue is also your greatest vulnerability. If you weren't so damned attentive to other folks' needs, especially Maggie's, you would probably drive yourself more stubbornly toward your own goals."

"Like what?"

"You say it all the time: doing something glorious. Isn't that right?"

John nodded and blew two perfect smoke rings at the fire. "Trouble is, I can't figure out what would impress Maggie the most."

"You make my point. Maggie respects strength, especially moral commitment and force. It confuses her when you defer to her every whim. That makes her wonder if you have no mind of your own. Tell me honestly; do you think you need her permission before you start on any project?"

"Hell no, Ned!" John frowned. "'Course, I'd enjoy any project more if she agreed that it was *truly* glorious! When we hashed out that benefits package for ranch families, that felt good, mighty good."

Ned nodded his understanding. "Of course. Your dilemma is that you two disagree fundamentally about what something glorious means."

"I wonder why?" John said wistfully.

Ned took his time while he set aside his pipe, ordered another glass of sherry and savored the first mouthful of a delicious chowder. "I think I know. Lily told me that Maggie's abiding childhood frustration was her father's indifference. Maggie believes her father almost never talked to her and never told her he loved her just because she wasn't an assertive, smart aleck little boy."

John thoughtfully examined his cigar, then placed it carefully in an ashtray. He took a spoonful of chowder, wiped his mouth, looked out the window to study a pair of robins hopping across the cold ground, then said, "So maybe that's the reason she's tryin' to prove she's an intellectual." A new insight struck him. "I'll bet that's the real reason she's drownin' herself in all that damned philosophy, tryin' to lead Davey to God. But...

but...."

"But she's also still trying to claim her father's approval." Ned added a dash of Tabasco hot sauce to his soup. "Does that make sense to you?"

"Yeah, Doc; it does." John's eyes were bright with this new understanding of Maggie's demons. "You're sayin' her victories have to be of the mind."

"I needn't tell you that her childhood also influenced her attitude toward men. Do you remember her confrontation with Fred Mackie at your wedding?"

"Vaguely."

"So that little drama didn't teach you anything, I suppose."

"Like what?"

"Like the central essence of Maggie's being."

"Which is?"

"Rebellion against all forms of injustice, especially China's injustice toward women, and suspicion of all forms of authority, especially male authority."

"That really confuses me. I thought Maggie loved everthin' about China."

"She did at first, she told me. She accepted the Confucian formula that sacred *li* (rituals) would guarantee both the attainment of *jen* (humanity), the highest level of moral development, and the *tao*, the path that would yield harmony between heaven and earth, the natural and the social order."

"Then what happened?"

"By the time she was twelve, she had seen enough cruelty toward women to feel outraged on behalf of Chinese women."

Fascinated by these revelations, John spooned his soup mindlessly. "Is that where she gets her passion for the underdog?"

"I think so. Trouble is, her zeal for the underdog conflicts with her search for harmony. Every moment she wavers between those two impulses."

Bemused, John stared at Ned. "Let's see if I've got this right. When she's in favor of harmony, we can get along. But if she's suddenly fightin' for the underdog against the enemy—men—she'll fight me over anythin'?"

"That's a good summation. In her search for reconciliation among her demons, the ranch has become her laboratory. Since she first arrived there, she has explored the affairs of nearly every human under your authority. I think Davey's birth reinforced her zeal to find the path of harmony."

"So you think she's usin' our marriage and the ranch and Davey to try to solve the problems of her childhood?"

"Don't look so surprised, John," Ned said quietly. "You're doing the same thing. Growing up on the ranch, you became highly educated and skilled according to old Nate's values. Courage and physical strength were necessary for approval, especially your father's approval. Are you getting my drift?"

John stared at Ned. "Jesus, Doc. No wonder we don't see eye to eye on a lot of things. I reckon I should have seen these things before we got married. But I adored Maggie; still do. It's just that... she's sometimes impossible to live with... or talk to."

"I can imagine. You really don't share many interests except Davey. Trouble is, you two approach Davey from quite different viewpoints." Ned pointed his pipe stem at John. "You want him to grow up in your image. You say to yourself that it's for his own good in a world of men. You also see your son as your only path to your father's forgiveness."

"Aw, Doc; I...."

"I know the whole story, John. It wasn't your fault; but the old devil made you believe you had killed your brother. That single lie has damaged you and your relationship with Maggie more than anything else."

"Why, Doc;... that's ridiculous!"

"No it isn't. You're a man of incredible courage and fortitude; but in memory of your mother, you guide your life in search of *everyone's* forgiveness. It's ironic; Lily told me that's what Maggie first found so attractive in you: a certain vulnerability, as if you needed the healing power of love."

"And now she's havin' second thoughts?" John motioned to the waiter and ordered coffee.

Ned squinted through his pipe smoke. "Maybe. Please understand what I'm saying. You're an intelligent, well-educated man. But she doesn't recognize that because you don't speak her language."

"Why Ned, I do the best I know how. But I can't think of anythin' to do that would inspire her respect."

"You told me you got into bicycles because you thought they would impress Maggie. So you turned ranch management over to Ramon. But she isn't very impressed with your bicycle business. So she's asking herself, 'What really anchors John's life? And where is he leading us?'"

"How does Davey enter into the picture?"

"Children either bond a marriage or stress it to break-point. Maggie thinks Davey is exceptionally gifted."

"What do you think, Doc?"

"It's a little early. But from what she's told me, he may be the brightest kid I've ever seen."

"He was mighty slow learnin' to talk. That worried Maggie."

"At first, I think Davey was far more fascinated with pictures in his mind than with Maggie's experiments with three languages or music or the lectures she gave him on philosophy."

"You think all that stuff hurt him?"

"Not a bit. Maggie told me he chatters constantly now. More interesting, he uses vocabulary that is way beyond a typical thirty-month old kid."

"I've wondered about that. Where do you s'pose he gets it from?"

"He's gifted with an eidetic—photographic— memory, John. He remembers everything he sees or hears. The time will come when Davey's mental gifts may stress your marriage the most."

John grinned. "Are you tryin' to scare me, Doc?"

"Not at all. No need to worry now. But when it happens, come see me before you fly off the handle."

"Let's get back to Maggie, Doc. What's your prescription?"

"It's very simple, John. Find your passion and follow it. Remember how you felt in the Rockies?"

"You mean I ought to hunt more?"

"Not exactly. I mean you should stop trying to impress Maggie according to her rules. Do what you love to do. If you're really happy with that, you'll encourage her to be happy with *her* passion—music, philosophy, politics, whatever. And Davey will benefit from both of you, learning from your strengths instead of choosing among your flaws."

John felt a stirring of hope like a faint glow from a first sip of brandy. A vision of a light engine floated across his mind. "What would you think if I tried to build the first light airship engine?"

"Never mind me... or Maggie, John. Forget your parents and Davey. What would *you* think? How does that idea feel to you?" Ned instantly had the answer in a slow grin and a light that suffused John's face. "O.K. So that's clear. But you and Maggie still have another issue to settle."

"What's that, Ned?" John's mood shifted to a warm tolerance as his imagination began to fill his mind with the possibilities of a new engine.

"Power. Authority. Control. Since you were seventeen, you've taken it for granted. You've been the patrón for quite a while. Maggie has only recently gotten a taste of it on the ranch and with Davey. Do you want to fight for it?"

John reflected on the question. Why bother? He really didn't have the time or interest to battle Maggie over Davey now. Why not let her do her job without his interference? As for the ranch, Ramon reported everything to him anyway. If he chose, he could quietly countermand any of Maggie's instructions. "No, I'd rather have her love and respect than her opposition."

"Maggie is a beautiful, vivacious woman. But you put your finger on the central issue when we were in the Rockies."

"Remind me."

"She has too much love in her. She wants to save the world. But she thinks everyone should be as energetic and as strong-minded as she is. I think she actually believes in the liberating power of Darwin's ideas, especially for the individual: competition; struggle and rewards."

"So do I; so does Teddy Roosevelt. Isn't that the spirit of the age?"

"Of course. But you don't really agree with her social philosophy. She's not a social Darwinist. She wants government to lay down rules and redistribute wealth so the struggle for survival isn't stacked against the poor."

"What's wrong with that?" John offered Ned a snifter of brandy.

"Hell man, you're already getting a taste of it on your ranch. In her zeal to help everyone, Maggie had to find out about their big problems, then their smaller problems and, finally, the last detail of everyone's life. Her style is obsessive research. Her knowledge combined with her authority is damned intoxicating, especially to someone with altruistic motives."

"So what should I do?"

"Compromise; delay, negotiate; you sure can't draw arbitrary limits."

"Why not?"

"Because she's smarter and prettier than you are. She'd run right through your limits or by-pass them. You probably won't win most of your battles."

"How about the ones I want to win?" He almost added, *Like bringing up Davey to be a man.*

"You'll have a good chance if you select them carefully. Even then, you'll have to be as devious as a politician." Ned paused to clean his pipe and think about the most awkward element of his advice. "You may not win those if you don't treat her like a real woman."

"What do you mean, Ned?"

"Maggie may be beautiful; and I know you're proud of her. But don't turn her into a goddess on a pedestal. You'll win more battles if you treat her like a human being with doubts and flaws like the rest of us. Spend more time with her. Let your assistants run the bicycle shop for a while. Try to rediscover your family, John."

CHAPTER THIRTEEN

CARMEL VALLEY
JANUARY—APRIL, 1898

Following Ned's advice, for the next month John tried to spend more time with Maggie and Davey. He often joined Maggie in the library while he researched light engines. On many afternoons, he heaved Davey in front of him on a saddle and took him for rides around the ranch, talking about horses, cowboys and Indians, the Civil War, the heroic achievements of Harrisons and the dream of first flight.

Sensitive to John's conciliatory mood, Maggie tried to welcome his presence in the warm library and made every effort to show some interest in his research. But it soon became clear to her that John's idea of an exciting conversation was how a thing worked; he simply had no head for abstract ideas or relationships. She desperately wanted to talk about something besides the ranch; but a shared interest was hard to find when their angle of vision toward themselves, Davey and the world was so different.

Then suddenly, one evening in February everything changed. Over coffee after supper, it started innocently enough. Conscious of Maggie's interest in foreign affairs, John focused on something in the Cuban situation on which he thought they could agree: Cuban civil rights. "The newspapers say the Spanish are wipin' out men, women and children in Cuba. Butcher Weyler is crowdin' ever'one into camps so they can't help the rebels."

Maggie was aware of the crisis in Cuba; but since Christmas, she had focused attention on Davey and ranch families. "What's wrong with the camps?"

"Terrible conditions! No sanitation; short rations; disease rampant. The President sent a special envoy named Calhoun down there last spring. Came back and said the garlics had burned houses, torched sugar-cane fields and cut down banana trees. He said the countryside was 'wrapped in the stillness of death and the silence of desolation.' Right poetic...."

"How awful." Maggie felt a surge of sympathy for the Cuban rebels. She had seen so much starvation in China that she could imagine the effects of the insurrection on innocent children in Cuba. "What did the President do after Calhoun reported?"

"Sent a public condemnation to the Spanish guvmint. Told 'em we have lots of commercial interests in Cuba. We therefore have a right to demand that they conduct their war accordin' to a civilized military code."

"Good for McKinley! Did that do any good?"

"Naw. The garlics told us to mind our own b'iness." John sipped his coffee thoughtfully. "They said they'll deal with the three-year insurrection as they see fit. But they *did* withdraw Weyler; and two months ago, they promised to break up the concentration camps."

"But surely there are civilized ways to force the Spanish to behave?"

"Honey, the garlics are bloodthirsty monsters. All they understand is force."

"How can you know that, John?" Maggie felt guilty that she had not studied the situation with greater care.

"Just read the papers! The *New York Journal* has reported all the gruesome details: the way Weyler murdered and tortured and raped women and children and butchered the weak and the crippled; the way garlic soldiers abused and jailed Evangelina Cisneros." He pounded his fist on the table in sudden anger. "We can't stand by and tolerate such brutality."

If those reports were true, *something must be done*. Maggie felt her rage rising at the intimidation of defenseless women and children. "Are you sure the reporting isn't exaggerated—like the airship craze?"

"Not the same! Not the same at all. Correspondents have gone to Cuba to see for themselves. Sure some of it's sensational; but it's mostly true. I think we should take an army down there and clean up that mess." John's enthusiasm for military action echoed the sentiments of thousands of young men flocking to recruiting stations.

Maggie glanced at Davey, who listened quietly to the conversation while he slowly finished his dessert of *flan*. Imagining him threatened by brutal Spanish soldiers, she didn't realize that her jaw was clenched, her fists tight. "I hope the President acts with firm determination."

"Don't see how he could do otherwise, now that the stupid garlics have blown up the U.S.S. *Maine* in Havana harbor. Killed over two hundred and sixty men. McKinley has asked the Congress for fifty million dollars to get the army ready for war."

"If the Congress declares war, what would you do, John?" Maggie held her breath, confused by conflicting preferences. She hated war and violence; but she thought she might hate the Spanish more.

"Why, I... I hadn't thought it through." He almost asked, "What would you *want* me to do?" Then he remember Ned's advice. "I'd be tempted to go."

"But what about the ranch and your moto-cycle?"

"I can postpone my research easily. Ramon has good control of the ranch; and Roger Macon can run the shop fine. I reckon I'd be mostly concerned about leavin' you and Davey."

John's priorities pleased Maggie. She heard herself rushing to remove all barriers to his service. "Why, Johnnie, you're always talking about something glorious. We...; I would miss you... terribly. But I would feel... selfish if I thought you stayed out of this... great liberation because of me... and Davey."

Now John was confused. "You mean you'd really *want* me to go?"

"I can't say it that way. No...; I wouldn't *want* you to go. But I'd be... proud to think that you had lifted your vision above money-making to do something so... daring for humanity." In a rush of fierce regret for her dissatisfying relationship with her father, she said, "If I were a man, I'd *have* to go."

Her enthusiasm filled his heart with hope. If she could respect a warrior in a just war, maybe Cuba would finally give him a chance to prove himself. He imagined himself coming home with a medal, maybe a battlefield commission for bravery. Surely that would capture her gratitude and respect.

From that night forward, they were in accord on the Cuban issue. John leaned naturally toward the military aspects of the situation while Maggie

accented social and political considerations. The more she learned about
Spanish repression of the Cubans, the deeper her resentment burned
away thoughts of international harmony and negotiation. On occasion, the
thought of John in battle would remind her that he might be killed. Instead of making her feel inadequate, such thoughts prompted her to seek
help from John. One evening in late March, she said, "If you really intend
to go to Cuba, Johnnie, maybe you better teach me how to balance the
books for the ranch."

John considered. For four years, she had been learning the tricks of
ranching. If she really understood the books, she would no longer need
him to manage the business. But she deserved to know. After all, he might
not come home a hero; he might not come home at all. "I'll show you
ever'thin', honey. In fact, before I go, I'll make sure that Ramon and
ever'one know you're to be in charge. I'll teach you the fundamentals of
the bicycle b'iness, too."

Maggie soon noticed a curious change in John. He rarely joined her in
the library or rode to Monterey or took Davey for walks. Instead, he and
Ramon rode off every morning for a week, returning in the middle of the
afternoon. She didn't want to seem nosy; but finally on April Fool's day after supper, she observed, "You seem to have turned your thoughts away
from us. I feel sometimes as if… as if you've already gone."

"Forgive me, Maggie. I've been remembering what Poppa told me
about battle. It kinda changes my priorities."

"Where do you and Ramon go every day?"

"Target practice! I can hit a bulls eye consistently at a hundred yards
now."

"So you're focusing your mind on killing?" Maggie said it as if John had
brought a dead skunk into the house.

John nodded. "I enjoy workin' with you, studyin' the situation there.
But when you come down to it, you'll be here with your philosophy and
Davey and the ranch and the shop. I'll have to forget about those things."

"Forget about us? Why?"

"I can't be worryin' about you while I face the heat and mosquitoes
and rain and… and screams from wounded men and horses and… jungle

snakes and lousy food and...."

"Stop it, Johnnie!" Maggie hadn't imagined such things. She had thought of what a pleasant relief it would be to run things her way without any interference from John. Now suddenly, he had reminded her of the price he would pay for her pleasure. "You don't really have to go, you know."

"Yes I do." John wasn't about to back down now that he had promised Mr. Roosevelt that he would go; now that he had seen how the prospect of battle had captured Maggie's respect; now that he had shot hundreds of rounds of ammunition and now that he had altered his priorities so radically that he had relegated everything except Cuba to insignificance. His father had told him that battle was something like hunting except for the fact that the enemy could shoot back.

Only one thing still bothered him: his promise to his dead parents to take care of Davey. Nearly three years old, the boy was beginning to intrigue John, who had been challenged by the boy's attitude that very night when John and Maggie put him to bed. When he had finished singing a medley of cowboy songs to Davey, he had asked, "What's this roundup business, Davey? You mentioned it at supper tonight."

"I do it every night, Poppa. I try to remember everything that happens all day. Then I put our brand on them."

"What is our brand, son?" *If it's a thing, it's my brand; if it's an idea, it's Maggie's.*

"Why, Poppa, it's love. Momma says if I love everything, everything will... harmon..., everything will be in harmony." In that simple statement, Davey used the most important word in his vocabulary.

Davey was too young to grasp any metaphysical meaning of harmony. He thought it meant the blending of voices the way the vaqueros sang songs. Indeed, his life seemed to be an ocean of inner and outer harmonies. If he had been asked the meaning of the word "God," he would probably have answered, "He must be the biggest harmony." He said to John, "Momma says everything has a part in the whole song."

"Isn't that a pretty big idea for such a little squirt?" John asked with a grin.

"Poppa, I know I'm small," Davey said. "But I hear music everywhere. You know what I mean."

It was then that John first suspected that Maggie's lectures on philosophy might have taught Davey ideas, as well as vocabulary. What kind of music was the kid talking about? John feared that something dark might threaten Davey's sanity. Could Maggie be trusted to handle it while he was gone?

A new controversy between Maggie and John about rearing Davey might have reached an explosion if fate had not intervened. On the afternoon of April 19, John was admiring his latest bicycle when a telegraph messenger raced excitedly into the shop. "Got a hot one for you, John!" he cried as he thrust a telegram into John's hand. John noted that he hadn't even bothered to seal the message in an envelope. The telegram read:

APRIL 19, 1898
CONGRESS APPROVED JOINT WAR RESOLUTION EARLY THIS MORNING
STOP. FORMING ROUGH-RIDER REGIMENT STOP. COME SAN ANTONIO
WITH UTMOST HASTE STOP. (signed) TR

Suddenly John forgot his personal vows to dead parents and his concerns for Davey's upbringing. Since the destruction of the U.S.S. *Maine* on February 15, John had accepted the conclusion of the New York *Journal*: "The warship *Maine* was split in two by an enemy secret infernal machine." War fever had kindled his own fervour and acted as a kind of antidote to his doubts about his wife, his son and himself. And Maggie seemed to support the war. Here, finally, was something he could do with gusto and confidence. He grabbed a bicycle and rode over to Ned Ambler's office.

"Ned, Teddy Roosevelt has sent me a telegram. He wants me to join the Rough Riders. Do you see any reason why I shouldn't?"

Ned's emotions were confused these days. One part of his mind thought John's marriage deserved attention; someone else could fight the Spanish in Cuba. But another part of his mind yearned for John to go to war, perhaps never to return. Only then might he have a chance to court Maggie. Insanity. "What about your obligation to your family?"

"Maggie thinks I ought to go, says she's sorry she's not a man. Why, she said she'd be proud to know I was liberatin' all those women and children."

Ned considered the whole venture an expansionist tempest in a teapot. He knew that John would normally feel the same way. However, the war in Cuba might bring him more glory than the one he was losing at home. Maybe both John and Maggie needed a holiday from the challenge of their marriage of four years. John especially needed to recapture his self-esteem and a sense of glorious purpose. Perhaps Maggie needed time to satisfy her hunger for power and to dream of Davey's future. And maybe Davey needed a vacation from their relentless disagreements. "I reckon you should go, John. Teddy liked you; maybe you can keep him from making a fool of himself."

Then John said something that filled Ned's heart with hope. "Will you watch over Maggie; try to help her over any rough spots?"

"Of course I will, John. Don't worry about things at this end."

With a whoop, John exploded from Ned's office and raced back to his shop. "Roger," he yelled at his assistant, "I'm goin' to war! Hold down the shop 'til I get back. I'll catch the train south tomorrow."

PART III

THE WAR

"It is well that war is so terrible; we would grow too fond of it."

GENERAL ROBERT E. LEE
AT FREDERICKSBURG, 1862

CHAPTER FOURTEEN

TAMPA, FLORIDA
MAY-JUNE, 1898

June 3, 1898

Dearest Maggie,

Please forgive me for my long silence. The past six weeks have been like a round-up in San Antonio. Dust and heat and confusion. Colonel Leonard Wood and TR called it training. Last November I told you a little bit about TR. But I had never met Wood, whom we call "Old Poker Face." I didn't know that he had won a Medal of Honor for tracking down that Apache, Geronimo, in 1886. He looks shorter than his 5' 11" because he is so stocky and tough looking with a big head, a bull neck, broad shoulders and a brusque manner. Between his short, gray hair and his dark, bushy mustache, he has the most intimidating eyes I have ever seen. With no sense of humor, he looks at you as if he's judge and jury with no tolerance for human frailty. I was surprised to learn that he was White House physician to President McKinley before he received command of the Rough Riders.

From the moment I reached the San Antonio railroad station on May 1 and saw "THIS WAY TO ROOSEVELT'S ROUGH RIDERS" on a sign, I felt like it was mostly one long party. At "Camp Wood," only two miles from the Alamo, Colonel Wood had rustled a mountain of equipment for us before the other regimental commanders even found the door. Instead of heavy wool uniforms, we got khaki with yellow cavalry trim. Each of us got a long-barreled Colt revolver and a new Krag-Jorgensen carbine with magazine. In our flannel work shirts, campaign

hats, blue polka-dotted kerchiefs around our necks and tough
canvas fatigues stuffed into boots or leggings, we felt
mighty cocky, but we didn't look—or act—very military.

I guess we were all too excited; and we were having fun
ragging all the blue-bloods that joined the regiment: people
like the former master of the Chevy Chase hounds; the two
best tennis players in the country; a strapping doctor named
Bob Church, who played football for Princeton; Bucky
O'Neill, the former sheriff and mayor of Prescott, Arizona;
Ham Fish, the grandson of President Grant's Secretary of
State; and full-blooded Cherokee trackers like Tom Isbell
and Ed Culver. A motley crew; but game, mighty game.

TR arrived in mid-May. He joined us on all our trail rides
through Texas dust and even bought us beer in a roadside saloon after a dry, hot afternoon of torture. I heard that Colonel Wood later cussed him for undermining discipline.
That's when TR asked me to stay close to him and try to keep
him from making a fool of himself. He said my experience with
cowboys had taught me how to treat men. I knew that it sure
doesn't pay to seek cheap popularity from men you will later
have to order into battle. The trouble was—and still is—that
TR thinks the sun rises and sets on this gang. He seems to
feel a deep affection for every trooper. I've never seen the
like.

On May 30, General Shafter sent a telegram to report to
Tampa. TR did a war dance in front of Colonel Wood! TR acts
like a ring-tailed bob cat from the high country. But I guess
everyone in the regiment is as eager for action as he is. The
Texicans gave us a dandy sendoff the night before we left. A
band was supposed to play "The Cavalry Charge." At just the
right moment when the music sounded like a cavalry charge, a
pistol detail was supposed to shoot blank cartridges. Our
regiment had loaded live rounds. At the signal from the band
leader, everyone fired and the civilians scurried for cover!
Someone told me we fired over two thousand rounds.

The train trip to Tampa was like a victory parade. At little towns all along the way, pretty girls waved the Stars and Stripes and threw us kisses. I even saw old rebs salute the flag. Poppa would have wept.

We reached Tampa today and it was quite a letdown. No one to meet us; no idea where we were supposed to bivouac; hotter than the hinges of hell; no chow or forage for man or beast. We finally got settled at a campground under the command of an old reb, General Joe Wheeler. White-hair and a white beard; can't be taller than five feet. TR said McKinley gave Wheeler command to show the nation that the Civil War is really over. The irony is that we have been put in the same brigade with Buffalo Soldiers, the 9th and 10th Regular regiments, composed of Negro troopers and white officers. I wonder what Poppa would think of that?

Words can't express how much I appreciate your letters. I miss you and Davey like thunder. Sometimes, when the day is over and the sun has gone down and I have a moment to reflect, I count myself the luckiest man alive to have my family safe and sound in Carmel. Give Davey a big hug for me.

Seated in the library, Maggie read the letter out loud to Davey and marveled at John's flowing prose. From his awkwardness in conversation, she had assumed that he simply couldn't communicate. It came as a surprise that, like many others, his thought process preferred the written word. She tried to imagine the sights and sounds and smells of John's great adventure "I just pray that he's all right, that nothing will happen to him," she murmured to Davey.

"He's all right, Momma," Davey said cheerily.

"I wish I could be sure." Now that John was no longer a physical presence in her life, she often felt unsure of herself, her authority, her responsibility for Davey and the ranch and the bicycle shop. She supposed she would have to experiment until someone said, "Stop."

"I'm sure, Momma. All I have to do is peek."

"Peek? Do you mean you can see your Poppa in your mind?"

"He's at a big house that looks like the Del Monte Lodge. He's sitting next to a big fat man and another man with tiny glasses. They both have mustaches. They're drinking and they look very hot. And Poppa is all right."

Maggie made a note to herself to ask John about the "big fat man" and the "big house" in her next letter. Despite all her theoretical work about paths to redemption, whether ascending or descending, she could think of no adequate explanation for the apparent reach of Davey's mind. She could not remember a single mention of such "remote viewing" in any of the great works that had obsessed her for nearly two years. She felt alone and a little frightened.

June 14, 1898

Dearest Maggie,

Now I understand what General Sherman meant when he said, "War is hell." For the past six days, we have sweltered in the bowels of a troop transport called the *Yucatan*. When Colonel Wood commandeered this hulk, we congratulated him for his bold initiative. We were sick and tired of waiting, waiting, waiting in our tents lined up on the hot sandhills of Tampa.

We didn't know we would have to wait even longer in this floating oven. Anything would be better than this cauldron that we have to endure until the navy can assure General Shafter that no Spanish warships will intercept our convoy to Cuba.

For a while, I thought TR would go crazy with the disorder of the situation in Tampa. A thousand freight cars stood in line: testaments to what it takes to send thirty thousand men, mostly Regulars, to one place. Because our supply officers failed to put bills of lading on the cars or even the boxes, we spent days just sifting through the boxes to find our rifles, ammunition and saddles. We finally assembled enough equipment to put on a formal review of the cavalry brigade a week ago.

I guess our 2000 bowlegs looked pretty good. But TR was mighty unhappy when he learned the same day that limited space on the transports would permit only two-thirds of our regiment to embark. The worst news was that there would be no room for our horses. Everyone except officers will have to fight on foot. TR will take his two mounts, "Texas" and "Rain-in-the-face." That evening beginning at six o'clock, we marched to the Tampa Bay Hotel to get our pay, all $2.10 of it. While we stood in line, I thought of you when I heard an orchestra playing "After The Ball Is Over" and "Sidewalks Of New York." It was almost ten o'clock by the time we returned to camp. Then we were ordered to pack up and prepare for embarkation. I rolled my clothes, a few personal things, my sleeping blanket and my poncho into a shelter-half and threw it over my shoulder. I put on my cartridge belt with 125 rounds. I threw a couple of haversacks over my shoulder and picked up my carbine. I didn't think about going to war or battle or such things. I was so hot that all I could think of was a cool, breezy ride on a train.

For two hours until midnight, we marched around hunting for a train to haul us down a single track to the pier at Tampa. It never showed up. It seemed there was no schedule, no allotment of times for each train. We were supposed to catch another train the next morning, but that one never showed up either. By then TR was apoplectic with rage. You have to hold on to your socks when he gets mad. At 5:00 a.m. he simply commandeered a bunch of coal cars and moved us down to Tampa in an hour. We were loaded aboard the *Yucatan* by midnight of June 8.

For the next two days, TR fumed and fretted. Everybody bellyached to him about no horses. He finally took me in a launch to see General Shafter at his headquarters on June 10. I couldn't believe my eyes. The General met us on the veranda of the Tampa Bay Hotel. It's a Moorish monstrosity. Shafter is such a heavy man—probably 300 pounds—that he didn't even try to stand up when TR and I approached him. Shafter just rocked back and forth in his rocking chair. I guess that's why the news correspondent, Richard Harding Davis, calls this the "rocking chair phase of the war." So we sat there and drank lemonade while TR tried to convince him that he must embark the entire First Volunteer Cavalry Regiment.

Maggie paused and referred to the date when she had read her last letter from John. June 10. Davey's imagination had not been working overtime. He had actually seen the little group of three men on the veranda of the hotel. She felt an icy shiver creep up her spine. *Oh God, please help me understand my son,* she prayed as she turned back to John's letter.

Shafter was adamant. The ships were already too crowded. He said he felt lucky to jam 16,000 men and 3000 horses and mules and 38 artillery pieces onto 31 transports. No room for any more anything! I don't claim to be an expert on the art of war. But I have no confidence in the War Department. TR says the brass in Washington spend their days arguing about who should get credit for some obscure flanking movement or frontal attack in the Civil War. How dare they rest on the laurels of that bygone generation of leaders? What does this generation have to crow about? The victory of a few younger men over the Plains Indians? I've heard a few Regulars talk proudly about "the Old Army." That's our trouble; the Army is so old, it's muddleheaded. Their performance at Tampa showed anyone with eyes that they have no conception of modern warfare, especially the burden it must impose on railroads and industry. It's criminal to issue Springfield rifles to our infantry. Gatling guns might compensate; but the sages in Washington are sending only four on this campaign. If the Spaniards have any such guns or some modern artillery, our medical service will be overwhelmed.

On the other hand, I was most impressed with the younger West Pointers I saw at the Tampa Bay Hotel: tough minded, practical men. TR told me their motto of service to "Duty, Honor and Country" is not an empty myth. They were having a kind of reunion in the Hotel while they waited for orders. Their camaraderie and high spirits made me a little envious. I wonder if Davey might ever join that "Long Grey Line"?

Maggie read the last sentence with a gasp. Her son a military man? Never! The thought of it made her clutch the letter in her fist with apprehension that bordered on panic. She continued reading.

My troop is quartered on three tiers of bunks on the second deck where coal had once been carried. Tight and uncomfortable and hot. For the past six days, the grub has been the same: hard tack, stringy, tasteless canned beef, canned tomatoes, beans and coffee. Like everybody, I'm glad we're finally going. We can't stand much more of this floating prison. In the hold, the smell of sweating men and manure has driven many of us on deck at night.

Ashore, I can hear the band playing "There'll Be a Hot Time In The Old Town Tonight." We will shove off any moment. I should feel tremendous excitement. But I'm so weary of the Army game, hurry-up-and-wait, that I'm just numb. I'll cut this letter short so that TR's orderly, Bill Saunders, can take it ashore with last-minute dispatches.

Maggie glanced at the calendar: June 21. It had taken a week for the letter to cross the continent. She wondered where John might be now. Howard Chandler Christy's marvelous illustrations in *Leslie's Weekly* helped her visualize the drama. And in Monterey she had seen "moving pictures" of "actual battlefield scenes" produced by Vitagraph, Biograph and the Edison Companies. They had sent correspondents to photograph the 10th Infantry Regiment training in Tampa and scenes of the 9th Cavalry watering horses in Cuba. But for details, she relied on each morning's paper for the latest dispatches from Davis of the *New York Herald* and Remington and Stephen Crane of the *New York World*. She thought it was ominous that the press had been silent for the past week.

June 21, 1898

My Dearest Maggie,

Today, I watched TR perform another of his war dances when he learned we will be among the first to land tomorrow at a place called Daiquiri. It is on the south coast of Cuba around fifteen miles east of Santiago. Each of us will carry three days' rations, a hundred rounds of ammunition and a blanket roll. As I write, a beautiful tropical night adds mystery to what we are about to do. In the distance, I can see fires at Daiquiri and Siboney. Admiral Sampson has bottled up the Spanish fleet in Santiago Bay; but he won't risk his ships against the guns of Morro Castle. So it's up to us to attack Santiago by land.

The trip was mostly a horror. We could only go as fast as the slowest boat. So we spent six days lumbering along at four knots. Foul water, spoiled canned beef, a form of rat poison that the canteen tried to sell us as drinking whiskey, the godawful stench and sea sickness laid a lot of fellows low. When we rounded Oriente Province yesterday at the eastern tip of Cuba, I could almost feel the whole army breathe a sigh of relief.

As it turned out, my trip was an unexpected eye-opener for my research on flight. I met two fellows who showed me a new weapon of war: the observation balloon. One of them, Ivy Baldwin, has been a dare-devil all his life. He's a small, trim man with shoulders and chest like a wrestler. Five years ago, he and his brother, Tom, visited the World's Columbia Exposition in Chicago and met Captain Thompson of the Signal Corps. That was about the time a bunch of experts—like Chanute and Langley—gathered in Chicago for an International Congress on Aerial Navigation. Captain Thompson brought the Army's new balloon, called the *General Myer*, to the Exposition for display. Needing a balloonist to fly it, they discovered that one of the experts, Tom Baldwin, was a famous aerialist who was the first American to ever jump in a parachute from a balloon. The Haight Street Cable Line in San Francisco had paid for his first leap in January, 1887.

Anyway, Captain Thompson hired Tom to take charge of the *General Myer* in Chicago. They made a successful ascension and the Secretary of War announced that the balloon had finally taken its place in the mechanism of war. In the spring of 1894, the Signal Corps shifted the whole aeronautics game to Ft. Logan in Colorado. Profits were thin so Ivy agreed to join the Army in November as a Sergeant to fly *General Myer*. On its first flight, it exploded because no one had taken good care of it, but the Army persisted.

When war clouds loomed in April this year, Ivy went to Ft. Wadsworth for more trials of a new balloon, called *Santiago*. As luck would have it, under the command of Major Maxfield, Ivy and his assistant, a Corporal named Zeke Harner, sailed on the *Yucatan*.

Now, you may ask, why does this story interest me so much? Because Ivy and Maxfield became real excited when I told them about my work on a small engine. They want me to design it for a war balloon like *Santiago*. I never expected to find official encouragement for my work in the sweltering heat of the Caribbean. Isn't that exciting?

I like Ivy Baldwin a lot. He's square. But Harner worries me. He's bent, somehow. He's a bully who thinks money and political influence count for everything. So I don't trust him. He tells me he has a wife and young son in Dayton, Ohio. If he's teaching his youngster to think like he does, the world will have another Harner to cope with one of these days.

It's getting late now and I had better turn in. God willing, our landing tomorrow will encounter no resistance. But if the enemy fights, I pray that I may behave honorably. I don't know which will be harder, fighting the enemy or keeping up with TR and Leonard Wood.

Maggie read the letter several times. She glanced at her calendar. It had taken nine days for the letter to reach her. Dispatches from Frederic Remington and Dick Davis had already brought her up to date on the unopposed landings at Daiquiri and the irresolute advance by Shafter's Fifth Corps to foothills east of Santiago. Today was July 1, 1898. What would he be doing today?

CHAPTER FIFTEEN

CARMEL
JULY, 1898

June 30, 1898

Dearest Maggie,

Did you know that over two hundred correspondents are covering this campaign? Astonishing! You must be keeping up with the fine dispatches by Remington and Richard Harding Davis. Dick has stayed close to TR throughout and tells an accurate story, I think. Nevertheless, I feel obliged to give you a personal perspective from the landing at Daiquiri until this moment, the eve of an attack against what we are calling Kettle Hill.

On June 22 at Daiquiri we were mighty lucky. I don't know if the Spaniards are stupid or ill-informed. Maybe they thought a feint west of Santaigo was our main attack there; or maybe the bombardment of Daiquiri by six of our warships frightened them, though it sure didn't do much damage. It never even touched a blockhouse on top of a high hill overlooking Daiquiri. Anyway, there was no opposition to our landing. Sticking close to TR as ordered, I went ashore aboard a yacht, the *Vixen*, commanded by TR's former naval aide.

Perhaps because of my responsibility for TR's safety, I felt a different personality seize control of me when we set foot on the pier. I have hunted all my life, as you know, but this was the first time in my life that I was the hunted. It feels like a thousand eyes are watching you, waiting for you to make one mistake. I could sense danger lurking in every

palm tree, waving high above the rest of the thick undergrowth. It was very hot and I began to sweat, but some of that
perspiration was nerves. TR stepped ashore like he was on a
picnic. *His* nerves are made of steel. Or maybe he doesn't
have sense enough to be scared.

We had few casualties among the men; and I felt terrible
to see some of the horses drown. Besides the fifty that died
on the voyage, we lost another six in the surf at Daiquiri.
When a bunch of confused cavalry horses turned to sea, a bu-
gler made them turn around by simply blowing "Recall."

We spent that first night out in the open. The next day,
two brigades of Lawton's 2d Regular Infantry Division moved
west along the coast to Siboney. I could hear occasional
small arms fire from the jungle where Castillo's Cuban guerrillas chased after the retreating Spanish rear guard.

Those guerrillas have suffered more than the law allows.
Armed only with machetes and old-style Remingtons and
Springfields, many of them barefoot, they are so thin that
they look like a bunch of year-old scarecrows, their rags
hanging on them like ribbons. I fear that their misery and
torture at the hands of the Spaniards have stolen their pride
and their humanity. After a greeting of *"Viva Cuba libre,"*
they beg us for anything we can give them: food, clothes,
weapons. Their cruelty to animals made all of us angry. Instead of simply shooting a bull for slaughter, they insisted
on stabbing the beast to death. Should we really turn this
country over to the likes of them?

After we seized Siboney around 9:00 a.m. on June 23, the
landing went on all night under searchlight from the transports. It was quite a sight. The men were so glad to be on
land again that they celebrated on into the night. To dry out
their uniforms, many men simply took them off and stood naked
around the fires. For most of them, it was their first bath
in seven days. If the Spanish had attacked us then and there,
we would have lost the war.

Like McClellan on the Peninsula during the Civil War,

General Shafter was afflicted with the slows. He had issued
an order to consolidate at Siboney unless the "senior officer on the ground" dictated otherwise. Old Joe Wheeler was
senior officer. He's a feisty bobcat and had no intention of
following meekly behind the infantry. I heard him hand out
the order for a reconnaissance-in-force to the north on June
24. He split his brigade into two columns. The east column
under General Young had eight troops: four from the 1st Regular Cavalry Regiment and four from the 10th Regulars, Ne-
groes. Young also had 2 Hotchkiss mountain guns. The plan was
for them to march north on a miserable trail just wide enough
for a wagon. The locals call it the Camino Real. It snakes
its way up a valley so dense with jungle that you couldn't
see through it on either side of the trail.

Perhaps a mile or two west of the Camino Real was a much
narrower trail. Our eight Rough Rider troops under Colonel
Wood were supposed to move up that trail.

I was dog-tired by the time TR and I turned in at midnight
on June 23. Reveille was at 3:15 the next morning. We had
rancid bacon, hard tack and thin coffee for breakfast. Young
started up the Camino Real at 5:45 and we started up our
trail at 6:00. The heat was fierce. I love the dry heat; but
that heat was so humid and sticky that I felt like I was in a
bathtub all day long. TR and Dick Davis rode near the head of
the column while I walked in front of them.

I thought it was unfair to be responsible for TR's safety.
Between the thick jungle vines I felt squashed and blind and
helpless and hot and angry. I was especially angry because
the men forgot their training and acted like they were taking
a stroll in a park. Worse, they chattered like blue-jays,
noisier than jungle birds, adding their chorus to the general disorder. I heard TR talking to Davis about the beauty
of the jungle, the names of flora and fauna. Maybe Colonel
Wood thought the Cuban guerrilla, Castillo, was providing
security to the front and flanks. The undergrowth was so
thick that flank security was impossible; but he finally

sent Ham Fish ahead as point.

Anyone who wasn't scared was either a liar or a fool—or trying to prove something more important than overcoming fear. I think that's what keeps TR going. Until he left Harvard, almost every day he had to prove to himself that he wasn't weak, even if his body was. That must have been how he developed the habit of will power. I've never met anyone else with such steely determination. I know now that he can be depressed like the rest of us, but his life-long struggle with his body has taught him that the only antidote to depression is hard exercise. He refuses to let the physical world rule his emotions. I guess that's why he wasn't alert to that puma back in Colorado.

At around 7:30, General Young's column spied some breastworks up ahead near a cluster of some strange hog-nut trees called *guasimas*.

The two trails came together at that point. Then I guess Ham Fish saw them too. Both columns halted. We immediately deployed with TR on the right of the trail and Major Brodie on the left. At 8:15, General Young fired his Hotchkiss mountain guns at the breastworks. The Spanish replied with a heavy volley from their Mausers. They sound like corks exploding out of a champagne bottle. Pop! Pop! Pop! TR wanted to get into the thick of it; but we couldn't see the Spanish. Then a runner came down the trail to tell us that Ham Fish had been killed. I tasted real fear then; it's a dry taste. No amount of water will rinse it away.

It was about that time that Dick Davis pointed through the trees to a bunch of conical hats. "There they are, Colonel!" he said. Suddenly a rifle bullet cut through the tree beside TR and splashed splinters against his glasses. A close shave. Then a heavy exchange of rifle fire warned us that the main Spanish position was on a ridge of trenches about 300 yards ahead. Firing from a standing position behind a tree, I may have picked off several Spaniards; it didn't occur to me that I was killing anyone. And then Captain Capron got shot.

That's when we deployed our entire regiment in a thin skirmish line until it was about a thousand yards wide. We had nothing in reserve.

And then a terrible rage seized control of me. I forgot about TR and my duty to him and the heat and even fear, I think. I joined the skirmishers who slowly advanced against those trenches. I walked steadily up that hill for a pace or two, then lifted my Krag and fired at any hat I could see. Everyone was cheering or screaming their anger, excitement and pain. I could hear the whine of Mauser bullets slicing through the bushes and the leaves. Whenever I heard a thud, I knew someone had been hit. I wondered if I would hear that same sound if I got hit.

It's impossible to describe the madness that takes hold of a man in that kind of situation. Even TR picked up a carbine and pitched in with the rest of us. When I saw that, I remembered my duty and stuck close to him again. At about the same instant, TR on one end of the line and Wood on the other decided to charge. We later called it "Wood's bluff" because we were actually much weaker than the Spanish force. We had less than a thousand to their fifteen hundred. We charged with such enthusiasm that the Spanish must have thought we were part of a much larger force. They skedaddled. The battle at Las Guasimas only took one hour but it felt like a life-time. It cost us 8 dead and 34 wounded.

That afternoon, I went with TR back down the trail to see what we could do to bring up supplies and food. We were astonished to see some wounded from the 1st and 10th Cavalry singing "My country 'tis of thee…." We saw Doctor Bob Church carrying wounded men on his shoulders to the medicos.

The next morning we buried the eight Rough Riders who were killed. We tried to do justice to Ham Fish and Capron and the others. But we were very tired. So a plaintive bugle call and silent mourners around the mass grave was the best we could do.

That single skirmish was important for two reasons.

First, it made Shafter decide to approach Santiago by the inland route instead of along the coast. Maybe most important, the correspondents gave TR the most credit for our "victory". That one hour may have paved the way for TR's political career for the rest of his life—provided the Spanish don't kill him first!

Because of a shortage of food and ammunition, we paused for six days while the engineers improved the road north from Siboney. Exhausted men and mules laid corduroy across mosquito-infested swamps, bridged small streams, filled depressions, removed boulders and widened the road. The medicos needed the time to cope with the wounded and the growing number of men with the Tennessee quickstep (diarrhea) and yellow jack. I went forward with scouts to a point called El Pozo Hill. From there to the west, we could see a range of hills and, maybe five miles beyond, Santiago. We could also see the Spanish digging entrenchments. TR thinks the Spanish will make their battle there because our approach to San Juan and Kettle Hills is open, dangerous country with easy avenues of fire for Spanish marksmen.

For the last six days, it has rained every afternoon. I spent the morning with Ivy Baldwin and Zeke Harner while they got the balloon ready for an ascent. What a sight they must have seen! About two miles across open country are San Juan and Kettle Hills, scarred with Spanish trenches; to the east, twelve thousand men in a narrow column wound their way westward from Los Mangos. We came here to El Pozo to spend the night in an old sugar factory. This afternoon at 3:00, the order came down to break camp and move out to assembly areas for our attack tomorrow. Tomorrow morning, five thousand men under General Lawton will attack El Caney to the north. The rest of us will attack San Juan and Kettle Hills.

It is a brilliant, clear tropical night. It makes me think of you and little Davey. Forgive me for the long letter. Between the lines, I send my love.

Feeling frightened and guilty, Maggie folded the letter and asked herself why she had supported John's enthusiasm for the war in Cuba. She had scarcely framed the question mentally when Davey spoke as if he had read her mind, "Momma, Poppa *had* to go fight the garlics."

"How do you always know what I'm thinking, Davey?"

"I hear you, Momma. I always hear you."

That assertion reminded Maggie of a fear that had been growing quietly for three months. It wasn't like her fears for John, which were sometime things. This other fear was like an unquenchable fire fueled by numerous daily reminders like Davey's last off-hand comment. It had all started in late April. Within a few days after John left, Maggie discovered that Davey could read her mind. In fact, by May, he habitually linked mind reading with another gift: finding lost articles. He might be glancing casually at a magazine when he would hear her mind ask, "Now where did I put those keys?" Without looking up, he would say, "They're in your jacket in your bedroom."

At first, Maggie had been amused by Davey's strange ability to pinpoint stray possessions around the house. She had almost become accustomed to, even dependent on, his curious skill until one night in mid-May when she and Ah-ying played a memory game with him. While Ah Ying had diverted him, Maggie laid out twenty items on the rosewood coffee table in the living room: a knife, a pair of scissors, a spoon and so forth. She had covered them with a towel and explained the rules to Davey. "I'll give you ten seconds to look at some things under this towel. Then, I'll cover them again and we'll see how many you can remember."

At the end of five seconds, Davey turned away and asked Ah Ying a question about the meaning of a *ch'eng-yu*. Maggie felt disappointed at his seeming disinterest in her game. "Isn't the game fun, Davey? Or is it too hard?"

"It's too easy, Momma." He then promptly listed all twenty items. Some he named in Spanish; some in Chinese; and the rest in English. In the next twenty minutes, he showed Maggie and Ah Ying that he could remember sixty items after only ten seconds of exposure.

Apprehensively Ah Ying had covered her mouth and shook her head in shock. "*Hsieh lou t'ien chi*! (He leaks knowledge of the divine world)."

Then Maggie had a brainstorm. She sketched the relative location of each object on a piece of paper. After she gave Davey ten seconds to view the objects, she covered them and asked Davey to turn his back. Then she removed the towel and jumbled the objects together. "O.K., Davey," she said. "Now see if you can put all these things back in the same place they were."

It took Davey only a few minutes to arrange the objects in precisely the same pattern they had occupied during his ten-second inspection.

There could be do doubt about it. Davey had a... what had Ned Ambler call it? ...an eidetic memory. His mind could photograph an image and retain it. The very idea of such a talent excited Maggie as she thought of Davey's coming schooling. Why, perhaps he could become a scholar, a renowned intellectual, perhaps even an *enlightened* scientist, surely a contradiction in terms, if not a miracle. His promising mental power had thrilled her until his accurate remote viewing of John in Tampa in early June warned her that he might be... different, even... abnormal.

Burdened by that possibility, Maggie decided that his bizarre talents came from his detachment from society. She resolved to force him out of his day-dreams. To carry through her plan, she decided to take him horseback riding every afternoon when she visited housewives on the ranch. Seated behind him on the saddle, she was not pleased at his disinterest towards strangers. In desperation, in mid-June she urged him to get out and play more with little Juan Cisneros, the son of the ranch foreman, Ramon.

An earthy, rough-and-tumble little boy, Juan was two years older than Davey. The boys soon became inseparable, while their fluent interchange of Spanish and English nurtured their sense of brotherhood.

Horseback rides, three languages, songs and little Juan Cisneros thus became Maggie's tools for forcing Davey into the world. But since her studies had confirmed her belief that the purpose of life was harmony, she didn't want him to lose his natural sense of rhythm. By early July, she felt she finally had succeeded in helping him craft a fine balance between his inner and outer worlds.

CHAPTER SIXTEEN

SAN JUAN HILL
JULY 1, 1898

I wonder if I have the guts to go up in that thing? Could Ivy arrange it? John Harrison's shirt hung on his shoulders like a wet dishrag, the cost of existence in the Cuban oven. "Are you goin' up this mornin', Ivy?" he asked.

"No, General Shafter wants Colonel Derby to go up and report on the Spanish dispositions." Ivy had just finished supervising the inflation of the *Santiago* in a clearing about 400 yards behind El Pozo Hill. In the bright morning sun, it was a dull yellow silhouette against the surrounding green forest. Several soldiers man-handled hemp lines to stabilize the balloon in the mild breeze, while Major Maxfield and Lieutenant Colonel George Derby, Shafter's chief engineer officer, stepped into the basket. Ivy was disappointed to be deprived of the view of the battle, but he tried to put a good face on it. "Anyway, I'll be more help on the ground than I'd in the air; I don't trust the way Zeke handles the lines. I won't put any man's life, especially mine, in Zeke's hands." It was the first hint that Ivy shared John's distrust of Zeke.

"I know what you mean. He told me he knows two brothers in Dayton, Ohio, who'll pay for Langley's secrets about flight. Do you think he's lyin'?"

"Don't pay any attention to him. He's talking about the Wright brothers. I know them. First, I don't think they're very interested in flight. Second, they are honest; they wouldn't pay Zeke a plugged nickel for anything."

"Does Zeke know them?"

"I reckon; he worked in their bicycle shop for a time before he joined the army." Ivy threw the dregs of his coffee on the ground and yelled, "Haul down on that line, Zeke; it's too slack!"

Ivy's mention of a bicycle shop interested John. "Who are these Wright brothers? Do they really know something about aeronautics?"

"Not any more than anyone else, I guess. They told me they've been reading the usual popular stuff for about eight years. The best scientist in the field was Otto Lilienthal. He died in a glider crash two years ago."

"But is Langley's research really so secret?" John stood beside Ivy while they watched the balloon begin a slow ascent above El Pozo Hill.

"I doubt it. Four years ago, a fellow named Chanute summarized just about everything there is to know in his book, *Progress in Flying Machines*. He reads every article he can find, runs meetings, writes in *The Aeronautical Annual* and generally keeps everyone informed on the race."

"What race?"

"Why, John, the race to be the first to fly a powered aeroplane. Whoever does that will go down in the history books." With that parting remark, Ivy ran forward to correct mistakes by Zeke and other members of the crew.

John stood rooted to the hillside as the import of Ivy's last statement sank in. The possibility of being first to fly a powered airship had frequently piqued his imagination ever since he and Maggie had seen the airship a year earlier. But he had focused his attention only on the engine because he also needed a light motor for his moto-cycle. Could Davey's destiny be first flight in an aeroplane? What were the technical problems? Was there some connection between bicycle manufacture and an aeroplane? Bristling with excitement, he resolved to talk more with Ivy about Chanute and others who had devoted their lives to the dream of flight. His mind was so aglow with promise that he forgot his first priority until the nearby thunder from Grimes' battery reminded him. He still had a battle to fight.

As he turned away from the balloon and walked towards the Rough Rider bivouac, he heard Colonel Derby yell, "Walk the balloon toward the Spanish. I've got to find a better approach for our attack!" The crew walked forward. The balloon ascended to about a hundred feet above the trees. Suddenly, Zeke Harner stumbled off the trail and fell down. His line became entangled in the thick undergrowth. Before he could disentangle it, the air was filled with shrapnel from Spanish artillery.

My God! John thought, *the damned balloon gives away our position. We're gonna smell hell now. I'd better get back to TR.* He raced down the hill to a ford across the Aguadores River where he expected to find the Rough Riders.

"Harrison, that damned balloon is drawing fire," Lieutenant John J. Pershing cried as he rushed his Negro troops past wild-eyed soldiers of the New York 71st Volunteer Regiment. Hovering directly over their heads, the balloon was attracting heavy enemy rifle and artillery fire. "You know those fellows; can't you bring it down?"

"It's already dying a natural death, Sir." John watched the balloon, riddled with holes from small arms fire, slowly sink into the trees. But the damage was done. Now, the Spanish knew the precise location of the main American force. John marvelled at the quiet confidence of the Negro troops. Stripping off extraneous equipment in preparation for battle, they ignored the green, demoralized New Yorkers. *No wonder everyone calls this Lieutenant Black Jack*, John thought. *He should be proud of them. They're professionals. They make those New Yorkers look sick.* At that moment, he saw Zeke Harner, terrified and white-faced, racing toward him and Pershing. Impulsively, John pulled out his revolver and jammed it in Harner's stomach. "Where do you think you're goin', Harner?"

Harner's eyes were glazed with fear. Saliva dripped from the corner of his mouth. His entire body shook in his torn uniform; but he was not wounded. "I...; I...; the Major ordered me to..., to.... I've got to get away; got to tell someone; there must be five thousand garlics right in front of us."

John glanced at Pershing, who made no effort to mask his disgust with the coward. "You son-of-a-bitch!" John growled. "You didn't even try to save Maxfield and Derby, did you? Just ran off to 'tell someone.' I've a good mind to kill you right here." He watched Pershing move away to take charge of his troops. "Turn your butt around and move forward there where Colonel Roosevelt is standin'. Stay in front of me or my Colt may fire accidentally." He assumed that artillery and rifle fire to the north must be General Lawton's attack on El Caney, the extreme left of the Spanish line.

At the ford, dead and wounded lay on the side of the stream. Shrapnel whistled through the trees and churned the water. The 10th Cavalry crossed and deployed as skirmishers to the right of the road. John took his prisoner to a position where Roosevelt conferred with Generals Kent and

Hawkins and Shafter's aide-de-camp, Lieutenant John Miley.

Just as John was about to join Roosevelt, Ivy Baldwin and George Derby crashed through the undergrowth. "General Kent," Derby said, "I know that balloon played hell with our approach. But I spotted a trail that leads to the Spanish right flank. If you fan out to the south, you'll be able to bring enfilade fire on Kettle Hill and San Juan Hill behind it."

"Now, Zeke, just get hold of yourself," John said while he watched the impromptu staff conference. "See those men talkin' like everythin's normal? You can stop shakin' now and gather your wits."

"What..., what are you going to do with me, Harrison?"

"I'll take you over to Ivy." John was sick of nursing Zeke Harner. "If you just behave yourself, I won't say anythin' about your disgraceful skedaddle. You stick close to Ivy and you'll be all right."

John quietly led Harner to Ivy, then stood behind Roosevelt and listened to the parley. He soon understood that the Generals were confused. Major General Kent, commanding the First Infantry Division, didn't know whether to advance or withdraw. Brigadier General Hawkins, commanding the First Brigade of Kent's Division, said that Spanish fire was heavier than anything he had experienced in the Civil War. Attack across the wide field of waist-high grass leading to the foot of Kettle Hill promised heavy casualties. On the other hand, retreat must cost even greater casualties because the single trail was jammed with troops. General Kent wanted to wait for an order from General Shafter. But Lieutenant Miley said that would take hours. General Hawkins wanted to attack immediately. Kent still hesitated.

What happened next astonished John. Lieutenant Miley, cool and unruffled in the face of both enemy fire and August rank, offered to order an attack in General Shafter's name. When that suggestion troubled Kent, Miley argued respectfully, "The heights must be taken. Any retreat now would be a disastrous defeat."

John wondered where the West Pointers got their grit and confidence. He heard Hawkins tell TR that he had graduated in '56. Miley had graduated eleven years ago. Almost every Second Lieutenant in the field graduated last year. Even the Gatlings were under a West Pointer. He wondered if Davey could ever get into the place.

Brows suddenly cleared. Backs straightened. Shoulders squared. A simple plan soon emerged. Kent would lead the New York Volunteers to the south. The Rough Riders under General Sumner would move north against Kettle Hill. John thought, *God help those green New Yorkers with their single-shot Springfields and that damned black powder. They don't have the grit for this job.* A few minutes later they cheered as the Rough Riders forded the Aguadores River.

"Don't cheer," Roosevelt growled. "Fight! Now's the time to fight."

John stayed close to Roosevelt while the Rough Riders used the undergrowth to move forward with the Aguadores River on their left. They started taking casualties almost immediately. Withering fire from the Spanish trenches on Kettle Hill reduced any advance by rushes to sporadic, disorderly movements by individuals. Like the others, John advanced on his hands and knees beside Roosevelt. The mile from the ford at El Pozo to Las Guamas Creek, the natural barrier beneath Kettle Hill, was the longest mile that John had ever covered, whether walking or crawling. "Captain O'Neill, you'd better take cover!" He had great respect for the troop commander of Troop H.

"Hell's bells," O'Neill answered. "The Spanish bullet isn't made that will kill me." A few minutes later, he lay dead with a Spanish bullet through his head.

Soberly, Roosevelt stared at O'Neill's body. "This is humiliating. We can't withdraw and we almost can't advance 'cause we can't see anything through this tall grass and scrub." He crawled forward and peered ahead at steady flashes of rifle fire from the military crest of the hill.

Slowly the Rough Riders pushed Spanish outposts back through the undergrowth. John saw them break across the creek and start up Kettle Hill.

Fifty feet to his left, he saw Black Jack Pershing lift his head to survey the situation. With the Spanish outposts on the run, he yelled at Pershing, "I reckon it's time to go, Sir."

Then he was appalled to see Roosevelt mount his horse, *Little Texas*, and cry out for his regiment—what was left of it—to assemble for a charge. *Is the man daft?* John wondered. *Maybe some people really are favored by the gods. Look at the idiot paradin' back and forth under enemy noses. I guess I'll have to be just as stupid.* With his carbine at high port, he tried to keep up with Roosevelt, who splashed across the creek ahead of other Rough Riders.

John and Roosevelt's orderly, Henry Bardshar, reached a wire fence forty yards from the crest of the hill at the same instant that Roosevelt dismounted.

With cheers and screams from the rest of the regiment ringing in their ears, the three raced for the crest. John felt marvelously calm as if he had found the quiet center of a hurricane, from which all discomfort from the heat and the dirt and the whine of Mauser bullets had disappeared. He saw a conical hat bob up fifty feet away. In one smooth motion he lifted his carbine and killed him. Bardshar killed a second and, in a rush, they were on the hill. Almost instantly, artillery and rifle fire rained down from San Juan Hill to the west. But on the southern extremity of that hill, John could see the determined advance of ribbons of blue: General Kent's brigade, including the New York Volunteers. At 3:15, a new sound erupted on the battlefield: *coffee grinders*, Lieutenant Parker's Gatlings. 600 yards from the Spanish positions, three of them lay down a withering fire at 60 rounds per second.

Roosevelt couldn't stand to be left out at the finale. He called for another charge from Kettle Hill across the valley and up the north slope of San Juan Hill. He, John, Bardshar and two other men crossed some barbed wire and started wading through the tall grass down the west slope of Kettle Hill, only to discover that no one had followed. Flushed with anger, Roosevelt turned back and shouted again. Soon Rough Riders and men from other regiments, black and white, followed him down the slope and up the steep sides of San Juan Hill. That surge of screaming banshees combined with the attack from Kent's division to drive the Spaniards off the hill.

But the enemy wasn't through fighting. A huge Spanish soldier loomed from the blockhouse and lifted his rifle to shoot Roosevelt. John thought of the puma as he killed him in a single shot. Roosevelt turned to him with a grin. "Saving my life seems to have become a habit of yours, Harrison. You'll get a CM for that; keep this up and we may have to give you a commission."

That pleased John, who knew that a Certificate of Merit was the only award for bravery other than the Medal of Honor. People must have been motivated by other passions to do some of the strange things he saw. While Dick Davis and Leonard Wood lay beside each other in search of cover against withering Spanish fire, Stephen Crane paraded around in a white raincoat. In vain, Wood urged Crane to lie down. Davis finally accused Crane of trying to impress everyone with his bravado and courage. Then Crane took cover. John accosted Fred Remington. "Just wanted to tell you how much I admire your work. Your sketch of Grimes' battery lungin' up El Pozo is fine, mighty fine."

By 4:30, a thin line held on to San Juan Hill and wondered if Lawton's men from El Caney might reach San Juan Hill before the Spanish counter-attacked. While John waited for precious food and water and ammunition that didn't come, he cleaned his pistol and his carbine and reflected on the astonishing day. After he and Roosevelt completed a roll call, they found that 132 Rough Riders were missing from the 400 who had started from El Pozo: one-third casualties, 86 of them dead. He learned later that the victory had cost 205 dead and 1200 wounded: ten percent of the American forces engaged!

But those numbers meant much less to him than the emotions that had welled up in that last assault as lines of color and class disappeared in the tangle of khaki and blue, rich and poor, black and white, Yank and Reb, all moving forward against probable death. He hadn't known this kind of feeling for men since that first roundup in the summer after his father's death. Courage and endurance... and something else. What was it that had bonded these men in such an unfamiliar halo of unity? The word came to John like a benediction: selflessness. He thought, *Men don't die for abstract causes; they die for one another*. Whatever the morrow might bring, he would remember this day with reverence for the rest of his life.

CHAPTER SEVENTEEN

MONTAUK POINT, LONG ISLAND
SEPTEMBER, 1898

John reflected on his five months in the army. Why did he still feel so sad... and so incomplete? Hadn't it all been a great adventure, an epic filled with improbable characters, including the mascots: "Cuba" the dog and "Josephine" the lion cub? Hadn't he won a battlefield promotion to Second Lieutenant and a Certificate of Merit? So why did he feel that he had done nothing noteworthy? How could he explain his sense of emptiness? Had the brief moment of excitement, larger than life, below Kettle and San Juan Hills failed to fulfill his appetite for glory? Was he resentful because the war had been so short? It seemed unreal that he had been recruited and trained in two months; hurled into combat for two weeks; decimated by disease for another month; then carried by the sick ship *Miami* to Montauk Point where the entire regiment was under quarantine and where he had wavered between life and death for a month. In his delirium, the whole experience vacillated like a roller-coaster between a fantasy at best and a nightmare at worst. For the first two weeks at Montauk, he had felt himself sinking ever deeper into a black pit of ennui and sense of failure. Failure to find a new identity in the promised glory of war. Failure to feel worthy of his promotion. Failure therefore to fulfill his dream of coming home as a hero instead of as an invalid, vegetating on the ranch at the bicycle shop or in reach of Maggie's pity.

And then one day the nurse told Ivy that John's fever had broken the night before. "His mind is clear today; he has some color in his cheeks, too."

That was the day John actually smiled a greeting to Ivy Baldwin, the day Ivy started telling stories quietly beside his bed. "You've been mumbling about 'first flight' for a week, Lieutenant," Ivy said. "Do you know much about the history of aeronautics?"

"Not really," John admitted. "Eighteen months ago, I thought a powered airship was impossible. No known engine was light and powerful enough."

"You sound like you changed your mind. What happened?"

"I told you on the *Yucatan*. I started to design a light motor. But now I'm so tired the whole thing seems silly."

"If you think a small motor is silly, you're daft," Ivy snorted. "Let me teach you a little history. I won't bore you with the long list of pioneers—and the even longer list of their illusions. In every age, a few scientists have been bitten by the flying bug. Most of them thought that, because birds flap their wings, any flying machine must have flapping wings also. For the last forty years of his life, even Leonardo da Vinci was obsessed by the idea of a wing-flapping mechanism."

In spite of his depression and fatigue, John found himself listening to Ivy, whose vibrant enthusiasm and epic story gradually diverted John from his own emotional and physical anguish. When Ivy left that day, John felt impatient to hear the next installment.

On the second day of Ivy's ministry, he said, "Now let's talk about a man named Cayley in England. While we were fighting for our independence, he identified the three main problems of flight: lift, control and propulsion. By the time he was nearly eighty years old in 1849, he had stumbled on practical ideas for lift and control. He built the first glider that could carry a boy."

"What about propulsion?"

"Elusive, mighty elusive," Ivy said. "In 1874, a Frenchman named du Temple built a steam-powered machine; but it failed to sustain itself in the air. Eight years ago, Ader actually flew another steam-powered machine nearly 200 feet in France. After Hiram Maxim made a lot of money with his new machine-gun fifteen years ago, the flying bug bit him too. He invested in a light steam-engine. Four years ago, he staged his final big test. It failed."

On the third day of Ivy's tutorial, John said, "Sounds to me like no one has licked the propulsion problem yet. Has anyone improved on lift?"

"That was Otto Lilienthal's game," Ivy said. "In Germany, he experimented with both lift and control. He set out to master the wind with gliders."

"Did his work amount to anything?"

"I guess his best discovery was the cambered wing. Cayley had thought about that much earlier. But old Otto's curiosity made him experiment with different cambers for optimum lift."

"What about control? Did he figure that out?"

Ivy shook his head. "Four years ago, even people like Samuel Langley at the Smithsonian Institution visited Otto to watch his spectacular glides. They exceeded a thousand feet from a hill northwest of Berlin. That's where he discovered that the wind could turn a glider upside down if the pilot's control couldn't maintain center of gravity. The best Otto could do was shift his own weight from side to side. The wind finally proved that technique wasn't good enough. He died in a crash two years ago."

"Did he leave any notes?" John asked at the outset of the fourth tutorial. The desperation in his voice reassured Ivy and John's nurse. It was evident that John had found a new passion.

"Some notes. More important, nine years ago, he published his findings in a book called *Birdflight As The Basis for Aviation*."

"Is there a way I can get a copy?" John asked.

"This is my gift to you." Ivy presented Lilienthal's book to John. "Tomorrow, I'll tell you about Octave Chanute. He is alive and he lives in Chicago. So you don't have to go to Europe if you want to bring yourself up to date on aviation."

John eagerly devoured Lilienthal's book for the rest of the day. Next day he asked, "How could Chanute know more than Lilienthal? I thought Chanute was just an engineer who designed the Chicago stockyards."

"He *is* an engineer. But more important, he spread the word about Lilienthal—and everybody else with the slightest interest in flight. In 1876, the same year as Custer's last stand, Chanute began to correspond with researchers all over the world. Beginning seven years ago, he wrote 27 articles which he finally published in a book, *Progress in Flying Machines*."

"So Chanute's book is really the most up-to-date discussion of all aspects of flight?" John's eyes sparkled with interest, a fact that greatly encouraged his pretty nurse and Ivy alike.

"That's right, John." Ivy reached into his knapsack, pulled out a volume and handed it to John. "And here is your copy. From now on, we'll use it for all our discussions."

For the next three days, John devoured Chanute's opus. He learned that, in 1896, Chanute and Augustus Herring had spent the summer working with experimental gliders on the sand dunes of Lake Michigan. They tried everything from a monoplane to twelve wings, each six feet long and three feet wide. By August, 1896, they had a glider with two wings that could carry a 155-pound pilot 150 feet. John thought, *Thank God for Chanute. If everyone had been as generous with his ideas as he is, we might have progressed faster, further. But then I would have missed my chance to design the missing piece, the best light engine in the world!*

"At about the same time that Chanute and Herring were gliding, Alexander Graham Bell and Samuel Langley of the Smithsonian Institution threw their hats in the ring!" Ivy said. "Langley had been experimenting with models since 1892. Compared to others, he had the advantage of funds, a staff and a good-sized workshop."

John remembered how Maggie had gleefully reported the Langley flight two years earlier. While Bell watched, he had flown a steam-powered model weighing 26 pounds over 3000 feet. He called his models "aerodromes." "Why hasn't Langley built an aerodrome that can carry a man?"

"Langley thinks he's learned enough about the principles of flight. For the sake of more knowledge, he doesn't think it's necessary to build a machine large enough to carry a man. Also, he doesn't have a light, powerful engine. The rumor is the War Department has offered him $50,000 to build a full-sized aerodrome. But he won't accept their invitation until he can find a reliable engine."

"Ivy, you've saved my life," John exclaimed ten days after Ivy had started preaching to him about flight. "I want to get in this game right now. I'll bet I can design that engine for Langley." Then a troubled expression crossed his face.

"What's wrong, John?"

"What should I tell Maggie? I'd love to see her and Davey, of course. But I'm so fired up about this that I think I ought to go see old man

Langley soon and stake my claim. There's not a moment to lose!"

Ivy was too wise to advise John how to choose between his family and his odyssey. Men had faced such a decision ever since Homer. But he could suggest, "Whatever you decide, you'd better write a letter to Maggie today, now that you're feeling better."

September 14, 1898

Dearest Maggie,

Even after you received the telegram from Ivy Baldwin, you probably wondered why you received no letters from me for two months. The explanation is simple. In Cuba, there were five hazards to a man's health: the Spanish, typhoid fever, dysentery, malaria and yellow jack. They told me they made me a Second Lieutenant for saving TR's life a couple of times. But I think I was promoted because all our junior officers fell sick. Finally, so did I. Like a lot of other fellows, I must have been bored with the two-week siege of Santiago after Admiral Sampson destroyed the Spanish fleet on July 3. While my platoon helped tighten our six miles of trenches around the city, the mosquitoes and rain and mud and filth and 100-degree heat and rotting mule carcasses and half-buried corpses and foul water and humidity and boredom tightened their siege around us. I knew I was in deep trouble when I came down with a raging fever and chills and nausea and delirium, back pains, terrible headaches and a swollen face.

I must have lost thirty pounds by the time they lifted me off the ship here at Montauk Point on August 15. If it hadn't been for TR, they would probably have left me in the ground in Cuba. He raged into the Red Cross supply depot at Siboney and corralled rolled oats and condensed milk and rice and dried fruit for us. By the time we left Cuba, less than half of the original regiment of Rough Riders were fit for duty. Four thousand men were on the sick list. TR leaked a personal letter to General Shafter so the press would know how miserable we were.

So in addition to credit for winning the battle of San

Juan Hill, he got credit for "bringing the boys home." Now he is reaping the political rewards of his service. He has decided to run for governor of New York State. As for the rest of us, we will lower the flag tomorrow for the last time and give TR one of Fred Remington's sculptures, "Bronco Buster," just like the one I have in the library. Then we will spread to the four points of the compass.

All of us have been in quarantine here until the medics could be sure we wouldn't infect New York City. So even though the war was over officially a month ago, and even though we now own the Philippines, Guam and Puerto Rico, and even though Cuba is independent, all the celebrations haven't meant much to me because I've been fighting for my life. I owe a special debt to Ivy Baldwin for nursing me through that long, hard spell. The nurses prescribed my medicine. He perscribed my books. He educated me,… no, he *inspired* me about the coming age of flight.

After John covered the history of flight for two more pages, he continued.

You know I was already interested in flight before Cuba. But now I'm inspired! I'm a good engineer. From work with bicycles, I know how to make light structures. Anyway, thanks to Langley's studies, lift doesn't seem to be as big a problem now as control and propulsion. I think I can design the small gasoline engine that Langley needs.

But there is a price I'll have to pay. All the experts are either in Europe or on this coast. I want to meet Langley and maybe those Wright brothers in Dayton, Ohio. Then, I'll have to go to England to meet a fellow named Pilcher. He has continued Lilienthal's experiments. Some of the most daring pioneers are in France. It may take me as long as a year. It's a heavy price because, while I was sick, I began to think that the only glorious thing I had ever done was marry you and sire our son. Maybe that should be enough; but I'd like to help the first man to fly. The very thought of it just makes

me tingle. Langley thinks someone will do it soon. Can I help
him beat others with my engine? I can only try.

John paused in his writing to consider the question, *Should I tell her the
truth? Should I tell her that the war gave me a taste of liberation from her preachy
tongue and critical eye?* Just thinking about the hum-drum routine of his bicycle shop and the ranch gave him a sinking spell. On the other hand, the
promise of first flight sent a thrill down his spine. He feared that even one
day at home would trap him in all of Maggie's real and imagined problems.
Why not let her and Ned and Ramon cope? What about his vow to his parents about Davey? Hell, he wasn't even four yet. Maybe it would be possible to get home by his fourth birthday in June, 1899.

I'll try to write every week. I guess I'll go to Washing-
ton first and see Langley. Then maybe I'll go to Dayton,
Ohio, to see the Wrights and then to Chicago to see Chanute.
If I can do all that before Christmas, I'll go to Europe in
January. Take good care of Davey and give him a hug every
night for me.

Six days later, Maggie studied the letter with a sense of dismay and
dread. What had Lin T'ai-chi said to her in Shanghai? "Your husband will
be a great river. He will sweep you out to sea. You will never recover the innocence of your childhood." She looked wistfully out the window to the
fading light over the distant hills and reviewed her achievements since her
wedding four years earlier. *I didn't want some man to take control of my life; I re-
sented a world dominated by men. I worried about John's return and his probable
protests against my ideas about the ranch. Now I've gotten my wish. Even though
Ramon runs things, everyone knows the ranch is under my direction. Didn't I want a
child whose potential I could stimulate and sculpt? So now I have Davey under my
constant supervision. Why, I have everything I ever wanted. So why do I feel so sad?*

Suddenly, her world seemed small and insignificant in comparison
with the great venture that John was starting. Well, there was nothing to
be done about it. For whatever reason—the war, ambition, John's competitive spirit—he had made his choice, his Holy Grail called an aerodrome in
preference to his family. Now she must make hers. And her first priority
must be Davey.

CHAPTER EIGHTEEN

CARMEL VALLEY
SEPTEMBER, 1898

The morning after she received John's letter, Maggie opened William James' 1890 opus, *Principles of Psychology*. Her reliance on *Principles* had reached a state of dependency. Every page had become a light guiding her through the anomalies of Davey's growing up. She believed James' ideas about consciousness were rooted in her favorite philosophers' speculations across two thousand years of history. In her current state of mind, she especially welcomed his emphasis on the empirical. She started each day with a reading in much the same way that a religious might read a Psalm from the Bible before facing the challenges of the day. She could not know that today, James' reassurance would forsake her. It would be her first experience with a "Davey Dream."

It happened that afternoon while she was having a picnic with her son. She had just pointed to a flock of birds when she noted a strange expression on Davey's face: a wooden, trance-like rigidity, unblinking eyes bright with expectation, the direction of his gaze apparently inward since the birds had quickly flown away. "Davey! Davey!" she said in a low voice. "Where are you? Come back. Come back this instant!"

"Here I am, Momma. That was really fun."

"What was fun, Davey?"

"Flying… flying with the birds. You never told me about that."

It was obvious that Davey thought everyone could fly with the birds. The very idea disturbed Maggie more than anything Davey had ever done with his other psychic gifts. "How does it feel, sweetheart? Tell me about it."

"You know. I just… fly. I could see everything: our house, the stables, the river, Monterey."

"You were really... up in the air?"

"Sure; that's more fun than any other game you ever taught me."

"Do you remember what you were thinking before you... flew?"

"Sure. I just wanted to be like a bird. I wanted to be a *bird*. And there I was."

Maggie tried to treat his experience as if it were normal, as if adults could do the same thing whenever they felt like it. "What fun! Let's call the game the 'Becoming Game.'" But her mask of pretense dissolved in a wave of terror that afternoon when she and Davey watched some vaqueros slaughter a steer.

At the instant the steer died, Davey said, "There's his smoke; there he goes."

"What smoke?" Maggie asked with a frown.

"Don't you see the smoke coming out of that steer, Momma? It's just like the smoke that comes out of flowers after you cut them." He shook his head sadly. "After you cut them, they don't have nice light all around them."

"Tell me about that light, Davey."

"It's just like the colored light you see around everybody, Momma. It's funny how it changes all of a sudden. Why does it change, Momma?"

Maggie tried to control herself. Davey believed everyone could see a glowing light around plants and animals and people. More startling, he seemed to "see" a thin spiral of smoke that announced their death. Should she order him to censor such visions? How could he stop doing what must be totally natural? "What happens to the color, Sweetie?"

"Well..., when you're happy, your color is silver and even a little like the vine in our patio."

"Purple?"

"Not so dark; you call it... violet, I think. Then, when you're mad or maybe scared, it changes to red like your color now. Are you scared?"

In a mild state of shock, Maggie dodged the question. "Do you see the colors all the time, everywhere?"

"Sure, Momma. That's why everything is so pretty all the time. People and flowers and animals are all like a big garden. Kinda hazy though."

"Does that hazy appearance ever disappear?"

"What does... disapp...? What does that mean?"

Maggie had talked to Davey like an adult almost since birth. He was so precocious verbally that she sometimes forgot that he was only three.

"Does it ever go away?"

Davey admitted guiltily, "When I get mad or scared, it goes away. If I feel real tiny, all my friends run away—even the children who sometimes come and play with me."

"Children? What children?"

"Why…, I told you about them. A little boy and his sister? Didn't I tell you?"

Maggie felt her fingernails cutting into her palms as she clenched her fists with growing anxiety. "Maybe I forgot; tell me again."

"They come almost every morning when I wake up. They tell me all about things. They told me to watch for the smoke when an animal or a flower dies. When I told them I didn't like the hazy colors around people to go away, they told me to love everybody and the colors wouldn't go away."

"That's just wonderful, sweetie." Maggie was determined to foster all these absurd talents in her son until she could get some advice. William James wasn't enough; she must consult someone who might know more than she could learn from a book.

Maggie visited Ned Ambler the next day in Monterey. She had taken great care to dress conservatively in something appropriate for a visit to her doctor. She wore a black alpaca shirtwaist dress. The only feminine touches were embroidered braid on the blouse, a sheer frill at her throat and a matching alpaca hat. But nothing she did could conceal her glorious auburn hair, full bust and willowy figure. "Do you believe you're a scientist, Ned?"

"Of course! I try to keep abreast of new developments in the sciences." Ned wondered where this conversation might be going. On the telephone, Maggie had sounded quite disturbed. Now she looked to be under considerable strain.

"Are you one of the new specialists who define science narrowly?" Avoiding Ned's eyes, Maggie nervously toyed with an ashtray on Ned's desk. "Or do you still welcome a wider set of boundaries?"

"Maybe I can answer your question by saying that I'm still a devoted student of William James. Two years ago he published a series of papers in which he reminded his colleagues at Harvard that the scientific method and religious experience aren't incompatible."

"That's hard to imagine." Maggie affected a frown of disapproval. "Most scientists think one is based on fact; the other is riddled with superstition."

Ned smiled at Maggie's feeble attempt to play devil's advocate. "Generation after generation has told stories of occult experiences. William James has written that science congratulates itself on its self-satisfied systems of logic and theory while ignoring certain facts that don't agree with those systems."

Maggie giggled nervously. "Maybe *those* so-called facts are just the products of active imaginations."

"Maybe—in some cases. But James says that whenever scientists and mystics compete, the mystics win when it comes to *all* the facts. The scientists win when it comes to their neatly coherent, usually wrong theories."

"Maybe he means simply that scientists haven't explained all the facts."

"If that were the only issue," Ned reasoned, "he might be more tolerant of fellow scientists. What bothers him is that many of the new scientists are afraid to even look at unexplainable facts."

"Ned, do any other scientists agree with him?"

"Yes; he's been in touch with the new British Society for Psychical Research in London. Several eminent scientists founded that society in 1882."

"I've heard of the SPR. Are its members... credible?"

Ned smiled at Maggie's skepticism. "You can't be more credible than people like Professor Henry Sidgwick, the eminent Professor of Philosophy at Cambridge; or his brother-in-law, the Society's Vice-President, the famous political leader, Gerald Balfour; or Gerald's brother, Arthur, who may well be the next Prime Minister; or the physicist, Sir Oliver Lodge; or the great classical scholar, F.W.H. Myers. An American Branch was founded five years ago."

The names were unfamiliar to Maggie; but they couldn't have attained such responsibilities if they were unbalanced. "Can you sum up their objectives?"

"At first, they wanted to know if paranormal happenings really exist."

"What do they mean by 'paranormal happenings'?"

"Let's see… such things as animal magnetism, so-called Mesmerism, magical cures, ecstasies, hypnotism, apparitions, divinations, occult powers, inspired discourses, telepathy, stigmata, demonic possessions…."

Sure now that Ned could help her understand Davey's extraordinary skills, Maggie began to relax. "What do they believe about such things?"

"They're all natural. They just don't know how to explain them yet."

"Have SPR members written anything?"

Ned wondered if she had become a spiritualist. He reached to his nearest bookshelf and handed a volume to Maggie. "I subscribe to their *Proceedings*. This is the first volume covering the years from 1886 to 1889. A few months ago, Professor James published a little book called *Human Immortality*. That sums up many of their beliefs, I think."

Maggie tried to think of other questions. She wanted to lay a firm foundation before she revealed her concerns about Davey. "What is their evidence?"

"The experience of common people. Before he died twelve years ago, an Englishman named Edmund Gurney, a classical scholar and medical doctor, led an investigation of supernatural happenings to determine if 'psi', as they call it, really exists. He surveyed over twenty-five thousand cases, which he called his 'census of hallucinations.'"

"Sounds like old wives tales. They could be just anecdotes told and re-told until they have less validity than rumors. Did Mr. Gurney write a book?" Maggie thought talk was cheap; anything worth remembering *must* be in print, preferably a thick book.

"Yes; *Phantasms of The Living*. It describes his procedures and conclusions. I treasure it; you're welcome to borrow it."

Now Maggie could feel excitement growing. "What does he mean by super-natural happenings?"

"When someone sees a form or hears a voice or feels a touch which no material presence can account for."

"And what did this Mr. Gurney find?"

"That over ten percent of adults in England and America have had such experiences." Ned was beginning to get the gist of Maggie's inquiry. After William James published *Principles of Psychology* in 1890, he focused on the more esoteric dimensions of the mind. From 1890 to 1896, he researched a twenty-page essay, *What Psychical Research Has Accomplished*. That essay was published in a small book called *The Will To Believe*, which established William James as the foremost student of the mind in the United States.

"Do *you* believe in hypnotism?"

"Of course. It was only in 1879 that the medical world finally accepted the undeniable fact of hypnotism. But science still can't explain it. Professor James has defended the practice of both hypnosis and mental healing. He supports the right of spiritualists and Christian Scientists to explore their beliefs. His motto is, 'Don't stamp out the facts; study them.'"

"But doesn't that attitude open science to all kinds of quacks and charlatans?"

"True. It also opens science to new discoveries. As Professor James has said, 'No scientific summary can contain the creative totality of the real'. He's trying to find scientific relationships among three fields: religion, mental healing and psychical research. Those are my keen interests, too."

Maggie suddenly felt a great weight lift from her mind. Ned had been her guide through philosophy. His encouragement had always been kind and gentle. Now she could think of him as an ally. "Then you *agree* with William James!" Maggie exclaimed triumphantly.

"That's right. We both think the most interesting aspect of science is what is still not classified. He calls it the fringe which 'floats like a dust-cloud of exceptional observations around the accepted core of science.'"

Maggie idly leafed through the first volume of the SPR's *Proceedings*. "And what does this ponderous tome tell us?"

"It reports on their experiments with hypnosis and their collection of information on thought-transference, what's called telepathy now."

"Did they find any valid cases?" Maggie asked eagerly.

"Rigorous scientific examination persuaded them that telepathy happens—repeatedly. They just don't know how or why." Ned thought to draw on Maggie's education abroad. "The Chinese have been at this longer than the Europeans. What's their view?"

"Eastern thought believes in many levels of consciousness. I think William James writes of only two levels: consciousness and subliminal consciousness. Can you explain the difference?"

"James thinks the subconscious or the hypnotic consciousness is a kind of mother sea that surrounds consciousness. He calls it the subliminal self. What do the Chinese call it?"

Maggie suddenly remembered the "smoke" that Davey had described when an animal died. "My Chinese professor calls it *ch'i*, a pervasive vitality. He told me that *ch'i* is the vital essence of all animate and inanimate things. At that level we are totally, unconditionally joined. That is our true identity. Ned, do you believe these levels really exist?"

"Oh, yes! At the SPR, that brilliant Frederic Myers thinks the level of subliminal consciousness is a vast array of paranormal powers. He says science *must* explore that level in order to gain a deep understanding of human personality."

"Does William James agree with him?" Maggie glowed with the feeling that Ned was surrounding her with allies.

"Yes." Ned tapped burned tobacco from his pipe and refilled it thoughtfully. "James believes the subliminal self is the storehouse of all earthly knowledge and memory. From that level of vital energy, we can draw incredible strength or knowledge when we need it at the much more shallow, focused level we call conscious or sensual reality."

"Does anyone outside the SPR agree with these ideas?"

Ned mused on that question for a moment. "A remarkable scientist named Rudolph Steiner thinks we live in three interpenetrating worlds: the etheric which is the life force, like the Chinese *ch'i*; the soul-body..., some call it the astral; and the intellectual soul. Some people see all three of those worlds as a kind of aura, a cloud of changing color around a person."

Davey's description of auras seemed to validate Steiner. Maggie was glad that Ned had mentioned Steiner's theories. This was precisely what she needed. "Has the SPR discovered a specific process to bring subliminal knowledge to the service of the conscious mind?"

"Not yet," Ned replied, "Actually, humanity has been linking all levels for thousands of years. James believes the links are very personal, very subjective. They seem to be associated with certain attitudes and actions."

"Like what?"

"Well, attitudes of selflessness... and mindlessness... and detachment from worldly desire... and love: not romance but a deep sense of trusting love. Some of the most familiar keys have been prayer... and meditation... and even simple games which divert the mind's attention temporarily from personal troubles." Ned suddenly looked directly at her. "Is this about Davey, Maggie?"

"Yes." Maggie tried to appear calm; but she felt as if her revelations might be a form of betrayal of her son. She feared that someone in authority could brand the boy "insane," perhaps even imprison him in some asylum. She decided to tell Ned the whole story. "I think Davey has learned how to communicate with his subconscious." For a half-hour she described Davey's gifts in the chronological order of their revelation: his mind reading; his skill at finding lost articles; his eidetic memory; his accurate remote viewing; and his most recent ability to "become" a bird and "see" the world from the air; his cognition of "smoke" at the moment of death and his natural perception of auras around animate objects.

"Did you teach him how to do those things? Do you blame yourself?"

"No to both questions. I think he was experimenting with these ideas before he could talk. At first I thought it was quaint, charming. But I don't like the way he still can't distinguish between make-believe and reality. Do you think he's is a disturbed child? Could his fantasies drive him over the edge?"

Ned tamped tobacco into his pipe and considered the situation. "I would say the lad has a highly developed sixth sense but nothing to worry about. He would delight William James, who pleads for a science of wholeness, not just Bishop Berkeley's *philosophy* of wholeness."

"What does 'sixth sense' really mean?"

"I mean he has an extraordinary awareness of Steiner's super sensible world. Your mind and memory are part of that world. When Davey tells you where to find a lost article, he's simply reading your memory. Telepathy. Thousands of cases. Nothing unusual."

"And what about seeing John at the hotel in Tampa?"

"Clairvoyance or clear seeing. He's gifted with what we might call extended perceptual ability. Nothing to get upset about—not once you read *Proceedings*."

Maggie nodded as if reassured. "That may also explain his perception of auras; but what about his flying with birds?"

"His flight is a form of what Gurney calls 'astral travel' in *Phantasms of The Living*. He cites over three hundred such cases. We all do it frequently in sleep. Sometimes a dream is so real, so three-dimensional that it doesn't feel like a dream."

"And the smoke at the moment of death? And his imaginary children?"

"I would say the smoke is the departure of the etheric body, the life-force, from the physical body. As to the imaginary playmates, a young Austrian doctor named Jung believes, like Steiner, that the super sensible world is objectively real, populated by beings who are independent of our minds. To reach that world requires what Jung calls an active imagination. When Davey sees auras and smoke and even the apparitions of little playmates, he is merely reporting what several serious scientists believe actually exist."

Maggie thrilled at Ned's explanation. If an engine and powered flight was John's passion, maybe Davey could fuel her study of human consciousness. "Ned, are we witnessing the dawning of an age of consciousness?"

The tone of conviction in Ned's response riveted her attention. "During the next century, Maggie, I think people like William James and Rudolph Steiner and Carl Jung and Edmund Gurney will lead a world-wide effort to find rituals and mind-games and maybe even drugs that help open the door to the mysteries of the subliminal mind. It's the last great frontier of science."

PART IV

THE ENGINE

"He put this engine to our ears,
Which made an incessant noise like that of a water-mill.
And we conjecture it is either some unknown animal,
Or a god he worships.
But we are more inclined to the latter opinion."

JONATHAN SWIFT, THE DRAPIER'S LETTERS

CHAPTER NINETEEN

WASHINGTON, D.C.
OCTOBER–DECEMBER, 1898

I wonder if the old man will invite me to join his team? On October 15, that question colored John Harrison's entire trip from Long Island to Washington, D.C. The same question occupied his mind while he rode through the twilight in an open carriage from the railroad station. He savored the glorious autumn air. He ogled the capitol building like any other tourist. But these were only brief diversions from his new obsession: an engine both light and powerful enough to drive an aerodrome. He consoled himself with the thought that, if his engine was too heavy for an aerodrome, at least it might power a dirigible. A steam engine would be too big and too heavy. He *must* persuade Langley to let him design an internal combustion engine.

For the next three days, John poured over pamphlets and books on engines in the Library of Congress. Only after the library closed each night would he return to his cousin Minerva Harrison for a late supper. On the morning of his appointment with Sam Langley, October 19, he dressed nervously in his best blue serge suit. He was so worried about his meeting that he could barely eat Minerva's splendid breakfast of kippers, sausage, scrambled eggs and griddle cakes. He knew she was offended, but he couldn't help it. Haunted by the fear that Langley might dismiss him after a few questions, he approached the Smithsonian with no conscious appreciation of its Romanesque and Gothic architecture. His heart was in his throat as he entered Langley's office: a dark room of wood paneling, shelves, wooden filing cabinets, two leather-covered chairs, a roll-top desk against one wall, a large conference table at the center of the room and a prominent photograph of the U.S. Naval Academy, where Langley had taught for several years.

The famous astro-physicist, already 65 years old, welcomed John into
the office. Stocky and showing his age with white sideburns and goatee,
Langley wore a slightly rumpled three-piece sack suit. He didn't seem to
realize that he was still wearing his straw boater. He had been executive
secretary of the Smithsonian for eleven years.

John came straight to the point. "Sir, I'm a mechanical engineer. I
know you need an engine for your aerodrome. Will you let me help?"

From John's letters and a discussion with Teddy Roosevelt, Langley
knew John had money, had graduated from Berkeley and had saved Roosevelt's life in Cuba. "Well... what do you know about the infernal combustion engine?"

John quickly sketched the history of the engine from its origins in the
late 18th Century to the production of the first Otto four-stroke engine in
1876 and the first Clerk two-stroke engine two years later. "I assume your
big problem is weight."

"That's right. Fifteen years ago, even small engines weighed more
than a thousand pounds per horsepower and could produce no more than
200 rpm." Langley placed a cup of hot coffee in front of John, took off his
boater and flung it at a coat rack by the door. The hat sailed across the
room and landed magically on a coat hook.

"You must have welcomed Daimler's 1886 engine." John knew it had
weighed 88 pounds per horsepower and produced 800 rpm. "Although it's
light for aerodrome purposes, its big advantage must be its new fuel, what
they call petrol."

Langley liked what he was hearing. Harrison had obviously done his
homework. "That's right. Petrol is a major advantage. It's volatile and
maybe a little dangerous; but it promises more power per pound than the
heavy steam engine. What do you think of de Dion's newest design?"

"Most promisin'," John replied, eager to show off his knowledge of the
latest advance made by de Dion in France only two years earlier. "I understand that engine put Daimler and Benz to shame with its splash-
lubrication, air-cooled, finned cylinders, electric ignition and its aluminum crank-case. Doesn't de Dion's engine deliver 1800 rpm?"

"True. Trouble is," Langley said with a frown, "it's still too heavy for
us."

"Is the weight of the engine your only problem?"

"No; many engine components aren't reliable. And the aerodrome as a whole is a symphony of problems. All of them must be solved with an eye to weight. We face too many unknowns. It's like a cat chasing its tail. Where do you begin your line of reasoning? We know so little about flight that we don't even know what speed we must maintain to sustain a given weight in the air."

John thanked his gods that he had studied Lilienthal's book thoroughly. "You mean you don't trust Lilienthal's drag and lift equations?"

"Ah, you know about those, do you?" Langley smiled with satisfaction. "I don't trust anything, including Smeaton's coefficient. But I believe a good, reliable engine is the major obstacle to a first flight in a heavier-than-air machine. Trouble is we're not sure how many horses we need to turn a propeller how many revolutions per minute. We're not even sure how to calculate the probable horsepower of a gas engine because engine output depends on a consistent mixture of air and gasoline injected into a cylinder. But no reliable carburetor is available."

John nodded sympathetically. "Horsepower also depends on compression of the mixture in the cylinder; but compression depends on the tightness of pistons in the cylinders. Do you have a machinist with the necessary skill?"

Langley grimaced. "No. The American Motors Company were supposed to have the best. But they gave up after six months."

John hesitated, then decided to blow his horn. "At the risk of sounding immodest, I've worked to mighty fine tolerances in my bicycle shop."

Langley stared out the window, his back to John. He was feeling pressure from Roosevelt, the War Department and his own staff to test his full-sized aerodrome, then under construction in Smithsonian shops. Without an engine, the finished craft would be useless. Worse, its failure to fly would make him and the Smithsonian the laughing stock of official Washington. This young enthusiast might be the answer. "All right, John Harrison, I accept your offer of help. When can you start?"

John's heart soared. He was in! "Immediately, sir. With all those unknowns, have you settled on a set of arbitrary specifications?"

"Yes. We want a six-cylinder Otto-cycle engine capable of around eight hundred rpm. It must develop twelve horsepower and weigh no more than a hundred and twenty pounds. And we want it in four months!"

John stared at Langley with disbelief. An engine producing a horse-power for every ten pounds? Wouldn't *that* be something glorious! If he could design it and bring it to production, his name would have a revered place in history. By God, *then* Maggie would have to take notice.

At that moment, a slender young man entered the room. He was several years younger than John. His pince-nez glasses deferred to a luxuriant mustache that added weight to an otherwise weak chin. He wore light blue workman's overalls over his suit.

"This is my new assistant, Charlie Manly," Langley said.

As soon as Manly understood John's purpose, he gestured to the conference table laden with blueprints and drawings. "On that table, you'll find the sum total of our creative energies. I'm afraid it's not very impressive."

Although he liked Manly instantly, John was disappointed. He had expected much more material for his own research. "What's in those filing cabinets?"

"Reams of useless notes and references," Manly replied. "Have you heard of Stephen Balzer of New York City?"

"No," John answered. "Is he a piece of the puzzle?"

"Maybe," Langley said. "He designs the best light automobile engines. We have decided to challenge him to make us an engine in his New York shop."

The three men were soon engrossed in a probing discussion of the many trade-offs that confront any engine designer, especially one whose major constraint is weight. The heavy, complex array of pipes and fittings and radiator needed to cool an automobile engine had offended Charles Manly's design sense as much as it had trapped the American Motors Company. They had discovered that an acceptable power-to-weight ratio introduced major questions like the strength of metal alloys and the reliability of components. Ignition, for example. None was very reliable or strong. De Dion's system was promising; but there was no such thing as a standard spark plug.

The most baffling problem of up-scaling from the steam engine that Langley had used on his successful models was the fact that heat would rise by the cube of the enlargement factor. So if they wanted to increase size to gain more power, they must also solve a much greater heating problem. Increasing disproportionately, vibration would be the inevitable price to pay for more power in each stroke and more strokes per minute, provided they could get larger valves and a larger carburetor to keep up a steady combustion of fuel as the engine produced more and more rpms. As vibration increased, they could expect greater wear on bearings, valves, valve springs and spark plugs, not to mention the aerodrome itself!

"You can see those design problems have already turned my hair white," Langley said with an engaging grin. "After our experience with American Motors, we think Balzer has the only machine shop for prototype production. Nothing can come off the shelf. We'll have to design every component of our own engine to fine tolerances under the personal direction of Charles Manly."

By the time that first day drew to a close, John knew he had been accepted as a member of the team. He had demonstrated that he could read engineering drawings with ease. He could discuss their shared problems in their language. Perhaps most important, they seemed to like and trust him. They agreed that John should design certain components while Charles would take the rest, examining each component of the engine for less weight and more reliability.

As they were about to leave the Smithsonian shop, John asked a question he had saved all day. "Do you feel competitive with others about bein' the first to fly?"

"I think Charles is more competitive than I am," Langley said. "I've already made my mark in the world with astronomy and physics. Why do you ask?"

"I have the feelin' that the competition will grow fierce. The rewards for the winner could be enormous: fame and even money."

For the next six weeks, Charles and John worked day and night to craft an ideal engine. After Balzer accepted Langley's challenge and agreed to come to Washington on November 30 to examine plans, they redoubled their efforts to be ready for him with the most advanced set of drawings. They argued, laughed, ate and, sometimes too exhausted to walk home, even slept at the Smithsonian. They interviewed metallurgists, chemists, electricians, other physicists and inventors. John felt Charlie's mastery of mathematics, electrical and mechanical engineering and especially high-voltage currents was little short of encyclopaedic, concluding that this time with Manly had been a crash course in prevailing science and technology. Under the stimulus of competition, they were trying to solve several major problems. Success in any *one* of them should have yielded satisfying recognition. But the big reward would come to the first person to blend multiple solutions into a single system—the flying machine.

Stephen Balzer was impressed with their work. Fair-haired and sporting a full mustache, he had an air of intense concentration while he pointed his beak of a nose at details of the drawings and asked questions. After he examined the drawings, he said late in the afternoon, "I propose a five-cylinder rotary engine, producing 12hp and weighing not more than 120 pounds. I'll use a high-tension, jumping ignition system; that is, spark plugs, instead of the more common, wiping, low-tension system."

"How long will it take?" Langley asked. "How much will it cost?"

"Four months," Balzer said with confidence. "I want fifteen hundred dollars."

That evening, despite flaws in their ability to control the yaw, pitch and rotation of the aerodrome, Charlie and John were ecstatic with the conviction that the new team could design and build the ideal engine. Indeed, flushed with the sense of a total systems breakthrough, they had said so that afternoon to a pretty secretary, Jenny Lowell. The next day, they strongly urged Langley to offer Balzer a contract.

John was reading a study of venturi's at 10:30 that evening when Minerva called him to the telephone. "Sounds like some kind of trouble at the Smithsonian," she said.

"You'd better get over here, John," Charles Manly told him. "Someone has ransacked Professor Langley's office."

Ten minutes later, John was shocked by the scene. At the entrance to the building, he passed a nurse hovering over a guard whose head was swathed in bandages. While police questioned the guard, John entered Langley's office to find all file cabinets open and papers scattered around the floor. "The engine design?" John asked Charles.

"They knew what to look for," Charles said bitterly. "All drawings and all our notes on the components are gone. A lot of it is preliminary, maybe even useless. But we'll still have to recapture everything."

"What did the guard say?"

"Only that someone brutally attacked him at around nine o'clock. He struggled with his assailant and tore this from his throat." Manly showed John a small *ankh*.

John carefully examined the cross. "What do you know about this cross, Charles?"

"The bottom t-shape or *tau* was a male symbol in ancient Egypt. The loop on top of it was a female symbol. The combination, called a *crux ansata* or *ankh*, symbolizes eternal creation and eternal life."

John suddenly remembered this particular symbol. He had seen it suspended around Zeke Harner's neck during their cruise from Tampa to Cuba. Zeke had valued the small icon as the only thing that his bullying father had ever given him. "Is this symbol unusual?"

"Not really. I collect crosses as a kind of hobby. You could find this identical cross in any junkshop in Washington."

"I believe I know who did this, Charles." John recalled that Zeke had sworn his dedicated belief in the sanctity of ends, regardless of means: the only lesson his father had ever drummed into him with his nightly beatings. "And I think I know where to find him. Did the guard say anything more about the assailant?"

"Said he was a short man, strong as a bull; smelled of garlic; and he growled. Does that help?"

"Maybe." John considered the slender evidence against Harner. It would have been persuasive if that particular *ankh* had been unique. But Zeke Harner was not the only one who wanted to win the race to first flight. What about those two brothers that he had worked for? What was their name? Wright..., in Dayton, Ohio. Could they have hired him? "Look, Charles; I've been thinkin' about going to Chicago to see Octave Chanute. But first, I want to make a little side trip to Dayton, Ohio. Let's talk with Professor Langley tomorrow and clean up this mess. Then I think I'll take a train to Ohio."

"Fine. If Mr. Langley agrees, my personal notes should be enough to prepare a contract for Balzer in the next two weeks. When you return, you can help me draw a new set of plans."

"While I'm gone, you better ask Jenny Lowell if she recalls talkin' to anyone who answers to the guard's description of the thief."

"You think Jenny was involved?"

"I doubt it. But it sure looks like an inside job. How else could the thief have learned about our progress and the specific location of our plans?"

On the morning of December 3, with Samuel Langley's blessing, John Harrison set out on a manhunt.

CHAPTER TWENTY

DAYTON, OHIO
DECEMBER, 1898

It was a cold overcast afternoon when John called from the Dayton railroad station to make an appointment with the Wright brothers. On his way to their shop, he reviewed his limited knowledge of his potential adversaries. He was sorry that he had not asked Ivy Baldwin more. Orville was John's age: 27; Wilbur was four years older. They had a younger sister, Katharine, probably around 24 now; Ivy had said that she was the bright one. If she had stuck to her schedule, she would have graduated from Oberlin College only five months ago. Could she be the real brains behind the plot? Their mother had died of tuberculosis nine years earlier. The father, Milton, was a Bishop of some church; John couldn't remember if Ivy had ever been specific. There were older children; but only the brothers and Katharine still lived with Milton at 7 Hawthorne Street.

For some people, the father's affiliation with a church might have been reassuring, but John had little respect for religion of any persuasion. As he had told Ned Ambler in Colorado, he believed that a man's religion was very personal and private. He thought all ministers and rabbis and priests were exploiters of human frailty and loneliness. Maggie's sudden obsession with philosophy and religion had only reinforced his resentment against mealy-mouthed preachers. Damn Billy Sunday and his ilk! The brothers' family background did not absolve them of his suspicion.

Why would such a family steal Langley's plans? On first glance, they did not seem even qualified as competitors. "They're well-read," Ivy had said. "But they never finished high school. Wilbur almost finished and Orville took some college preparatory courses, but they don't believe in titles and degrees. They're not stupid or ignorant. In fact, they are two of the most practical, methodical men I've ever met. As I recall, they excel in science and math; not pure science, not *why* things work a certain way but *how to make* things work. They have a fine library at home; but I never saw any of the standard books on flight. I think Zeke Harner was mistaken in Cuba; I don't think they're especially interested in flight. Bicycles are their game."

Wilbur and Orville Wright seemed bewildered when they welcomed John to their shop at 1127 West Third Street. "Why do you want to see us?" Will asked.

"Well, like I said when I called from the station, I build bicycles in Monterey, California. I guess the airship craze two years ago planted a seed. Now I want to build a light engine for a flyin' machine. I thought maybe you had been bitten by the same bug."

"Because we build the Van Cleve bicycle?" Will Wright frowned. "Doesn't make sense. There are over three hundred bicycle shops in this country, fourteen in Dayton. Why'd you pick us?"

Hoping to deflect their suspicion that he might be investigating them, John was prepared for that question. "Why, in Cuba Ivy Baldwin told me that you might have some interest in flight."

The two brothers exchanged surprised, questioning glances. Beginning a year earlier, Will had begun to feel dissatisfied with his life in a bicycle shop, but had forgotten what he told Ivy. "We enjoyed Ivy's dare-devil exploits from his balloon," he said. "But we have no special interest in a heavier-than-air machine. Should we?"

"Why, not necessarily. I guess it seemed reasonable to me."

"Why?"

"Bicycle manufacture is excellent experience for building aeroplanes, I think," John replied. "I've learned four things in my shop are relevant: the idea of balance; the idea of positive control; how to build light structures; and how to use chain-drives for linking engines with propellers."

It was evident that Will Wright was intrigued by John's reasoning. With a high forehead on a balding head, lively eyes and a firm straight mouth, his whole demeanor reflected an orderly mind given to routine, except for his clothes: rumpled suit with baggy knees and skewed tie, whose color clashed with his shirt.

As for Orville, John thought he was a striking contrast with Will: fussy about form, perhaps too sensitive about his appearance to the point of being spiffy, a clothes horse, a fashion plate. With a balding forehead and bushy mustache, Orv's pale, narrow face and pointed chin gave an impression of doubt and diffidence, even weakness of will. It was only later that John learned that Orv was recovering from a long and vicious bout with typhoid fever.

John decided to confront them with a test. If they reacted guiltily, he would know they were implicated. "I'm workin' with Samuel Langley to design an aerodrome for the Army."

The brothers showed no particular interest in Langley or the aerodrome. "Are you and Mr. Langley making any progress?" Orv asked politely.

"Some, but there are lots of problems. They make buildin' a bicycle seem like small potatoes." In later years, John would swear that his remark lit a fire in the dry kindling of Will's probing mind.

Will stared at John as if he had been challenged. "It seems to me that the problem is a bunch of trade-offs among these factors." He took a pencil from his pocket and wrote:

a. Shape of the airfoil

b. Size of the wings

c. Type and location of stabilizing surfaces

d. Structural strength

e. Light-weight materials

f. Engine

g. Control mechanism

h. Light weight

John read the list with astonishment. From his own intensive reading, he had decided that the essential problem of flight was a systems approach: balanced attention to all three aspects of flight: lift, control and propulsion. Ader and Maxim had stressed power. Lilienthal had stressed lift. Chanute had missed control. Will Wright had leaped instinctively to the systems approach. John thought he was either a damned genius or hand-in-glove with Zeke Harner. "Trade-offs?"

"Of course," Orv answered. John would later become familiar with the brothers' disconcerting habit of speaking as if they represented one mind.

"You would have to accept less strength for lighter weight; compensate instability with more control, that sort of thing."

For the next hour, the three men discovered each other through their common interest in bicycles. John felt quite at home in the clean, well-organized workroom, which contained everything that he had bought for his own small plant in Monterey: a heavy metal lathe, a drill press and a power saw, all powered by belts from an overhead shaft; a substantial workbench with a large vise; a stack of bicycle wheels in one corner; assorted bits and sprockets on shelves against a wall. He was beginning to relax and enjoy the two brothers when his eye fell on the corner of a manila envelope almost covered by two magazines about bicycles. The return address of the Smithsonian Institution had caught his attention. While the brothers were occupied with the drill press across the room, John lifted the magazines and stared at the envelope with shocked recognition. The manila envelope belonged to him. It was adorned with his own scrawled instructions: "KEEP IN LANGLEY'S OFFICE."

John could feel a flush of outrage on his face as he jerked the envelope from its hiding place and stared at the Wrights with hard, accusing eyes. He did not include tact and diplomacy on his list of talents and skills.

"This is *my* handwritin'! It was stolen from the Smithsonian last week. I believe a feller named Zeke Harner took it. In Cuba, Zeke told me that you would pay him for Langley's secrets."

"May I look at it, John?" Wilbur asked. A glance told him this was damning evidence. He handed the envelope to Orv. "Have you seen this before?"

"It's new to me," Orv said. "Where did you find it, John?"

"Over there on that chair by the door. It was under two magazines." John was furious and deeply disappointed. He felt betrayed by two men whom he had been ready to trust. "Do you have any explanation for this?"

"None whatsoever," Will said with indignation. "Zeke Harner *did* work for us before the war. But we never promised to pay him for espionage or theft. As I said before, we have no special interest in flight. I can only assure you that we have never seen this before. We will confront every member of our staff."

"In the meanwhile," Orv added with a glance at Will, "I hope you can stay in Dayton until we get to the bottom of this. You must not leave with even a small cloud of suspicion in your mind."

Will nodded. "Someone has played a cruel joke on us."

"Do you think you can prove your innocence without goin' to court?"

"We certainly intend to try," Will said. "We're not thieves, Mr. Harrison."

If they were, John thought they were superb actors. Maybe they really were innocent, or they sure were mighty cool customers. "I'll be glad to stay here until we can clarify this bi'ness. I assume you won't object if I take my property back to my hotel?"

It was Katharine who broke the case on the second day of the investigation. She reminded her brothers that she had included Harner's wife and son in her occasional visits to poor families in Dayton. In April, when she was home on spring break from Oberlin, she had learned that Zeke planned to enlist in the army. She persuaded her brothers to donate a bicycle to Lizzie Harner so that she could go out and collect laundry. A fine seamstress, Lizzie had desperately needed some way to supplement her pitiful income.

"I met Zeke on the same day I brought the bicycle, just before he went into the army," Katharine said. "I was surprised at the way he acted."

"What do you mean?" Will asked.

"Well, you would have thought it was the first gift anyone had ever given him. He kept touching it and smiling and flushing with embarrassment and acting quite childish. He wanted to know if he couldn't do something in return. He seemed... upset, as if he couldn't bear the burden of any obligation."

"You pegged him right, Miss Katharine," John said. "He once told me that obligations of any kind imprison a man."

Katharine nodded, her eyes brimming with tears. "I thought he was afraid of simple human kindness. Lizzie had told me that Zeke hated any generosity, even my small donations. Maybe the bicycle broke down all his defenses."

"Do you think his idea was to square his debt with Mr. Langley's plans?"

Katharine took off her spectacles and twirled them between her right thumb and forefinger while she stared thoughtfully at the fire. "Yes, I do. I remember now that he wanted to know what Will and Orv were most interested in." She flushed self-consciously and lifted her left hand to her throat as if to reassure herself. "I don't know what got into me. Maybe it was a remark that you made to Ivy Baldwin, Will, when he visited. Anyway, I said you were fascinated by the prospects of flight."

Astonished, Will stared at Katharine as if she had lost her mind. "Did you discuss it very much?"

"No. But I remember that he put on a smug little smile and said simply, 'Good; that's real good.' And then I left."

"But after you graduated from Oberlin, you kept going back there week after week while Zeke was in Cuba, didn't you?" Orv asked.

"Of course. That bicycle has saved Lizzie's life. And her little boy, Dale, is a strong, happy little boy, just about four now."

John shook his head. He would never have believed that Zeke Harner could feel so indebted to anyone. More unbelievable was the way Zeke had tried to repay the debt—anonymously. Any sane person would want credit for repayment. Or was this just Zeke's first installment? If so, God only knew what else he might do to repay the Wright family for simple philanthropy. "You had better be on your guard against any more favors from him. He's big trouble. In fact, I think I'll confront him tomorrow."

Next morning John descended upon the Harner family. The house was a tiny, run down clapboard structure in a poor district. Only a border of painted stones outside the unpainted fence testified to at least one person with self-respect in the family. From what Katherine had said, John suspected Harner's wife could claim credit. At his knock John was surprised to confront Zeke Harner when he opened the door. Unshaven and wearing a dirty undershirt, Zeke looked like he was suffering from a hangover.

A glance at John warned Zeke that this was not a social call. "Hello, Harrison. What d'yuh want?"

"May I come in, Zeke?" John asked.

"No. The house is a mess. And I figure this ain't a friendly visit. After I get a coat, we can talk outside."

Before Zeke reappeared, John heard him say abusively, "I don't want you to see 'im. You and the kid get lost." Furious, John confronted Zeke without any preliminaries. "Harner, in Cuba, I saved your cowardly hide once 'cause I thought you might still make somethin' of yourself."

"What d'yuh mean, my cowardly...?" Harner began.

"Shut up!" John warned. "I know you stole plans from the Smithsonian. So you're a thief. Then for some reason you planted them among papers in the Wright's shop. That means you're a stupid thief. Did you honestly think you could get away with it?"

His back to the door, Harner did not realize that it had opened slightly to reveal his wife and son bearing witness to his humiliation. "So what are yuh gonna do about it?"

"You admit you stole the plans?"

"Sure." Harner's derisive smile was a taunt. "Who cares? No harm done."

"I care. And the Wrights care because you almost injured their reputation. If they hadn't asked for lenience, I'd send you to jail right now." At that moment, John noticed the woman and her son, a look of shocked horror on their faces. Although sensitive to the situation, he could think of no way to soften his indictment. "For their sakes, I won't stick around here and prosecute you. But if I ever hear of your crimes again, I'll track you down and throw the book at you."

Paralyzed by the intensity of John's accusation, Zeke could think of nothing to say. Nor did he have to. The blaze of hatred in his eyes spoke volumes. He turned toward the door to see his wife shaking her head in scornful reproach. Without another word, he slipped past her and closed the door.

For the first time since John's arrival, the burden of suspicion was lifted. Now he could stop playing detective, jury and judge and could meet the Wright family on friendly terms. In the give and take of conversation that evening, he decided to repay their hospitality with his own enthusiasm. He showed them his two treasures: Lilienthal's book on lift and airfoils and Chanute's book that portrayed the whole exciting turmoil of the burgeoning field of flight.

"The key to flight is control, John!" Will exclaimed after supper.

"That's where you should focus your attention."

The comment surprised John, who shared Langley's belief that a reliable motor was the missing piece of the puzzle. "Why do you say that, Will?"

"Because competent scientists have already explored lift with good results but they haven't emphasized positive control of an inherently *unbalanced* machine, just the way a cyclist could use handle bars to balance a bicycle."

"What about propulsion?" John asked. Were he and Charlie Manly barking up the wrong tree?

"Important, of course," Will said. "But we can assume that an adequate steam engine or even a small motor car engine will suit when everything else is ready."

"That's right," Orv added. "What's missing is a system for positive control. And *that* is something we could patent!"

Reflecting on this conversation later, John concluded that Will was interested in the technical challenge of flight; Orv seemed most interested in money.

During four days and nights of conversations, John's contagious enthusiasm gradually captured not only Will's interest but—most important—his friendship. It wasn't so much their knowledge of mathematics and engineering that impressed John. In fact, they had some catching up to do. He was most impressed by the way their minds worked.

When they focused their attention on a subject, their mutual encouragement seemed to foster a speed-up in thought and language. Repeatedly, John watched a conversation start with a question, move through speculation and then accelerate into high gear with a verbal staccato like machine guns barking at each other with short phrases that only another quick mind might understand. Also, they were magicians at converting abstract ideas into concrete shapes.

One evening stood out in John's mind.

"We must counteract the wind," Will said after Katharine's excellent supper. "And we can't do it the way Chanute and Lilienthal have done it, by just shifting the pilot's body from side to side."

"If the wind forces up one wing tip," Orv added, "maybe we could devise some leverage on the other tip to correct the imbalance."

"We'd have to change the shape of the wing on that other edge," Will mused.

"Why not make it move like a rudder?" Orv asked.

And then before John's eyes, the two brothers sketched a box-kite. For an hour, they chattered about controlling the kite's upper surface. In the flow of mutually stimulating suggestions, they demonstrated the creative process for which they would become famous: drawing on existing knowledge and their own experience to visualize a new application.

While Will sketched, they both talked.

"The kite must be controlled from the ground," Will suggested.

"But each top wing-tip must be controlled independently of the other," Orv added.

"So why not use two sticks instead of only one?" Will asked.

In a fury of excitement, they mentally stripped away enough inter-strut structural wires to permit slight warping of the upper wing, whose tips would be controlled by strings to the sticks.

In an instant, John saw the technical feasibility of their system. Weeks and months might be required before the concept could be translated into full-scale reality. He could even imagine improvements with certain sprockets and linkages to give the pilot positive control. But the brothers had teased a vital new concept out of each other's minds by simply playing, a habit of dialogue that they had discovered in childhood. Encouraging each other to visualize alternative applications of a familiar system of flight—the controlled box-kite—their creative conversation had proceeded methodically without any radical changes to a conclusion that was stunning in its simplicity and its feasibility.

"Why don't you build a model and try it?" John asked.

"I think we will!" Will answered with a light in his eyes. "What will you do next?"

"Now that you have confirmed my suspicion of Zeke Harner and I've recovered our plans, I think I'll go on to Chicago to see Chanute. Then I'll return to Washington or New York to help Stephen Balzer and Charlie Manly design a light motor. Then maybe I'll go to Europe in the summer."

"You're determined to design a new engine?" Will asked.

"That's what I do best. While I'm designin' an engine next year, why don't you work on your ideas about control? You said no model can substitute for the real thing. Did you mean that?"

"Why, we sure did," Orv replied. "Only personal experience can reveal problems that models often conceal."

"Then build your box-kite!" John said with a smile. "Write to Charlie Manly for some books from the Smithsonian."

"Maybe we will." Will's eyes gleamed with suppressed excitement. "Maybe we will."

CHAPTER TWENTY-ONE

CARMEL VALLEY
DECEMBER, 1898

On Christmas Eve, after Maggie put Davey to bed, she indulged herself in a glass of claret in front of the fire and idly thought about John's passion for an engine. Would he go on to Europe in the spring, as he has planned? She prayed that he would change those plans and come home instead. She was ready to relinquish the management of the ranch. And Davey had become a handful; he needed his father. But finally, she missed John, even missed their arguments. She turned off the light in the living room, made sure the fire screen was secure against the chimney, then made her way past Davey's bedroom. She had almost passed the door when she heard a sound from within. She quietly opened the door and listened.

Davey was singing! The lyrics of his song were English and Mandarin and the tune seemed to be his own composition. He was relating his whole day as if he were sharing it with a familiar friend. When he had finished, he asked a question. "Do you think she will give me a telescope?"

Maggie heard no answer to the question. Opening the door a bit wider, she could see that Davey was standing at the foot of his bed, looking at the gentle glow of full moonlight outside. Was this the way he conducted his nightly round-up? Who was he talking to? She glanced furtively around the room; but could see no one else.

"When will Poppa come back?"

Maggie wished she could hear the answer to that question. She couldn't be still another moment. She entered the room, knelt down and put her arms around her son. "Davey, who are you talking to?"

"Hi, Momma. I'm talking to my friend."

"I don't see your friend. Is he very small?"

"No, Momma. It's pretty big."

"My goodness. Is he bigger than the chair?"

"Yes, Momma. But it's not a "he" or a "she.""

"Oh!" *It must be a presence,* Maggie thought. "Bigger than I am?"

"Yes, Momma."

"Bigger than a giant?"

"Bigger than the whole world. And it talks to me whenever I want it to."

Maggie felt that she had arrived at some critical moment in her relationship with Davey. This was a new twist. In the *Proceedings* of the British Society for Psychical Research, she had read about thought transference. If Davey would only share his experience now, perhaps she could finally explain all of his strange behavior. "Does it ever play with you?"

"Sure, Momma." Davey pointed to a photograph on top of a dresser.

Maggie could feel the hair stand on end at the back of her neck as the photograph moved from one side of the dresser to the other. It performed a stately dance while it floated to the doorway, then returned to its normal position. *Classic psycho-kinesis*, she thought. *Thank God Ned gave me the Proceedings to read. Otherwise, I'd be terrified, not just shocked.*

Davey clapped his hands and giggled. "And watch this, Momma," he bubbled. He pointed his little forefinger at a toy cast-iron horse-and-buggy on the floor across the room. In a moment, the buggy began to move. Wheels turning, it clattered across the floor and came to a stop at Davey's feet.

Maggie thought. *I wonder how long this has been going on. No wonder he loves his "round-up" time. He commands the whole spirit world to entertain him.* "What fun, Davey. What were the answers to your questions?"

"It said I'll get a nice telescope for Christmas and Poppa will come home for my next birthday."

Maggie could attest to the accuracy of only one answer: the telescope. For Christmas, she had ordered the best French telescope available at Sears and Roebuck. It had a magnifying power of fifty-five diameters with a quality that the Sears catalog said was unobtainable from American optical shops. It could reveal the satellites of Jupiter, mountain ranges and craters on the moon, the rings of Saturn, the canals of Mars, and spots on the sun. With the astronomical eyepiece, the power could be increased to eighty diameters. Maggie had paid the extravagant sum of $20.35 for the introductory instrument that would further open Davey's mind to the glories of space exploration. Only time would tell about the fact or fiction of Space Travellers and John's return. "Do you think you could sleep now? It's past nine."

"O.K., Momma. Anyway, I finished my round-up."

"And did it say goodnight to you?"

"No. It said I'm never alone and I must never forget who I am."

"And who are you, sweetheart?"

"It says I'm love."

Still shaken by the awesome implications of her son's revelations, Maggie tucked Davey under the sheets, closed the door and quietly went to her room. On impulse, she called Ned Ambler on the telephone and begged him to come by the ranch the next day. He reminded her that it was Christmas Day which he hoped to spend with his family. But he agreed to join her for lunch on the day after Christmas since he had calls to make in the valley.

Boxing Day of 1898 was clear and cold in the Carmel Valley. While Davey chattered in Mandarin with Ah Ying in the warm kitchen, Ned Ambler tried to calm Maggie's frayed nerves. During lunch, they talked about John's adventures and speculated about when he might return. Finally, they moved into the library where they both savored fresh-ground coffee.

Maggie was so nervous that she had to stand to present her case. "For the past eighteen months, I have reported to you about some of Davey's curious games. You may recall that, just after John left last summer, he showed me his prodigious photographic memory."

Ned stared at the fire over his cup. "Yes. Wasn't that when he also became your official 'finder?' Does he still have a nose for lost keys and such?"

Maggie nodded. "I also told you about his mythic children, his companions. I've forgotten what you called that dialogue."

Ned smiled. "I said Jung calls it active imagination: just simple mediumship."

"*Simple* mediumship? Ned Ambler, there's nothing simple about it. This is not a case of his overworked imagination." Maggie dabbed her eyes with a handkerchief. She couldn't decide which she felt more strongly, anger or fear.

Ned wanted to comfort her. He was grateful that he had followed William James' lead and subscribed to every issue of the SPR's *Proceedings*. At least he had a command of their language; he also knew what they *didn't* know. "I don't mean to minimize the seriousness of the situation, my dear. I am simply using widely accepted definitions to diagnose Davey's... er ah... skills."

Once again, Ned's voice had its desired effect on Maggie. His sense of the normalcy of Davey's gifts calmed her mind. She stopped pacing in front of the fire and took a seat. "Are you saying that clairvoyance is widely accepted even in this country of money-grubbing materialists?"

"You surprise me, Maggie." Ned accepted a refill of his coffee from Ah Ying, who had peeked in to see if they needed anything. "Look at Cleveland, Ohio. It's a city of three hundred thousand. The twenty or thirty clairvoyants in that city have listed themselves in their own category in the city directory. I'm told that they make a good living at the game."

"But surely many of them are frauds?"

"Of course. There are frauds in every field. Truly gifted people must always suffer the burden of both frauds and friends. The former ruin everyone's reputation. The latter expect too much."

"What else do you know about interest in esoteric knowledge in this country?" Maggie asked.

"Well, four out of five books sold today are about fortune telling, palmistry and such. The field is more popular than fiction. In St. Louis, one of their newspapers devotes a whole page every week to psychical happenings."

"That's the common herd," Maggie said contemptuously. "What about educated people?"

"How about Samuel Clemens—Mark Twain? He has a zealous interest in these matters. And the American Society for Psychical Research in Boston—William James is the President—has over five hundred members."

"What has that society achieved?"

"They say their greatest achievement is the discovery of Mrs. Piper, one of the greatest mediums and clairvoyants of the age, and what they call her 'control:' Dr. Phinuit. She may be as good as Helena Blavatsky."

Maggie was surprised at Ned's mention of Madame Blavatsky, the founder of the Theosophical Movement. "After the scathing attack by Richard Hodgson on Madame Blavatsky, do you still believe in her? Why, she's a trickster and a fraud, isn't she?"

"I don't think so." From the bookshelf Ned handed Maggie two copies of a journal entitled *Borderland* edited by someone named W.T. Stead. "In this magazine she regrets that she used phenomena to attract attention to serious principles of theosophy. She fears that she may have damaged the reputation of the Theosophical Movement." Ned paused to gather his thoughts about the famous—or infamous—Russian seer. "But the fact is that I believe in her ideas as much as I believe in anything else in this strange field. Do you know how she wrote *The Secret Doctrine?*"

"No."

"All automatic writing. Not a single reference. Friends attest to the fact that page after page of profound insights would appear on her desk when she would have nothing at hand except perhaps a French novel. She usually had no idea what she was writing until she had come out of trance."

"Is Mrs. Piper really credible?"

"I don't know. The British and American SPR's have recently turned their attention to the question of survival of human personality after death. Mrs. Piper's skills have been enormously helpful. She has convinced many fine minds that she's in contact with departed spirits."

"But you have doubts about her honesty?"

"No.... She's not a fraud; she's been investigated thoroughly by the SPR here and in England. But William James questions whether her information is derived from a spiritual source or her own subconscious."

"But Ned, where do *you* think Mrs. Piper or Madame Blavatsky get their information?"

"That's the unanswerable question. As I said before, many students of the subject think she communicates with living experts in many fields. But others challenge that idea and assert that she is in touch with ultimate knowledge. I would say that, thanks to the combined efforts of the SPR and Mr. Stead, the weight of informed opinion is on the side of spiritual, not physical sources."

"But I've been told that *The Secret Doctrine* is packed with accurate references, footnotes and allusions. She didn't research those in libraries?"

"Apparently not. Sometimes she might ask a friend to check on the accuracy of some fact that had come through from her Master. But the process is unimportant, finally."

"How can you say such a thing, Ned?" Maggie's tone challenged Ned's calm dismissal of Blavatsky's "automatic writing" skills.

"Because her teachings are what count, Maggie, not the process by which they have come to light. Did it matter to you how your great philosophers arrived at their conclusions?"

"I see what you mean." Maggie somehow felt consoled at the reminder that process was less important than substance. She looked at a magazine he'd handed her. "What's this *Borderland*?"

"It was first published in January, 1894. I think it's time for you to get a closer view of this field. By now, you must know that all the philosophers in the world haven't been able to explain most of the occurrences that are discussed in the SPR's *Proceedings*."

"Will *Borderland* help me understand Davey?"

"Maybe. At least you may be comforted to know that his behavior isn't unique. And you will become familiar with the boundaries of the debate. The magazine covers all major subjects in the psychic field: hypnotism; telepathy or 'thought transference' as some call it; clairvoyance; automatic writing; out of body experiences, like what you call Davey Dreams; astrology; palmistry; dreams; crystal-gazing; and even psychometry. Authors in *Borderland* are renowned scientists like Professor Oliver Lodge and F.W.H. Myers and public figures like Arthur Balfour and George Curzon."

"What's the point of all the debate?"

"Basically, Maggie, the SPR wants to know if the field is all fraud or if it is worthy of scientific scrutiny."

"But aren't fortune-telling and palmistry and astrology just nonsense?"

"Sir Oliver Lodge seems to agree with that judgment. But others think those so-called disciplines help connect the conscious mind to the subconscious."

"The way Davey seems to connect?"

"It appears that Davey connects naturally. He doesn't seem to need any mental discipline. That's why he's so astonishing."

Then Maggie told Ned about Davey's conversation with an angelic presence on Christmas Eve. She described the psychokinetic photo and toy. "I try to be abstract about such things, Ned. But I feel very alone and... very frightened."

"Well, my dear, Davey is obviously gifted. Your experiences the other night demonstrated two forms of psycho-kinesis: both relatively common in the literature." Ned couldn't restrain a delighted smirk.

"What's so funny, you wretched man?" Maggie was in no mood for humor, especially at her expense.

"It just occurred to me that you would be the envy of every student of human consciousness in either the SPR or *Borderland*. Davey is a walking, breathing laboratory. While John is studying something so pedestrian as engines, you have a chance to study questions that are far more baffling than anything he is likely to encounter."

"Questions? Like what?"

"Well.... Try this one for size. Is the reality that Davey talks to an objectively separate reality, a kind of parallel universe? Or is it a fantasy, merely a product of Davey's rich unconscious mind?"

"Do you think we'll ever know the answer to such a question?"

"Yes; but only if we challenge superstition and fraud and do what the SPR and William James want to do: explore the subject with an open mind and scientific rigor." Ned was pleased to see an expression of curiosity and—something else—on Maggie's face. What was it? Where had he seen a similar expression before? And then he had it. Teddy Roosevelt's face also shone with some inner light when his mind contemplated a great cause. *John Harrison had better watch out,* Ned thought. *He only wants to make a machine; she wants to understand the full range of power available to a human being. And she has the making of a zealot.*

CHAPTER TWENTY-TWO

QUINCY, ILLINOIS
DECEMBER, 1898

I hope this trip isn't a wild goose chase, John thought. Octave Chanute's bright-eyed enthusiasm had persuaded him to make this 260-mile side trip to Quincy from Chicago. Chanute had said, "Tom Baldwin is a treasure of information. If your purpose is to find a shortcut to knowledge about flight, a day with Tom will teach you more about balloons than you could get from weeks of polite discourse with even Santos-Dumont in Paris."

As the train sped past a wintry scene south of Galesburg, Tom wondered why he should care about balloons? Why not keep on through Ft. Madison, cross the Mississippi and go home?... But if he did that, he feared he'd *never* get away from the ranch and his family again. He *must* help Balzer and Charlie design the new engine. Then, in the summer, he'd go to Europe and see all those people that Chanute had mentioned: Pilcher; Santos-Dumont; Benz; Mercedes. He *had* to meet those fellows. He just hoped this fellow Baldwin would be all that Ivy and Chanute said he is.

Tom Baldwin was waiting at the railroad station for John. Weighing over 200 pounds, Tom was nothing like John had expected, certainly no acrobat. A man in his mid-forties; chunky, even a little rotund; a shock of dark hair, flecked with gray; kindly but appraising eyes; clean-shaven face with a wide mouth, a square head and small ears. He wore a soft cap and an ill-fitting three-piece blue serge suit under a heavy wool overcoat. His welcome and enthusiasm were genuine. "When Ivy wrote me about you, I couldn't wait to meet you, Mr. Harrison."

"It's my pleasure, Mr. Baldwin; and please call me John. I hear you train parachutists."

"That's right. We'll drive right out to the park."

For the next two hours, Tom Baldwin proudly displayed his 32-acre Baldwin Park at Thirteenth and Maine streets. "Seven years ago, I set out to model the place after Denver's famous Elitch's Gardens. When we finished, we surrounded the whole place with a twelve-foot fence. We have a clubhouse where Ivy sometimes tended bar and told whoppers about aeronautics. We also have a big amphitheater, a baseball diamond, ponds, fountains, a hotel, a floral hall and a beautiful home for my family. We've added a bowling alley and summer cottages."

Although everything was obscured with new snow, the size and diversity of the operation impressed John. *My God*, he thought. *He's a businessman. Ivy is the real performer.* "This place must have cost a mint!"

"It cost plenty, but I could afford it. I got into the aeronaut business at just the right time, in the eighties." Tom led John into the welcome warmth of the clubhouse. They threw their coats on chairs and sat down facing a window through which they could watch a light snow begin to fall. Both men were soon warming their hands around mugs of Irish coffee.

"Was tight-wire walking so profitable?" John asked.

Tom shook his head. "That didn't make much money, but the parachuting really hit pay dirt. Eleven years ago on the Fourth of July, I made my first free ascent here in Quincy. I jumped from two thousand feet. The city fathers and mothers were so impressed that they showered me with medals and money. Later, I met Bill Cody, a great showman. He told me to go to England."

John suddenly felt at home with this easy-going bear of a man. He was glad that he had decided to come down here. "Ivy said the Prince of Wales gave you a diamond ring there."

"Yeah; I went there ten years ago. They were real nice to me, especially another showman named Farini. They called him the Barnum of England. He taught me a lot. I jumped every Thursday and Saturday evenings. The Balloon Society of Great Britain gave me their first gold medal."

John knew that part of Tom's history. But he wanted to hear the whole story. Somewhere in the story was a piece of information, a nugget of gold that John needed. Otherwise, why would Ivy and Octave Chanute send him all this way to the Mississippi River? "Is that when you took your world tour?"

"That's right. My wife, Carrie, and I took the *Oroya* to Australia. I jumped there and in New Zealand." Tom's grin was disarming. It had a naughty, conspiratorial quality that made John want to lean forward and share a secret with his host. "I also tied on the feedbag. When we got back in the spring of eighty-nine, I was too damned heavy to keep it up. I decided to become a showman and let younger fellows like Ivy do the jumps."

John thought Baldwin must have inspired daredevils everywhere to join the race into the air. Perhaps the names of key contacts was what John was supposed to get from Baldwin. "Ivy said you went to the Far East in 1890."

Tom smiled as he looked intently out the window as if to conjure up scenes from his past. "That was one hell of a great tour. In Japan, half a million people would gather to see a single parachute jump. The Japanese army ordered a balloon from me. Ivy jumped before record crowds in Shanghai, Hong Kong, Macao, Singapore, Burma, Saigon and Calcutta."

The snow was heavier now. John wondered if he was drinking the coffee fast just to counteract the *impression* of cold outside. He deliberately pushed the Irish coffee aside and resolved to nurse it a bit. No point in getting drunk. "Ivy told me that he really likes to jump."

"He's crazy!" Tom drained his coffee and ordered a second without any hesitation. "He's a true acrobat; loves the risks. When he was in Mexico in ninety-two, he advertised how dangerous it was—drew the crowds like flies. Sometimes he even scared the hell out of me. That summer back here in Quincy, he loved to hang a ring forty feet below the balloon. He'd grab the ring and swing like a pendulum until he felt like jumping."

"By then, your focus must have shifted to balloon manufacturing." Slightly bemused, John decided that jumping couldn't be the reason for his visit.

"That's right. I began to see that jumping was just a form of good advertising for my balloons and the park's other attractions. If it's good weather on a Fourth of July, we can attract ten thousand people and gross maybe four thousand dollars." Tom smiled at the memory. "We'd have dancing, pie-eating contests, tub races, cake walks, balloon weddings, that sort of thing."

John wondered if Tom really knew the details of a balloon. Or was he just a showman? "How do you make the balloons?"

"The size of a balloon obviously depends on the weight it must carry. My biggest balloons generally have a capacity of thirty thousand cubic feet with a lift of about a thousand pounds—on a sunny day. We use sail cloth treated with linseed oil and turpentine. My preference is gas-filled aerostats; Ivy likes the hot-air variety. We cover a balloon with netting from which we suspend a rope system to carry the basket."

"Where do you get gas?"

"We fill it from the gas main at Twelfth and Jersey downtown. Then we walk it to the park for its ascension."

"Do you have any foreign customers?"

"Sure. We get orders from Europe and the Far East. Through his jumps, Ivy met some businessmen in Mexico who owned a flawed French balloon called *The City of Mexico*. They invited me down there to fix it in the autumn of ninety-two."

"What was wrong with it?"

"Hell, it was poorly made. Gas leakage exceeded an allowable two percent."

"What does that mean?" John had a vision of the balloon collapsing in Mexican jungle.

"It means that it would cost around six hundred dollars a day just to keep it inflated. And that would be the low if they understood gas. The French engineers didn't. They probably wasted over sixty thousand pounds of sulfuric acid the first time they filled it."

Suddenly, John felt the conversation was finally moving in the right direction. "Were you able to fix it?"

"Sure. The job forced us to stay there into the spring of ninety-three, but those fellows thought the world of us when we left. Those French engineers weren't worth squat. When we finally repaired it, it could carry sixteen passengers. It was a profitable trip. Unfortunately, when I got back in April, I learned that tornadoes had wrecked this park."

"Why'd you rebuild it if the money isn't there any more?"

"It's the balloons and parachuting that have lost their novelty. There are probably four hundred parachutists in this country today. A parachutist is lucky to get twenty dollars for a jump. But the park still earns good money. The amusement park business is sweeping the country."

John hadn't thought about that. "I wonder why they're so popular?"

"That's an easy one. A park or a centennial is one of the few places—not counting vaudeville, of course—where young men and women can go for decent public entertainment while they're meeting one another. Thirty years ago, amusement parks and enclosed baseball diamonds didn't exist. Today, every town in the country has its amusement park."

For the next four days, John warmed to Tom Baldwin's unusual personality. Across Main street from the Hickman Hotel, Tom showed him his factory where employees sewed up sections of sail cloth or silk. A self-made man who had been orphaned at twelve, Tom's conversation revealed a curious mixture of rough down-to-earth tolerance and urban sophistication. He had met Princes and Queens and had gained financial success. But something weighed on his mind. At home during evening meals, he made no effort to conceal his strained relationship with his wife, Caroline, a cheery, slender, attractive woman who liked wide-brimmed hats and responded to all of Tom's schemes with a pull on Tom's ear or a toothy grin of tolerance. Their son, Tom, Junior, was an energetic seven-year-old who filled the Baldwin house with his laughter and energy.

After supper on John's final evening with the family, he asked, "What's your next big project, Tom?"

"I think you're the answer to my prayers, John. I've talked to Chanute about my idea. Maybe that's why he sent you down here. I want to mount a small motor on a balloon with enough lift to carry two or three men. If Ivy had had such a rig in Cuba, things might have been different."

"What about heavier-than-air? Why focus on balloons?"

"Forget about Langley's aerodrome!" Tom snorted. "It's a dream. You won't see a man in an aerodrome for another ten years, maybe longer." Tom paused to light a cigar. He had a way of pursing his lips when he wanted to make an important point. "John, you need to understand that there are two races going these days."

John sipped some fine port that Tom had learned to drink in England. "Two races?"

"You betcha. There's the race for the first man to fly an aerodrome, but that's pie in the sky. There's no quick money in that race. The money is in military ballooning—powered airships."

John was reminded of the yellow *Santiago* in Cuba. A lot of fine men had died because it was so unmanageable and so visible above the Rough Riders. "I'm not sold on spherical balloons."

"I'm not either. They bounce and buck around too much in any wind. The military spherical balloon probably sang its swan song in Cuba."

"Then what's the alternative?"

"They don't need to be spherical. Look at the Germans; for the past two years, they've been using sausage-shaped tethered balloons."

"What about Graf von Zeppelin? Isn't he ahead of the game?"

"Hard to tell. Last year, a feller named David Schwartz showed the German army the possibilities when he powered a small dirigible with an Otto-cycle engine. But the German military don't like Zeppelin's idea of a rigid airship. They want to be able to carry it deflated to the field, inflate it and launch it. I think I can do that before the competition if I can only find a good engine."

When Tom said that, John could smell a business opportunity. But he wondered if Tom Baldwin was technically qualified or was he just a showman? "What's your cheapest balloon?"

"I can make a seamless hot-air balloon for a hundred and fifty dollars. I use thoroughly varnished imported pongee silk."

"You feel your factory downtown could meet the demand?"

"Absolutely! I can sell forty balloons in a good year right now; I can get as much as two hundred and fifty dollars for a small balloon. For a big one like *The City of Mexico*, I could get eight hundred dollars."

John thought about that. At forty balloons a year, Tom's minimum gross income must be $6000, probably a lot more. If balloons could be powered, the sky would be the limit. "What does a customer get for his money?"

"With every balloon, I throw in five hundred feet of tether rope, twelve ballast bags, twenty-five feet of hose to conduct gas into the balloon, all the netting needed to cover the balloon, a valve top and neckpiece. For an extra twenty-five dollars, I'll even add a windlass to raise and lower the balloon."

"Has General Greely ordered any more balloons for the Signal Corps?"

"No; but that's because no one has figured out how to drive them. I don't think navigation is a problem. All we need is a small engine. If we can rig a small, reliable engine to a balloon, we'll get orders from every army in the world."

If John had had any doubts about the proper focus for his energies and skills before, this conversation with Tom Baldwin erased all of them. For the first time, he understood why Zeke Harner and his Wall Street masters were so willing to commit mayhem to get a small engine. It was the key to a huge fortune—not sometime in the future when an aerodrome might emerge from Langley's drawing board or the Wright brother's kite. That fortune was waiting right this moment for the first man who could build a light, powerful engine. "Are the Europeans serious competition?"

"Not yet. Earlier this year, Santos-Dumont flew a dirigible over Paris with a pair of DeDion engines in tandem. But that whole rig is too heavy for their mere three-and-a-half horsepower. And his dirigible factory at St. Cloud can't solve the problem."

John closed his notebook and took a sip of port. "So is your idea to start a new b'iness?"

Tom chewed on his cigar and eyed John thoughtfully. The lean Californian appealed to Tom. So did California. That's where he had been given his big boost, and that was where he might return if his family situation didn't improve soon. "My hope is to team up with you. I make the best balloons in the world. If you can make the engines, we could go fifty-fifty. What do you say?"

"Would you keep the factory here?" John asked the question just to buy some time. In many ways, Tom's idea appealed to him. But he couldn't commit to anything until he returned from Europe.

"I was thinking of setting up in San Francisco. Is location important?"

"I guess not; but I'd like to see a partner once or twice a week—not once a year." If Tom was right, if the army put its money into powered airships before a commercial aerodrome could be designed and built, maybe it would make sense to keep a foot in each camp. Hell, aerodromes and airships both needed a light engine. Tom's plan merely added a string to John's bow. If he and Charlie Manly and Stephen Balzer could develop a good engine, suitable for either airships or aerodromes, they might benefit regardless of the rate of progress in the two races.

Perhaps more important than his appreciation of the commercial value of the Balzer engine was John's new sense of timing. During his visit with the Wright brothers, with Chanute and finally with Tom Baldwin, John had concluded that there was a pace, a rhythm to invention and applied science. Nothing happened overnight. Prevailing technical knowledge must be the foundation for the ultimate emergence of an aerodrome. If that was so, then powered balloons could be the technical bridge to an aerodrome. He must listen to people like Tom who understood air currents, had looked down on the world from two thousand feet and had mastered the construction of reliable airships.

Another thought crossed John's mind: secrecy. Balzer's engine was clearly of vital significance for the future of either powered airships or the aerodrome. But Manly and Langley had not even thought about securing their plans until John had suggested it. Now that John had proved the culpability of Zeke Harner, security must be given even more attention. John decided he must spend the winter and spring of 1899 in New York City, not only to help design the engine but especially to guard against the Harners of the city.

"I'll join you, Tom; but I can't promise an engine until I see what comes out of our contract with Balzer. And even if we produce a powerful motor in the next four months, I'll have to get Sam Langley's permission before we could use it on one of our balloons."

Tom was gratified that John had adopted the word, "our," so quickly. "But of course, John. I don't want a patent. I just want a fine little motor. Go work with Balzer; go to Europe. But when you get back, let's talk again."

CHAPTER TWENTY-THREE

NEW YORK CITY
FEBRUARY, 1899

From his spacious room in the Plaza Hotel, John Harrison looked out on Central Park, adorned with a blanket of fresh snow. If it weren't for the twilight traffic down Fifth Avenue, he could have sworn that he was looking across a beautiful valley, populated by only a handful of people. The ice skaters had given up in the fading light; only a few calashes or hansom cabs still moved briskly through the park. This time of day was always the hardest for him; this was when he missed Maggie and a son he hadn't seen for nearly a year. After finishing his weekly letter to them, he wrote to Charles Manly, with whom he liked to share progress.

Dear Charlie,

Since I arrived here on Monday, January 2, I have watched Balzer's genius flower. He has accepted our suggestions with a gracious spirit and, as I have related in past reports, the results have been more than promising. Indeed, I have every confidence that he will fulfill his contract on schedule. Please thank Mr. Langley for his sketch of the aerodrome and his proposed mounting for the engine. By the end of April, you should have in your hands one of the finest, most powerful small engines in the world. It should more than suffice to power the aerodrome.

John paused and reflected on that last sentence. Did he really believe that Balzer had solved most of the intricate problems with which he had been wrestling since he signed the contract in mid-December? Certainly the work that John and Manly had done gave Balzer a running start towards the impossible goal of a horsepower per 8.31 pounds of engine weight. But solutions to a few technical issues were still locked up in the mathematics and mechanics of Balzer's radical concept: the first 5-cylinder, rotary engine in history.

I'm glad that Mr. Langley likes the full-scale drawings that we sent to you a month ago. But I am still dubious about Balzer's concept of a rotary engine. I would prefer a stationary radial because I think many of our problems come from the vibration and centrifugal forces of an entire engine in motion. Here are is my list of our main problems:

1. The carburetor would challenge divine wisdom. I think we must devise a system to pre-heat inlet air since evaporation cools it too much now.

2. Our ignition system is primitive. As you know, we're using a heavy battery and coil with each cylinder. That make-and-break "wiping" system is much too heavy. I think we ought to return to Balzer's original idea of a "jumping" system: De Dion's high-tension sparkplug idea. Of course, we would have to make our own sparkplugs. I've been tinkering with a distributor that could feed current to each sparkplug in sequence.

3. The valve train needs to be simplified. Unfortunately, the centrifugal forces of a rotary are likely to throw the valves out of kilter and foster unreliable air-fuel mixtures. I'm working on that problem also. If the engine were not rotating, our existing valve train would probably be adequate.

4. The pistons should be lighter. Balzer's ball and socket design to link each connecting rod to the piston is too heavy, I think. I would prefer to use a wrist-pin to link pistons to connecting rods.

5. We need some radically new master-rod and slave-link system for driving the crankshaft.

6. Finally, we will need water jackets around each cylinder. I don't think it is possible to cool our motor adequately with air.

Those problems notwithstanding, I am so confident that I'm afraid I boasted about our prospects the other night to one of J.P. Morgan's aides: Gerald Ashley. At Theodore Roosevelt's urging, Ashley sought me out and invited me to a night on the town. I welcomed the invitation because, during nearly six weeks of intensive research, complicated calculations and draftsmanship, I gave myself only a few days to explore Coney Island's Steeplechase Park, the "Canals of Venice," the "Giant See-saw," the iron steeplechase and its many restaurants, freak shows and shooting galleries. Usually, I'm so tired at the end of a day that I have no interest in any entertainment.

Ashley is a dedicated theater-goer. When we first met for lunch in my hotel, he must have taken my measure instantly. As you know, I'm just a country boy more at home in the canyons of Colorado than the canyons of New York City. So when he rattled off names like Eddie Foy and Marie Dressler and Nellie Melba, my ignorance gave me away. He knows all the theaters and attends the musicals, farces, operettas and vaudeville almost as a duty. I think he dines out every night. Maybe that's one of his responsibilities with J.P. Morgan: entertaining clients. When I fell into his hands, he must have decided to fill a terrible gap in my education.

At first, I was afraid he would take me to the Metropolitan opera. He did mention that some singer named Lotte Lehman had won everyone's heart with her performance in something called *Tristan*. And he admitted that some woman named Eames would be singing in *Faust* that evening. I think he was trying to locate my cultural center.

I had no desire to impress Ashley. From our Christmas season together in Washington, you know very well that I'm uncomfortable around swells. And I make no effort to conceal my disdain for them. Ashley, with his pomaded, slicked-down hair and faint aroma of lavender, qualifies as a relentless swell. So I frowned my disapproval at the very idea of opera or—even more boring—ballet. All I wanted was a good time. I told him I'd be delighted with one of the popular coon shows either at the Casino on 39th Street or at Koster and Bial's on 23rd Street, which featured the Kings of Koon-dom last autumn. Even Proctor's 23rd Street vaudeville house would have been fine. I love all those soft-shoe dances, ballads, acrobats, minstrels, skits, animal acts, magicians and mind-readers. But Ashley finally insisted that we see *A Romance of Athlone* at the 14th Street Theater. Chauncey Olcott's rendition of "My Wild Irish Rose," made me wish Maggie was there.

After the theater, Ashley took me to the famous Delmonico's restaurant at 26th Street and Fifth Avenue. Del's doesn't accept reservations so we would have had to wait if Ashley's boss, John Pierpont Morgan himself, had not invited us into a private dining room. I was surprised that Morgan would use such a public place as Del's for a private dinner since everyone knows that Morgan is sensitive about his unsightly nose, deformed and bulbous with acne. Ashley told me that Morgan thought Del's would be the best neutral ground for several of his guests. Also, some of them had vowed never again to set foot in Morgan's "Black Library," his personal study at 219 Madison Avenue, where he has reputedly ruined more people than I can count.

That dinner was more dramatic than the theater. For about an hour I kept my mouth shut while I tried to keep up with some veteran gourmands. They acted as if their capacity to gorge was a measure of their manhood. I reckon they waded through ten or twelve courses of oysters and soup and fish and beef and lamb, all of it drowning in savory sauces. I'm not a hearty eater, so I listened to the conversation while I nibbled.

It soon was clear to me that these fellows were among the most powerful men in New York, maybe in the whole country. I had heard of some of them. But I never expected to meet Morgan or James Hill or Harriman or William Vanderbilt or Jay Gould or Harry Whitney or John Jacob Astor or the presidents of several utility and insurance companies. It didn't take me long to understand that these moguls were concerned about Teddy Roosevelt's threat to tax utilities and insurance companies. They angrily reminded themselves that they had been paying "Easy Boss" Tom Platt to protect them from such taxation. Between courses they expressed outrage that Governor Roosevelt should dare to challenge their special perquisites.

I was stunned—and confused—by their ambitions. They think oil, electricity and autos are the coming thing. They agreed that oil *must* exist somewhere besides Pennsylvania. They're sure the country needs more than the single 5000hhp generating station we have; and they're convinced that our 8000 automobiles are just a beginning.

I soon realized that the focus of this supper meeting was the railroads. What impressed me was the way Morgan quietly warned Hill and Harriman that they must not allow their competition for control of the railroads to damage innocent businessmen across the country. Hill tried to explain that, since the big depression of '93, investment bankers like Morgan were forcing many smaller railroads to sell out to combines. Morgan didn't buy that argument. He quietly suggested that, if Harriman and Hill didn't settle their differences peacefully and soon, he, Morgan, would settle them, perhaps not so peacefully. When a man with that much power quietly puts a threat on the table, you can hear a pin drop. He suggested further that seven major railroads might be about the right number to manage our 200,000 miles of lines efficiently. It didn't take a scholar to see that the seven principals were sitting there, nodding their heads in agreement.

Then they got on the subject of steel and, once again, Morgan had his say. He struck me as a master of mergers. He said that steel was so vital to the country's future that a steel war among producers could plunge the country into another depression. I think he has some idea up his sleeve about creating a huge combine to insure that steel production doesn't lag. I imagine Andrew Carnegie would have something to say about that….

Now comes the part that is a little embarrassing; but I have to get it out. After about two hours of high-powered talk, I was stuffed with food and champagne. I shouldn't touch that stuff. But I had to do something with my hands since I didn't feel qualified to do anything with my mouth, except eat and drink. So I kept sucking down liquid courage until I reached a point where I thought our motor and the aerodrome deserved some attention.

During a brief silence while everyone was wiping his mouth and belching and wondering who would die first of a heart attack, I asked, "What about the aviation industry?"

All heads turned towards me in surprise. I guess Harriman echoed the general view when he asked, "The *what* industry?"

Well of course, I had to make a fool of myself. We Harrisons are not known for our reticence when challenged. Right away, I knew that you and Langley and Chanute and the Wright brothers and Tom Baldwin had taught me more about flight and its possibilities than any of them could even dream of. So I launched into a lecture that turned into their evening's entertainment. They laughed so hard that some of them were crying! Gould said I was Darius Green come to life. I didn't like to be compared to a fictional character.

By then it must have been two in the morning. I should have shut up; I should have gone home to bed. But they started asking questions. So I told them about Langley's contract to produce an aerodrome. Some of them already knew about that and had no confidence in Langley. I got angry and said that Langley was an unrecognized Edison. Hill said that Langley was good for only one thing: star gazing.

That angered me more. So I had to explain how a great race had started for conquest of the sky. I described the work of Lilienthal and Chanute and Langley. I told them that the only obstacle to our winning the race was a small engine. That's

when I said that small engines driven by gasoline would reveal the inefficiencies of steam engines someday.

"Are you talking about a flying buggyaut?" Harriman
asked.

"What's a buggyaut?" I asked him.

"That's what they call the Duryea brothers' buggy that
won a motocycle race three years ago on Thanksgiving Day," he
said.

Then I noticed that old Mr. Morgan was listening intently. That old man exudes wisdom and something else—maybe
it's the smell of awesome power. He asked, "Are you saying
that you think the gasoline engine can beat the steam engine
as a source of power for small machines?"

Hell, Charlie, what could I say? I didn't have the exact
figures on recent motor car production. But I knew that only
a few hundred built last year were powered by gasoline. At
least a thousand were powered by steam or electricity. So I
launched into a description of the Balzer engine. Some of
those fellows are engineers. None of them is stupid. The
laughter quieted down and they began to listen. An aerodrome
was a subject of speculation to them; and they weren't convinced that the race for first flight was worth running. But
a small engine was worthy of their attention. By the time I
finished boasting about Balzer's genius and the fine progress we were making, I noted that Vanderbilt, Whitney and
Astor had shrewd expressions on their faces. Through a thick
haze of cigar smoke, I could see that they wanted to know
more. So I told them that we expected to test our engine
within a week.

Then I realized that I had violated every pledge of secrecy that I had ever made to you and myself. In light of Mr.
Langley's recent decision to make George Wells responsible
for securing all drawings and notes and books in the
"Aerodromic Room" and his plea to us to be especially attentive to the confidentiality of our project, I felt like a
damned fool.

"Do you think Balzer could be another Selden?" William Vanderbilt asked.

That single question set them off. You probably already know about George Selden; but I had never heard of him. They revealed that Selden, a shrewd lawyer, and a machinist's assistant named Gomm manufactured a three-cylinder gasoline engine twenty-one years ago in Rochester, New York. Thanks to Selden's knowledge of patent law, he designed and patented a horseless carriage to be driven by their engine. He never actually built his "road engine." But he amended his patent every two years until 1895, when he pushed through his final patent. The rascal intended to use the patent to sue anyone who used a gasoline engine to power an automobile. He recently sold his patent rights, on a royalty basis, to a syndicate in New Jersey called the Electric Vehicle Company.

Now, why were these rich men so interested in Selden and patents? I'll tell you why. A Federal Judge named John R. Hazel has just found in favor of the Electric Vehicle Company, which sued two automobile companies for patent infringement. Instead of paying legal fees for endless infringement lawsuits, nine automobile manufacturing companies have just formed an association which has agreed to pay Electric Vehicle Company over 1% royalty on each vehicle they manufacture. That means that Selden and that company will make money on every automobile that will ever be made in this country for eternity!

The party broke up soon after my drunken speech. I thought maybe I hadn't done too much damage to our cause since only William Vanderbilt came up to ask me questions. Of course Ashley questioned me on our trip back to the Plaza. I think he was just trying to be polite since he seemed very casual about his questions. So I'm praying that my big mouth did not get us into any trouble. Anyway, I defended Sam Langley to the best of my limited ability. Please tell him so when you read him this letter.

CHAPTER TWENTY-FOUR

NEW YORK CITY
MARCH, 1899

At noon on a bitterly cold day in March, 1899, John Harrison trudged into the New Brighton Dance Hall and Restaurant on Great Jones Street. He was startled by the sheer bulk of the maitre d', a giant who liked to be called Eat-'Em-Up Jack McManus. John was further intimidated by the opulent interior of mirrors, brass railings and sparkling chandeliers. Curiously, he felt most uncomfortable by the smiling, one might say willing availability, of so many nearly naked waitresses. But he took a firm grip on his homburg and stifled his misgivings; the situation called for desperate measures.

At first, he had thought that the snail's pace of Stephen Balzer's recent progress on the motor could be ascribed to complex technical issues that challenged his competence. But Balzer's behavior since mid-February convinced him there was another reason for Balzer's languor. When John had voiced his suspicions to Teddy Roosevelt, TR said, "When I was head of the Board of Police Commissioners, I met a Tammany chieftain, an Irishman named Michael Coyle. If it's information you need, Big Mike can find it if anyone can—or will." After John and Mike sparred over origins, accents and motives at two earlier meetings, Mike asked for time to sort out what he called his options. John prayed that Mike had come to the decision to help.

Whether or not Mike would help, John liked him, liked his no-nonsense intimidation of thugs and gangsters and his contrasting compassion for women and children, especially Irish immigrants south of Delancey Street who would have died without Mike's weekly supplies of food and clothes. Republicans might argue that Mike simply did the bidding of the Tammany machine, which would reap its rewards for his small generosities when a critical vote might be needed. But Roosevelt had seen behind such a cynical explanation of Mike Coyle. Mike, loved what he called his "ward-healing role" with some of the 26 million immigrants who had just arrived. Despite the popular joke that a shotgun fired at random in any direction at the five corners would miss an honest man, TR's faith in Mike, and John's need, fostered John's belief that Mike was honest and a man of his word. That Mike also loved his four-year old son, Patrick, above all else was reassuring.

John handed his overcoat to a redhead and sat down opposite Mike Coyle, who was wearing an impeccably tailored three-piece suit. His conservative dress and quiet tone confused John, who saw contradiction between the clothing and the scarred, battered face, a map of many street fights.

"Now Misther Harrison," Mike said with his impish Irish grin, "tell me agin about your little problem." Since the first of their three meetings, Mike had learned to like John even if his ancestors were Scots. More to the point, John had powerful friends in Albany; namely the Governor hisself, old "Four-eyes" Roosevelt, who had licked the Tammany machine by a mere 11,000 votes last November. By focusing his campaign on Tammany boss, Richard Croker, for tampering with the New York State judiciary, Roosevelt had taken his reform-minded energies to a stunning and disturbing victory.

"As I said last month, my charges are hard to prove."

"Ye don't have to prove nothin', Misther Harrison," Mike growled. "I jes need to know what ye're afraid of an' what ye want to do."

"Well...; you know this motor is critical for the Langley aerodrome." John felt as if he had repeated the story a hundred times. "I've told you about this race we're in to beat the Germans and...."

"Sure, and to beat the goddam English. If I kin do anythin' to twist their tails, I'll do it jes for the sheer pleasure of it. Go on." Mike was so hungry he could eat a horse. Where the hell were the crabcakes?

"I've been here three months to help Stephen Balzer design and build the motor. I thought we were doin' right well 'til he suddenly slowed down last month. It was bafflin'! Suddenly, he seemed... almost indifferent; didn't seem to care whether or not he fulfilled his contract with the guvmint."

"Is he stupid? Or is he jes runnin' short of cash?"

"He's not stupid. He has one of the best minds I know for motors. I've made a few contributions; but he's the genius. I like him and I trust him. Oh, money may be a small problem. But he knows that I can get more of the necessary from Sam Langley if we really need it."

Mike Coyle studied John's face with renewed interest. When they had first met, Mike had feared that the cowboy's problem would be just another routine favor. But their dialogue had tickled his curiosity. What had started as a political favor had turned into something else—maybe even a friendship. "So you think someone else is slowin' him down?"

"Yes. Balzer is at least intimidated if not terrified. But he won't talk about it."

"Where is his shop?"

"At 370 Gerard Avenue. I go there ever' mornin' to work on the motor. Last month, tough lookin' bozos began to stand across the street and watch the house. I'll have to admit they bothered me too."

"Gerard is a hell of a long way from here. But your watchers sound like a lot of my... friends down here. So what's your diagnosis?"

"I think someone—maybe on Wall Street—has discovered how close we are to success. They must know the motor is what will lose or win the race. I think they want to win by delayin' or stealin' our motor."

"Wall Street! Hmm. Are ye talkin' about lots of money?"

"Money and maybe power; certainly industrial power and probably political and military power."

"A devil's brew if there ever was one. If Wall Street investment bankers or insurance companies are involved, that's bigtime swindling."

"You won't help me?"

"I din't say that. I'm jes sayin' I only know about petty graft and corruption down here. Do ye know anythin' about how we run the wards?"

"Not even a glimmer. I bow to your superior knowledge."

"It's a long story. All ye need to know is this. South of Times Square, Tammany runs New York by makin' deals with the gangs."

"Deals? What kind of deals?"

"Oh, little compromises. Like I said, 'Live and let live.' We pay off the police an' keep 'em off the gangs as long as the gangs behave themselves. Not *too many* murders and robberies. Not *too much* mayhem or the good citizens will rise up and commit an atrocity like electin' Roosevelt." Mike's grin masked his sense that he was tutoring a child. No New Yorker would need such an explanation. Mike was grateful when his crabcakes arrived so that he could pause for fuel before continuing his little tutorial.

John thought his lamb chops looked suspicious, but Mike had said that this place was one of the best restaurants on the East Side. Maybe he could drown any stray bacteria in beer. "I'd think a few folks would protest anyway."

"They do now an' then. We had an investigation in ninety-four an' they tried to dismiss Captain Big Bill Devery. But the state Supreme Court set it aside an' ordered the police commissioners to leave him alone. Now he's Chief of Police. I suspect another investigation is comin' next year because Big Bill and Police Inspector Williams have made a mockery of the Eleventh Precinct judicial system."

"Beggin' your pardon, Mike; but how big is the Eleventh Precinct?"

"Sure an' that's the whole Lower East Side, bounded on the west by the Bowery down to Chatham Square, Division Street on the south, Clinton to the east and Houston to the north."

John took an exploratory bite of lamb chops only to discover that they were tender, juicy and delicious. The vegetables seemed fresh and not overcooked as he had expected. Anywhere else, he would have complimented the chef. The quality of the meal disarmed him, as did so many other aspects of life on the East Side of New York City: violence and compassion as intermixed and as unpredictable as the cultures of its citizens. "Is it really so bad here?"

"Depends on your point of view, m'boy. All ye need ta know is that Tammany owns a lot of the judicial and political and especially the police appointments here. We count most of the police force as dues-payin' members of Tammany."

John suspected San Francisco was run the same way. "Even the police pay dues?"

Mike paused, a generous portion of crabcake on his fork. "Listen boyo, the whores pay patrolmen for the privilege of solicitin'. Sneak thieves, burglars, pickpockets, gangsters, footpads an' damn near anyone who wants to do a little bizness an' stay healthy pay a little bizness tax to us. Nuthin' happens down here that doesn't come to our attention, especially if we kin tax it."

John suddenly realized that Mike was telling him something of the utmost significance. Tammany did not simply have its hands around New York's throat; it also had access to information, almost any information that could be obtained by fair means or foul. And Mike was now the personal conduit between John and that vast encyclopaedia spread across the streets of the New York City. "Are we talkin' about a lot of money?"

Mike grinned innocently. "Oh, just pennies. But Inspector Williams has saved enough pennies—he claims they come from his investments in Japanese real estate—to buy a yacht, an estate at Cos Cob, a large house in the city and he has several fat bank accounts. Are ye gettin' the picture?"

As John finished his meal and reached for a cup of excellent coffee, he realized that he was enjoying himself. He would have to tell reformist Maggie about Mike Coyle. While men like Roosevelt grappled with corrupt state legislatures and the trusts, the likes of Mike were the only force for some semblance of order in the Lower East Side. Without Mike, chaos would prevail. "So how does this little lesson in civics relate to my motor?"

"Ye need one more little piece of information. Then ye can answer your own question. There are hundreds of small clubs and gangs down here; but most of them like Johnny Spanish an' Biff Ellison an' Kid Dropper owe allegiance to one of two powerful gangs: either the Five-Pointers, run by my good friend, Paul Kelly, or the Eastman's, run by the great Monk Eastman. I s'pose the Gophers count for somethin' since they plunder a domain that stretches from Fourteenth to Forty-second Streets between Seventh and Eleventh Avenues. But the Gophers can only field five hundred first class thugs in a crisis." Mike paused to savor a trifle, his favorite dessert.

"Five hundred *armed* men?"

"Of course they're armed. No self-respectin' thug goes into the street without one or two revolvers, one or two brass knucks, a Bessie—that's a blackjack—and at least one knife. Johnny Spanish generally carries four revolvers. An' five hundred men is nuthin'. The Five-Pointers number over fifteen hundred. I guess the Eastman's could field twelve hundred before a drunken weekend. New York is a battlefield, John. Don't ye ivver forget it!"

John wondered if Maggie should send him his new '96 Winchester and

Colts, or maybe a few Comanche hunters. But they would feel helpless in the tangled filth of the Bowery. "It must be hard to carry all that artillery."

Mike grew thoughtful. "Ye're right. A lot of the lads keep spare weapons in cigar and stationery stores. But the best system is to have yer woman nearby. She can carry a spare revolver in her muff or in her jacket. I've even seen one concealed in that hairdo called a Mikado tuck-up. One woman I know uses a revolver instead of a rat for her pompadour."

"Is that little story about the gangs the final piece to my puzzle, Mike?"

"Almost. Paul Kelly, who owns this restaurant, can help and here he comes."

Over the next ten minutes, John was astonished to hear the ruthless Paul Kelly, chief of a domain that stretched between the Bowery and Broadway all the way to 14th Street, sprinkle his conversation with phrases from four languages: French, Spanish, Italian and English. John learned that Kelly had been a bantam-weight boxer in his youth but rarely would stoop to hands-on mayhem now. Nothing must damage his carefully tailored blue pin-stripe suit, his manicured nails and his cosmopolitan manner. Then John asked Kelly if Monk Eastman was well educated.

"Monk Eastman is a twenty-five year old Neanderthal, Mr. Harrison," Kelly replied mildly. "As far as I can tell, he has never been in the vicinity of an education. With his bullet-shaped head, his cauliflower ears, his broken nose, his sagging jowls and his short, bull-neck decorated with numerous knife scars, he *looks* like the thug that he is. The oaf has been shot so many times that he boasts that his weight comes from bullets still lodged in his body."

"Why does Tammany tolerate such a man, Mike?" John asked with a frown.

"Because he's a genius at election time, m'boy. He dominates all dishonest—and even a few honest—voters east of the Bowery from Fourteenth Street south to Monroe an' all the way to the East River. Where would the Wigwam be if Monk didn't dragoon his gangsters to the polls and blackjack any honest citizens who might want to vote their conscience?" Mike explained John's problem to Kelly, who listened intently.

"Are you thinking what I'm thinking, Mike?" Kelly asked.

"Sure an' why not? It's that new man from Ohio.... What's his name?

The one that looks like Monk's twin brother?"

"His name is Harner. Ezekial Harner."

John stared at Mike in shock. Harver again! Was he some kind of nemesis?

Mike chuckled. "He sez he fought with the Rough Riders. One of my spies told me that he keeps bragging about a big windfall that's due him any time."

"If Monk likes him, I'll be glad to despise him," Kelly said. "Who is he?"

For the next ten minutes, John told the story of Zeke Harner. When he ended, Kelly and Coyle smiled at their iron-clad diagnosis. "It's plain as the nose on yer face," Mike said. "This feller Harner or one of Monk's lads has put the heat on poor old..., what's his name? Buzzer?"

"Balzer. So what can I do? We're desperate for this motor!"

"Do you really want to get yourself mixed up in New York politics?" Kelly asked gently. Unlike Coyle, Kelly politely turned his head away before blowing a smoke ring.

John squirmed in his chair. He had never run from a fight before. He wasn't going to start now. And the engine was critical to Langley's success. In fact, he had to admit to himself that physical threats from competitors, even bunglers like Harner, only added spice to the greater lure of fame... and maybe even a fortune. But he knew that he could do nothing without help from Kelly and Coyle. "Do I have an alternative?"

"Can you fire a weapon?" Kelly asked.

John told them about his marksmanship. It was no time for false modesty. He even told them the story of Roosevelt's puma in Colorado. He mentioned a few of the incidents in Cuba.

Through a cloud of cigar smoke, Coyle and Kelly exchanged looks of great satisfaction. Harrison might be an innocent in New York; but he had seen the elephant and could be relied upon to stand his ground if necessary.

"Let us study on it for a week or two, John," Mike said.

"But Mike," John protested, "time is precious!"

"True; but ye don't want to rush off half-cocked. We need to find out whose sticky fingers are in this stew. Maybe your friend Harner is workin' for an investment banker. Let's hope he's workin' his own graft. That we kin handle easy. Who else might know about yer motor?"

"At a dinner party in Delmonico's, I told Morgan an' Gould an' Harriman an' Vanderbilt an' Hill an' one of Morgan's henchmen, Ashley."

"Jaisus!" Mike protested. "That complicates things a bit. Kin ye button yer lip for a while?"

"So what should I do?"

"Just keep workin' with Buzzer and let us see if we kin find a way to persuade Mr. Harner to back off."

CHAPTER TWENTY-FIVE

NEW YORK CITY
APRIL, 1899

For the next month while he waited for word from Mike Coyle, John Harrison surrendered himself to Jerry Ashley's inspired tutelage. By a brilliant spring morning in late April, John had become a veteran of New York's night life: the theater, late suppers and even later clubs with the children of the Four Hundred. Those young men and women had taught John many things. But his most important lesson would last the rest of his life; namely, that education and breeding were no defense against the seductive, irresistible power of physical pleasure. That was a fact that could be discussed in polite company—within limits, of course. What John could not yet discuss, even with himself, was the depths of his own hunger for liberation from social convention. It would take several years for him to realize that Jerry Ashley had deliberately challenged his capacity for self-indulgence—and self-hate. Prideful of his endurance, he had demanded ever more from Jerry, who knew that diversity was less dangerous than quantity: too much food too much alcohol and too much cocaine. As a kind of graduation exercise, Jerry had cemented their friendship two nights before by arranging small quantities of all three stimuli, plus the prospect of limitless sexual exercise with two extraordinary French expatriate prostitutes: Marie and Mathilde, "M and M."

It had taken John all of the next day to digest that experience, which had all but destroyed the few illusions about himself that he still nurtured. By the end of that day, he found shallow consolation in the thought that his appetites for food and alcohol and even cocaine were still under control. That was because he had found the limits not only of their pleasures but especially of their painful effects: floating ecstasies of mind followed by everything from prolonged bowel-wrenching nausea to nerve-shattering pain in the head, the eyes, the stomach and the joints.

But M and M taught him that he barely understood the delights of co-itus. They introduced him to the idea that its pleasure varies with the rhythm and sophistication of stimulating games before its climax. They taught him that his level of sex education from vaqueros around Carmel and sophomores at Berkeley was so primitive as to be nearly non-existent. The furtive urgency and fumbling to climax that John had understood as the sex act they rejected out of hand. Instead, they insisted on discipline from him—even when his hormones were screaming for release. They re-minded him of, even demanded from him, a certain obligation to share his pleasure with his partner. Their use of every sense, of vision and touch and sound and smell and even taste, was so gentle and carefully orchestrated that he was able to sustain an erection for a full hour before one of them consented to intercourse.

Then, exchanging a look of satisfaction for releasing John from child-hood fears and inhibitions, they got down to the serious business of physi-cal therapy. For the rest of the night, through conversation and experimentation, they taught him how to "make love." By the end of that night, they had opened John's awareness to a dimension in himself that he had suppressed for many years. He had always enjoyed hard physical con-tact with nature; but social convention had warned him away from any such contact labelled "sex." With Maggie, he had behaved as if guided by a book of etiquette. M. and M. quietly led his mind to the realization..., no, the *conviction* that sex could be, *must* be just as natural as—and potentially far more rewarding than—football, polo, a roundup, a hunting trip or al-most any other form of human endeavour. Moreover, in contrast with the price that one must pay for excesses with other appetites, the physical af-ter-effects of prolonged sexual athletics were sweet and natural: relaxation and sleep. And if one made a slight adjustment in one's personal code of behaviour, the negative emotional effects, especially guilt, could be avoided.

And so John had awakened late on that spring morning with a sense of deep gratitude to Jerry Ashley and a liberated zest that propelled him through breakfast and inspired a new resolution to complete the Balzer engine.

Following a habit that had emerged from his dedicated investigation of New York night life, John Harrison arrived at 370 Gerard Avenue at noon. He was astonished to find Stephen Balzer still in bed. When John's angry protests finally forced the dispirited Balzer to show his face, that tired, ravaged countenance shocked even John, whose frequent outings with Jerry Ashley had inured him to almost every extreme of beauty—and depravity.

"What the hell's gotten into you, Balzer?" John raged. "Have you given up on the engine? You promised a full test a month ago. It never happened."

Balzer pouted and refused to face John's accusing eyes. "You know it's overheating."

"O.K. So what are you goin' to do about it?"

"I don't know. Each cylinder needs more cooling area. Maybe we should use radiating fins. Or maybe we should double the number of cylinders to ten."

"Hell, man, you're just procrastinatin'." John couldn't restrain his disgust.

Balzer turned bloodshot eyes away from John and collapsed on a kitchen chair. "You have no idea of the pressures I'm under, Harrison."

"I think I do. I've avoided the issue because I wanted to give you a chance to work it out for yourself. But Manly and Langley are going to cancel the contract if you quit. Then where will they go?"

"No contract is as valuable as a man's family." Balzer offered that opinion with a vehemence that forced John to reconsider his own determination to confront Harner or whoever it was that was intimidating Balzer.

"Just as I suspected," John felt equal parts of sympathy and exasperation. "Has someone threatened your family?"

"Yes. I can't take it much longer." Balzer stood up, carefully drew aside the kitchen curtains and searched for the watchers across the street. "They aren't there today; but I know you've seen them."

"Where is your family? I haven't seen them for some time." For the first time in weeks, John noticed that the house was suffering from indifferent maintenance: dust on the tables, unwashed dishes and the odor of spoiled food. John suddenly felt guilty; while he had worked in the shop during the day and had enjoyed New York's many forms of entertainment at night, Stephen Balzer had sent his family away to safety and suffered alone.

"Do you know who's behind the threat?"

"No." Balzer shuffled into the living room and opened a desk drawer. He retrieved a sheet of paper on which the following message was printed from newspaper clippings:

"If you finish the engine for Langley on time, your family will pay for that achievement with their lives. Look out your window tomorrow for proof that we mean business."

"When did you receive this message?" John asked.

"In late February, just about the time I told Langley that a test in late March should yield twenty horsepower."

"Twenty-horses?" John sneered. He felt guilty, as if he had failed Balzer in some way. "Why this piece of trash won't yield more than eight. Why didn't you show me this warning then?"

"I was afraid you would try to force me to go forward. I was frightened and confused. Now I'm exhausted and even more frightened."

And we're way behind schedule, John thought, his mind a mix of anger, guilt and compassion for Balzer. *Poor devil! This is much more serious than I thought. It takes a lot of money and influence to keep up this kind of pressure on Balzer. Who could be behind this campaign of intimidation? Whoever it is, Mike Coyle hasn't been able to help much. So it must come from outside of Tammany. Maybe Jerry Ashley would have some ideas.* "Don't worry about the motor. I'm sorry I wasn't payin' attention. Try to relax today and let me call on a few friends for help. I'll get back to you tomorrow with a plan."

CHAPTER TWENTY-SIX

NEW YORK CITY
APRIL, 1899

That night, after Jerry and John had ogled the sublime Lillian Russell in Offenbach's *La Belle Helene*, they stood outside the Casino and searched for a hansom. "Usually, we might join the crowd at one of the better restaurants, perhaps Luchow's on Union Square," Jerry said. "But we have an invitation to something special. Have you ever heard of Monk Eastman?"

The question startled John. Hadn't Mike Coyle and Paul Kelly said that Zeke Harner had been seen with Eastman, even looked like him? "I've heard of him—mostly bad. Why do you ask?"

"Monk may look like the devil; but he's a man of startling sensitivity. Why, I believe he has over a hundred cats and maybe five hundred pigeons in his house and his store on Broome Street." Ashley hailed a hansom and held the door for John to enter. "Anyway, Monk has invited us to a racket at his place on Chrystie Street near Canal."

"What's a racket?"

"A dance. The women are usually selected from the most beautiful prostitutes in the Bowery. The men, though armed and a bit rough, are properly dressed, maybe even over-dressed. I think you'll find it amusing."

By the time they reached Chrystie Street, the racket had spilled out into the street. Several hundred people were dancing to two orchestras. John noticed that perhaps fifty bicycles leaned against Monk Eastman's headquarters.

"Why so many bicycles, I wonder?" John murmured to Jerry.

"Oh that's one of Monk's sidelines. They probably belong to Crazy Butch's 'Squab Wheelers.' Monk has let it be known that if you're a friend, you'll rent a bicycle from him at least twice a week. So Crazy Butch organized the Squab Wheelers. He lives around the corner on Forsyth Street."

The range of Jerry's knowledge—and acquaintances—once again astonished John. They paused at the entrance of Monk's headquarters to survey the street scene. Suddenly, John felt a presence behind him. He turned to face one of the ugliest men he had ever seen, unquestionably the redoubtable Monk Eastman. While many were elegantly dressed in tuxedos, Monk's dark wool serge suit had not been near a pressing or cleaning for months, maybe years. A thin black necktie against a dirty, soft-collared shirt was Monk's only concession to the festive occasion. His head resembled a melon that had suffered so many bruises that its puffy welts and folds concealed its original shape. Unshaven with uncombed hair, Monk startled John because of his extraordinary resemblance to Zeke Harner.

"Monk!" Jerry said with a delighted smile. "Allow me to introduce my friend, John Harrison. He makes bicycles in California."

"I heard about dat." Monk's attempt at a welcoming smile with his puffy lips became a grimace with overtones of a sneer. "But youse is most famous for yer new motor. Come wid me."

John and Jerry exchanged bewildered looks and followed Monk up a flight of stairs to a private office. The walls were adorned with an enviable collection of street brawling weapons: Bessies, knucks, lead pipes, revolvers and even several shotguns. The aroma of unwashed bodies permeated the room. John suddenly felt the air was stifling with menace. Monk took a seat behind an ancient desk while three of his henchmen stood at the door.

"I don' like violence," Monk started. "I like de kits and de boids and almost anyone who likes de bikes. But a friend tells me dat youse is pushin' Buzzer to finish wid de motor. Iz dat right?"

"I say, Monk," Jerry protested, "what's this all about? I thought you invited us to this racket to have fun?"

"Shut up!" Monk was clearly in no mood for small talk. His mouth held an ominous pout and his right hand rested on a lead pipe. "I invited youse here to give you a personal warning. Me and my friends want you to go back to California. Leave Buzzer alone."

"What if I tell you to go to hell?" John asked with a rage that he could barely restrain.

Monk turned a cold eye on his three henchmen, who had simultaneously reached for weapons after John's unfriendly outburst. "Youse is a tough guy, Harrison. An' yer family is far away. But Buzzer takes de heat if youse don't listen to me. New York ain't good for your health any more."

John looked at Jerry Ashley with dismay and anger and disgust. So it had come to this. Should he take the case to Roosevelt? No, he was much too busy to annoy with this trifle. Should he go back to Mike Coyle? Then he remembered a note that he had received from Mike that afternoon. With apologies for the delay in replying to John's case, Mike had said that he and Paul Kelly had been ordered to back off from the whole situation. No more help from that quarter. Should he ask the police to protect Balzer? Why should the likes of Commissioner Williams lift a finger? John couldn't even identify the real brains behind all the intimidation. Certainly the thug in front of him had no interest in the motor. He was merely acting for someone who had enough power to stifle even Tammany and the chief of the Five-Pointers. Maybe he could get Monk to tell me him who that is. "What do you care about the damned engine, Eastman?"

"Dat's none of yer b'iness," Monk snarled. "I jes want youse out of town. Youse can have one more week to clean up yer affairs. Then we go after Buzzer and we go after his family." Monk's face made another small effort at a smile. "He can't hide dem. I got watchers watching dem right now." His face was a map of arrogant confidence. His own lead pipe close at hand, he seemed to be torn between impatience to get back to the party and a certain subtle eagerness to spread some blood—John's blood—around the room.

His senses at a high state of alert, John suddenly smelled musk, a rancid odor exuded by filthy clothing, stiff on the outside with the residue of spilled food and dried blood from old battles, moist on the inside with nervous sweat, redolent with a myriad of effluents from unwashed bodies and highly efficient as a means of communicating a bio-chemical blending of squalor and terror.

No wonder Jerry Ashley douses himself in cologne! John thought idly. *That's his only defense against these hoodlums.* If he had been in the Rockies facing a grizzly, John would have felt safer. At least he would have had a knife and a Winchester. He wondered if Jerry had any experience with street-fighting. Probably not. What were his chances against these thugs? Were they really as brutal as their reputations? He remembered a story about one Patrolman Dennis Sullivan who had been set upon by several Eastmans one night on Greenwich Street. After taking away his nightstick, his revolver and his shield, they beat him senseless with stones and blackjacks. Once he had lost consciousness, four of his assailants ground their hob-nailed heels into his face as a permanent reminder of their disrespect. The memory of that story suddenly turned John's quivering rage to a debilitating sense of helplessness. He made a decision. "Suppose I design my own engine in California?"

"Youse can do any damn t'ing youse wants t' do out dere. Jes stay away from Buzzer an' his health won't suffer."

"Let's get out of here, Jerry. I think we've concluded our business with Mr. Eastman." For a moment, John thought the other three "Eastmans" would defy their boss and attack. He edged his way towards the wall of weapons.

But Monk stood up abruptly and led the way out of the room and down the stairs. John could feel the menace at his back until he breathed the balmy April air on the street. Boiling with frustration, he failed to notice an exchange of smiles as Jerry Ashley handed Monk a narrow brown envelope.

"I'm terribly sorry, old man," Jerry said. "If I had had any inkling of such an outrage, I would never have brought you down here."

"It's not your fault, Jerry," John said soberly. "The fact is that we have run into some serious technical obstacles anyway. I don't think Balzer can solve them, not with his rotary design."

"So what will you do? Go on to Europe?"

"I have to talk to Charlie Manly first." John had never felt so stung by defeat. His mind was a turmoil of fear, resentment, guilt and a raging hunger for some decisive act that might obliterate Monk Eastman, Zeke Harner... and obscure faces on Wall Street, just for good measure. "Manly and Langley are already unhappy with our progress. If we were closer to success, maybe I'd take this problem to Roosevelt. But I think it would be criminal to proceed at the risk of hurtin' Balzer's family. It's not worth it."

"So you'll leave before the end of next week?"

"I reckon so. Maybe I'll go to Rochester to see that feller, Selden. If I design a different kind of engine in Monterey, his advice about patent strategy might be right useful."

"Good idea," Jerry said almost too quickly. "I'll certainly miss our nightly trips around New York; but your departure sounds like the better part of valor."

CHAPTER TWENTY-SEVEN

NEW YORK CITY
MAY, 1899

When he awakened late next morning, John discovered that a shattered dream has a distinctive taste of bile and bitterness. His dream-filled night before this worse-than-hangover taste was the first of many sleepless nights that would painfully reprise the might-have-been's and the should-have-done's of his confrontation with New York's comfortable conspiracy among its underworld, the Tammany Wigwam and Wall Street. As he lay in bed, he reflected whither his glory road now that it had led him over a cliff? Must he abandon forever his dreams of a small motor, his golden key to something glorious?

His faith in himself—not to mention Balzer and Manly—might not have been so damaged if he could have indicted only Eastman and his shadowy (Wall Street?) master. But his innate honesty warned him that the roots of his failure were deeper than any financial flim-flam or Bowery gang intimidation. At some deep level of his mind, he told himself ruefully, he had anticipated failure. My God he wondered. Could Maggie be right? Do we already know our own future?

While he closed his eyes and luxuriated in a hot bath, he played with unfamiliar ideas, *Could free will be merely our right to rearrange the props, the stage set of our lives, so as to excuse or explain something that's already pre-destined? Are we just pawns in a larger game?* The thought appealed to him momentarily as a lovely rationale, not only for his failure but also for all sorts of childishness in what Maggie's philosophers' graciously called "the human condition." If God had already discounted human frailty in His plan for their redemption, why blame one's self for living up to one's reputation with God? Let *Him* worry about the Great Plan, whose paragraph labelled "Damage Control" must have anticipated humanity's propensity to sin.

But such a facile excuse for irresponsible self-forgiveness didn't rest easily on his mind. In fact, that line of thought led him to a searing self-indictment. Why had he been so angry at Balzer for slowing down? What about his own dedication? After February, at the peak of his optimism, had he buckled down to work like a Trojan? Had he tried to solve the problem of multiple cylinders joined to a single crankshaft? Had he offered any advice on the location of an oil sump when the bottom of the crankcase had to be open for at least one cylinder? Had he proposed any method for cooling the cylinders except by the variable speed of the aerodrome? Had he suggested anything to reduce drag? Hell no! He had played all night, slept all morning and worked less than half a day every day for six weeks. And he had boasted about their progress at the top of his lungs to the most ruthless crowd of financial cut-throats in the city. To escape from his own doubts, had he just begged for someone to interfere?

Burdened by such guilty thoughts, harsh judgments and too many questions, John rubbed himself on a fleecy hotel towel, wrapped himself in a terrycloth bathrobe and strolled to the door for his morning paper. Two letters caught his attention. One was from Tom Baldwin, which he opened instantly.

Since you left five months ago, I have thought a lot about your interest in an engine for an aerodrome and your experience with bicycles. Because of my own interest in powered airships, I have gone out of my way to learn about the progress of engine builders here and in Europe. As I told you when you were here, when I tried a Pierce-Arrow engine five years ago, it was too heavy. French engines weren't powerful enough then.

John reflected on the simplicity of everyone's fundamental problem. Up to that moment, a century of fumbling and bumbling had yielded many deaths and many more failures. But there was still a race for a small, powerful engine. He refused to believe that he had been eliminated from the race.

Even Count DeDion and the German manufacturers haven't made much progress on either a reliable engine for a motor car or a smaller engine for an airship, not to mention an aerodrome. So I urge you to reconsider your idea of going to Europe; I think you would be disappointed. Of course, if your purpose is only the pleasure of travel, I would encourage you....

Allow me to suggest an alternate plan. Please consider returning to your original objective; namely, designing an engine for a moto-cycle. If you can do that, you could then aim at a somewhat heavier power plant for my airship. Why am I so interested in moto-cycles? Because they are the ideal machine for racing. And racing will attract large crowds. And I know how to handle large crowds, including separating them from their money.

My research has uncovered two good leads for you on your way back to California. The first is a bunch of bicycle-racing enthusiasts in a little town at the southern tip of the finger lakes, south of Rochester, New York. They call themselves the Hammondsport Boys. I hear that they race every weekend at a place called Stony Brook Farm where a fellow named Champlin breeds trotters. Why not stop off at Rochester and detour south for a few days to see if the Hammondsport Boys can teach you anything?

My second lead is a company in Buffalo called the E.R. Thomas Company. They are already making small automobiles. They're also developing a moto-cycle called the "Thomas Auto-Bi." Why not check into it to see if you and Thomas can teach each other something?

Finally, I have decided to join you in California.... I'm too old to keep up a steady quarrel with Carrie, who seems to think I'm playing around with our housekeeper. It may take me a few months to wind up affairs here; but I would hope to reach California within another eighteen months. If you can have your own engine in operation by then, we can start building powered airships as soon as I get there. So I say: forget Langley, the rotary engine and the aerodrome. Design your own on different principles, maybe a stationary engine: a radial.

The second letter was from Ned Ambler. It was brief and to the point.

You should high-tail it back here and build a moto-cycle. The enthusiasm here for racing is growing every day. All your friends are asking, "Where's John? Why can't we get a moto-cycle from him?" I would be the last person to interfere with your dream of an engine for Langley's aerodrome. Maggie has kept me fully informed about your progress. But if success isn't staring you in the face right now; or if you are dissatisfied with your progress, COME HOME.

The coincidence of the two letters startled John. Why *should* he tie his kite to the Balzer engine? Could Monk Eastman, some unknown Wall Street mogul, Tom Baldwin and Ned Ambler be members of some strange conspiracy, all dedicated to returning him to his proper destiny? He wouldn't allow his mind to follow such speculation very far; it reminded him too much of the way Maggie's mind worked. But he could feel the pressure pointing him home.

That afternoon, he walked through Central Park, went to the zoo, fed the pigeons and helped a small boy win a race with his beautiful model sailboat. The enthusiasm of the boy and his young mother, as vivacious as Maggie in form and spirit, capped the day with an excitement that John had not felt for a long time. At least he had been diverted from a fog of confusion that obscured his vision of the future. The brilliant blue sky, fresh air, joyful spring flowers dancing in the wind and the aroma of new-mown grass had awakened sweet memories of Carmel.

When he returned from Central Park, John was mildly surprised that Jerry Ashley had not left a message. John had come to think of Jerry as a friend. He had expected Jerry to call, perhaps to offer another evening with Marie and Mathilde as consolation for the Balzer motor fiasco. That night, he ate a quiet supper alone in the Plaza Hotel. He felt that it was just as well that Jerry had not called because he had no appetite for the theater or slumming or rich food or—and he was mildly astonished to admit this to himself—another lesson from M and M.

At noon next day, John joined Stephen Balzer for lunch in the Plaza to say goodbye. Balzer told John that he had talked to Charles Manly on the phone the night before. He had once again postponed any test on the grounds that the engine needed radiating fins. He pleaded with John to say nothing about the threats . "I've lost nearly all my money on this project," he complained over coffee. "But even worse, I've lost my confidence. Maybe I should abandon the engine for a while and learn to live again without the constant threat of attack against my family."

"You can't do that! You must continue—somehow. What about the Europeans? Could we learn much from them now?" John wondered if Balzer might validate Tom Baldwin's judgement.

"The current issue of *Scientific American* describes in great detail the only engine worth attention. It's a single cylinder gasoline engine designed by De Dion and his engineer, named Bouton."

"How does it differ from our engine?"

"Two big differences: the ignition system and the cylinder head. For ignition, it uses the high-tension, 'jumping' technique: the sparkplug. For cooling, the cylinder head has many fins to increase the area of radiation. I think it will become a very popular engine for small vehicles like De Dion's tricycle. I wish we were as far ahead as they are."

"Don't fault yourself," John pleaded. "You've made some major advances. And you've taught me much about the limits of the rotary design. I'll call Manly and try to buy some time for you. I'll also keep you informed of my progress in California."

They parted friends and John went back to Central Park in search of more clarity and self-renewal from nature. After supper that evening, he nursed his wounded ego with a Mark Twain novel. The next morning, to his surprise, he once again found two letters under his morning paper. One was from Maggie; the other was from Wilbur Wright.

Maggie's note was brief and plaintive.

Today marks the anniversary of your departure for the Spanish-American War. Are you ever coming home? Everyone misses you: the ranch hands, Ramon, Davey and me most of all. Carmel has never been so beautiful. The ice plant is in full flower; around the house, my honeysuckle is so sweet that you think you have fallen into syrup. There is a mysterious magic to the mix of your favorite aromas: gum trees and seaweed and wild flowers and succulents and the familiar ranch smells.

Have you forgotten that your son will have his fourth birthday at the end of this month? He has adopted an expression of habitual sadness because he no longer believes me when I say "Soon" in answer to his question, "When will Poppa come home."

We don't simply miss you, John. We NEED you.

John held that letter in his hands for a long time while he stared unseeing at Central Park and saw the road from Monterey across the Aguajito into the Carmel Valley, saw the long, low house hugging its hill, saw the lyrical, well-remembered sweep of Carmel Bay from the Peninsula, saw dramatic images that traced his life from his childhood to this moment. He felt unaccustomed mist in his eyes. Now there was no question; he *must* return to California.

Impulsively he reached for the telephone and called Charlie Manly to explain the pressure under which Balzer had been working.

"Hell's bells!" Manly replied. "We don't have to tolerate such nonsense. We'll grant him an extension and bring him down here to work with us."

Then John explained that family pressures demanded his return to California. He would catch a train to Rochester the next day. Despite Manly's warm appreciation of John's situation, John felt defeated and deflated. He idly opened the letter from Wilbur Wright.

I want to express my gratitude to you for putting my life back on the right track. Last November, your own hunger for flight inspired me more than you can know. Don't ever give up! And thanks for your help with the team at the Smithsonian. Charles Manly sent us a rich treasure of pamphlets and books and we have been pouring through them eagerly.

We have made a bamboo model of the kite that we sketched that evening when you were here. The model has three pairs of struts, one pair at the center and one pair at each end.

We're using a modified Pratt truss like the design that Octave Chanute used in his two-surface glider. To maintain the
rigidity of the kite, we retained the Pratt trusses to join
each pair of end-struts to the central pair. But we have removed the small trusses between each pair of struts so that
we can experiment with wing-warping.

So far, the small model has taught me a lot. I will now
begin to build a larger kite, a simple biplane with a wingspan of about five feet. I plan to use pine for the structure. I'll cover it with a fabric that I'll seal with
shellac. The wings will have an arch to them. With any luck,
I should complete the kite by the end of July. I expect to do
most of the construction. For the moment, Orv doesn't seem to
be as passionate about this project as I am.

As for the motor, I'm not going to worry about it now.
We'll pray that you will have designed the perfect motor by
the time we are ready for it.

PART V

HOMECOMING

"'Mid pleasures and palaces though we may roam,
Be it ever so humble, there's no place like home;
A charm from the skies seems to hallow us there,
Which sought through the world is ne'er met with elsewhere."

JOHN HOWARD PAYNE HOME, SWEET HOME

CHAPTER TWENTY-EIGHT

HAMMONDSPORT, NEW YORK
MAY, 1899

John Harrison hid in his Pullman compartment as his train made its way west from New York City to Rochester. No amount of sleep and day-dreaming and good food could banish his sense of failure and, worse, cowardice. Would he ever recapture the promise of an engine as his key to something glorious? He felt no confidence in such a prospect. He could think of no reason at all for going to Europe. Even this side trip to Hammondsport seemed futile if not silly. What could a bunch of bicycle racers possibly offer him in his current despairing state of mind?

As a smaller train carried him south from Rochester along the western edge of Lake Canandaigua, he consoled himself with the vision of spring-time feathery green across the countryside. From Bath, he took the nine-mile Bath and Hammondsport Railroad through acres of vineyards to the southern tip of "Crooked Lake," Lake Keuka. From the tiny lakeside depot, his first glimpse of Hammondsport, population 1100, made him grin with satisfaction. Nestled at the lake's edge between two hill masses, it seemed the apotheosis of small-town America. It reminded him that more than half of all Americans lived in towns with a population of less than 5000.

He strolled from the station into a beautiful little park, criss-crossed by a sidewalk, surrounded by small shops and adorned with a band stand at the western edge and a Civil War monument at its center. Colorful awnings cast shade in front of westward-facing shops. Horse-drawn carriages tied to railings in front of the shops proclaimed the park as the commercial center of the village. A strident whistle suddenly disturbed the peace and announced the imminent departure of a steamboat, bound for Pen Yan twenty miles away at the northern end of the lake. John's senses inhaled the lively busy-ness of the town's sounds and smells and sights. His tensions seemed to drain away while he strolled from one shop to the next.

When he paused in front of Saylor's photographic studio, it occurred to him that the photographer must be well informed about local events. As soon as he entered the shop, he assessed a tanned, lean young man behind the counter. For all his youth—John thought he couldn't be older than 20 or 21—his balding head, serious eyes and thin mustache conveyed an impression of sober maturity. He wore a clean white shirt with a dark tie twisted in a permanent knot and a cloth workman's cap on the back of his head. "How do," John said. "My name is John Harrison."

"I'm Glenn Curtiss. What can I do for you, John Harrison?"

"I've heard of a crowd of bicycle racers called the Hammondsport Boys. I'd like to meet them, maybe see them race."

"Why? Are you a betting man? Do you race bicycles?" In one burst of energy, Curtiss revealed two habits of a lifetime: define every situation in terms of reasonable options and learn every shred of relevant information before choosing one.

"Yes to both questions." John had never raced bicycles; but he thought his reply was more likely to lead him to his goal. "I make bicycles in California. I plan to put a motor on one to see what will happen."

For a moment Curtiss stared at John as if to stimulate more revelations. When they weren't forthcoming, he began to quiz John about bicycles. "Have you heard of the Stearns racer?"

"Can't say that I have. What does a Stearns weigh?"

"Seventeen pounds."

"Does it win?"

"Whenever I ride it, it does." Glenn could be forgiven for his pride. John soon learned the story of Glenn's local fame. After "Tank" Waters first persuaded him to join the Hammondsport Boys four years earlier, when Glenn had been a Western Union messenger, he had won many cash prizes at county fairs and racing meets. Jim Smellie, a pharmacist, had encouraged Glenn's passion for speed by arranging for him to buy a $100, yellow Stearns racer at a price of $50, which Glenn had paid for by installments. Now Glenn was the leader of the Hammondsport Boys. "The Hammondsport Boys will race at Champlin's racetrack tomorrow. You're welcome to come along if you like."

"Fine! Can you direct me some place to stay the night?"

Curtiss studied the stranger shrewdly. An honest face with good eyes: grey and steady with some pain behind them. He might find a room at any one of the several small hotels in town. But why let *them* take John's money when Lena could use it to better advantage. "My wife, Lena, and I live near here with my grandmother. I think the women would be glad to rent you a room." After a moment's reflection, he added, "I'll borrow a bicycle for you and we can go to my place right now... unless you have something else to do first?"

"Not at all. I'd be pleased to stay with you."

That evening, John learned something of Glenn's history from his quiet, attractive wife of fourteen months and Ruth, his energetic grandmother. His father and grandfather had died within a year of each other. Six years later, in 1888, his mother, Lua, had moved to Rochester to watch over his sister, Rutha, who had enrolled in Zenas Westervelt's Institution for Deaf Mutes after meningitis had stolen Rutha's hearing. To finish the eighth grade, the end of his formal education, Glenn remained under his grandmother's indulgent supervision for three years. In 1892, he moved to Rochester to help his mother. He worked for the Eastman Kodak Company for a year before he became a Western Union messenger and succumbed to a growing obsession with speed and bicycle racing, first among the messengers and later as one of the Hammondsport Boys. A born tinkerer, Glenn diffused his energies among photography, bicycle repair for Jim Smellie, harvesting Catawba grapes from his grandmother's vineyard, racing his heart out every weekend and loving Lena and Ruth.

John awakened early the next morning and walked outside to survey the splendid vista from the plateau on which the Curtiss home stood. He could see the lake and the bustling little village nestled between spring green hills covered with vineyards. He thought the hills looked like crouching sentinels, standing guard over Pleasant Valley and its "port." For a moment, Monk Eastman, Stephen Balzer and Jerry Ashley seemed a million miles away. He cleared the New York catastrophe from his mind and simply surrendered to the balm of springtime in Hammondsport.

After a hearty breakfast of eggs, smoked bacon, crisp toast, cold grape juice and black coffee, he and Glenn Curtiss set out on the three-mile ride to Stony Brook Farm. They had raised a thin sweat by the time they reached the farm, to find two dozen other competitors tinkering with drive-chains, tires and seats. The racers wore corduroy or wool knee britches or trousers clipped at the shoes. Against a nip in the air, over striped cotton shirts they also wore light wool coats or sweaters. Each of the "Boys" sported a red and white baseball cap with the initials "G.H." on the bill.

For two hours they raced free-for-all, by pairs and finally by teams of four. John realized that he could hold his own with everyone except Glenn Curtiss, whose Stearns racer clearly had the edge. By the time they broke for lunch, courtesy of Harry Champlin, the owner of the farm, John knew that the others accepted him as a strong competitor. He asked, "Have you ever considered makin' your own racers, Glenn?"

Glenn frowned when several of his friends snickered at the question. "Don't mind them; and you might as well call me 'G.H.' All my friends do. They're just teasing me 'cause I've designed something I call 'the Hercules.' I think it'll leave the Stearns in the dust."

The Hammondsport Boys grinned and nudged one another and rolled their eyes at the very absurdity of such a thing. John munched on a spicy meatloaf sandwich and washed it down with Champlin champagne. "Why don't you build it?"

"Are you serious?" Glenn asked. "It takes money, money I don't have right now."

John looked speculatively at Jim Smellie, whittling on a willow stick and listening to the conversation with calculated indifference. Glenn had told John two things about Jim. First, he liked to bet on just about any gamble from bicycle races to the probability of a change in wind direction. Second, his pharmacy business was expanding so well that he was thinking about getting out of the bicycle repair and spare-parts game. "How much would it take to get started? Would a thousand dollars move you off dead center?"

Glenn and Jim Smellie stared at John. Jim could feel an itch on the back of his neck, a reliable warning of an investment in the air, maybe a bet. He asked idly, "Now where would G.H. get a thousand dollars?"

John studied Glenn thoughtfully. The key to victory in any race was not just fine equipment. The rider must also bring special qualities to the game. The past two hours had demonstrated Glenn's endurance and his remarkably strong legs. But did he have a winning spirit? Did he have grit? "How important is winnin' to you, G.H.?"

"Shoot, what's the use of racing if you don't think you can win?"

"Do you think you and I could win a race against twenty-four men?"

"What kind of race?" Jim Smellie forgot his pretense of the idle whittler.

"G.H. and I compete with the rest of you. He and I alternate on the Stearns bicycle for twenty-four laps around the track, twelve laps each." John figured he was good for six miles, twelve laps around Champlin's half-mile track, before his dissipation in New York might catch up with him. "At the end of each lap, a fresh competitor waits until we can trade off the Stearns. That way, we start each race from a standin' start. The winner is whoever wins thirteen laps. I put up the thousand dollars for our team."

There was a long silence while everyone thought about the idea. This was clearly not a test of bicycles. Of course the Stearns would give Glenn and John a slight edge. But the race would be a test of endurance of two men against the physical stamina of the entire club. Jim Smellie knew the strengths of everyone there. He was inordinately proud of Glenn's many victories, but he had a hunch that Glenn and the stranger would wear down before they could win so many laps. "What do you say, G.H.?"

Glenn regarded John with new interest. What were this stranger's motives? If they won, would they split their winnings? And what had he, Glenn, done to capture the stranger's trust? What made John think that he wouldn't lose deliberately and later split John's money with his own friends? Well, by God, he would vindicate such trust! "I'm in, Jim; how about you?"

"I'll put up the thousand; but the winner must win fifteen laps. And I manage the Boys. If either team fails to win fifteen, it's a draw." Jim figured he would race the weaker members of the club for the first eight or nine races; the Stearns would win them anyway. But then he could sandbag the tiring challengers with increasingly strong club members. If his team could win just two of the first twelve races, fresh, strong riders should be able to steal the march on at least eight of the last twelve. Those ten victories would make it a draw. He thought his bet was well hedged.

"Tell you what, Jim," Glenn said. "We'll agree to that if you'll throw in all your spare parts if we win. That way, I can start my own bicycle business with my share of the winnings." He was pleased that John readily assented to his proposal. It had the effect of reassuring John that Glenn had the incentive of a bonus for winning, not losing deliberately.

"I'll agree to that," Jim said. "But there will be no breaks, no rest periods."

The first race went as predicted. Glenn easily outdistanced Lou Hazard, a newcomer to the club. But John lost the second lap while he tried to accustom himself to the delicate balance of the Stearns racer. He also cursed himself for miscalculating his stamina. As the heat of the day climbed, the champagne that he had guzzled for lunch also sapped his strength. He gritted his teeth and swore to win the fourth lap after Glenn once again sailed around the track far in advance of a fresh competitor.

John lost the fourth lap almost instantly when he pushed too hard on the pedals while the front wheel was turned aside. His weight promptly knocked the Stearns racer to the ground. By the time he had retrieved his balance and his dignity, his competitor was far ahead. While Glenn won the fifth lap, John pondered the situation. A pre-cognitive sense warned him that his physical condition and the unfamiliar bicycle were a formula for disaster. He consoled himself with the thought that Glenn could probably pull twelve victories out of his twelve laps. That meant that John must win three. He did ten push-ups and twenty deep-knee bends before massaging his thighs and lower legs. When he retrieved the Stearns from Glenn's third victory, he willed himself to relax. His opponent was a stocky young fellow who was already breathing heavily before Harry Champlin fired the starting gun. John sailed home with a solid victory for the sixth race, giving him and Glenn a score of 4-2.

Once again, Glenn won the seventh race without a whimper. *Iron man!* John thought. *Why, he's hardly sweating! What the hell have I let myself in for?*

Farm hands from the Champlin farm had gathered around the track. Some of Harry's friends had arrived and were placing side bets with Harry

Champlin and Jim Smellie.

John managed to win the eighth race by about ten yards. But the experience had wounded him. He collapsed on his back and spread-eagled himself in the tall grass. He tried to remember his endurance in his glory days: hard rides in the saddle in the Rockies; roundups and fighting the Spaniards in Cuba. But his legs complained about the unaccustomed exertion and his heaving chest reminded him that New York had not prepared him for this torture.

Glenn casually sailed around the track for their seventh victory. When Harry Champlin touched John for the tenth lap, he groaned silently and seized the Stearns from Glenn. At the quarter-mile, he knew he was in trouble. He was neck-and-neck with a fresh competitor who gradually pulled ahead to win. The score now stood at 7-3.

While Glenn took off for the eleventh race, John thought, *Fourteen more laps. If Glenn even wins three, it'll be a draw.* The growing crowd on the sidelines evidently had reached the same conclusion. John could hear excited voices responding to Jim Smellie's quotation of changing odds. *Well, what the hell,* John thought, *tonight I'll either be famous or infamous. But this beats the opera and Madison Square Garden and Delmonico's and all the whorehouses in New York. I had forgotten how much I enjoy it.*

After Glenn won the fifteenth race and made the score 10-5, the Boys could no longer win. Gleefully, Jim Smellie deftly shifted the bets to "win versus draw" and the crowd began to smell blood. While Glenn's stamina sustained his extraordinary run of victories during races seventeen, nineteen, twenty-one and twenty-three, ever stronger club members handed John four defeats in a row. They taught him painfully how far he had allowed his body to drift from peak efficiency. A dry mouth, a pounding heart, glazed eyes and an ache in every muscle in his body warned him that he had reached a dangerous level of over-exertion. He offered Glenn hoarse congratulations for his twelfth consecutive victory after the twenty-third lap.

The score stood at 14-9.

In a kind of floating despair, he climbed on the Stearns racer only to feel Jim Smellie seize the handlebars. "I'm sorry, John. We have to wait a moment. My twelfth team-member has been called away on an emergency. I have to decide who will ride the last race against you."

Anxiety and excitement written across the faces of onlookers warned John that this unexpected climactic twenty-fourth lap would be a hostage to heavy money. For the next half-hour, Smellie's gambling instincts savored the situation like nothing he had experienced in years. For the final round of bets, it lay within his power to shift the odds one way or the other merely by his selection of the final rider. Even though some bettors had already lost or won earlier rounds of bets, the drama of the final race compelled everyone to stay and face the outcome. For a moment, Jim had history in his palms. He knew that he also had his own reputation for even-handedness riding on this race. Only he knew that he had already won more than $1000 on side bets. And he also *wanted* to give his bicycle business to Glenn. So how could he arrange for Glenn and the stranger to win without obviously throwing it away? What precedent could he use to validate his selection of the club's final competitor?

"Ladies and gentlemen," he announced finally. "As temporary team manager for the Hammondsport Boys, I've come to a decision about their final racer. But I'm disqualified to calculate odds for another round of bets. After I announce our team's final competitor, I'll give Harry Champlin another half-hour to offer new odds and take bets on the race." He looked at his watch. "It's now three o'clock. The race will start promptly at three-thirty."

"Who's your boy, Jim?" a voice rang out from the crowd.

"And why?" another voice followed.

"I think it's only fair to use the rules of our national sport: baseball," Jim said. "The Boys have followed a batting order today. In the absence of the last batter, I must call on the first racer for the team to go to bat again."

"Hell, Jim, he's fresher than anyone. Look at John Harrison; the man's dog-tired. Why, you're throwing the race to the Hammondsport Boys."

But John had discovered a second wind. The half-hour of wrangling had been a god-send for his tortured body. His heart no longer complained as if it might explode from his chest; the rest and the balm of the warm afternoon sun had muted his muscle soreness; and his mouth seemed almost normal after he had rinsed it repeatedly with grape juice.

Glenn Curtiss gave him an added boost. "Don't let 'em get you down, John. Let me tell you something about Lou Hazard, your competition. He's new at racing. He can't stand it if you tail him. He might win if you're just in front of him. But if you just stay right behind him until the last two hundred yards, he'll be so exhausted from holding on to his lead that he won't have any zip left. Try that strategy and John...."

"Yeah?"

Glenn offered his hand and a heart-warming smile. "Good luck!"

At precisely three thirty, all bets were in and Harry Champlin fired his gun. John felt surprisingly good, limber almost. He made no effort to get ahead of Lou, who was pedalling like a demon. At the quarter-mile post, Lou held a slight lead but he couldn't widen the slight gap that John maintained behind him. As he approached the 220-yard marker, half way home, John felt as if he could ride the little Stearns racer forever. He couldn't remember ever feeling quite so steady before. He felt like a river of energy pacing itself for optimum power without any sense of urgency or panic. With the slightest increase in his rhythm, he began to pull ahead of Lou Hazard. He did it almost casually. While he became aware of a distant roar somewhere near the finish line, it seemed only incidental, an afterthought for his leisurely acceleration. When he sailed across the finish line, he was three bike lengths ahead of Lou.

In later years, John would always remember that victory as his official welcome into Hammondsport society. Glenn Curtiss had tears in his eyes when he embraced John and pounded his back. Jim Smellie conducted a victory ceremony on the spot, congratulated the winners and gave them a thousand dollars in cash. Before Glenn Curtiss could object, John made an announcement. "Before this race, G.H. and I agreed to split the winnin's. But I din't know how important this race would be to me at this particular time. It's taught me a lesson—not so much about racin' as about... livin'. So I herewith donate my half of the winnin's to my partner and his new bicycle b'iness. We'll hear great things from him one of these days."

The crowd went wild with approval. It was a small gesture; but it was offered with sincerity. When John and Glenn returned to Castle Hill that afternoon, the celebration with Lena and Ruth became a high point for John's one-year absence from Carmel. He knew the victory was only a thin scab over his raw emotional wound from New York, which he expected to fester long after a bicycle race faded into memory. But the race had revived his spirit of competition, a gift beyond price. It reminded him that the only way he could ever eradicate his sense of failure in New York would be to build a brilliant motor *before* Balzer or Manly or anyone else. After supper, John asked, "So where'll you get a motor for your Hercules?"

"From the E.R. Thomas Company in Buffalo. That's the future. Why, does a motor interest you?"

"More than you could imagine." John explained his association with Manly and Langley and his interest in a small engine. "As soon as I get home, I'll start work on a new design. I'll keep you informed. Maybe one of these days, we can be partners again."

CHAPTER TWENTY-NINE

CARMEL
MAY, 1899

John Harrison timed his departure from Hammondsport to make connections at Bath, Rochester and Chicago. He sent telegrams to Ned Ambler and to Maggie. He calculated five days from Chicago to Monterey, including an overnight stop in Oakland. Settled into a comfortable Pullman compartment in Chicago, he was grateful that the Attorney General had been able to settle the 1894 dispute between Eugene Debs, the head of the American Railway Union, and the Pullman Palace Car Company, even if the settlement did cost the lives of several union strikers. He couldn't imagine a more luxurious mode of travel as he savored the sights along a route that swept through Iowa and Nebraska to Cheyenne, crossed northern Utah, turned south at Winnemucca, Nevada, started climbing at Reno, poked through the mountains at infamous Donner Pass and finally completed its twisted, tortured passage through the Rockies to reach the welcoming downhill glide through Sacramento to Oakland.

Whether dining in a first-class dining car or gazing vacantly at the passing scene, he reflected on his year of wandering through the drama of war and the more curious drama of competition for a light engine. As he idly watched Iowa and Nebraska plains turn to the greener canyons and foothills of the Rockies, he rearranged the story of the year to explain away his worst mistakes, including his failure to take this five-day trip at least once to see his family. He could rationalize that grievous decision only by underscoring his dedication to the motor—a risky story line since, for the moment at least, it had ended in failure. By the time he stepped down from his Pullman in Oakland, he had concluded that he shouldn't make that one dramatic failure the financial—and emotional—keystone of his post-war past. Thanks to his small victory at Hammondsport, he could now treat it as merely a setback. If he thought of it that way, it could become the foundation for a renewed effort in Carmel. It all fit together rather nicely, he thought, as he assigned heroic or brutish roles to the many personalities who had aided or obstructed his quest. As he thus rebuilt his self-esteem, it was perhaps as well that he couldn't even conceive of frightening new challenges waiting for him at home. His adversaries in Cuba and New York had only tested his pride in his skills. In Carmel he would have to face a challenge to his very sense of reality.

At noon on the last day of May, his heart lifted when he stepped down from the train in Monterey to see Maggie, Davey, Ned Ambler and Ramon Cisneros. Maggie's slender beauty stirred him more than he had imagined. Remembering John's preference for simplicity, she had selected a lacy white shirt-waist, tucked into an ankle-length, rust-colored, cotton skirt, whose light green leather belt accented her petite waist. She had rejected a bustle and the pouter-pigeon look for clean lines and her naturally full bust. But John saw only her light green Bolero jacket and her shining, up-swept auburn hair, surmounted by a ridiculous little yellow straw hat. He removed his own Stetson, held her at arms-length for an instant, whispered, "Maggie, my love!" and crushed her in his embrace. Then he turned to shake hands with Ned and Ramon. "Were you able to find it, Ned?" he asked.

Ned nodded happily. "Just what you wanted, John. Welcome home!"

"Find what?" Maggie wondered. Had Ned and John been conspiring? She felt vaguely troubled by this hint of change in a familiar pattern of authority.

"I'll tell you later, sweetheart." John shook Ramon's hand and inquired in Spanish about his wife and his two sons, Jaime and Juan. Then he finally turned to Davey, who seemed confused about this big man in dark boots, buff corduroy trousers, matching jacket and wide Stetson hat. Momma had told him they were going to meet his Poppa. But this tall, grey-eyed figure was not what his usually impeccable memory recalled of his father.

"And you must think I'm a total stranger, huh?" John asked as he went down on his knees and stared directly into Davey's eyes. "Do you think you could risk a little hug for your Poppa?"

Davey's shy grin masked a suspicion that this man was an impostor. How should he respond to such a heroic figure? John's gentle smile invited Davey to give him a hug, especially since Momma and Ah Ying had warned him to be on his best behavior at the railroad station. At least *they* understood that he was really more interested in the hissing, steaming monster of an engine than he was in the social ritual of a homecoming.

John noted Davey's fascination with the engine and instantly took the first step towards recapturing his son's heart. "You want to see how it works, son? Well, come along with me and I'll explain it." For the next ten minutes, while Ned and Maggie exchanged comments about John's pallor and surprising weight-gain, John honored a four-year old with a simple explanation of a steam engine. Much to Davey's delight, the engineer stepped down from the cab and joined John in the game. By the time John and Davey had thanked the engineer for his help, Davey lost his shyness and was firing questions with a startling grasp of detail that delighted John. In the next instant, John swept Davey high above his head and settled him on his broad shoulders. "If you want to get down, just pull my hair, you hear?"

Davey's wide smile of excitement was a tonic for both Ned and Maggie, who had wondered how the boy might welcome his father. With warm affection, Maggie put her arm around John's waist and hugged him while the party moved to the family carriage. *It's going to be all right,* she thought with an inner smile. *He's a stranger to all of us, but if he will just keep loving Davey, I can handle anything else.*

"What say to a lunch at the Del Monte?" John asked with a smile. "Could you join us, Ramon?"

The invitation astonished both Ned and Maggie. Before he had gone to war, John would never have invited his ranch manager to lunch at the Del Monte lodge. *Who is this man?* Maggie wondered. *Has he suffered some memory-loss about the way we do things around here?*

Ramon was even more flustered by John's gracious invitation. *"Mil gracias, Señor. Pero..., al rancho, tengo muchas obligaciones."*

"Of course, Ramon," John said in Spanish. "I just wanted you to know that I think of you as family. I'm mighty glad to see you. Tell the vaqueros and everyone that I'll want to talk to each of them when I get home."

After fond goodbyes and thank you's, Ramon mounted his own horse. John helped Maggie into a new "American Beauty" buggy. He seized the reins and placed Davey in his lap. "Now you hold onto the reins too, Davey, so's you can see how a horse's mouth feels when he's pullin'." Luggage stored in the rear, the three made their way to the hotel. Ned followed in his own buggy.

CHAPTER THIRTY

CARMEL VALLEY
JUNE, 1899

Next day, Davey celebrated his fourth birthday. He was overjoyed to see Lily Wang. His feelings for "Aunt" Lily were beyond his powers to understand or express. It was not simply their habit of speaking in Chinese. It was a language behind the language that bonded them. It was as if they had known each other much longer than four years. Davey couldn't explain it; it was enough that he adored her.

Lily swept Davey up in her arms and said in Mandarin, "*K'e-aide Da-wei* (lovable David), I have brought you a friend to help celebrate your birthday. You will have to speak to him in Chinese because he understands no English. He is a very wise man and has agreed to tell your future! Isn't that exciting?"

John greeted Lily warmly and waited with curiosity to meet her companion. Lin T'ai-chi was a slender man of medium height, a smile of greeting on his round face. His eyes seemed to glow like embers concealing banked fires. They took in the scene as if their intensity might consume everything in sight.

"I know you remember Mr. Lin, Maggie," Lily said. "He arrived last night from San Francisco to see my father and to discuss the political situation in China. I thought it would be great fun for him to read Davey's '*chi*' on his birthday. I hope you don't feel it's an imposition!"

Behind Liu's mask of a pleasant grin and sparkling eyes, Maggie sensed the same incredible power that had awed her when she had first met him in Shanghai. On the other hand, John saw a rather unimpressive man, seemingly intelligent, who nodded his head as if he had inconvenienced them all. John noted that, throughout introductions Lin focused his attention briefly on each person. However, when Lily introduced him, he could have sworn that Lin probed into him as if to discover some ingredient, some vital essence. He felt himself squirm uncomfortably under Lin's scrutiny.

Finally Lin said quietly to Lily, "We have all been together through many lifetimes. It is so pleasant to meet again."

Maggie wondered nervously how John would react to Lin. Since her avid consumption of *Borderlands*, her zeal for the esoteric equalled John's passion for a small motor. But she didn't want to confront John so soon with their differences. How might Davey react? She reasoned that if she, Lily and John were present, Davey shouldn't be fearful. And it might be good for John to experience a master like Lin. "John, I told you a little about Mr. Lin. He mastered Black Hat Tantric Buddhist studies in Tibet and is now an advisor to the Imperial Court in Peking. His reputation has spread across the world among Chinese circles." She turned to Lin and welcomed him in lilting Mandarin. "Please come out on our terrace. Across the river, the vaqueros will stage trick riding and horse races today. Then we will have a lunch for everyone on the ranch."

After they were seated on the wide terrace overlooking the river and the Santa Lucia Range, Lily noticed that Lin directed most of his attention to Davey. Davey split his energies between explaining the races to Lin and showing some of his sketches to Lily. It was a balmy day, the temperature in the low 70's—perfect for an outdoor feast. After the racing had ended, Maggie led everyone to the south lawn where a huge table groaned under the weight of Mexican dishes: stacks of hot tortillas, stuffed chile-peppers, mounds of rice, tureens of paella-a-la-Valenciana, pungent barbecued beef, large platters of fresh fruit from Ed Berwick's fruit orchards and assorted vegetables. In the shade of the overhang along the entrance to the house, Ramon's three younger brothers strummed guitars and sang the haunting songs of their culture. By one o'clock, over hundred people had gathered together.

When all guests had stuffed themselves to bursting, Ramon announced that it was time for the *piñata*. In this old Mexican tradition, the birthday child is blindfolded, armed with a long stick and charged with breaking open a clay jar, which hangs from a tree and contains many gifts. Maggie said in Spanish that she had changed the tradition slightly. She had carefully wrapped a gift for every child at the party. In later years,

Davey would remind friends that this was the reason he always gave gifts to friends on his own birthday. Encouraged by the other children, Davey soon had demolished the *piñata*, its largesse tumbling out onto the ground.

Lin smiled his approval when Davey stood back and let the other children have first choice of the many toys and small gift packages strewn across the tiles. Then, as if to reward his patience, a vaquero led a beautiful Shetland pony forward.

That was John's cue. He whispered to Maggie, "This is what I asked Ned to find for me." He reached out for his son and lifted him to the pony's back.

"There you are, buster. There's your first mount, all your own with a fine new saddle and bridle."

Davey was so overwhelmed that he couldn't speak. Then he turned to his father and said, "It's the best gift in the whole world... Poppa! Thank you. I'm gonna call her Su-su."

By four o'clock, all guests had said their goodbyes, staff had cleared away the food, and Lily, Lin, Maggie, John and Davey gathered in the library.

"Now I give you my gift, Davey," Lily said. "Mr. Lin will tell you a story in Chinese. I believe you will understand him, but don't hesitate to ask any questions; there is no rush. Maggie can interpret for John." Then she turned to Lin, "Please proceed, Master. He is ready for your lessons."

Lin looked into Davey's eyes with rapt attention. "Please turn your head from left to right several times." After Davey had done that in a smooth, sweeping motion that completed over 200 degrees of a circle, Lin began. "Please understand that the '*ch'i*' is the energy of your life. Some people call it your true Self. That is who I will describe for you now."

"Remember what I told you, Davey?" Lily asked in Mandarin. "Your *ch'i* is the part of you that never dies."

"Like the smoke, Momma?" Davey asked in Mandarin.

Maggie nodded, grateful that John couldn't understand the Chinese language and therefore need not be exposed too dramatically to Davey's inner world.

"It is the sum total of all your lessons through all your past lives," Lin continued. "And you have been blessed with many, many lives. *Your ch'i* energy is focused very high on your forehead. This means that you have already found an unusual understanding of yourself in nature. This is good."

John listened to Maggie's translation in growing astonishment. How could a four-year old kid understand this silliness? "Davey, do you understand what Mr. Lin is sayin'?"

"Some of the words are too big, Poppa. But I think I know what he's saying."

"The earth element of your nature is very high. This means that you have great integrity. There is a clarity between your thoughts and your actions that permits no doubt about their essential unity. This is also good."

Like John, Lily also wondered if Davey was understanding Lin's Chinese. The boy's alert attention suggested that he was having no trouble with the ideas.

"The wood element in your nature is neither too high nor too low. That means that you may listen to instruction and criticism from many sources. But you are a strong oak with deep roots in your *ch'i*. Although you may bend and twist before public pleasure, your integrity cannot be pushed around by fear."

By now, Maggie was whispering a simultaneous translation in John's ear. Whether or not John approved of or believed in the theory of *ch'i*, he welcomed Lin's last comment. It reassured him about his son's manliness.

"The still water element of your nature is a wide lake. It is deep and clear with clean boundaries—no moss or undergrowth at the water's edge. That means that you are very hungry for learning—from everyone and everything."

John wondered how Lin could possibly know these things. How could he be so confident? *Jesus, I wish he had been with me in New York. What would Jerry Ashley say? Probably would ask him to predict the stock market.*

"Your understanding is not simply from the teaching of other people. You draw information from all sources, including your deepest identity, your *ch'i*."

Feeling vindicated, Maggie smiled at John. Perturbed, John nevertheless returned her smile with a warm grin and a squeeze, as if to reassure her. He might be abashed by this little trip into cuckoo-land; but he didn't intend spoiling his homecoming now. He was too happy just to be home with a sweet memory of tender love-making the night before. Maggie felt a rush of gratitude for Lin's reading. It seemed to be the ideal introduction to Davey's psychic gifts. She had wondered how she could explain to John her long battle to help her son craft a mental balance between his physical and metaphysical realities.

With education, Lin continued, you will learn words for what you see and feel. But you don't need my words because you have already learned the trick of becoming. With that skill of empathy, you know that your best sources of learning are not words."

Sometimes, Lily would whisper a single English phrase if she thought Davey might not understand. But she spoke infrequently. She didn't want to interfere with the flow of Lin's thoughts into Davey's mind.

"The running water element of your nature is a wide, long river flowing down to the sea. This means that your life will be filled with friends from not only your own land but even from the ends of the earth. These will not be simply acquaintances. Your relationships will be deep, founded on trust and love."

At first, John had been suspicious of this curious Chinaman. Could Lily have briefed Lin on the family? On Davey's personality? However, by now, he was listening intently to Maggie's translation.

"The fire element of your nature is medium. That means that you are not easily seduced by anger. You have an even temper. But the embers of your fire can be stirred by injustice. Once angered for a just cause, you will not be able to let someone else correct the situation. You will act decisively based on your sense of the dynamic harmony among many factors. That is good."

At this point, Maggie bubbled with questions. John was still so skeptical that he had resolved not to validate this superstitious proceeding with a question.

Lily anticipated Maggie's curiosity. "Let's wait for Lin to finish his reading of Davey's spiritual nature and its implications for his future."

"I see no problems on the horizon with your physical health. You will grow in strength of body and mind, slightly shorter than your father but strong enough for any challenge." Here, Lin paused and said the words that captured the essence of young David Harrison for an entire lifetime.

"You are a warrior. You have always been a warrior. You will always be a warrior. This means that, once again in this lifetime as in so many others, you will have the courage and the strength to fight against all negative forces that would impede your destiny." Gravely, Lin added, "By warrior, I do not mean a killer. Indeed, your warrior spirit is the summation of all the elements of your nature that I have described. Because you are so grounded in an unconscious awareness of your spiritual identity, you are fearless."

After Maggie translated the last few sentences, John smiled slightly. Maybe Lin did know his apples.

"For this reason, you will be a healer. You will help people banish their fears, all of which are self-made. You will be a great leader because you will help people discover within themselves their own warriorhood, their own path home. Their hunger for this discovery of themselves will prompt them to trust you and follow you—even into battle and into the valley of death! I am finished."

As Maggie interpreted to John, she trembled with apprehension that Lin's words had reached into a deep part of herself where she sheltered truth. *Into battle and the valley of death?* She felt her eyes misting and, for a moment, she couldn't speak. Then she said, "Lily, you have given us a memorable gift. I'm overwhelmed."

Throughout Lin's presentation, Davey had not moved. He seemed to accept Lin's statements without any facial or other reaction. Although Momma had talked with him for hours about the nature and power of love, this was his first direct experience with a fortune teller. Now he asked, "How can you know all about me?"

Lin chuckled with pleasure. His eyes sparkling, he said to Lily, "Didn't I tell you? He is not going to be satisfied with my insights. He wants to steal all my knowledge, as well. Everyone is his teacher. I will not get off easily." Turning to Davey, he replied gravely, "My knowledge cannot be explained in a few words. However, I promise that you will acquire the same knowledge as your life progresses. For the moment, I can only tell you that each of us has access to a deep level of understanding. Unfortunately, each of us makes a little self that fights against such profound knowledge."

"Why?" Davey asked. "What are people afraid of?"

Lin smiled. "Knowledge—and God, who is ultimate knowing. It takes great discipline to release the little self from its many fears and to welcome deeper levels of understanding."

John thought Lin sounded like some of the things Maggie used to say. Could he and William James have studied from the same book?

Lin continued, "As you get older, you will discover what I am talking about. That's because your parents will nurture your fearlessness with their love. Never forget that Love is always waiting, always present. Even if you forget to be aware of it, it will always sustain your search along your path."

Recalling his own communion with nature, Davey asked, "Do your ideas come to you in words or in pictures?"

"What I have said has appeared in my mind's eye as clearly as the books in this library. Your spiritual nature is unchanging; but your life experience will certainly expand your awareness of your spiritual identity; for that is the only purpose of a life."

Much of what Lin said reminded Maggie of her discussions with Ned Ambler. The conscious mind must be like the visible part of the solar spectrum. The *ch'i* must be like the invisible part of the spectrum. "How does his *ch'i* relate to his ego?" she asked.

"I have described his spiritual strengths, the pattern of his *ch'i*. The *ch'i* is permanent, it is his essence. His ego is transient like a pair of spectacles for perceiving and responding to life situations. He will design his own ego to learn those unique spiritual lessons that are already imbedded in his life's destiny." Impishly, Lin added one last bombshell. "The reason that he loves Lily so much is because he was her husband in his last lifetime."

Lily giggled and seized Davey in her arms. John and Maggie both laughed at the teasing absurdity of such an idea. But Davey nodded as if he had already known this in some obscure part of his mind.

"Master Lin, how does our science relate to the theory of *ch'i*?" John asked.

After Maggie translated, Lin answered, "Your science does not yet have the confidence to include these invisible energies in its boundaries. These energies embrace a far wider range of human powers and skills than your science and ordinary consciousness can contemplate." Suddenly Lin frowned.

Maggie saw the change in his expression and refused to let him make excuses for his silence. "You must tell us what perturbs you, Master Lin."

Lin paused. How could he avoid an honest answer? He must speak the

truth in response to Maggie's question. He would have preferred a metaphor; for he believed that all of life's experiences were metaphorical tests
and lessons about inner truth. But no metaphor would suit this situation.
"The clarity of your son's *ch'i* has confirmed for me my worst fears for our
countries," Lin said sadly. "A great war is coming. Your son will be in this
war. I do not understand how this will come to pass; but he will fly through
the air."

Perhaps it was at this moment that Maggie's mind first began to turn
against John's fascination with engines and flying machines and the lure of
their great promise to her only son. She felt deeply shaken by a wave of fear
and rage. She didn't dare look at John, lest he discern her moment of hatred for the male infatuation with competition and battle. She knew it was
easy to be skeptical about *ch'i-gung* Masters like Lin. But she had seen too
many of them to doubt their skills. Finally, mustering her courage, she
asked, "Will he live through this war?"

At this question, Lin smiled. "Oh yes! Your loving nature will guide
him through very sorrowful times. He will bring you beautiful grandchil-
dren."

CHAPTER THIRTY-ONE

CARMEL VALLEY
JUNE, 1899

After Lily and Lin departed, John, Maggie and Davey sat down to a light dinner. Maggie could feel John's silence like a heavy pall hanging over the waning hours of Davey's birthday. She tried to strike a cheery note. "What did you think of Master Lin, Davey?"

"I like him." Davey gobbled Ah Ying's spicy shrimp fried rice in peasant fashion, his left hand tilting the bowl slightly at his mouth and his right hand shoveling deftly with chopsticks.

"Did he scare you?" John asked.

Davey stopped gobbling and gave the question some thought. "No, Poppa; but it felt kinda funny for him to know so much about me without asking any questions. Will I change?"

"Don't you think people *can* change?" John asked.

Davey paused to swallow. "I guess people change a lot on the outside. Like eagles and animals, they get bigger, don't they. So people can change the way they talk and act. Momma told me that was their... personality. But Mister Lin wasn't talking about that, was he?"

"No, Davey," Maggie said. "He thinks your *ch'i* is your fundamental nature. Do you understand the relationship between your *ch'i* and your personality?"

"Not really."

John felt a mindless agitation when he saw that Maggie was about to explain that relationship. His role as host had forced him to tolerate the episode with Lin. But the experience had revived all his early doubts about Maggie's infatuation with philosophy and religion before he left for Cuba "My God, Maggie, are you taking that man seriously?"

"What do you mean, John?"

"I hope you won't try to stuff Davey's head full of Mr. Lin's mumbo-jumbo." For some reason, John suddenly felt threatened. "Davey, aren't you confused about all this stuff?"

Maggie could feel her anger rising. Was John still so close-minded? She was glad that she had never written to him about Davey's psychic skills. But neither had she warned Davey to hide them.

"Poppa, I don't understand lots of things." Davey screwed his forehead into a frown. "I guess I'll know more after I grow up."

"On that note, it's your bedtime, young man." Maggie led Davey to his bedroom, sang two songs, kissed him, closed the door and returned to John.

"Maggie," John asked, "how could Lin know so much about him? Where does he get his information?"

Maggie sighed and took a quick sip of port. "Johnnie, after you went to Cuba, I asked Ned the same question. He gave me books on human consciousness."

"What did you learn?"

"I learned that we have three ways to gain knowledge: from the senses; from thoughtful analysis of experience and…" Maggie hesitated. Would John keep an open mind? She had to risk an explosion. "… and from a mystical connection with ultimate knowledge."

"So you think Lin has made such a connection?" John gulped his brandy and tried to suspend his own disbelief. "How does he do it?"

"Persuasive explanations are very hazy. But I think Mr. Lin knows how to reach into that part of a person—or an animal—that wants love. He's like a lighthouse that sends love in all directions."

John thought that answer sounded like more Oriental clap-trap. He set that thought aside, determined to discipline his doubts. "Can you explain more?"

"Ned and Lin T'ai-chi could explain these ideas much more clearly than I can. Lin thinks that children know how to… connect … more easily than adults. Unfortunately, we destroy their skill by teaching them fear."

"Maybe Davey *needs* a little fear," John mused. "How will he survive in a competitive world without sensible fear? He also has to learn to climb the same mountain we all must climb to the ultimate fear."

"What's that, John?"

"Why, the fear of death, of course!"

Maggie frowned. "I'm not sure of that. Lin thinks that fear, especially fear of death, blinds us to other realities."

During their courtship, this kind of comment had charmed John. Now it reinforced his doubts about the effects of such thinking on his son. He said, "Reality is what we touch and see and measure. Anything else is an illusion."

"Oh, Johnnie, we're much more than that!" Maggie exclaimed. "Do you honestly think we're just skin and bones, biological and chemical formula?"

"I'm just an engineer, Maggie," John replied stiffly. "If there's somethin' more to what you call nature than physical reality, I'd need a barn of evidence before I'd believe it."

Maggie stared at him. How could she express herself without patronizing or antagonizing him? "William James believes the unconscious is a storehouse of all earthly knowledge and memory. From that level of energy, we can draw incredible strength or knowledge when we need it at the more shallow level we call conscious or sensual reality."

"Maybe I should go to my unconscious for help on my engine."

"Maybe you should! It could be the wellspring of human creativity."

"How do I get there? Where do I catch the train?"

Ignoring his stab at humor, Maggie pleaded, "You're really asking the right question. How does Lin escape the noisy babble of the conscious to find the serene wisdom of the unconscious? Whatever the process, if you'll just listen it will empower you."

"What gets me, Maggie, is that you say these things as if you know they're true. Do you think Davey has connected with his unconscious mind?"

"I don't know." She hesitated. Should she mention a Davey Dream or tell what happened when Davey seemed to enter a flying bird's brain? "Freud says each of us should find a unique balance between our inner and outer worlds before the age of four. Perhaps we didn't push Davey hard enough to join the world when he was a baby."

"Perhaps you pushed him in the wrong direction while I was gone." John didn't want to blame Maggie for anything. But Lin's ideas threatened the very foundations of the known, as he saw it. "Philosophy is one thing, but how could an intelligent woman like you believe in a fad like the new spiritualism?"

"I'm not a faddist, John. I believe this is the dawning of an era, an age of consciousness." Unsmiling now, Maggie's expression warned John of the intensity of her conviction.

"I thought the subject was riddled with anecdotes and several thousand years of fraud?"

"True, but this era is different because reputable scientists are examining these things for the first time in human history."

Maggie's tone riveted John's attention. To him, the idea of spiritual power was utterly useless for approaching practical problems. It was exasperating that Maggie should even compare her mind-games with the tangible value of a fine engine. Later, preparing for bed, he curbed his irritation and decided to gather more information before jumping to conclusions. He chuckled and turned to Maggie with a smile. "Let's not argue about this now, Maggie. Give me a chance to think about your ideas. I don't want to compete with you."

Maggie quietly brushed her hair. With searing clarity, she suddenly grasped the essence of their differences. To John, his engine designs and established scientific principles defined his place in the world. Maggie was not disdainful of those principles, but like Lin T'ai-chi, she believed they had application only to a narrowly-defined system of thought within a much larger system. It was her pleasure to speculate about the nature of the larger system. She felt yet another fear lurking behind John's protests. His notions of masculinity might be at stake here. She suspected that he considered her open-minded musings to be a sign of weakness, of feminine hysteria: signs and portents, emotional instability, and so forth. Did he think Davey might emerge from childhood without the proper masculine convictions? "You don't have to compete with me, sweetheart."

"I know, but I felt we were in competition when I went to war. We're just teachin' Davey different patterns. I can call my patterns science or engineering or anythin' I choose. It's possible they're just part of a much bigger pattern which you call love. Lin calls it 'ch'i.' Some call it God. It's way beyond our notion of science right now."

"It's a levels question," Maggie said as she slid under the cool sheets. "My levels of interest are mostly non-physical. I use words like 'thought' and 'love' and 'ch'i' to try to explain why things happen a certain way. Maybe we can figure out some connection between my patterns and your patterns."

"I can't imagine that," John replied thoughtfully, "I believe in the laws and mathematics of the physical level." He propped his head against the headboard. "It's the common blackboard that all the other levels write on. I'll be grateful if I can learn *how to think* about that blackboard."

Maggie persisted, "William James says, 'Salvation lies in accumulated acts of thought.' If you try to connect with non-physical levels more, maybe you'll learn to apply them to the physical plane, to something like your engine."

"I wonder if that's why Davey is so interested in rhythm and harmony."

"I think Davey believes everything already harmonizes." Maggie replied. "Instead of correcting *him*, maybe we ought to change *our* perspective. To find harmony, we may have to learn some new lessons."

CHAPTER THIRTY-TWO

CARMEL VALLEY
JULY, 1899

John's indulgent reaction to William James and Lin T'ai-chi did not deceive Maggie. She would not feel safe until he had experienced a "Davey Dream" with tolerant equanimity. But she decided that John would have to work that out with Davey. John was a grown man, fully capable of his own judgments. She saw no reason why she should try to censor his exposure to something that had challenged her sanity for fourteen months: Davey's extraordinary inner world. Nor did she see why she should change her playful acceptance of their son's baffling insights and perceptions. She reasoned that father and son needed something from each other. It was time for them to discover the nature of that "something" without interference from her.

Through his first month at home, John led Davey on Su-su for long rides through hidden valleys and across bubbling streams. They lunched together almost every day under the shade of a live oak or a willow. After lunch they talked, mostly about the coming age of flight. Then, they would often swim in a small pond or behind a beaver dam. At first Davey's technique struck John as primitive thrashing. But the boy soon responded to his father's instruction. By July he could dive, swim underwater and perform a fair breast-stroke.

Whether armed with fishing rods or a football or baseball gloves, ball and bat, or kites of radical design, father and son became a familiar sight around the ranch. Davey's admiration for his father soon amounted to hero-worship. If Maggie had permitted, Davey would have slept in John's boots. Through Davey's fresh perception of the ranch, John rediscovered enthusiasm and novelty and even his own childhood. He could not remember when he had been so contented. For a charmed instant, his life seemed to have found a joyous equilibrium. Except....

Nothing in John's experience could explain Davey's baffling insights and skills. Davey was smart, but no four-year old could be *that* smart. In disapproving silence, he watched Maggie indulge... no, *encourage* Davey's fantasies, especially "the Game." *I've got to be patient,* he persistently told himself. *At least with that strategy I'll avoid fights with Maggie.* Cuba and New York had taken a lot of fight out of him.

By mid-July, constant exposure to Davey's eidetic memory, his casual mention of smoke rising from dying animals and his pre-cognitive visions forced John to conclude that patience was too passive an approach to the boy's bizarre sense of reality. That conclusion had been reinforced by John's sense of alienation from the Game. He was especially bothered by Davey's startling perceptions, which transcended mere childish curiosity. Sometimes, as in their conversation about Lin T'ai-chi, his insights reached a level of wisdom that shook John with its childlike simplicity and, worse, its unassailable validity.

After they put Davey to bed one evening at the end of July, they went into the cool living room where John filled two glasses of port. "Maggie, we need to talk about some of Davey's ideas. For the past two months, I've felt... excluded from what he calls the Game."

"How could you feel excluded from us?" Maggie protested. "Davey worships you."

"That may be," John replied. "But sometimes he seems lost in the clouds."

"Give him time, Johnnie," Maggie pleaded. "He wants nothing more than your approval. When you left last year, I thought his heart would break. That was when I first tried to teach him to think big, to reach out with his mind, to find you and comfort you."

"*Find* me? Hell, he barely remembered me when I returned!"

Maggie frowned. "Maybe I was wrong. On the very day you left, I decided to get him more involved in the world. But I knew he would be comforted, too, if he thought he was near you." Then she told him about Davey's vision of John and Teddy Roosevelt on the veranda of the Tampa Bay Hotel.

The story staggered John. It was one thing to speculate about levels of consciousness. It was quite another to accept Davey's behavior as validation of those theories. "Why do you call his behavior a Game?"

"For two reasons. When Davey's psychic skills first appeared after you left, I was afraid I'd crush his fantasies if I didn't understand him. Ned thought his connection with the subconscious was just a phase. He said it was normal for a three-year old to mix up make-believe and reality. Since Ned thought it was just a form of play, I called it 'the Game.' More important, Ned persuaded me that the idea of what we call reality may be a nightmare, a dream, compared to the beauty of Davey's reality."

John shivered at the thought that the world of Newtonian physics might be a nightmare, some kind of anthropomorphic dream. He dared not predict the fate of a human who acted as if human endeavor and human achievements were mere illusions compared to some metaphysical reality. Even if it were true, belief in such a thing would be disastrous for the believer. All the priests and rabbis and ministers in the world would never persuade him of such a reversal of the proper order of things. "Can you hear what Davey hears?"

"No. But Mr. Lin said that I shouldn't expect to hear the same music others hear. Each human teaches himself to use the five senses in a unique way. Each of us must also screen out certain sixth-sense sounds and images. Finally only selected images pass through the filter of the brain."

"Surely this is all just imagination gone amuck?"

"No! The facts aren't speculation. Only our understanding of the process is. At first I didn't believe the stories either. But I've watched Lin dissect a total stranger's personal history as if he were a next door neighbor. Once he told of an event taking place thousands of miles away as if he were watching it with his eyes. Later, a letter confirmed the details of his description. When we were in our teens in Shanghai, he taught me and Lily that such skills merely reflect different levels of awareness. He says that at the deepest level communication is literally instantaneous."

The scientist in John rebelled. "How can communication be instantaneous? It must travel through a medium, which offers some resistance. It must take time to travel distance."

"Not always," Maggie replied with stubborn confidence. "Mr. Lin said that when the past and the future disappear, time becomes a single point."

The implications of that statement stunned John. How could time be a variable? What would happen to all the critical measurements of science if time collapsed to a single point? "If the past, present and future were a single point, we would know the future."

"Probably. That's why Davey's dreams sometimes terrified me when you were gone. I asked myself, 'Can these dreams be pre-cognitive?'"

"And what was your answer?"

"Confusion. A vision or a fantasy may predict the future at some distant time. But if time disappears at that level, it must be very hard to locate the vision precisely in what *we* call time."

"Why didn't Lin teach you how to do the same things?"

"He tried. But I was afraid I might lose my mind. Lin insisted that I'd find peace only after I banished fear from my mind."

John thought So we're back to fear. *Maybe I'll finally get a fix on Davey's mental state.* "Is that why Davey is so... psychic? Because he's fear-less?"

"John, you can't imagine how hard I've worked to keep fear out of his mind."

"What did you do?"

"I tried to teach him that he's never alone. I wanted him to feel joined with nature, seeing nature as his friend."

"Do you ever try to listen to animals and trees and such?" John asked.

"No, I'm better at listening to another person's essence. That's why I fell in love with you."

"Why, because I'm brilliant, handsome and rich?"

Maggie grinned; had they reached a truce for the evening? "I love you and married you because you have an innate sweetness that somehow survived all your education. Everyone thinks you're a tough guy because you spend your time with wranglers, horses, blacksmiths and engineers."

From harsh experience, John observed with conviction, "You have to be tough to deal with those characters."

Maggie smiled. "That's just your mask. They don't see and hear what Davey and I see and hear in you. You just play our game with different toys. But down deep you understand exactly what we hear and see and feel. At least you understand it as much as Davey and I do."

CHAPTER THIRTY-THREE

CARMEL VALLEY
JULY–DECEMBER, 1899

The conversation with Maggie weighed on John for the next week. He felt that his enthusiasm for life, especially the shop in Monterey, was under siege by dark forces that eluded his understanding. He could list at least four issues that still challenged his confidence: Davey's rich inner life, from which John felt excluded; the implications of the Game for his own sense of reality; his gnawing sexual frustration; and his relentless sense of failure with the Balzer engine.

With respect to the first two forces, John decided that the proper course of action with Davey was to persuade him to abandon his fantasy world by tantalizing him with the world of complicated machinery, especially bicycles. He asked Davey to accompany him to Monterey at least three days a week until John could sense a satisfying change in Davey's viewpoint.

For Davey the trips were fun. And he more than met John's challenge. Between July and September his instinctive grasp of levers and gear ratios would have done credit to an adult. Most important, John's sense of exclusion from "the Game" faded as he noted Davey's evident enjoyment of workmen's endless discussions. How trim weight off the bicycle? How add more power and speed? In August, shop dialogue about a moto-cycle revived the issue of a light, reliable engine. So John began to explain the internal combustion engine.

By mid-September, after many lectures on the workings of an engine, the boy could draw crude sketches of cylinders, pistons and crankshafts. John had never encountered such a sponge-like mind, ready to soak up any tidbit of trivial information. He proudly confided to Maggie that Davey had become a good luck mascot at the shop and on the ranch. Whenever

Davey was around, new ideas seemed to come to the surface of John's mind effortlessly. The men would hum and buzz and find a lighter mood for their work. Davey would simply look, listen and "help out." On the ranch, Ramon said, "He opens our eyes to beauty." When John asked how, Ramon shrugged. "It's hard to explain. My son, Juan has tried to explain it to us; but he is too young. He only says, '*Es el amor de Dios.*'"

"Does he mean David's love for God or God's love for David?" John asked.

"I don't know," Ramon replied. "Maybe it's the same thing. In any case, his way of asking hundred questions makes everyone feel very wise."

"I know what you mean," John agreed with a grin. "To explain things, I have to go back to basics. Then a light goes on in my mind and suddenly I see the problem, the question, and the answer from a new perspective." By the end of September, John had almost forgotten his concerns about Davey's bizarre dialogue with the spirit world.

And then one afternoon in early October, when John and Davey were several miles from the ranch house, Davey suddenly said, "Poppa, we better go home. Mister Mackie is comin', I think he needs to see you."

The confidence in Davey's voice startled John. "How do you know he's comin', Davey? Did Momma tell you Fred Mackie wanted to see me?"

"No." Davey wore a puzzled expression on his face, as if John's question was absurd. "I can see him, Poppa. Can't you?"

"If you can see him, tell me what he's wearin' son. Is he ridin' a horse or is he in his buggy?"

"He's in his buggy. He has on that dark blue suit he likes. There's a gold chain hangin' across his tummy. If we leave now, we'll get home before he gets there."

When they reached the ranch, John was perturbed to see Fred Mackie in his buggy only two hundred yards away. He wore his favorite three-piece blue suit with batwing collar. His watch chain hung across his ample belly. Despite Fred's happy report to John about the healthy status of John's bank account, John felt haunted by the implications of Davey's vision. His effort to capture Davey's attention through the summer had been premised on the belief that Davey's youth and loneliness had fostered mere

fantasies. He had condemned Maggie for her mystical bent, which he believed had potential for damaging their son. But now he could no longer
deny the possibility that Davey's astonishing inner world *was* another reality. If so, John felt that he must do something decisive to confirm Davey's
different realities.

The third force at work on John's heart, mind and body was not suitable for candid discussion with Maggie. Maybe it was his yearning for Maggie that had awakened John's sleeping beast—an addiction that had
destroyed many more experienced men. It was lust; and before M and M,
John had never known its power. What a pair! John could not believe that
anyone could have used his body to tease out such ecstacy.

During his first week at home, John had carefully restrained himself
with Maggie since he knew that she was an indifferent partner in bed. Furthermore, Parisian courtesans weren't ladies. He had read somewhere that
the way to handle women was to treat whores like ladies and ladies like
whores, but he couldn't bring himself to such cavalier behavior. His
mother had taught him to treat ladies with respect and gentle fingers, just
the way you would treat a fine horse. He simply could not spend his lust
with Maggie the way he had in New York. As a result of his restraint, his
sexual relationship with Maggie grew increasingly frustrating. There was a
hunger building up in him that was becoming a monster of desire. He
couldn't look at a young woman without mentally undressing her and
imagining a wild passion they both could share. At odd moments Marie
and Mathilde would return to summon up the demons. He would suddenly grow hard in a reverie of tangled legs, arms and breasts.

As fantasies of lust recurred with increasing frequency, John wondered
if he was ill. When he could not banish his irrepressible needs with a combination of polo, hard physical work in the shop—and Maggie, he knew
that he must seek help. But who could he talk to about the situation?
Where could he turn? Should he visit San Francisco like some of his friends
and pay his respects to an elegant, red plush parlor house or one of the
many houses of prostitution on Morton Street? Too complicated and too
dangerous. The Barbary Coast was still notorious for its parlor houses,
dance halls, cribs, Chinese slave girls and rampant venereal disease.

Maybe he should find someone nearby who might satisfy his powerful appetites....

Despite his imaginative revision of his story during his homeward trip from New York and the stimulus of Davey's interest, John's sense of failure with the Balzer engine remained as relentless as his lust and his memories of M and M. He wondered if Balzer and Charlie Manly had solved the problems of the rotary design. Should he resume his work on a different kind of engine? Charlie Manly gave him the answer one afternoon in mid-October.

October 9, 1899

Dear John,

You probably thought Balzer's engine would be done by now. Well, it isn't. In May, after you told me about the intimidation that you and Balzer were facing in New York, we brought Balzer to Washington for a month. I didn't tell Professor Langley about Eastman and his thugs. I just persuaded him that we should scrutinize Balzer's work more closely. I thought the safety of Washington and the extended contract would stimulate him to finish it. He went back to New York in early July. You may imagine my disgust when I paid him a surprise visit later that month to discover that he was working on an automobile engine. The aerodrome engine was gathering dust in a corner! He argued that heat and ignition were still troubling him. He used the shortage of funds as an additional reason for his slowdown. If I gave him more money, he said he would thoroughly test a single cylinder by August 1. I arranged a partial payment for him from his fee.

Wonder of wonders! He actually tested a cylinder on August 4. He claims that it produced 4 hp. That means that five cylinders theoretically could produce 20hp. But he said the cylinder head overheats after running fifteen minutes. It starts pre-ignition then. He could cool it down only by wrapping wet cloth around it. Nevertheless, he promised to test a complete engine by September 22. He said he would need a mount and a clutch to throw on a load (a propellor?) for a real test of brake horsepower.

He finally subjected the entire 5-cylinder engine to a test on September 26. It could only produce 8hp! Because of poor lubrication, the crankshaft froze. So he would have to obtain new bearings before another test.

I had lost so much confidence in Balzer's word that I visited New York again a week ago. Fortunately, I found five men working on the engine. We designed a mount. Then I described the whole mess to Mr. Langley at the Metropolitan Club. I should add that I was somewhat surprised to see several unsavory characters lurking around Balzer's shop. One of them followed me to the Metropolitan Club. I wonder if they were some of Eastman's men?

Though short, this letter is meant to let you know that we have an engine. But I don't think it will satisfy our requirements. I don't think any rotary can do so. Some time next year, I may try to persuade the Secretary (Langley) that we should take over the whole project in the Smithsonian shops. If we do, I'll adopt your original recommendation: make it a stationary radial. And then I'll need all the advice you can give us. No one else knows that engine as well as you do.

The letter had two effects. First, it redeemed John's sense of failure with Balzer. If more money and much more pressure from the Secretary and Charlie had failed to accelerate Balzer's production schedule, very real technical problems must have added their weight to Monk Eastman's thugs, who were apparently still watching and waiting. Second, the letter revived John's ambition to build his own engine.

Through the rest of October, John felt a new zest in his work as he re-thought the array of problems that must be overcome to design a radial engine that could yield one horsepower per nine pounds of weight. Davey, by his side either in the shop or on the trail, showed no new evidence of mind trips into cuckoo land. Instead, his evident interest in metal lathes, boring tools, horses, racing bicycles and flying machines persuaded John that his son had finally joined a man's world with gusto. Then he received another letter in early November. This one was from Wilbur Wright.

November 9, 1899

Dear John,

Everything takes longer than expected. But I'm not complaining. One day last August, I personally tested our full-scale kite. Only a flock of curious schoolboys were witnesses. I must have presented a bizarre picture: a grown man in a business suit manhandling a large kite.

It more than fulfilled our expectations! I think the wing-warping idea can assure full control of any machine's tendency to roll. Orville was so pleased that he soon joined me in designing a full-scale glider. To our astonishment, we ran into more problems than we had bargained for. Some of them pertain to control. Those issues are relatively mechanical, like simple mechanisms for the pilot to warp the wing-tips while aloft. Before we can build a single component of a full-sized wing, we must learn how to give the pilot the power to make the center of gravity of the machine coincident with a moving center of pressure of the wind. Only when those two pressures are coincident will the machine have equilibrium in flight. We think there are two ways to make that happen: by giving the pilot some control over a horizontal surface in front of the wings; and by building stability into the wing airfoil.

The more complicated problems relate to lift. Remember how we thought Lilienthal and Chanute had solved the lift component of flight? I think we were wrong. "Aerodynamic efficiency" will probably give us much more grief than control problems. How big should the wings be? The wing airfoil is the most challenging problem. We think Lilienthal's idea of a curved or cambered wing is better than a flat wing. He preferred a camber of 1:12. That means, as you will recall, that the height of the camber or arc of the wing should be 1/12th of the width of the wing. But we are beginning to think that such an arc is too high. You might check it with a model. We think that a flatter camber will reduce the amount of downward pressure that the wind can exert on the top of a curved wing.

But the really challenging issue is: where should the curve peak? At the center of the arc? Or somewhere else? We think the peak of the arc should be close to the leading edge of the wing. That will give the wind only a small surface on which to exert downward pressure on the top of the wing. In other words, we want to limit the distance that the center of pressure can move. To play with different arcs, we will build a wind tunnel and test different model wings to find the most efficient airfoil.

To control pitch, we will use the same system that Penaud used twenty years ago. Only we plan to use the "canard" arrangement with the horizontal stabilizer in front instead of in the rear. We think the canard system will have several advantages. First, it may protect us from Lilienthal's fate—a nosedive. Second, if we get into a nosedive anyway, when we strike the ground the forward stabilizer will be a buffer for the pilot, just like the engine and front bumper of an automobile. Third, if we mount the forward stabilizer on curved runners, it may facilitate soft landings, and we might be able to use it somehow to foster lift. And, finally, we think it may help the pilot to recognize the instant the machine tilts at an angle to the horizon. We might need to flex the stabilizer. To do that, we'll give the pilot some kind of simple control mechanism.

How are you coming with your engine? If we can satisfy our need for the most aerodynamically efficient airfoil, we should have our first full-scale glider in the air sometime next year—maybe in the late summer. It would be wonderful if your engine was ready for our use by the summer of the following year, 1901. But perhaps your agreement with Mr.

Langley will preclude our access to your engine.

Never mind. We think the race is quickening. But it will never undermine our friendship with you and Octave Chanute, with whom we plan to share our many problems.

When can we see your engine?

A full-scale glider! The very idea thrilled John and set his mind churning with the possibility of building his own glider, perhaps in the barn. Didn't he have all the books that the Wrights had? Weren't Lilienthal's airfoil data and other data from Chanute's gliding experiments on Lake Michigan freely accessible in their books? Didn't he have all the drawings of Langley's aerodrome? John re-read Wilbur's letter as if to answer the question, "What do Wilbur and Orville Wright have that I don't have also?" His heart raced with the thought that he also knew more about engines than either Wright brother. He reasoned that he could work on a better engine in the shop while tinkering with a glider in his barn. The one should not preclude work on the other.

Through the month of November, John outfitted the barn for glider building. Within three weeks, the barn had a floor, a huge wood-burning stove and insulated walls and ceiling for winter occupancy. There remained the job of filling it with woodworking tools. During John's enthusiastic upgrading of the barn, Davey never left his side. And Maggie frequently visited to give encouragement.

As if to reinforce John's new zeal for a radial engine, a letter from Glenn Curtiss arrived on the last day of November.

November 22, 1899

Dear John,

That scoundrel, Jim Smellie, decided to wait until next year to turn over his bicycle shop to me. So much for our winnings in a bicycle race! But Jim isn't welching. He just needs some time to make a smooth transition.

In the meanwhile, I'm still hunting for a good engine for my moto-cycle. I believe Lena is right; I've been afflicted by the god of speed! Pedalling isn't enough any more. The E.R. Thomas Company in Buffalo swears that it will demon-

strate a Stearns racer with a small engine at the Pan American Exposition in Buffalo in 1901. I don't know if I can wait
that long.

Can't you produce something for me sooner than that?

All the Hammondsport Boys send greetings. And my grandmother and Lena send their love.

Two weeks later, John received a letter from Tom Baldwin. It added
fuel to John's renewed ambition for the most efficient small engine in the
world.

December 6, 1899

Dear John,

Our summer fairs and performances drew huge crowds this
year to see Greenleaf jump in his parachute. His two daugh-
ters, Ruth and Florence, may follow in their father's footsteps one of these days.

The balloon factory has also done very well this year. Now
we know how to make "figure balloons": almost any shape you
want. I've been negotiating with a scientist named E. B.
Baldwin (no relation) to supply him with a bunch of balloons
for an arctic expedition in 1901. He wants 16-foot, bright
yellow balloons for messages and identification markers. He
has a lot of experience; so I'm trying to do a good job for
him.

You may not know that Ivy will leave the Signal Corps in
the spring and come here to join us. He keeps reminding me
that he wants credit for starting you on the road to a flying
machine!

That's most of the good news. The bad news is that Carrie
is convinced that I've seduced the affections of our
half-witted, 16-year old maid, Ernestine. I feel insulted
that Carrie believes Ernestine meets my high standards! If I
didn't feel obligated to set Ivy up and organize an orderly
transition, I would leave here now and come west. I'll try to
do that before the end of 1900.

I expect you'll have your engine fully tested and operating by then so that we can power our airships right into the War Department!

The letter made John smile. Life suddenly offered exciting possibilities: airships, gliders, aerodromes, motorcycles. And all of them seemed to be waiting for his engine. Well, by God, he would deliver that and more, much more. He would design and build a complete flying machine. As if to affirm his commitment, Octave Chanute wrote him a letter which arrived on the day before Christmas.

December 18, 1899

Dear John,

Since your visit last year, you have been much on my mind. I have tried to keep abreast of developments in aeronautics all over the world. The sheer volume of participants in the race for first flight is astounding. I can name several men in almost every state of the Union who are testing gliders and seeking the bubble reputation. The spirit of competition is in the wind. In your own state, you must meet Professor John Montgomery of Santa Clara.

I believe you did the right thing in staying in New York instead of going to Europe. You might have met dare-devils like Santos Dumont and Sir Hiram Maxim and Clement Ader or scientists like Frederick Lanchester and James Glaisher and De Dion. I especially wanted you to meet Percy Pilcher, who had experimented with Lilienthal. But you must already know that he was killed on September 30 while testing his bamboo Hawk. In any event, I don't think any of them, with the possible exception of De Dion, could have helped you much in your search for a suitable engine.

After I met you, I felt that your education in engineering had armed you with an unusual advantage over most of your competitors. With your additional experience with Sam Langley, Charles Manly and Stephen Balzer, you should not hesitate to invest your very best mental and physical energies to win this race. Until recently, I thought the keys were still control and propulsion. But the Wright brothers have about persuaded me that lift still holds mysteries for the designer. If I can ever be of any assistance, please do not hesitate to call on me. I pray that we both live to celebrate that grand day when a human first controls a powered flying machine.

Encouragement from such an illustrious authority in the field acted like a surge of adrenalin to John. If he had had any doubts before, Chanute's faith removed them all. Monk Eastman and Wall Street and intimidation faded into some deep well of memory and the creative juices started flowing again. Now was the time for the best he could give.

By the last day of December, John had installed woodworking tools in the barn. It had been a month of hard work. But he could survey his lathe and his power saws with satisfaction. He felt like a hunter, hot on the trail again. While Davey sketched and questioned his every move, Maggie watched them with pride and pleasure. From dawn to dark, they filled the barn and their home with exciting chatter. How to make a certain linkage on a new racer? How to test an airfoil for center of pressure? What kind of glue to use on the first model glider wing? How to bore a stock steel cylinder to thinner tolerances? How to make a reliable sparkplug?

Maggie knew that such problems only made John happy. He seemed to have forgotten his fear of exclusion or alienation from either their son or from her. She exulted in the sense that, at last they were a family. While she busily prepared for Christmas, she felt a fulfillment that she had feared might elude her when John had left for Cuba eighteen months earlier. Her zeal to unlock the mysteries of life through philosophy or mysticism or psychology seemed to have waned. Like John, she thought this was a time for living, for doing, for decorating, for planning. She had never been so happy. On New Year's Eve, with a deeply satisfying Christmas week behind her, she said to John and Davey, "Tomorrow, let's ride to the highlands and celebrate New Year's Day. Ah Ying can prepare a salmon for us and we can welcome in 1900."

PART VI

THE GLIDER

"The heights by great men reached and kept
Were not attained by sudden flight,
But they, while their companions slept,
Were toiling upward in the night."

LONGFELLOW, THE LADDER OF ST. AUGUSTINE

CHAPTER THIRTY-FOUR

CARMEL VALLEY
JANUARY, 1900

So this was where nearly six years of marriage had brought them, Maggie reflected as she guided her horse eastward up the Carmel Valley, the Carmel Highlands and the eagle incident behind her and a supper with Lin T'ai-chi ahead. If she could believe Professor Lin's predictions in Shanghai, the next seven years would be even more challenging. Maybe Lin could give her some private guidance that evening. She watched Davey negotiate dry washes, steep gullies and scrub oak with easy grace. He and Su-Su seemed to be one organic unit. It appeared that he had total trust in Su-Su's mincing steps down the steep slopes that drifted into the coast road to the Carmel Valley.

John's first exposure to a Davey Dream and the eagle incident at the Carmel Highlands had revived his fears about his son's sense of himself and the world. He wondered if there could actually be some kind of parallel world. And if Davey was in touch with it, could that be a good thing? Could a person live in both worlds without scrambling his brains or becoming a circus freak? The prospect of dining with Lin T'ai-chi that evening reminded John that he could no longer blame Maggie for Davey's strange insights and skills. In the past six months since his return from New York, he had seen enough to know that Maggie had tried to adjust *her* sense of reality to Davey's behavior. He warned himself that if he didn't do the same thing, he and Maggie might tear Davey apart with their arguments.

By the time the Harrisons reached the ranch, the sunset was sending its glory across the sky, fingers of scarlet, gold and pink reaching eastward where deeper shades of violet and purple promised nightfall. From the entry to the ranch, it was only about a fifteen minute ride to the ranch house.

Davey loved the final approach to their home, especially the Austra-

lian gum trees that stood at attention on either side of the road and welcomed the riders with their astringent aroma. He loved the way tendrils of
cooling fog reached eastward from the coast and coiled around ice plant
hanging from bluffs and cutouts, where the Carmel River carved its way
through a hillside. Impatient for a rubdown and supper, Su-su pulled on
the bit and began a gentle canter home.

Two hours later, Maggie greeted her guests and presided over a round
table complete with lazy susan at its center. Opposite her sat Ned and
Amy Ambler, John, Davey and Lily. On her left sat Lin T'ai-chi; on her
right in the place of honored guest sat Lily's father, Wang Lao-chih, (Wang
of Venerable Wisdom), called "Larry" by his American friends and English
partners. Larry spent most of the year in Shanghai, where he supervised
his complex business interests and hosted occasional visits from business
partners, principally Americans and English. Now he was anxiously on his
way home from a long trip to Europe. He had agreed to spend a month in
Monterey with Lily, provided that she accompany him back to China to
help him navigate troublesome times. From Larry's house high in the
Aguajito, one could observe a spectacular 360 degree view of the coastline,
the Monterey peninsula, the lovely old town of Monterey and the Carmel
Valley. The home's geomantic position was exceptional, Lin had said
when he first saw it in May, 1899. It brought the *feng-shui* (wind and water)
of this site into harmony. From Lily's viewpoint, it was a place of peace and
inspiring beauty. She much preferred it to the humid chaos of Shanghai or
Hong Kong or Canton.

Lin had just completed a six-month trip around North America and
wished to travel home with Larry. After one more week in Monterey, they
planned to embark on the long ocean voyage to China. Only one ticklish
problem remained before their departure, and the Harrisons had a critical
role to play in the resolution of that problem.

At dinner, Larry quickly saw that John was not familiar with Chinese
protocol at formal dinners. In his clipped British accent, he therefore
asked politely if he might lead several rounds of toasts before Ah Ying
served her twelve courses. Maggie had managed to unearth (figuratively,
not literally as might have been the case in China) several bottles of mel-

low *shaohsing* wine. Larry quickly toasted the host and hostess, the guests and Lin T'ai-chi, by tradition honored for coming together from so far away. "*You yüan ch'ien li lai hsiang hui; wu yüan dwei mien bu hsiang feng.*" (No distance can sever those whom fate unites; no nearness can join those whom fate severs). After that toast, Larry quickly toasted the first dish, then tried to strike a note of levity lest John Harrison feel displaced as host. "When I was a young man," Larry said, "I made a terrible mistake once at a formal Chinese dinner."

"Oh, tell that story!" Lily exclaimed. "It shows our slavery to protocol."

"Indeed it does." Larry nodded graciously at his daughter. "I must have been no older than twenty. I had been invited to dine with several proud officials and their wives, eleven very traditional, conservative men and women alternating around a round table. I knew good manners dictated that the men should serve their dinner partner."

John was grateful that Larry Wang had deftly seized the initiative. At a time when many of his friends were clamoring for restrictions on Chinese and Japanese immigration, John really wasn't sure how he should behave toward either a soothsayer like Lin or a powerful businessman like Larry.

"So I boldly used my chopsticks to serve the lady on my left, a very beautiful former courtesan who was then married to the Commander in Chief of our navy. Her husband was watching us from across the table." While he spoke, Larry thrust his chopsticks into a platter of shrimp sizzling on browned rice and transferred several portions onto Maggie's plate on his left.

John followed suit by serving Amy on his left. Lin T'ai-chi served Lily's plate while she quietly interpreted from Larry's English to Chinese for Lin. John had sensed a change in Maggie since Larry Wang had come in the house. By some physiological miracle, Maggie actually looked Oriental. Wearing a tight-fitting, bright green *cheong-sam*, a long, silk Chinese gown with delicate gold embroidery around the high collar, her figure was as spectacular as he had ever seen it. Then he remembered that Larry had played the role of Maggie's father for two years in Shanghai until both girls were ready for college. Nevertheless, Maggie's facial expressions and her charming use of her head and eyes to express respectful deference aroused his jealousy, an emotion that startled John more than Larry's story.

"I did the same thing with several dishes until I happened to notice a frown on the August naval person's face. The lady on my left seemed amused. I finally whispered, 'Am I doing something to offend your husband?'"

Lily lifted her napkin to her mouth to cover a fit of giggles. She obviously knew the story well. To control herself, she took a sip of *shaohsing* wine.

"My dinner partner smiled at me and said, 'You are doing beautifully, except for one thing.' 'And what is that?' I asked."

At that moment, Ah Ying brought in the second dish—orange-flavored dry slivered beef. Larry dutifully toasted the new dish and the chef and begged everyone to, "*gan bei*" to drink the glasses dry. He then reached for the long chopsticks resting in that dish and served Maggie again. "She said, 'If you had served me with the long public chopsticks in each new dish, you would be telling the world that you and I are merely acquaintances.' I stared at her while I held my own chopsticks over her plate, where I had just deposited her share of the new dish. She went on, 'If you had use *my* chopsticks, you tell the world—and my husband—that we are only good friends.'"

John had a sense of what was coming and couldn't restrain a grin. He had decided that he liked Larry Wang, a man of the world. In his Bond Street, exquisitely-tailored dark serge suit, Larry's tall, lean figure and round moon-face conveyed a charming blend of Occidental commercial energy and Oriental cultural tolerance.

"So when she said, 'But when you use *your* chopsticks to serve me, you are saying publicly that we have a very intimate relationship. Perhaps that's why my husband looks confused.'" Larry was a master mime. He adopted an expression on his face as if to say, "What would you have done?" Then he finished the story. "I turned beet red and dropped my chopsticks in her plate. I knew my reputation was ruined forever. I left the table to collect myself. From the veranda, I could hear my dinner partner regaling everyone with the cause of my discomfort. Soon they were all laughing."

"And what happened to your reputation?" John asked.

"Very curious. From that day forward, I was welcomed everywhere. It was as if I became the target for social redemption by every hostess in

Shanghai."

Lin T'ai-chi smiled. "That's your splendid karma! I wish we could re-solve our other problems in China with equal speed." He was referring to the deepening confrontation between the ineffectual Chinese central government and the major foreign powers, which were demanding more concessions, including "sphere of influence" with near political autonomy in key areas of China.

"When I met with Secretary of State John Hay last month in Washington," Larry said, "he assured me that he would bend every effort to get support from all the major powers for an 'open door' policy towards China."

"What does that mean?" Amy Amber asked.

"It's a policy of equal opportunity for all commercial interests without spheres of influence. Without such a policy, I fear that China will be di-vided into petty states, echoing the squabbles of Europe and publicizing the near impotence of the central government in Peking."

"What do you think will happen?" Maggie adored Larry Wang and wor-ried about his safety in China. It was only because of Larry that Lily had escaped from foot-binding when she was quite young. Larry had firmly prohibited the custom until it was too late and Lily's feet were perceived to be hopelessly ugly compared to the "golden lilies" of all upper-class women.

"The Boxers will soon confront the court and the foreigners with vio-lence," Lin said with confidence. "The court will support the Boxers be-cause the anti-foreign faction can see no other way to retrieve honor."

Maggie was startled to see that Davey seemed to follow the conversa-tion as if he had a personal stake in the future of China. "Surely, the vio-lence can be contained?"

"Perhaps," Lin mused. "The troubles are mainly in the north, where foreign influence has been most insulting. But times are bad and the court has lost the Mandate of Heaven. The Boxers burned the Paoting-Peking railway last May. Now they seem to be mobilizing for a direct attack on the foreign legations."

"Do you see any cause for hope, my friend?" Larry asked Lin.

"I do not, Lao-chih. I see only a long period of military violence and a terrible destruction of our land and our people. I see civil war and foreign invasion at least through the next fifty years."

Larry looked at his daughter. "By then the responsibility will fall on Lily's generation and even the next generation."

"We are our own worst enemies," Lin added, "because we give too much of our loyalties to the family and have none left over for the country."

Larry agreed. "We are like Germany before Bismarck forced unification."

"Many soldiers in China will try to emulate him over the next thirty years," Lin observed sadly. "They will all fail, finally. We are too rebellious and selfish and independent. We will pay with blood and treasure!"

Throughout the evening, John had been fascinated by Lin's quiet confidence and clarity. Despite an uncomfortable skepticism, he could no longer restrain himself. "You seem very sure of your vision of China's future, Master Lin."

Lin smiled at John through shrewd eyes. "Just as sure as I am that the race for first flight will be won by whoever masters control of a flying machine, not those who seek only the perfect motor."

After Lily had translated, John's shock stopped his chopsticks in mid-air above his plate. How could Lin know that? John wondered if he knew of John's support for Langley's motor? Or did he know that the Wright brothers believed control of the airframe, especially the wings, was more significant? "Do you think the motor is unimportant?"

"The winner of first flight will not need the finest motor," Lin said. "A simple motor will be enough."

"But... but... that's where I've put all my energies!" John exclaimed. In pursuit of the mythic perfect engine, had he wasted nine precious months in Washington, New York, Chicago, Dayton, Quincy and Hammondsport? "What should I do?"

The expression of compassion on Lin's face stirred Maggie's heart with fear. In that instant, she knew two things: John's plea for Lin's advice meant that he had moved closer to her own beliefs in a discarnate world. Even more startling, Lin's expression suggested that John would not win the race to first flight.

"Master the problems of control and structural balance. With your knowledge of both engines and structures, you *will* win a great race." Then a frown creased Lin's brow. "But don't expect public recognition for your victory."

Yet another validation of his decision to build both an engine and an aeroplane, John thought. His expression of gratitude compelled Maggie to offer a favor in return. "We are most grateful for your vision, Master. May we do nothing to repay you for your support?"

The time had come for the test. Lin already knew the answer. But he must let Lily represent him. "Master Lin's favorite niece is a five-year old named Lin Mei-yin. Her parents were killed last year. Her mother, Lin's youngest sister, deplored foot-binding and many other Chinese customs. She hoped that her brother might save Mei-yin from such barbarisms. She had begged Master Lin to bring her daughter to America if anything should happen to her or her husband." Lily paused with embarrassment at the favor she was about to seek from Maggie and John.

For the first time that evening, Davey opened his mouth and, once again, revealed a knowing that defied easy explanation. "Momma, Aunt Lily and Master Lin want you and Poppa to take care of Mei-yin until Aunt Lily comes back from China. Mei-yin will come to San Francisco next week."

Maggie felt a thrill of gratitude when John answered her questioning look with a smile and a nod of assent. "Of course we'll take Mei-yin. We are honored that Master Lin should place such a treasure in our safekeeping."

"Until I met the Harrisons six months ago, I was baffled." Lin's eyes shone with love for Davey. "Now I feel the utmost confidence in Maggie to give her love and a home to Mei-yin and to begin her education. She should be no burden."

"No, at least not with Immigration," Lily said. "All of her papers are in order."

"Splendid," Larry said. "We can all go to San Francisco next week. At the same time, you can wish us a peaceful road and welcome little Mei-yin."

CHAPTER THIRTY-FIVE

SAN FRANCISCO
JANUARY, 1900

On the morning of January 7, they traveled by buggy to the Del Monte Lodge for lunch. Then, they took a tallyho to the Monterey depot and boarded the Del Monte Express for the three-and-a-half hour trip to San Francisco. As the train entered the city and proceeded slowly north down Harrison Street, Davey felt a familiar confusion. Had that street been named in honor of his family? After crossing Alabama, the tracks turned east onto Townsend and finally stopped at the Ferry Station, north of China Basin. The trip had taken the entire day between departure from the Carmel Valley ranch and arrival at Leander Sherman's home on Green Street. Sherman, Maggie's former piano teacher, opened his home to the Harrisons.

This was Davey's first trip to San Francisco. Maggie thought he would burst with all the information he was trying to digest. From their top floor room, she pointed out main points of interest: distant Angel Island, where most Chinese immigrants suffered through days, sometimes weeks of internment; the railroad town of Tiburon next to Angel Island, where travellers could catch a Northwest Pacific train for points north along the coast; the towns of Berkeley and Oakland across the bay to the east; Telegraph Hill and the bustling ferry building at the foot of Market Street from which everyone could travel to all points of San Francisco Bay.

John suddenly exclaimed at an announcement he was reading in the *San Francisco Chronicle*. "Maggie, gather up Davey. I'm gonna show you a huge surprise."

A half-hour later, they were plunged into the darkness of the Orpheum Theater to see Mr. Edison's latest magic machine, the vitascope, the first-ever projection of a moving picture on a big screen. They saw boxers, waves pounding a beach, skirt dancers and, most naughty, a sixteen-second closeup of two actors kissing.

Unimpressed, Maggie said later, "It was just a big peep show; there was no story, not even funny skits. The projection machine broke down twice and the film was grainy and jerky."

To compensate for that disappointment, John took everyone to supper at Mayes Oyster Saloon and Chop House. In the midst of their supper, Maggie excitedly nudged Lily. "Look over there. Isn't that Enrico Caruso? Mister Sherman predicted that he might be here."

During a pause in a lively conversation about the New York, London and San Francisco theater, Lin asked Maggie, "Please look in my eyes and tell me that you are *truly* happy to take Mei-yin."

Maggie smiled. "Oh, Master Lin, *yin shwei sz yüan* (Be grateful to your benefactor). This will give me a chance to repay you and Mr. Wang only a fraction of my debt to you for my education in Shanghai after my parents were killed. Without you, I would never have attended college; I would never have had such a wonderful sister like Lily. It will be my pleasure to carry on the tradition. I know I will love Mei-yin with all my heart."

By the time they ended their meal, it was time to go down to the docks, where Mei-yin's ship would be arriving. It was a magical, starlit evening. A full moon cast silver pennies across the bay and filled the cold, windy streets of San Francisco with beauty and mystery. While the group stood patiently waiting for Mei-yin to appear, they watched the first class passengers, whose gaiety and smiles expressed their gratitude at setting foot on land after so many days at sea. Finally, a lovely, well-dressed young Chinese woman stood at the gangway, a little girl tightly holding her hand.

"There they are!" cried Lin, who moved forward swiftly to greet them. In a moment, a confused Mei-yin, dismayed and shy at all the attention, tried to hide behind her companion. Before Maggie, John or Lily could do anything, something happened then that all would remember for many years. Davey took charge. He took one of Mei-yin's small hands in his and said in fluent Mandarin, "Welcome to America, Mei-yin. And welcome to Old Gold Mountain (the Chinese name for San Francisco). I am called Davey and I am your friend. I will take care of you." He drew Mei-yin from behind the defenses of her escort's skirts and went through the introductions as if she were a princess. "This is my father; this is my mother; this is your Aunt Lily; and this is your Uncle Larry; you already know Master Lin. Give them a smile!" And she did.

Lin whispered to Maggie, "Now I'm convinced. She will be very happy with you. You should be proud of your exceptional young son, but then I can see that you are. Someday perhaps I'll be able to repay you for this great gift. For now, you must take your son to Mary Stewart for an astrological reading."

"Mary Stewart? I never heard of her." With the prospect of Lily's departure, Maggie's emotions were very fragile. She wanted no fight with John now.

As if reading her mind, Lin replied, "You mustn't worry about your husband. Mary is truly gifted. The reading will be part of his own education."

"Isn't Davey too young? Will he understand?"

"Maggie, Davey's body may be young, but he's a wise old soul. Remember, he understood me."

"But... his vocabulary?"

Lin chided Maggie gently. "Have you forgotten all your lessons? Surely you remember that our most treasured knowledge comes nonverbally."

"When should we go?"

"Go there immediately after our ship leaves tomorrow. Your *ch'i* will need the comfort of Mary's gifts. She lives in a small house on Pacific Heights."

The next day at eleven o'clock in the morning, they made their way across a noisy, busy, crowded dock to board the 12,000-ton, Dollar Lines' S.S. *Numinous*. Its interior had been designed to equal the elegance and 20-knot speed of the Cunard Line's Atlantic liner, *Campania*, built in 1893. As if she had designed the great liner herself, Lily boasted that *Numinous* could carry 600 First Class, 400 Second Class and 1000 Third Class passengers plus a ship's complement of over 300 sailors, engineers, firemen and stewards. Lily proclaimed the *Numinous* to be a floating palace. She showed them first to the 100-foot long, grand dining saloon, capable of accommodating nearly 500 passengers. Its richly carved walls of dark mahogany supported a white and gold ceiling and a crystal dome rising thirty-three feet above the deck. She led them to the drawing room on the promenade deck. Its walls were satinwood and cedar. Spacious and lofty, it was decorated in Renaissance style with a fireplace, an organ and a grand piano. With its leather overstuffed chairs and couches and its paneled walls of fumed oak, the first-class smoking room resembled a club for men. Lily showed them the palatial ballroom, the many smaller lounges, the library and, finally, their elegant first-class cabins.

"You'll be spoiled rotten by the time you reach Shanghai, Lily," Maggie teased.

"It's a long trip, Maggie," Lily replied. "Hawaii will offer a little break from the boredom; but after that, we'll have to entertain ourselves with books and deck chairs and promenades and food, food and more food."

Pity the poor steerage and Third Class passengers crammed below decks, Maggie thought as she recalled the three steamer trunks that Lily had filled with the latest gowns by Worth, Felix, Revillon, Paquin and Raudnitz that her father had brought from Europe. Maggie felt dowdy beside Lily's elegant outfit, a Felix blue serge, ankle-length dress, that resembled a coat with separate waist and skirt. The black braid down her leg-o-mutton sleeves and skirt made her resemble a petite zebra, but the edging was exquisite: a white silk bias band with red and gold velvet strips.

Suddenly gongs and bells and loud speakers interrupted their chatter with the announcement, "First call! All ashore that's going ashore; all ashore that's going ashore." In a panic, Maggie wondered how an hour could have passed so quickly. She stared at Lily with shock; she might never see her again! Neither had realized how deeply bonded they had become until they faced the awful moment for departure.

After she, John, Davey and Mei-yin walked down the gangplank, Maggie felt forsaken. She stifled a sense of overwhelming grief while she watched a tug slowly pull the great ship away from the pier. As long as she could see Lily's tiny figure at the bow, she could pretend that this wasn't happening. Even after the tug had released the ship to proceed under its own power, she could focus on Lily's progress from the bow to the stern where she kept waving until Maggie could no longer discern her figure from the rest of the liner's superstructure. Then she turned away and buried her head against John's chest. Uncontrollable surges of sobbing wracked her body while John held her in his arms and tried to comfort her. Davey talked quietly with Mei-yin and waited for his mother to calm herself.

"Shall we go home, sweetheart?" John asked gently.

"No; we can't. Master Lin told me that we must see a woman named Mary Stewart before we go home."

"And who is Mary Stewart?"

"She's an astrologer." Maggie's eyes pleaded with John to indulge her, to let her have her way without argument. "She lives on Pacific Heights. We could have lunch first at Fisherman's Wharf. Then we could go see Mary, spend one more night at the hotel and go home tomorrow."

"Anything that pleases you, Maggie." John was shaken by Maggie's public demonstration of grief and loss. He had not realized the extent of their devotion to each other.

By the time they telephoned Mary Stewart to confirm an appointment, ate a light lunch and found their way to Mary's home on Pacific Street, not far from Leander Sherman's house, Davey had charmed Mei-yin into a brief escape from any sense of isolation. Chattering like magpies through lunch, Davey answered questions as if he were the official—and authoritative—host.

Mary Stewart was a motherly woman in her forties. She greeted the Harrisons with warm smiles, patted Mei-yin's cheek and complained that she had only had a week in which to prepare an astrological chart for Davey. Mr. Lin had given her the necessary information immediately after the Harrisons had agreed to accept Mei-yin. "But I have a peculiar rule, I'm afraid," Mary said. "I will tell *only* my client what I see in the stars."

"Do you mean that we can't share your vision?" Maggie asked.

Mary looked at Maggie thoughtfully. "Davey can certainly tell you what we talked about. But I will preserve my written reading until your son is old enough to decide who else should see it."

Maggie went to her knees and hugged Davey. "Very well, Mrs. Stewart. May we remain by the fire until you have finished?"

"Of course. Davey, you come with me and we'll have a nice chat." Mary led Davey into a small study with its own cheery fire. She asked him to sit on the floor where he could see a chart with concentric circles and lots of lines, mostly on the left side of the chart. She then began to summarize the ten pages of writing which she would keep for her "client" after the session had ended. "You are a very, very independent young fellow, aren't you, Davey?"

"Inde..., indepen...?"

"Oh my, we're going to have to make this very direct and simple, I see. Do you do mostly whatever you feel like doing?"

"Yes, ma'am. Momma says I'm mighty... willful."

Mary smiled and caressed Davey's cheek. "Well, that's just the way you're supposed to be. So keep right on being as willful as you want to be. You must try to be your own boss even if others try to make you obey their rules."

"Even if my Poppa wants me to pretend that I can't hear voices or see what's going to happen next day or... sometime?"

"I don't want you to disobey your father. But he doesn't understand how you like to talk to birds and cows and horses. Someday soon he'll understand. Until then, you must discover for yourself who you are; you don't have to pretend to be exactly like your father. *How can I tell him that his father is merely frightened but will continue to test him into his teens? Maybe his mother will be able to help.* "Do you talk to all the animals?"

"Yes ma'am. I don't think Poppa likes it much; so I don't tell him about it. And Momma said I should never, ever tell Poppa about my invisible friends."

"Invisible? That's a pretty big word."

"Yes'm. Momma taught me. It means that most folks can't see them. They're just kids like me. They teach me all kinds of things."

"I'll bet they do." Davey was reassured that Mary didn't seem the least surprised at his story or his candor. "Well, you keep on talking to them. Because your going to have to talk to a lot of people in your life. So it's a good thing that you're so smart. Did you know you were smart?"

"No ma'am. I'm not old enough to be smart yet. But I can read a little 'cause Momma taught me. And I talk Chinese with Ah Ying."

Lin was right; he's gifted and doesn't even know it yet. It's too bad that his father fears love. I'm going to have to be very nurturing with this one. "You don't like arguments, do you?"

"No ma'am. I like to help people talk about their problems. I like people to love each other."

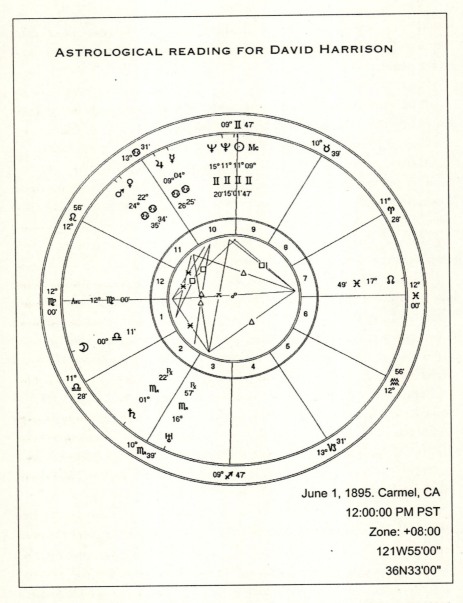

ASTROLOGICAL READING FOR DAVID HARRISON

June 1, 1895. Carmel, CA
12:00:00 PM PST
Zone: +08:00
121W55'00"
36N33'00"

He'll be a conciliator all his life. He could be an academic or a religious. But his fa-
ther will force him to put high value on more worldly achievements and career success.
That Saturn in retrograde.... That's this lad's sense of personal responsibility. His fa-
ther will use that as a powerful lever. Davey will have to cut short his childhood; he'll
have to mature early and find a compromise between his love of spirit and the world's
infatuation with ego.

That Jupiter.... "Do you ask what things mean all the time, Davey?"

"Yes'm. Every night I have a round-up of my day. I kinda..., I sing about my day and ask my friend to explain what it meant."

He'll never be shallow. That passion for detailed information will lead him to high position some day. What about Venus and Mars in conjunction in his eleventh house? Hmm. Great charisma; lots of friends. But slow maturing where women are concerned. He'll idealize them too much. That'll get him into trouble! Virgo rising.... He'll love work; endless projects. "Do you like to work with your father?"

"Oh, yes ma'am. I work in his bicycle shop. Then I work with Momma in the library. I ask questions and she looks up the answers. And now Momma and I are hunting for Space Travelers. They come from the stars. Momma gave me a telescope for Christmas."

Astonishing! Absolutely astonishing! Let's see.... He'll be a pinch-penny even though he'll be surrounded by wealth. But that won't stop him from starting great projects, meeting lots of people. Just a ball of energy! Very creative and very social. "You're going to have lots of friends, Davey. And you're going to be a leader, a special kind of leader. Would that surprise you?"

"No ma'am. I just like to take care of people. Is that wrong?"

"No. That's what you're supposed to do. Always do what your invisible friends tell you to do. They love you to care for people."

How reconcile Capricorn in his fifth house and Neptune in his tenth house? He'll be very practical, down to earth. That's his father's influence. But he'll be in constant communication with his mystical guides. A compassionate, practical concili-ator; service to others will be his ideal. Limited sense of humor; oh well, can't have it all. "Do you like jokes, Davey?"

"Sometimes. I like to laugh; but not if the joke hurts someone."

Aquarius in his sixth house. He'll be a visionary, highly intuitive. With educa-tion, he'll aspire to high position. But not for himself. He's an ideal candidate for some great cause. It's too bad that his mother must battle his father over Davey's soul. Lessons, lessons. I suppose those battles will strengthen this sweet child's charac-ter. "Well, Davey, I can tell that you and I will be great friends." She showed him ten pages of detailed explanations including two pages of pre-dictions about his life. "Someday you might find these pages interesting. Would you like your parents to read this story now?"

Davey's answer startled even Mary Stewart. "No ma'am. I want you to keep it for me until I need it."

"Can you tell me why you don't want them to read it now?"

"Yes'm. I think they would argue about it; don't you?"

Mary smiled at his youthful wisdom and his confirmation of her reading. "Quite right, Davey. I'll put it in an envelope and wait until you ask for it."

By the next evening, the weary foursome climbed down from their buggy and entered the welcoming, cool embrace of the ranch house. Ah Ying added another welcome to Mei-yin who, by now, seemed to have lost her shyness and had a comment for everything and everyone. She was surprised to know that she would have her very own room, next to Davey, with an east view across the wide lawn to the mountains. When she had settled into bed and was about to fall asleep, she was interrupted by Davey, who started a tradition that would continue for over five years. Sitting beside her bed, each of the Harrisons sang a song to her.

CHAPTER THIRTY-SIX

CARMEL VALLEY
JANUARY–MARCH, 1900

Mei-yin's arrival in the Harrison household was a turning point in everyone's life. She brought a subtle shift to the deep undercurrents of relationships in the family. For such a little girl, it was astonishing how she accentuated the *competitive* balance between masculine and feminine forces. That might not have happened if Davey's innate curiosity had not lured him toward John's quest for the ideal glider. And Maggie still might have fought Davey's seductive sirens—and perhaps his destiny—if she had not yearned for an adoring daughter and if Mei-yin's inquiring mind had not diverted her with questions, spoken first in Mandarin.

Mei-yin's energy was apparently inexhaustible. With a zeal and enthusiasm that would brand her personality for life, she hurled herself into a university of new experiences and challenging lessons. With help from Ramon Cisneros, Davey and Juan, she learned to ride Su-su. In late February, Ramon gave her a gentle pony. But he permitted the three youngsters to ride only in the paddock. Juan taught her Mexican and English songs. Thus did her English and Spanish acquire a lilt, a rhythm whose origin in childhood songs she would forget. When Davey and Mei-yin were alone, they fell into the habit of speaking Chinese. By late March, Ah Ying and Maggie had taught the children 100 characters. Their calligraphy would expand to over 2000 characters over the next five years.

By March, just as Davey followed his father everywhere, so Mei-yin dogged Maggie's footsteps. To Maggie's surprise, she found her new protegé enchanting and stimulating to the point that she fell into the oldest parental trap of all: crafting a clone of her better self. It became so habitual for her to turn to Mei-yin to explain some detail of decoration or cooking or art or whatever that she would feel mild resentment when the little girl wandered off to play with Davey.

Maggie also encouraged the work of several young local writers. She spent hours discussing both their manuscripts and the crop of new books, some non-fiction, many more fiction. Most novels were romantic tear-jerkers whose hero was invariably an artist or journalist trapped in a loveless marriage. But the typical hero's confrontation with selfish and frivolous "high society" or "the interests" sustained Maggie's yearning to emancipate humanity, especially women, from the crass materialism of the age. Over the next five years, Maggie would become familiar with a host of young authors, mostly women who wrote of escape from the prison of poverty, of small-town pettiness, boredom and routine and of masculine insensitivity, which *Atlantic Monthly, Independent* and *Century Magazine* validated when they rejected Maggie's stories. Maggie agreed with young Ellen Glasgow, who had just published her first novel, *The Descendant*. Ellen's rebuff by the New York literary monopoly had caused her to write, "They have created both the literature of America and the literary renown that embalmed it..., encouraging one another in mediocrity."

As the elections of 1900 approached, Maggie's interest in politics flowered. While John pursued his design of a glider, she pursued local political leaders. She had learned already that John did not share her interest in either politics or politicians. In fact, except for his experience with rare birds like Mike Coyle, he believed that politicians were as relentless as religious zealots, including priests and rabbis, in their exploitation of the gullible. His years with vaqueros, soldiers and common laborers had taught him a high tolerance for man's exploitation of man; therefore he had a high threshold of political outrage. As long as he could exercise some control over his immediate environment, especially his family and the ranch, he felt no need to fight injustice. His motivations—and his social vision—were those of the common man who expects little more than the status quo and is grateful to avoid the hypocrisy of the self-inflated political leader, dripping with self-anointed charisma.

On the other hand, Maggie's experience with Chinese peasants had planted the seeds of a lifetime commitment to a square deal for the underdog. She was ever alert to inequity and injustice, ever ready to defend a victim of greed and cruelty and insensitivity. Her motivations were *on behalf* of the common man. Like other socialist philosopher-kings across the planet, her conscience and a collection of fierce grievances—some real, most imagined—demanded change, preferably instant change.

John's education and experience, especially in New York and Cuba, had taught him to *accept* "the system" and to navigate around the evils of the day. If they would just leave him and his family alone, he would be content to seek beauty from an engine's form and function. Maggie's experience had taught her to confront evil, and *change* "the system" through confrontation and the dynamic creativity of human relationships.

One evening after a blustery day in late March, Maggie told stories from *San Kuo Chih* (*The Romances of the Three Kingdoms*). Like all small Chinese children, Mei-yin already knew many of the stories well since her mother had coached her on the dramatic story-line. After Maggie finished, Mei-yin told another story, which Maggie identified as a traditional myth from *Shui Hu Chuan (All Men Are Brothers)*, the great Chinese epic about a band of robbers whose exploits on behalf of the poor against the rich reminded Davey of the Robin Hood tales. Like Robin Hood, the stories revealed Chinese perceptions of the ancient conflict between free will and fate, good and evil, life and death, love and hate, honor and shame. The telling of great Chinese tales—the basis for all Chinese opera—became a regular Saturday night tradition. Juan Cisneros was frequently included among the wide-eyed listeners. Through such stories and through play, the bond among Davey, Juan Cisneros and Mei-yin deepened. They became almost inseparable. Davey especially began to feel a sense of kinship with his "sister," with China's culture and with her country's hopes and fears, failures and achievements.

CHAPTER THIRTY-SEVEN

CARMEL VALLEY
APRIL, 1900

Maggie greeted Ned Ambler with a warm embrace. "How nice to see you *Doctor* Ambler. Are you calling for business or pleasure?"

Ned Ambler frowned at the question. "These days, I find no clear distinction between the two. When I'm on a professional call, I'm a doctor. But when I *think* I'm calling for pleasure, my host often forces me to play either doctor or alienist in search of mental pathologies."

"Why Ned, even if it was all decked out in Fourth of July bunting, I don't think I could detect a mental pathology. Can you?"

Ned glanced behind him toward his buggy and the Carmel River, shimmering in the early afternoon sunlight. He wondered if he should share his concerns about Davey or should he continue his investigations a little longer? "I thought to see John for a moment. Has he lost interest in his moto-cycles?"

"Where did you get that idea?" Maggie ushered Ned into the foyer, took his coat and hung it on a coatrack. "And even if it were true, would his change of mind qualify as a mental pathology?"

Ned grinned, delighted with her pixie humor. "I don't think John is any more sociopathic than most of us; but I wondered what has diverted him from his second love. You are first, of course."

"If that's all you came for, I can give you the answers. In his shop, he is still hot on the trail of the most powerful small engine in the world. But in our barn, he's designing a kite."

Ned stared at Maggie with astonishment. "You can't be serious! A kite?"

"Yes. He's spent the past two months in the library studying the mysteries of things called airfoils and cambers. I don't pretend to understand any of it. All I know is that a kite is supposed to emerge from all that... cerebration."

"And where might I find the great kite designer?" Ned asked dryly.

"He's moved his books and notebooks and foul cigars to a shop in the barn. You'll probably find Davey and Juan Cisneros there, too."

"And Mei-yin?"

"She's helping Ah-ying bake a cake for lunch." Maggie said with mixed pride and amusement. "That means she's licking the icing bowl. She's the one you should examine for possible pathologies. Her specialty is political manipulation."

"Who would dare teach her such things in this household?" Ned asked with a side-long glance at Maggie.

"Don't blame me, Ned. She's on her own ground when she persuades Davey and Juan to give her *their* share of a custard pie. I wouldn't have believed it if I hadn't seen it yesterday."

Ned walked through the south door of the old barn to find a surprise. Floored in solid oak, the room was occupied by all the equipment of a fine carpenter shop: power saws, vices and two heavy work tables approximately six feet wide and thirty feet long. Racks along the east wall held long one-inch thick sheets of spruce and one-inch square ash and spruce rods. Along the west wall, rolls of sateen hung suspended on spindles. The entire room was flooded with sunlight that poured through a south-facing skylight. The north wall of the room offered a windowed-door. Ned peeked through it to see John, Davey and Juan at work.

He walked into the room to see that the north wall of the barn was framed in glass through which a steady light gave sharp clarity to a large drafting table and several long flat tables. Behind him, the south wall of the room was adorned with sketches of kites, many of them obviously the rough, primitive work of Davey and Juan. Along the west wall, several large flat file drawers offered space for drawings and blueprints. Along the east wall were suspended many slotted racks, on which several model wings, about 30 inches wide, were resting in the slots. Using a wood template, Davey and Juan were cutting out wing-ribs from stiff cardboard. Ned noted that each of the boys used a pencil to mark the same number on each rib. On one of the long tables at the center of the room were over fifty wooden ribs. John hovered over the drafting table, where he appeared to be drafting full-scale rib designs. In an instant, Ned could see the process. *John designs a master rib, gives it a number, reduces it to a model scale, then hands it to the boys. They make paper copies from which a model wing can be glued together.* "Violation of child labor laws carries severe penalties, John."

"Hello, Ned!" John stood up from the drafting table and shook hands with his best friend. He glanced at the two boys, who offered a quick smile to the visitor, then returned to their careful work with scissors. "It's worse than you think. I don't pay 'em a damn thing. Yet they keep comin' back for more."

"What's going on here? Looks like you're building a fleet of kites."

"Maybe I'd better start at the beginnin'." John handed Ned a cup of hot coffee and lit a cigar for himself. He stared out the north wall of glass to the distant mountains and collected his thoughts. "First, you must understand that I'm really designin' a glider that can carry a hundred-and-sixty-pound man. Before I build the real thing, I'll use model kites to test different sizes and shapes of wings."

"I thought you said Lilienthal and Langley had worked out detailed tables for their gliders. Why go to all this trouble?" Ned hated waste; this whole set-up reeked of excess—a typical Harrison project. He couldn't conceive of the money that John must have already spent on his shop. "Why don't you just build a full-scale kite and be done with it?"

"Hell, Ned, nobody knows the best airfoil camber and aspect ratio. So my team..." John gestured to Davey and Juan... "and I are engaged in great research." He pointed at a chart and the wings already slotted into the wall-racks. "Each pair of wings will be unique in size and shape."

Ned studied a chart of numbers on the wall next to the racks.

WING NUMBER	CAMBER	ASPECT RATIOS			
1	1:12	3:1;	5:1;	7:1;	10:1
2	1:16	"	"	"	"
3	1:20	"	"	"	"
4	1:24	"	"	"	"
5	1:28	"	"	"	"

"O.K., John, I'll bite. What are camber and aspect ratio?"

"Camber is the ratio of the thickness of a wing to its width. Lilienthal recommended a wing thickness about one-twelfth of its width. Wilbur Wright thinks that's too chunky. He thinks a thinner camber of about 1:22 will reduce drag and increase lift. Aspect ratio is the ratio of the wingspan to the width of the wing. The ideal aspect ratio and camber must be a mix that gives the most lift for least drag."

Ned glanced at the chart. "So you're going to build kites with wings as fat as 1:12 and as slender as 1:28. Long, narrow wings; short, broad wings." Ned thought John's approach was altogether too primitive. "Sounds like a mighty hit-or-miss approach. Don't you have some equation to work with?"

"Sure." John grinned at Ned's impatience for science. These days, everything had to be scientific. "The equations are right in front of your nose..."

For the first time, Ned noticed a placard with three equations on it.

$$F = kV^2S$$
$$L = kV^2SC(l)$$
$$D = kV^2SC(d)$$

"...I'm workin' on 'S': the ideal surface area of the wings in square feet. But we're suspicious of 'k'," John said with a frown.

"Who's 'we'? Davey and Juan?"

John smiled as the two five-year-olds looked up from their work and grinned at Doctor Ned's joke. "Yes, my two men plus a long line of theorists and engineers and would-be flyers from as far back as the mid-sixteenth century."

"I had no idea, John!" Ned savored both his coffee and the beauty of the golden champagne carpet of dry grass sprinkled with Monterey oaks that rolled away from the barn toward the distant mountain range.

"Galileo laid the groundwork in the sixteenth century when he took an interest in thermodynamics. Isaac Newton kept up the game in the eighteenth century along with Smeaton. All of them were tryin' to measure things like water pressure and the resistance of an object movin' through fluid."

Ned thought it was interesting that Maggie and John both liked history, the one for the history of ideas and the other for the history of physics. What did they talk about? "I've heard of Galileo and Newton, of course. I can see why you might be suspicious of their findings. But who was Smeaton?"

"John Smeaton was an English engineer who studied windmills. He came up with a very critical concept in 1750, so far back that even his equipment is suspect." The expression on John's face was grim, as if he blamed Smeaton for leading all would-be flyers astray, as if he had killed Lilienthal.

"What was the concept?"

"Look at that top equation, Ned. That's our Bible. Smeaton stuck flat plates into moving water and discovered the profound truth that the force (F) or pressure in pounds on the edge of the plate varied with the square of the velocity (V) of the water in miles per hour."

Ned's scientific mind began to leap across the centuries to John's problem with wings. He had seen similar streams of thought emerging from trickles to become torrential discoveries in medicine. "What is k in the top equation?"

"That's Smeaton's critical constant, called the Smeaton coefficient. It's a factor called a 'constant of proportionality.' Each medium, like air and water and oil, has its own constant."

"Makes sense. So Smeaton's coefficient is for air?"

"That's right. He said it must be .005."

Ned's mathematical brain performed a quick calculation. "My God, John. If that coefficient is only slightly wrong, your calculation of Force could be very badly out of kilter."

John nodded. He liked to have someone intelligent to whom he could explain his problem. Maggie had shown no interest whatsoever. "Fifty years after Smeaton proposed his coefficient, a feller named Vince studied the effect on pressure or F if he slightly changed the angle of the plates toward the flow."

Ned's mind took an instant leap of understanding. He was surprised that it so excited him. "I see. You're saying that that variation on Smeaton's work could be used by wing designers today to calculate lift."

Ned's quick understanding delighted John, who slapped Ned on his knee. "I always knew you were right smart. That C(l) in the second equation is the coefficient of lift. Lilienthal gave his life to calculate and publish pages of coefficients of lift, which changes with every angle of attack."

"And the third equation must calculate drag based on a similar coefficient of drag?"

John lifted a thick book from the drafting table. "This is Lilienthal's book. It contains tables of coefficients of drag as well. You've got it all, Ned. Now, that wasn't so hard was it?"

Unaccountably, Ned felt infused with curiosity. He had intended to stay only a moment. But he was captivated by a spirit in the room that he couldn't name. He hadn't felt this way for a long time. It was a mix of fun—the models maybe—and mystery and challenge and... the stunning possibility of flight! He had read that hundreds, perhaps thousands of men in barns and stables and shops across the country were caught up in a passion for flight. There was a competitive angle to the whole thing. But the lure of the sky was far more compelling than winning or losing first place. This was not the first time that John's mind and stubborn will had captured Ned's attention. A question positioned itself at the center of Ned's consciousness: *Should I offer to help?* "Let me summarize. The equation tells us that the ability of a glider to lift a given weight in pounds—the weight of the glider and a pilot—is equal to the Smeaton coefficient times the wind velocity squared times the wing surface in square feet times one of Lilienthal's coefficients of lift."

"Then you gotta subtract drag." John offered Ned a cigar even though he knew that Ned hated them. "You calculate drag from the third equation."

"How about the drag of an engine and the struts?"

"I'll figure that later. Right now, I'm just testin' cambers and aspect ratios. I'll assume Lilienthal's coefficients and Smeaton's ratio are right."

"Why only a pair of wings on each kite?"

"Two reasons. First, I trust Will Wright; his glider is a bi-plane. Chanute is still messin' around with multi-wing contraptions. But I think they're too heavy and too hard to control."

"And the second reason?"

John suddenly felt mildly embarrassed. What the hell, he might as well confide in Ned. He told him about Davey's dream at the Carmel Highlands. "Those machines were bi-planes."

Ned successfully masked his astonishment at John's respect for Davey's vision. Did this mean that John had come to accept the boy's startling psychism? Ned suspected it was more like pragmatic open-mindedness to see if its benefits might outweigh its risks. John was nothing if not an empiricist. "Those are both good reasons, John. Your lift and drag equations are great, assuming that Lilienthal's coefficients of lift and Smeaton's coefficient are right. But how do you fix V, the velocity of the wind?"

John's forlorn expression was answer enough. "I *can't* fix the wind. But I can measure wind speed with my anemometer. I'll try to do my tests on days when the wind speed seems to be around twenty miles per hour."

Ned turned the equation over in his mind and thought about its implications. He was struck suddenly by the fact that the key to everything might be speed. "Did you and Langley concentrate on the engine back in New York because you wanted lots of horsepower to give you plenty of speed?"

"That was the idea. Enough speed or 'V' could compensate for minor flaws in either coefficients of lift or Smeaton's coefficient. Hell, someday we'll probably have rockets with no wings, no airfoils and no cambers at all. The equation will be all horsepower and tremendous speed."

"So you're shifting to more efficient wing design because you don't expect to get your engine soon?"

"Not exactly, Ned. I'm also workin' on a radial engine design based on the Balzer engine. If I can design—and control—the most efficient glider and if I can build my own simple engine, I'll win the race for first flight."

"Are you in touch with the best minds in the field?" Ned asked. "And do they share their work with you?"

"So far, so good. Wilbur shares everthin' with me and Chanute. They're movin' along fast."

"How fast?"

"They're buildin' their first full-size glider right now. Usin' a spruce and ash framework. They'll cover the wings with French sateen, the same stuff I have in the shop. They expect to test it in September." Thoughtfully, John looked at the distant mountains. "With my own glider, I'd like to beat that schedule by a month."

Ned blinked. *He wants to fly a full-scale glider in August? Impossible!* "I wonder where they'll test it?"

"Place called Kitty Hawk on the North Carolina coast. They consulted the National Weather Bureau to find a place with a strong, steady wind.

They want the same fifteen to twenty-mile-per-hour breeze that I want. And Kitty Hawk has two other advantages."

"What's that, John?"

"Privacy and a lot of soft sand for rough landings." John frowned. "Trouble is, they've hired a scoundrel named Zeke Harner to watch over their shop while they're gone."

"Why is he a problem?"

John took a half-hour to tell Ned the full story of Zeke's theft of Langley's plans and interference with the Balzer engine. He had never told the story to Maggie because he didn't want her to worry about the possibility of assault by a New York gang member. "In his last letter, Wilbur said he and Orville had forgiven Zeke because they wanted to help Zeke's poor wife and son."

"Do you feel threatened by the man?"

John gave the question some thought while he took a final puff on his cigar. "Yes. Wilbur said Zeke recently *promised* the Wrights that no one would be allowed to interfere with their race for first flight."

Ned suddenly realized that John needed an ally. He could play with Davey and Juan, but they weren't old enough to be his intellectual partners. They were only old enough to cut ribs and maybe glue wings together. "Have you chosen a spot for your trials yet?"

"No. First, I have to build a bunch of one-eighth scale kites. The wind up on the ridge line is fairly steady. So when I have ten or a dozen kites ready, the boys and I will ride up there and runs some tests before I start my full-sized glider. Wanta help?"

"John, I would be honored and delighted. Where can I start?"

John filled Ned's cup with coffee and handed him a pair of scissors.

CHAPTER THIRTY-EIGHT

CARMEL VALLEY
SUMMER, 1900

Before lunch on June 1, Davey's fifth birthday, it was a strange group of six—three adults and three children—that urged their horses up Los Laureles, just north of the Harrison ranch house. Behind the saddle of each horse, a wooden framework carried two delicate kites. John also carried assorted instruments in a pair of saddle bags that hung loosely in front of his saddle horn. He was bursting with excitement as he reflected on the work of the last six weeks. He thought the airfoil with the best drag-to-lift ratio must be hiding somewhere among these twelve kites. His hunch was that he would get the best ratio from wide slender wings—not the fat stubby ones. But tests today should dispense with guesswork once and for all.

While the three children chatted, Ned Ambler marveled at the beauty of the scene. To the west down the Carmel Valley, he could see a fogbank withdrawing across the Pacific Ocean. Several eagles, coasting on steady, warm updrafts from the valley floor, were clear silhouettes against a brilliant blue sky. Wild flowers sprinkled a riot of colors across the slopes. He thought, *Even if these tests fail today, it's pure heaven to be out in this sparkling air close to the most beautiful woman on earth.* The thought revealed the love for Maggie that he had suppressed for several years out of respect for John and out of fear for his own mental stability. He had learned to live with his passion, masked by a thin veneer of gratitude for the several occasions when he could be helpful. At the age of 42, he had sense enough to know that he was fully qualified to make a fool of himself over a ravishing woman fifteen years his junior. He also had calculated the likely cost of any aggressive pursuit of his devotion: anguish and probably heartbreak for Amy; divorce; separation from his children; banishment both from polite society and probably his beloved Carmel; loss of patients perhaps to the point of bankruptcy; and for what? If successful, perhaps a decade of brief happiness before age overtook him. If unsuccessful, a humiliation that would haunt him for the rest of his life. So he had learned to draw small satisfaction simply from being near her.

Maggie also felt the promise of this celebration, a change from Davey's customary birthday party for the whole ranch. He had begged her to keep it to a small family affair and to make kite-flying the central attraction. She agreed because, in early May, John had invited her to join the team. She and Mei-yin had stretched fabric across the sturdy wings and had helped fasten them together with struts and wire. They had also named each kite. Those with fat cambers like 1:12 and 1:16 and aspect ratios lower than 3:1 they called by masculine titles: Grumpy Gus; Bully Ben; Fatty Frank and so forth. They used watercolors to paint somber earth tones on the leading edges of those kites. Kites with slender wings and slivers for cambers they gave feminine names like Elegant Ellen; Slender Sal; Rakish Rachel. Those kites' wings were painted silver and light blue and dove grey. Maggie didn't care if the tests were successful or not. It was pleasure enough to be on such an outing with her family. A picnic would have done just as well, but the men needed the illusion that something serious was at stake. Maggie could not bring herself to believe that kite-flying should be taken seriously. However this was no day for arguments. After all, regardless of John's obsession with their "aspect ratios" and "cambers," the model kites were quite beautiful. John had sanded the leading edges of the wings to reduce something called "drag." For the same reason, even the struts between wings were rounded. Privately, Maggie hoped the long, slender models would win—whatever winning meant to John. "I don't like the boxy, chunky kites, Johnnie," she cried after an hour of testing.

"Why, neither does my chief engineer: Davey. What's wrong with them?"

"They don't behave gracefully. They dart about from side to side as if they want to crash. They'd make me so seasick, I couldn't control it."

After two hours, Maggie's observation proved accurate. The erratic behavior of the chunky kites persuaded John that he must build a full-scale kite with a wingspan between four and five times the width of the wing. His imagination leaped to a vision of a glider with 400 square feet of wings, each wing approximately 30 feet in span and around six feet in depth. He was surprised to find that a camber of 1:18 gave the best performance. He resolved to make his next set of kites with a narrow range between 1:18 and 1:22.

While they were eating a delicious picnic lunch, John noted two horsemen on a ridge to the west. One of them appeared to have a telescope. "Give me your binoculars, Ned. I'd like to know about those fellers."

The one with the telescope was clearly comfortable in the saddle. However, his clothing was eastern: buff jodhpurs, shining riding boots, a tweed jacket. His only concession to western custom was a Rough Rider campaign hat, which obscured his face. *If I didn't know how much he hates horses, I would say that's Jerry Ashley. But why would he come here without first contacting me? Why would he come here anyway? And why would the likes of Ashley go out in public with that second character?* It was the second man whose appearance sent a shiver down John's spine. His outfit was a brown checkered sack suit. And he wore a derby. *Monk Eastman? Impossible. Monk wouldn't leave his birds, cats and bicycles; but he could certainly send one of his toughs across the country.* "Ned, I want to check those fellers. I think we've learned enough about gliders for one day. If you take Maggie home, I'll go see what they're up to."

John mounted his horse and rode directly to the stem of Los Laureles. He had barely reached that range of hills when he saw that the two strangers had disappeared. With Ned's binoculars he searched the ridge line in vain. They were gone. Thoughtfully, he worked his horse down into Carmel Valley. Were he and his family under some kind of threat? Or were they only under Monk Eastman's surveillance? Should he approach the sheriff with the situation? No, the sheriff would be powerless; there was no law against riding around Los Laureles. Furthermore, the strangers might not be associated with Monk Eastman. But he couldn't dismiss the thought of his vulnerability to the likes of Eastman. Should he warn Maggie? No, he had never told her about Monk Eastman, no need to excite her now. Until he could gather more evidence, he must be on guard.

He paused in his speculations as he guided his horse across a deep arroyo, moved along his own fence line and dismounted at a gate to enter his ranch. He rarely rode fence, leaving that boring duty to younger vaqueros. But today it gave him pleasure to see all posts firmly seated and all barbed

wire taut along the northern boundary of the ranch. He returned to his re-
flections about possible backers behind Monk Eastman.

How could Wall Street expect to make money out of first flight? When
he recalled that only thirty patents had been filed regarding aviation devices before 1890, the simplicity of the answer stunned him. Ownership!
That must be their goal. They must want to own the patents on the best
small engine, the design of the best airframe and the devices for controlling stable flight. Forget fame. The winner of first flight *could* have the
keys to a chest full of treasure: royalties on every similar engine or instrument sold across the world, same as that lawyer feller, what was his
name?... Selden, who was getting a royalty on every auto made—army
contracts, foreign sales.... John's mind whirled with the potential financial
power that might come to the owner of critical aeronautical technology.
No wonder greedy men might resort to intimidation, even death threats,
to capture a fistful of early patents. It came to him that even this day's two
hours of testing might have yielded findings subject to patent.

In later years, when John told his story, he would trace his zeal for ownership and competition for patents to that first day of testing, and the arro-
gance and damnable audacity of two strangers—*Easterners*! From that day
forward, he locked up all plans and models in the barn. He resolved to
share his work only with those who were equally generous. At that point,
among hundreds of men who thought they were competing for first flight,
John thought only four Americans deserved to be on his short list: Sam
Langley for his friendship and his work with models; Charles Manly and
Stephen Balzer for their work on the finest small engine in the world, and
Wilbur Wright for his work on controls. As he stabled his horse, John realized that none of them was far ahead of the others. If they shared their
work, they might achieve what no one else had done in history.

John included three other men on his list of friendly observers, deserv-
ing of general information but no details. Octave Chanute headed that list.
He deserved some information because he had given so generously to everyone, but his very generosity was a disadvantage to anyone who wanted
to preserve secrecy pending grant of patent. That was because he was a
publicist as well as an aviation enthusiast. He simply could not keep a secret! Tom Baldwin and Glenn Curtiss were interested only in building an
engine and, so far, they were simply potential customers for his motor.

By the time John started walking from the stables to the house, a strategy had taken shape in his mind. He would pursue a more vigorous correspondence with the two men whose work he respected most: Manly and Wright. In his Monterey shop, he would press ahead for an improved version of the Balzer motor. In the barn, after a summer of model-testing, he would build a full-scale glider. He imagined that a full-scale glider would reveal strengths and weaknesses that his small models had obscured. He suspected that Samuel Langley was devoting little new research to the full-scale aerodrome. By the summer of 1901, John hoped to make a trial first powered flight. He sent off letters to his two colleagues in mid-June. Then through July and August, he continued to experiment with model kites.

For Davey, it was a magical summer, the best kind of summer before submitting to the mysteries of First Grade. Besides building and testing models with his father, Ned Ambler and Juan Cisneros, he spent at least two days a week in the Monterey bicycle shop. He came to think of that shop as the metals shop, in contrast with the woodworking shop in the barn. In the metals shop, while he didn't care for the metal filings and the acrid smell, he watched precision grinding and boring of engine components with growing respect. He quickly learned the difference between a rotary and a radial engine, since his father denounced the former as inefficient and promised a big jump in brake horsepower rating for the basic Balzer engine if it were only stationary. That test would come sometime in the autumn.

Davey much preferred the sawdust and shavings and silk-covered wings of the models in the barn. For one thing, he could keep an eye on Mei-yin, for whom he felt some responsibility. For another thing, he could wander over to the stables and talk with the vaqueros, who were amused to educate him in the mysteries of honor and death and *machismo*. Stories of their dubious heroism in fictitious escapades filled his mind with the same themes of glorious selflessness that he heard from his father about the Civil War. In late August, he stumbled on a new talent, a variation on "the Game." It had started as hide-and-seek. Bored with the game, Davey said to Mei-yin, "Let's see if I can help you find where I hid something."

"How could you help without just telling me?" Mei-yin loved Davey's ideas for games. Just to keep them sane, she usually designed the rules.

"After I hide something, I'll come back to you and I'll try to become you!"

"How could you become me? I never heard of such a thing."

"I can become almost anything—in my head."

"Then what happens?"

"If it's a bird, I can fly; if it's a horse, I feel like running very fast. So if I could become you, I could tell you where I hid something. OK?"

"And what are the rules? Should I go there? Or what?"

"I'll get some paper and you can draw a picture of the place."

With Mei-yin's agreement, Davey found Juan Cisneros and persuaded him to take part in the great experiment. The boys carried a sombrero to an oak whose isolated position on a knoll commanded the full view of the ranch.

When they returned after ten minutes, they raced into the house through the kitchen to the library where they found Maggie reading. She did not usually like to be disturbed in the late morning, but the excited children aroused her curiosity. "Now what's this visit all about?" she asked with an indulgent smile.

"Dawei has hidden something somewhere," Mei-yin said in Mandarin, "and he's gonna try to tell me where it is."

"Why don't you simply tell her?" Maggie wondered what was so special about the game.

"'Cause I want to see if I can help her see my mind," Davey answered. "But you mustn't tell Poppa. He'll get mad." Too often since the eagle incident, Davey had heard his mother's futile attempts to mollify John's fears about Davey Dreams. Davey had concluded that only certain subjects were safe with his father: the Civil War; the ranch; the gliders; the engine and the War with Spain, especially the heroic performance of West Pointers.

Maggie put down her book and studied Davey with love and concern. Had it come to this? Had her nightly arguments with John alienated Davey from his own father? "No promises, Davey. Your father loves you just like I do and wants to hear about all your games. Now show me how this game works."

Davey placed a pad of drawing paper in front of Mei-yin, sat next to her and asked her to close her eyes and try to "hear" his voice. In the ensuing silence, they could hear a dove cooing in the meadow. Maggie noted that Davey's eyes seemed to be boring into Mei-yin as if he wanted to devour her.

For a moment, she was immobile and tranquil. Suddenly, she opened her eyes and smiled delightedly. She started sketching a scene on the pad. She hastily drew the hill. Davey was about to say something when she held up her hand and superimposed an oak tree. Then, with a final flourish, she sketched a large sombrero on top of the tree.

Davey threw his arms around her and hugged her with delight. "You got it! Wasn't that fun?" he asked in Mandarin. Turning to Juan Cisneros, he said in Spanish, "She got it. See? Every detail, just the way we left it."

"Now wait just a minute, Davey," Maggie said, wide-eyed at this new "gift." "Are you telling me that there really is a sombrero in the branches of an oak tree nearby?"

"I only knew he was going to hide something," Mei-yin said.

Maggie felt vaguely troubled by the experiment. "How did it feel to you, Mei-yin?"

"Nice. The picture... seemed real. Like I was sitting in the tree with the sombrero right next to me."

CHAPTER THIRTY-NINE

CARMEL VALLEY
AUGUST, 1900

On the Saturday morning before school started, Maggie piled Davey and Mei-yin into a buggy and drove to Carmel to meet their teacher, Julie Simmons. She lived in a lovely cottage located on a small rock outcropping. One side looked south along the Carmel Coast and was bathed in bright sunlight. A huge north-facing window offered a magnificent panorama along the coast. This window was the source of Julie's steady light for her studio. Here the children found her painting a seascape. When she spied her guests, she jumped up and enfolded the two children in her arms.

"I'm so glad you called about bringing the children over today," Julie said to Maggie. "I really prefer to meet my students before the first day of school"

While she poured cold lemonade and offered a plate of cookies, Davey asked if she would show them how to paint clouds and sea. Her amused response to Davey's request was warm and.... *What is it that she exudes?* Maggie mused. *It's more than hospitality and welcome. She has a kind of magnetism, an aura that just envelopes the children, especially Davey. Why, if Davey weren't so young, I'd swear she's flirting with him! Is that the way school teachers behave back east?*

Davey felt Julie's energy. He wasn't sure that he liked it; it felt... invasive, possessive. He supposed she was pretty. He wasn't old enough to know that she was more than pretty. Her coal black hair, tied back in a careless pony-tail, her flashing dark eyes, the faint olive tone of her flawless skin, and her tall, beautifully shaped body seemed to have stepped out of Spain—El Greco's Spain of drama and mystery. Her long skirt twirled around her slender waist and legs as if guarding against—yet inviting—male scrutiny and exploration. Her simple blouse could not hide the full lift of her bosom, especially since she had opened it at the neck for relief from the heat. Her eyes twinkled with laughter and provocative challenge. She didn't mean to be provocative. It was simply that her joyous femininity colored her every movement and turned men's brains to mush.

"So you want to paint sky and sea," she bubbled gaily. "Well, look at these for a moment." Her paintings captured the changing light of seascapes along the variegated coastline. While satisfying in detail, each held a mystical quality as if the artist had seen the subject through a dreamy haze.

"But..." Maggie stared, fascinated. "They're... marvelous, so... alive and vibrant. Where did you study?"

"Self-trained at first. Then I had a lucky break: two years with Thomas Eakins at the Pennsylvania Academy of Fine Arts. He armed my dubious talent with essential tools. He also kindled my passion for nature." Julie related how she was one of the handful of young artists who had helped form the Philadelphia Art Students League. Before coming to Carmel, she had joyfully accepted Eakins' insistence on both male and female nude models, and had heeded Eakins' caution to study nature. Later, under the influence of Robert Henri, she had sought all manner of experience, that her art might be steeped in reality and the new consciousness. Of all the things that Henri had told her, she was most inspired by his simple admonition, "I have little interest in teaching you what I know. I want your art to tell me what *you* know."

What she knew was that she was afflicted by her childhood, an affliction so deep-rooted that it seemed beyond healing. After watching her father abuse and dominate her mother, Julie could not even imagine submitting herself to another human being, male or female. In fact, her determined defense of her independence was a unique mix of hedonism, narcissism and a relentless disdain for men. Her sense of rebellion against male-dominated society had been reinforced by Greenwich Village, where she had translated the philosophy of Eakins and Henri into a determined liberation from polite society's apologies for her woman's body and its appetites. Indeed, her spectacular body and her attitudes toward men had armed her with the necessary tools to first capture, then destroy any man who dared to believe he could possess her. At the first such sign from a male partner, Julie didn't hesitate to throw him out—or leave. She had thus left an impressive trail of young men's broken hearts.

Her experience had fostered a sense of herself that was amoral. She was not infatuated with sex. But her dedication to self-expression gave her a license to do almost anything. These attitudes; her vivacity, her stunning physical beauty; her experience with sex; and her hunger for adventures qualified her as the proverbial tender trap. She was a magnet, sending forth its energies in search of loose iron. That search had brought her to San Francisco in early 1899. That summer, she had discovered Carmel and resolved never to leave it. She was as close to a "liberated woman" as Carmel—and Maggie—would see during the first decade of the twentieth century. She was waiting for them when the rest of Carmel's liberated artists began to arrive.

For several hours, the three listened and practiced. Julie generously corrected their brush strokes and patiently explained ways to capture the many moods of ocean and sky. As she talked and watched, she discovered that Davey was going to be far ahead of his classmates in first grade. Although he had to struggle, he already could read Mark Twain's stories, especially Huck Finn. He was probing the more complex language of Jack London's novels. On a sudden impulse, Julie asked him if he would consider helping her with the first grade in September. This new class promised to be so large that she had been asked to concentrate on First grade only instead of her usual grades 1 through 4.

"Oh, he would be a wonderful teacher," Mei-yin announced, her mouth stuffed with cookies. "He has taught me so many things."

In fact, Julie had not thought of Davey as a teacher. She only hoped he would help her keep the large class under control. If the class could respect Davey half as much as Mei-yin seemed to adore him, she and Davey would still have their hands full.

Davey was surprised at Julie's proposal. But his mother's apparent respect for her prompted him to agree to help in any way he could.

CHAPTER FORTY

CARMEL VALLEY
AUGUST, 1900

After a light lunch, Maggie regretfully dragged the children away from Julie Simmons' magnetic personality. She had so enjoyed herself that she vowed to see more of Julie, not just to keep track of her children's progress but perhaps to add another person to her still short list of friends. When she reached the ranch, she was astonished to find John galvanized with enthusiasm.

"Maggie, just look at all these letters! Why, accordin' to them, I may be leadin' the pack! I'm certainly in good shape to start buildin' my glider."

"What do they say, John?" Maggie was tired and really didn't want to spend time on John's toys and hobbies. Yet she didn't want to belittle his eagerness to share them with her. She knew his passion for the best small engine in the world had become an obsession.

He grabbed her hand and led her into the library. "You've been gone all day with that new school teacher. Just give me a few minutes and see for yourself the way things stand now. I'll get you some cold cider.... Start with Charlie Manly's letter."

August 21, 1900

Dear John,

It's hard to believe that over a year has passed since you left New York and dumped the Balzer engine in my lap. When you left, you and I both hoped to see a fully operating engine soon. Promises, promises. In my March letter I told you how Balzer had guaranteed an engine by February and how that promise, like so many others, failed to materialize. Balzer pleaded sparking problems and unreliable cooling. But a more ominous factor was at work. From my many visits to New York,

I could confirm your story that something other than technical issues was dragging at Balzer's spirit. I told Langley
about the unsavory characters lurking around his shop.

In March, Balzer claimed that he couldn't get good workmen. He said that he had actually seen workmen turned away by
some of the thugs outside his shop. He showed me a letter
from a potential employee, complaining that his family had
been threatened if he went to work on the engine. You may
imagine how low shop morale has been. The situation persuaded Langley to hire three new men to speed up progress in
our Washington shop.

By mid-April, I had to conclude that you were right. The
central concept of the rotary is the basic flaw which af-
flicts every aspect of Balzer's otherwise brilliant design.
The turning motion of the entire engine brings unacceptable
stresses to all parts. In your recent letter, you said that
you are building the same engine for stationary operation.
My experience over the past four months has convinced me to
try the same thing. But I share your concern about the essential problem of a stationary radial: cooling. Air cooling is
one of the few advantages of a rotary. With the radial, we
may need pipes and cooling jackets around each cylinder: all
threats to low weight.

By May, Mr. Langley was furious over the whole situation.
It might not have been so bad if completion of the aerodrome
were not totally dependent on the Balzer design. As you well
know, if we have to replace Balzer's engine with something as
heavy as a steam engine, we will need to redesign major components of the great aerodrome. In fact, we have actually
finished enough that only about a man-month of labor re-
mains. But until we can reach clarity about the engine, that
man-month might as well be a man-year! Balzer's poor brake
test on May 20 (a mere 8hp) did nothing to improve Mr.
Langley's humor. Even under the stimulus of his contained
fury, Balzer's June 13 test still failed to beat that unacceptable rating.

So with Balzer already $3000 in the hole (his own money on
this failing project), Mr. Langley decided to go to Europe to
see if any manufacturer there might be able to beat Balzer.
He figured that if thugs (whether from the Bowery or Wall
Street) had Balzer under their thumbs, their reach would not
extend to Paris and London. Before late June, when Langley
was scheduled to leave, I tried to solve the faulty exhaust
and inlet valve problem, with which I know you are familiar.
I also examined the possibility of substituting a steam engine for the gas engine. I concluded that, aside from persistent, annoying defects, the basic Balzer engine is still
better for power-to-weight than anything steam could offer.
I said as much to Langley on June 19. But to confirm that
judgment, Langley ordered me to join him on his trip.

My trip was an eye-opener. We left on the *Germanic* on June
27 and returned from Liverpool on the *Cymric* on August 3.
Langley instructed me to act as if the Balzer engine was a
failure and to examine all European alternatives for a
20-24hp engine capable of fitting the current design for the
great aerodrome. You may be sure that we saw all the best designers in Europe. Although we saw them a year after you had
planned to see the same people, I can validate your decision
last year. You would not have learned as much there as you
did under Stephen Balzer's direction!

First, Hiram Maxim denounced the rotary concept because
of difficulties of oiling and sparking. Second, most of the
thirty different automobile companies in Paris use the De
Dion-Bouton design. We met De Dion at the end of July; he
speaks excellent English. He absolutely condemns the rotary
system because centrifugal forces drive oil to the end of the
cylinders. The oil fouls up gases. Nor does he have any faith
in the radial design, which he labels "radical." Instead, he
believes we could get 20hp from four of his cylinders stacked
side by side with a cooling system made with a light-weight
aluminum alloy.

In London and Berlin, I found nothing more advanced than

the De Dion engines. However, the reason that I believe your decision to stay in New York was a good one is that De Dion has never designed an engine for a flying machine. All of his engines are for automobiles; he has no suitable engine for sale. Thus, you, Balzer and I probably know more about light aviation engines than anyone in Europe, maybe anyone else in the world!

I returned to New York under instruction from Langley to close down the Balzer project unless his final test promised a quick break-through. Since that test yielded only 6hp, I am now in charge of the next phase. I have resolved to try your approach with a stationary radial engine. I'll use temporary water jackets to cool the cylinders. If this system yields higher horsepower, I'll design a permanent cooling system. If that doesn't work, then I will be forced to try De Dion's side-by-side arrangement.

To summarize, until we have a reliable engine, our construction of the great aerodrome is stalled. So pray for us; the next two weeks will be critical! I will welcome any ideas from you with gratitude and respect.

Frowning, Maggie said, "Why Johnnie, it sounds like they've made no real progress for a year! How can they complete their..." she hesitated while she searched for the word. "... airframe without the right engine?"

"That's the critical question, honey," John answered triumphantly. " I think Wilbur Wright is right." He snickered at his pun. "The engine shouldn't be designed to compensate for airframe flaws."

"I don't understand."

"The airframe design should follow well-established principles, the same principles that I've been testin' on my models."

"And are you satisfied with your tests? Are you really so confident?"

"I think I've learned everthin' the models can teach. As to bein' confident, until I received that second letter in your hands, I still was jittery. Now, I think my design for a full-scale aeroplane will carry both a hundred and sixty-pound man and a hundred and twenty-pound engine."

Maggie glanced at the letter from Wilbur Wright.

August 19, 1900

Dear John,

I was delighted to hear of your decision to build your own kites and models. I have found that there is no substitute for hands-on experience when grappling with questions that have defeated hundreds of theorists. For example, I share your suspicion of the Smeaton factor and Lilienthal's ideal camber of 1:12. But only upcoming tests of our first full-scale glider will prove me right or wrong.

Maggie felt a mild thrill of self-congratulation for having even a vague idea of the meaning of "Smeaton factor" and "cambers." She had not been conscious of the fact that three months of kite building and flying had taught her a language in which she had no more than a passing interest.

Until this past June, I focused my kite tests on the critical issues of optimal camber and aspect ratio. My tests convinced me that a curved airfoil was essential with the peak of the curve near the leading edge of the wing. But the best camber remained in doubt until I learned that your tests confirmed mine. In my plans for the first full-scale glider, I'll aim at 1:22, a slender wing-rib indeed. I want a lift area of about 200 square feet. So each wing of the glider will have a span of 20 feet and a chord of 5 feet, thus yielding an aspect ratio of 4:1. I figure the glider will weigh 52 pounds, excluding the weight of the pilot, of course (unless I could find a small boy to try first).

Maggie felt a startled intake of breath when she read that. Could John have some insane idea of seating her son in one of his kites? Suddenly challenged, she read on with growing apprehension.

In June, I was so confident of my calculations that I confronted Orv with the pressing—and heretofore much neglected—question of pilot control. To solve that problem, we spent many hours discussing the proper arrangement of all the components of our glider. I believe the pilot must be treated as an integral component of the whole structure.

Have you given that any thought?

The theoretical problem can be stated simply. Depending upon the angle of attack of the glider into the wind, the "center of pressure" (CP) of lift will vary. Similarly the "center of gravity" (CG) of the glider may shift slightly with different angles of glide. If the CP is pushing up in front of the CG, the glider must climb. If CP is pushing up from behind the CG, it will dive. We reason that stability in flight can be achieved only when CP and CG coincide. How can we help the pilot achieve such coincidence?

We know that Lilienthal tried to do it by rolling his body from side to side; too primitive and unreliable, especially for a big wind from some unexpected direction. You already know about wing warping to control roll. In an earlier letter, I told you how we propose to control pitch: with a small wing in front of the pilot. We will give him the ability to alter the angle of that "wing" so as to counteract any shift in CP due to a sudden wind.

I have also decided that the pilot should lie face down between the wings and directly behind the canard small wing. I know that Chanute and Lilienthal and others liked to sling the pilot under the glider in a sitting position. But such a position is dangerous for the pilot, may have a pendulum effect on the distribution of weight (and therefore the CP) and may create more drag than a prone position would offer.

I am now finishing plans for my first glider, which I expect to build in early September at Kitty Hawk, North Carolina. Before we go to Kitty Hawk we will cut our wing chords from ash strips which we will steam-bend to our desired camber. At Kitty Hawk, we'll buy white pine for the leading edge spars and another piece of white pine to connect all ribs. Instead of binding the whole structure rigidly together, we plan to sew the structure into a single layer of unvarnished sateen. Thus the wooden wing will "float" inside the covering. I think the wings need such flexibility to facilitate control for the pilot: wing warping. He will warp the wings by pushing on a cross-bar at his feet. He'll control the canard wing with levers.

Pray for our success, John! Orv is finally showing some interest in my dream, the origin of which I trace to your fateful visit in the winter of '98. I will always be grateful to you for reviving my life.

Pensively, Maggie looked through the windows to the gentle afternoon shadows over Los Laureles hills. *John is serious about this. And he actually may win! He's building his full-scale glider at the same time as the Wrights; and he's slightly ahead of Manly with the engine. I wonder if anyone else is even close?*

As if he had read her mind, John said, "Now read the third letter from Chanute; there's a fourth competitor."

August 20, 1990

Dear John,

Since I began corresponding with the Wright brothers last May, I have found a new hope for achieving first flight in the next decade. I doubt that I can make much of a contribution technically. Their approach is so sane that I have little to offer except perhaps news of other developments.

Of those, a serious new competitor has just come to my attention: Gustave Whitehead. My informant is an engineer and a respected resident of Bridgeport, Connecticut, where Whitehead lives and tests flying machines. A year ago, he came to Bridgeport from Pittsburgh, where he reportedly actually flew in May last year! Unfortunately, no witnesses. Unlike Sam Langley, he has only limited financial resources. But my informant tells me that he is so passionate about flying that he only works enough to save a little cash for parts for his small engines and airframes.

He told my informant that he has already built 54 machines, including gliders. Of special interest is that his preferred design is a monoplane, not the bi-plane which my work has made so popular. Whitehead calls his latest design "Machine 21." He hopes to fly it late next spring. Like everyone else, he believes his principal problem is a suitable

engine, which he is currently designing.
I will keep you informed about further developments.

"Now, Maggie, what do you think I should do?"

"What do you mean, Johnnie?"

"Well, should I go to Connecticut to see this fella Whitehead? Should I go to Kitty Hawk to help Wilbur Wright? Should I go to Washington to help Charles Manley? Or should I stay here and work on my own rig?"

Those options quickly flashed through Maggie's mind. Did he want her to think about them? Or was his question gratuitous, a prelude to informing her about some decision he had already made? She could imagine advantages to his absence; but she had also become accustomed to his presence, even with their arguments about Davey's state of mind. From his viewpoint, she thought that he would gain greatest satisfaction from winning the race alone, not as an assistant to someone else. "It's hard to advise you, Johnnie. But if it were me, I'd correspond with *all* of them. I'd offer to help *all* of them; that's the only reason for them to help you. But I'd stay here, put my own knowledge and skill to the test and reap the rewards of winning... if there are any."

John thought he detected a challenge in Maggie's voice. Was she telling him to be a man and take some risks? In his pocket, he clutched a fourth letter that contained a vital piece of information, information that he preferred to keep from Maggie. It was only brief; but Mike Coyle had written to confirm that Jerry Ashley had been the mastermind behind the campaign of intimidation against John and Balzer in New York. Mike warned further that, desperate to clear the field for the Wright brothers, who knew nothing of Wall Street's behind-the-scenes dance for patent control, Ashley might indeed come to Carmel with instructions to stop John Harrison at all costs. *What the hell,* John thought, *I'll handle them here easily. No need to frighten Maggie about them. And I'll win this race in spite of them.* "I like that advice, honey. It'll mean hard work in the barn and in Monterey. Will you indulge me?"

Maggie smiled. "Don't I always? Run your race, John. I'll bet on you."

CHAPTER FORTY-ONE

CARMEL, CALIFORNIA
SEPTEMBER, 1900

Ramon Cisneros frequently despaired of his older son's future. Jaime Cisneros, at the age of twenty, was a smoldering mixture of prickly pride and frustration. A fine cowboy and too handsome for his own good, he believed that he knew enough to run the ranch without his father's advice. Indeed, Ramon appreciated his son's skill, but not his judgment. His snap decisions and his reputation as a crack shot had attracted the allegiance of other fiery young vaqueros. They gambled too much, usually on horse races; they wasted too much of their slender pay on silver finery for their saddles and boots and bridles; they hungered too much for risk; and they whored too much at Mama Rosa's. Ramon worried that little Juan would follow in his brother's wayward, self-indulgent footsteps. And so he withheld from his older son a position which even John Harrison had recommended: deputy ranch manager under his father.

Jaime's resentment and Mama Rosa's fiery tequila had built a small furnace in his mind on the night of September 10. While he lounged at the bar and teased one of Mama's prettiest whores, he slugged down his fifth drink and scowled at a noisy stranger, arguing with Mama.

"Madam," the stranger in a derby hat growled, "I always pay my bill." When John "Derby" McGee had first entered the bar three hours earlier, he had felt right at home. Cigar and cigarette smoke and a hundred unwashed bodies had yielded an aroma that reminded him of several favorite haunts around the corner from Monk Eastman's headquarters. The hum of a hundred humans huddled over rough-hewn, candle-lit tables; the tinkle of mugs and glasses of liquid courage; the flirtatious advances of pretty prostitutes, whose skirts of red and green and lemon yellow offered colorful accents against the drab working clothes of cowboys and common laborers; and the mood of subdued gaiety had sustained Derby's initial sense of warm welcome. But after three hours of guzzling and pinching and smiling and incomprehension of Spanish accents, his natural mood of sullen pessimism had asserted itself. He had become increasingly wary of the whores' glances of scornful amusement, of vaqueros' frowns of disdain and of Mama Rosa's expression of distrust. Now he felt trapped, adrift in a sea of hostility—*Mexican* hostility. He could feel its palpable energy distilled into tense confrontation over his bill. *Goddamn these Spics and Wops to hell!* he thought as he searched his tequila-clouded brain for a map of escape.

"You may leave as soon as you pay your bill," Mama said quietly. "But you may not pass Toro until you have paid."

Toro Martinez, the massive bouncer, stood like an immovable boulder permanently jammed into the doorway. Jaime knew what Toro could do to a customer who refused to pay. Indeed, Jaime had memories of a sore head and multiple bruises when he had attempted to take advantage of Mama's famous generosity. Now he watched the scene with growing interest.

"I've already promised you full payment soon."

Mama affected a scowl of scornful disbelief, her eyebrows arched in a deep V, her hands on her hips. This drama was beginning to amuse her as she saw its possibilities for entertaining her customers. "And what is your collateral, man-of-many-promises?"

Derby hesitated; he was so drunk that he could barely stand. He was tempted to draw a small derringer and force his way through the ring of intimidation that had gathered to enjoy themselves at his expense. But even if he shot Toro, he knew that Ashley would tear him to pieces if he made a scene. His clouded brain could not clearly sort out the priorities among several threats; but he had never met anyone as casually ruthless as Jerry Ashley. Even Monk Eastman had helped him when he was in need. But Ashley had never shown a shred of pity for anyone. Now, he just wanted to leave this whorehouse with the least fracas. "I have a secret that's worth lots of money, Mama. May I tell you what it is? Then you can decide if it's collateral enough."

"Who does your secret concern?" Mama's interest was aroused. She bartered secrets like a pawnbroker. Carefully handled, a secret could bring at least the power of gratitude and, at most, a small fortune in money or blackmail.

"Come over here to the bar and I'll tell you." Mama's smile reminded Derby of his mother, long dead from drowning in New York's East River. With extravagant deference, Derby led Mama to a position so close to Jaime that he could overhear every word. "My secret concerns a fella named Harrison."

Mama restrained a grin and glanced knowingly at Jaime, one of her favorite customers. She decided to be coy. "There is nothing valuable about John Harrison that everyone doesn't already know. Why should I give you a loan when you couldn't know anything new. Why, you're a complete stranger...; and a *borracho* stranger at that."

Derby hat flushed. *Jesus, if I don't get out of here soon, I'm gonna collapse. I'll jes tell her a little, enough to get me past that bruiser in the door. I've got to make this woman trust me or I'm a goner.* "My boss is gonna pay me lots of money after I destroy Harrison's bicycle shop."

"You are a fool, senōr." Mama sneered at him and gestured to Toro to come over and give her some backing. "Why should anyone care about John Harrison's bicycles?"

When Toro's hulk towered over "Derby," he whimpered, "I don't know the reason; nobody told me that. But the money is here now; my boss has it. As soon as I destroy a small engine in Harrison's shop, I'll get a thousand dollars. Now, doesn't that make sense?"

Jaime's brain suddenly cleared. Maybe this was the chance to prove to his father and the Patrón that he could make sound decisions. His father had told him about the Patrón's stubborn passion for a small engine and a flying machine. It seemed quite insane to lavish money on such foolishness. But who was he to tell the Patrón how to waste money? Every man to his own poison; Jaime much preferred whores and tequila. "Mama, you know how much I despise that John Harrison. Will you allow me to pay this man's bill? In fact, with your permission, I will give him another drink for the road."

Mama tossed her head as if to dismiss Toro, then fixed a stern look at the stranger. "You are in luck; this vaquero may even help you since he hates Harrison so much. I advise you to trust him so that you don't get in any more trouble around here. Go with God."

In another hour, Jaime learned that Derby and his boss were planning to set fire to the bicycle shop soon. They were waiting only for proof that all plans and the engine were inside the shop. "Maybe I can help you." Jaime poured tequila into Derby's glass. "I can come and go in that shop whenever I please. Would you like me to tell you when the time is right?"

After they agreed on Jaime's role and a mode of communication, Jaime helped Derby navigate through the door to his hotel. It was past midnight when he related the whole story to his father at the ranch.

Early the next morning, while Jaime held his sombrero between his hands and listened, Ramon gave the story to John for breakfast on the patio. Fortunately, Maggie was still sleeping and learned nothing of the new development.

"Boys, don't tell Maggie about any of this; and don't tell Ana 'cause she tells my wife ever'thin' that goes on here. Can I trust you?"

Ramon and Jaime quickly assented.

"OK. First, I want to thank you, Jaime, for doin' the right thing. I can't tell you how much I appreciate your loyalty and your good sense."

Jaime felt his chest swell. It was good to hear such praise in front of his father. Maybe luck and the Blessed Virgin had finally smiled on him.

"Here's what I'm gonna do," John continued. "I'll ride into Monterey this mornin' with Jaime. We'll give Sheriff Taylor the whole story. If possible, I want the law to handle this. But Taylor is so fat and lazy that we'll probably have to take matters into our own hands."

Sheriff Brad Taylor listened to John with growing apprehension. He had looked forward to a leisurely afternoon of fishing off Pop Halloran's dock. Surely this was a joke. Man and boy, he had worked both sides of the law in Monterey for forty years. He had participated in cattle rustling, legal and illegal hangings, saloon shootouts, ordinary murder and too many trials about all of the above. But arson was serious; in the right wind, a fire could burn the town to ashes. "Boys," he said with a weary adjustment of his 280-pound frame, "I don't rightly see what I can do. This calls for surveillance. But my only deputy is taking a prisoner to Denver to stand trial for murder. I can't watch over your shop night and day, John; and I don't have any money to hire some temporary deputies."

John frowned with exasperation at Brad's predictable plea of helplessness. The damn town was so law-abiding that no self-respecting lawman would consider wasting his years on mere town drunks. "Look, Brad, why don't you just deputize me and Jaime here. You don't have to pay us. If we learn of the most likely date, I'll let you know so you can be in on the kill. We'll do all the work and you'll get all the credit. What say?"

Brad eyed John warily. It sounded too easy. Brad had survived a succession of life-threatening crises by damage control, especially damage to himself. On the surface, John's proposal was appealing. John was a level-headed citizen and could probably manage the wild Mexican. Besides, John and Jaime were better shots than he was—if it came to shooting. If he did nothing and a fire burned down half of the town, he would never hear the end of it. He probably wouldn't get re-elected; might even be tarred, feathered and ridden out of town on a rail. "Very well, John. Here are a couple of badges. I'll swear you in right now."

"So we wait, Patrón, until I hear about their plans?" Jaime asked after Brad Taylor had locked the jail and sauntered away, a smile on his face and a fishing pole on his shoulder.

"No, Jaime; we don't wait. We go first to my shop, and then we tell the editor of the *Monterey Cypress* a tall tale or two." John led Jaime around two corners and through a narrow alley to his busy bicycle shop. He was pleased to hear the raucous sound of his "Balzer-Harrison" engine on a test bed.

Roger Macon was a young, West Coast version of Charles Manly. If John had not forced Roger to go home every afternoon, he would have slept in the shop when he wasn't tinkering with short-circuiting sparkplugs, valves, cams and leaky water jackets. "You were right about a stationary radial, John," Roger announced eagerly when John and Jaime walked in. "I'm getting a steady sixteen horsepower now, but it's not because we converted a rotary to a stationary radial."

John had learned to trust Roger's insights. He was definitely a godsend when it came to refining engine design. "What do you think is the reason?"

"I think Balzer's valves weren't tight enough or strong enough. And his camshaft was a piece of junk."

Roger's opinion caught John's attention. Stephen Balzer had made the same argument to Manly, who had refused to believe that the valves were the principal flaw in the engine. "Have you strengthened the valves since they collapsed last month and smashed several other components?"

"Yep, valves are fine now. And I added weight to the flywheel to cut down vibration. Last week the engine ran steady for ten minutes at 950rpm. Even though the flywheel was out of true, it still developed twenty horsepower."

John was worried about holding the engine under 120 pounds. An additional 25 pounds of water; probably two flywheels weighing 20 pounds; a 17-pound condenser; 12 pounds of sparking coil and dynamo and various connections could bring the total weight to 200 pounds. "What about weight?

I'll simplify Balzer's whole valve arrangement. It'll take only about three weeks."

John consoled himself with the thought that Charles Manly was having all the same problems. Weak bearings; faulty carburetion; ill-timed electric spark and poor lubrication also bedevilled Charlie's engine. John thought many of those problems could be resolved if he could get zero vibration. "You can have those three weeks, Roger, if you'll give me a special performance for the next five days."

"What kind of performance?" Roger was already accustomed to John's sudden changes of direction each time he received another letter from Dayton, Ohio, or Washington, DC.

"I want the engine to sound fully operational ever' mornin' and ever' afternoon. Can you do that for me?"

"Why, I reckon.... How long does it have to run?"

"Just a few minutes at each test; just long enough to annoy the whole neighborhood."

Roger grinned. "Should be easy; the complaints are already comin' in."

Jaime marveled at John's audacity. The vaquero needed no script to know what he must tell Derby McGee. And if Derby checked around the neighborhood, he would find plenty of evidence of imminent success from irate neighbors. The night of September 17 should be interesting....

Roy Emerson, editor of *The Monterey Cypress*, listened to John with interest. He had heard rumors about John's zeal for powered flight. He had intended interviewing him; maybe his crazy ideas would provide a little comic relief when all local news had disappeared. So John's visit was a godsend. "You have actually built the smallest, most powerful engine in the world?"

"Right. I plan to ship it to an East Coast customer on the eighteenth, just five days from now. It's already delivering twenty horsepower and weighs only sixty pounds. I tell you, Roy, it will revolutionize all sorts of things. It's big news for Wall Street, too."

"Well, John, sounds like you've got a bear by the tail! I'll give it a big play in tomorrow's edition. Congratulations. I wondered what the racket was in your shop. Lots of folks will be glad to hear that it's leaving town soon."

CHAPTER FORTY-TWO

MONTEREY, CALIFORNIA
SEPTEMBER, 1900

After three days of rave notices in the newspaper, Jaime Cisneros' reports to Derby and Jerry Ashley and a growing outcry from neighbors against the noisy engine, John warned the sheriff that the arsonists would probably take action on the night of September 17. That afternoon, to John's pleasure and surprise, his new radial engine actually lived up to the enthusiastic hyperbole of the *Monterey Cypress*. By four o'clock, it had produced 18hp at a steady 800 revolutions per minute for an hour without overheating. Roger's new water jackets seemed to handle the heat efficiently.

Before John locked the shop doors, he familiarized Jaime and the sheriff with the location of tables, plans, the engine, machinery, overhead belts and light switches. Having never been in the shop before, Brad Taylor was confused about the best location for each man. It soon became clear to John that the sheriff wanted to locate himself far away from possible gunplay. So John advised him to sit on the floor behind a table near the front of the shop. "I think they'll break in from the rear 'cause it opens on the alley. No one is likely to be there and the buildin' will mask any noise they make. So Jaime and I will hide near the rear door."

"John, I don't like the looks of things," Brad said. "Too much equipment to hide behind. What if they duck? A gunfight in here could be sheer murder."

"Get down on your knees, Brad," John said. "Your best firin' position will be close to the floor. The place only looks crowded when you're standin'. But on your knees, you'll see clear across the shop."

Brad kneeled to confirm John's advice. "Why so you can, John. Clever. What made you think of this tactic?"

"My son, Davey. I play on my knees with him sometime. When you're down at his level, the world looks a lot different. So this afternoon, I had the men clear all boxes and materials away to the side of the shop."

An hour after sunset, John, Jaime and Brad Taylor quietly entered the shop through its rear door. Brad positioned himself against a side wall and near a front corner so that he could observe the front door. Jaime sat in a similar position near the door at the center of the rear wall. John's position opposite Jaime would permit them to bring cross-fire against the rear half of the shop.

As one hour became two, the quiet of a morgue descended on the shop. Jaime and John cleaned and checked their guns several times, reviewed all warnings and signals of the past three days and reassured themselves that their trap had not been compromised. By eleven o'clock, only the sound of Brad Taylor's snoring disturbed the peace.

John walked over to Brad to find him on his back, a faint aroma of bourbon on his breath. John's hard punch awakened him and reminded him of his duty. Brad grumbled but resumed his sitting position with his back against the wall. John was about to return to the rear of the shop when he heard a sound at the rear door. Through the window he could see two figures silhouetted against a distant street light. He quickly moved to Jaime to alert him, then faded into the shadows.

The sound of a crow-bar and splitting wood announced the entry of Ashley and McGee. "Go get the kerosene, Derby," Ashley growled. "After we spread it all over the shop, it should burn down before any help can come."

John cursed silently. He wanted to act before there was the slightest threat of fire to either his shop or adjacent buildings. But he had to wait until Derby returned lest he be warned by any premature shooting.

As soon as Derby returned with a container and stepped into the room, John yelled, "Stop right there! You're under arrest for attempted arson." That was his first mistake. He had forgotten that Jerry Ashley prided himself on his quick draw and accurate shooting.

Jerry instantly dropped to his knees and fired a shot in the direction of John's voice. "Start the fire now, Derby!" he cried. "I'll take care of this one."

Derby had dropped the kerosene when Ashley fired the first shot. He also fell to his knees to retrieve the can.

Jaime had a clear vision of Derby's outline against the open door. He saw Derby open the can of kerosene and begin to spread it across the floor. *That one has bigger cojones than I imagined*, he thought. *Well, let's see if the liquid courage I gave him tonight at Mama's can handle lead.* From the hip, Jaime fired and caught him in the shoulder.

Crying out in pain, Derby dropped the kerosene and drew his pistol, returning fire in Jaime's direction.

Now John's plan for cleared fields of fire close to the floor paid off. From his prone position in deep shadow, he could make out Ashley's kneeling form, his left hand resting on a work table. For an instant, John hesitated. Was he capable of cold-blooded murder? Then memory reminded him of a rage that he had barely suppressed for too many months. Ashley had exploited and betrayed their friendship, had humiliated him and had very nearly shattered the central article of his faith in his destiny to do something glorious. He leveled his pistol and fired two shots into Ashley's chest.

"Oh my God, Derby, I'm hit," Ashley groaned. "Strike the match, man. Start the fire; then get away."

Derby was in no shape to strike a match. From his wounded right shoulder, blood was already draining away his life as he leaned against a table leg and tried to understand what had gone wrong.

At that moment, the sheriff switched on the lights; John and Jaime stood up; and John moved quickly to Jerry Ashley. After grabbing Jerry's gun, John kneeled and said, "Well, Jerry, looks like you've screwed the pooch. Are you crazy? Did old man Morgan put you up to this?"

Jerry stared at John dazedly. "Is that you, John? I... can't seem to see so well. I think...; it hurts like hell, John."

John suddenly saw how much damage he had done. Blood had already soaked through Jerry's vest and trousers. "Jaime!" John yelled, "run for the doctor. Tell him we have a man shot in the chest and gut."

"He's a goner, John," Brad Taylor said matter-of-factly. "You sure called the play. They fired first; no need to even have a hearing. Pure self-defense."

"For God's sake, Brad. A man's dying here and you talk about the law. Just shut up, will you. Go tend to Derby; see if you can bind up his shoulder." John kneeled beside Jerry and said, "Take it easy, Jerry. The doc should be here any minute."

"Not much time left, John," Jerry gasped. "Not... Morgan's fault... just... other folks' little sideshow." He began to wheeze as blood bubbled out of a punctured lung.

John watched Jerry's complexion fade into wax. It was impossible to stop the flow of blood. Even if a doctor walked in this instant, he wouldn't be able to do much for Jerry. "Is this all about patents, Jerry?" he asked bitterly.

"Yeah. They... they want the Wrights to win. They'll... toy with Langley... then sabotage his... great aerodrome. It's you... they worry about most." Jerry found it increasingly difficult to credit his senses. Sound seemed very distant, John's voice fading in and out. "M and M; something I should tell you about them, John; but ... can't remember. They ought to turn up the heat in here; damned cold. No feeling in my legs. Guess this is it. Watch out for... watch out... Zeee.... He's ugly... ver' ugly, ver' bad. So sorry, John. I...."

John sensed the instant that death took Jerry Ashley. He exhaled for the last time with such grace and gratitude that a peaceful calm spread across his face and wiped away the lines of strain and fear and hate. His sightless eyes seemed to stare into himself and, for a brief period before rigor mortis began its relentless process, his body relaxed as it was released from the torment and vitality of life. John lowered Jerry's head to the floor and closed his eyes.

When the town doctor arrived to bind up Derby's shoulder, John surveyed his shop. The only evidence of the gunfight was the pool of blood under Ashley. Then John noticed the stain of blood on his own clothes. While Jaime wiped up the kerosene, John reflected. *What the hell will I tell Maggie? If she sees me like this, she'll know I didn't spend my evening with cattle buyers, like I told her. Jaime's about my size; maybe I can throw these away and borrow some of his gear when we get back.*

It never occurred to John that the press would have to announce the whole story. *The Monterey Cypress* could rarely offer its readers excitement such as a murder in self-defense. Nor did John anticipate the efficiency of the rumor mill at his own ranch. By the time he had awakened the next morning, the ranch was buzzing with his heroism. When the paper arrived early that afternoon, the cat was half way out of the bag. When Davey returned from school in late afternoon, his enthusiasm unleashed Maggie's fury.

"Momma, Momma," he cried as he rushed into the kitchen. "Did you hear how Poppa killed a man last night? Isn't it wonderful?"

"And why do you think murder is wonderful, young man?" Maggie asked.

"Why... I thought...." Deflated for an instant, Davey searched for reasons. "The man and another fella had guns. They shot first." Davey stared at Ah Ying, drew imaginary pistols from his hips and cried, "Bang! Bang!" Then he held up his fingers to his mouth and blew away the imaginary smoke.

Ah Ying smiled at the pantomime, but Maggie felt something snap in her mind. This new violence was symptomatic of all her secret fears and everything she disliked about her life: her cat-and-mouse game with John about Davey's psychic gifts; the tedium and loneliness of ranch life; its relentless isolation from music and the arts and the theater; her sense of irredeemable loss of a musical career; her new fear for Lily Wang in China, where Boxers had beheaded two English missionaries on Davey's birthday; and this new paean of praise for brutality in her own home. Was the world going mad? The Tsungli Yamen in Peking had just suspended relations with eleven legations; three thousand foreigners were vulnerable to the disgusting "Fists of Righteous Harmony." And even that enlightened Professor Woodrow Wilson had said blandly that American political and commercial expansion seemed only natural. The planet's accumulated toxicity suddenly ignited her rage. "Never, ever do that again in my presence, David Harrison. You are not a hoodlum, a gunman. There is nothing heroic about killing another human being." She seized him by the shoulders and shook him until tears came to his eyes.

"Why, Maggie, why does Davey deserve such a shakin'?" John asked as he walked in.

"He thinks you're a hero for your gunfight last night. I thought you were meeting with cattle dealers."

John could not remember the last time he had seen her so... exercised. "Now, Maggie, calm yourself."

"No!" she cried. "I want you to apologize to all of us for risking your life like that! Why couldn't you let the sheriff do his job? Why must you test your courage over and over? Hunting in the Rockies! Fighting in Cuba! And now gunfighting here! You terrify me, John."

Davey stared from one to the other in confusion. He had heard them arguing at night after they thought he was asleep. But he had never seen such despair on his mother's face. And why did Poppa stare at the floor like he was guilty? Why didn't he tell her the story? Everyone at school knew he had to fight for his life against two armed men.

John seized Davey's hand and led him to bed. When he returned, he sat down at the kitchen table and sighed. "The story goes back to New York a year ago, Maggie." He then related what he had learned about Jerry Ashley's role in intimidating Stephen Balzer and his family in order to delay the completion of the rotary engine. Avoiding his own humiliation at the hands of Monk Eastman, he ended his story with the details of the shootout.

"Jerry was utterly ruthless. I was afraid he might come against my family. So I brought ever'thin' to a head last night. I didn't want to torture you with the threat; I... I wanted to keep even a whisper of danger away from you and Davey."

Maggie shook her head as if to clear her mind. Something was very wrong, very sick here. "I said I would support your race for first flight, Johnnie. And I will because I know it's a cause that challenges your soul." She caught her breath for a moment. "But does it justify murder? You must all be insane: the Wright brothers; Manly; Langley; Tom Baldwin; that new nitwit, Whitehead. Does the promise of flight curdle a man's brain like a drug?"

John smiled; maybe he could defuse Maggie emotions. "Maybe it does. But at least I *tried* to keep ever'one else's insanity away from you. I figured mine was enough for one family."

"Don't you think I have a right to be informed about such dangers, both as your wife and Davey's mother?"

John suddenly felt deeply confused and slightly offended. "You mean you're mad 'cause I tried to handle the danger alone? Or 'cause you think I deceived you?

"Oh Johnnie, sometimes I think you're totally blind to my needs and my values. I...; I don't care about what you call fun." She thought, *We don't have a single thing in common—except Davey. And we disagree so much about him that even he may become a battlefield. What could I do? I'll have to work underground. I must not let Davey fall too much under John's spell.*

"So what *do* you care about?" John asked, his jaw flexing and his eyes hard.

"The only thing in our marriage that has brought me joy: Davey. If you think I'll allow you to turn him into a rootin', tootin' gun-slinging cowboy like Jaime Cisneros...." Maggie paused to collect her thoughts, to find some language that would open John's eyes to her own deep conviction.

"Davey's goin' to be whatever *he* wants to be," John replied coldly. "Not what you and your dead philosophers think he should be."

CHAPTER FORTY-THREE

CARMEL VALLEY
SEPTEMBER–OCTOBER, 1900

After Maggie's public indictment of John's insane obsession with first flight, their routine changed little on the surface. She continued her morning studies in the library. In the afternoon, she met with pro-McKinley and pro-Roosevelt politicians. Or she visited sick women and children on the ranch. John continued to closet himself in the barn, where the full-scale glider slowly emerged, its ribs steam-bent to his preferred camber. One day a week, he went in to Monterey to confer with Roger Macon about the engine, which seemed nearly ready. Davey and Mei-yin became familiar with the routine of school and soon found themselves at the head of Julie Simmon's class. A stranger might have said that theirs was an idyllic existence.

But like a balloon with a slow leak, a subtle vitality slowly escaped from their marriage. Mutual suspicion made Maggie dispirited and John sullen. Suppers became mostly silent unless Mei-yin or Davey had something exciting to tell about school. The children felt the fraudulence of the adults' polite cordiality but they had no idea how to make things right. Nor did Maggie or John.

Unwittingly, John only accentuated the breach one brilliant Saturday in late October when he, Ned, Davey and Juan Cisneros loaded a wagon with the completed glider and carried it to a highland meadow for its first test. On the way, John tried to bolster his confidence with yet another review of his recent calculations and his correspondence with Gus Whitehead and Wilbur Wright. "Will said he did all the glidin' at Kitty Hawk, which convinced him that wing-warpin' could control roll and his canard wing was perfect for pitch."

"Then why worry?" Ned Ambler asked. "Did something go wrong there?"

"Yeah. I got Will's letter yesterday. At first, they spent hours flyin' it like a kite. It crashed two weeks ago 'cause the winds were so variable. Then they rebuilt it and Will actually flew *in* it after the eighteenth."

"So what's the problem?"

"Well, they measured lift and drag with regular grocer's scales, just like we did with our models. Lift registered much too low. They're not sure why; but they plan to use a more robust camber—Lilienthal's one to twelve—in their next glider 'cause they think their one to twenty-two was too narrow."

"I see, you're afraid our one to nineteen may also be too thin?"

"I just don't know, Ned. The whole damn glider may not be big enough. Wilbur said their second glider would have to be much bigger."

Ned nodded in sympathy. Through the summer, he had come to realize that first flight meant much more to John than a challenge to his imagination and his knowledge of mechanics and physics and thermodynamics. He had made the aeroplane a symbol of his self-worth, perhaps even his very identity. Ned feared he was setting himself up for a hell of a fall. What would John do if it failed? "Tell me again the dimensions of *our* glider." Ned accented "our" in hopes that he might help his friend carry the burden of possible failure.

"Thirty foot span; five foot chord. Aspect ratio of six to one." John turned to stare at the pair of wings resting on the bed of the wagon. For a moment, he brooded disconsolately over the hours that he had already spent thinking about, talking about, designing and finally assembling those wings—four months! It didn't sound like much. But if the effort had cost him his marriage, the price was too high. "Three hundred square feet of lifting surface; nearly twice as much as Will's first glider. The thing weighs a hundred pounds."

Ned figured an aeroplane would have to lift 400 pounds, a 200-pound engine and a 180-pound pilot. "We're still ahead, aren't we, John? Didn't Whitehead tell you he's still studying captured sea gulls?"

The mention of Whitehead brought a smile to John's face. "That man beats all! Since he has no money and no trainin' in mechanical drawin', he has to make almost ever'thin' from scratch in his basement."

"He must have been grateful for your money." Ned still couldn't believe John's generosity. "Didn't you send him a thousand dollars? Hell, that would be a handsome income for a family for a year."

"Probably the best investment I ever made." John grinned with pleasure. "He built a shop in front of his house, next to a church; started improvin' the steam engine he brought from Pittsburgh; uses compressed air instead of a boiler. Now he has the idea to use two motors."

"Why *two* motors?"

Apprehensive about his own glider, John could summon instant enthusiasm for Whitehead, whose natural genius John admired enormously. "He designed a kind of boat-shaped body with four wheels. One motor will drive the wheels like an automobile to move the whole rig to the test site. When it's movin', he folds the wings against the body. At the test site, he mounts the wings with wires tied to a steel mast in the body. The other motor is for his propeller."

Ned gasped as their wagon bounced over a large stone. *Thank God we've reached our meadow; I can't take much more of this cross-country climb up Los Laureles.* "Whitehead's rig must weigh a ton!"

"I don't know its weight; but it's bound to be heavy 'cause his materials are primitive: wooden wheels, poor spark plugs, faulty homemade generator, most parts made by hand. But I tell you, Ned, the man's a master. He's had flyin' on his brain almost from the day he was born." Just like Davey, John thought. Only Davey would be an *educated* engineer.

"His system seems to be trial and error," Ned suggested critically. "And he has no concern for patents or any other benefits of our great civilization."

"True. That's why I'm bettin' on him. He doesn't waste hours like me and Will Wright goin' blind with theory and math. He just builds, tests, fails, throws it away and builds again. By feelin' his way along his own line of imagination, he swears he'll fly next summer. I'm gonna try to beat him."

"That would be miraculous, truly miraculous." It was the first time that Ned had heard a firm target date. "I suppose he's returned your generosity?"

"Yep. Just like Maggie had predicted. All his best ideas, his sketches, even the way he works. And I'm helpin' him design a slick calcium carbide engine." John pulled back on the reins, stopped the wagon and paused to savor the heart-lifting vista down the Carmel Valley. A steady wind blew across the meadow. "Even if we have no agreement, I think of him as a partner."

"I'm glad you see it that way, John. When you think about it, it's a race among design methods—not just prototypes."

"What do you mean, Ned?"

"Well, at one extreme, you have the great scientist, Langley, with his money and his theory. At the other, you have Whitehead with no money, only a passion to fly all the way to God. In between are you and Will Wright. By feeding your knowledge and some money to Whitehead, you and he may combine the best natural talent and engineering knowledge to win."

"Hope you're right, Ned. Well, let's unload this beast." He and Ned easily unloaded each wing. They tethered the lower wing to the ground, set struts in place and mounted the top wing, stabilizing the bond between wings with guy-wires. When the glider seemed to be ready, John cried, "Let's see if it will lift itself off the ground as a kite. Raise it up, Ned."

At a steady twenty miles per hour, the wind was ideal. John and Ned had barely raised the glider to their shoulders when it started to lift.

"Hold your rope, Ned!" John yelled. "Now, let it out a foot or so at a time. Let's see if it will stabilize in this wind."

Both men stood entranced as their kite lifted higher and higher without apparent effort. It rode the wind like a song. John couldn't believe his good luck. His face broke into a wide smile that would stay there for the rest of the day. He felt as if *he* were the kite, dancing on the wind, its wings dipping occasionally only to resume a level position. John thought the camber must be perfect. Jesus, he had never had so much fun!

"How long do you want to let it fly, John?" Ned asked after twenty minutes. "It has a hell of a pull; my arms are tired already."

"Ok, Ned. Let's pull it down and discuss our next move."

While the kite rested, its leading edges tethered to stakes, the two men marveled at their initial success. "You'd think we were veterans at this b'iness, Ned. Isn't she a beauty?"

"I'm truly impressed, John. Your calculations must have been right on the button. So what should we do now?"

"I want to warp the wings and see what happens. Then I want to attach the canard wing and see what effect it has."

For the next hour, everything proceeded with astonishing ease. Everything that John's models had shown him and that Wilbur Wright had recommended paid off. After a brief lunch, John was ready to mount it himself.

He and Ned dragged the glider to the top of a small rise. "Now boys," John said, "I'm gonna lie down between the wings. You two pull on one wing and Ned will pull on the other. Let's see if it can lift me." As Wilbur Wright had instructed, he lay down between the wings and waited for the pullers to start the glider down hill. Nothing happened. Despite a fair speed as the glider's skids moved across the ground, it simply could not lift John's weight.

John insisted that they try four or five times; to no avail. He finally had to admit that he might need more experience at the primitive controls. Baffled, he said, "Let's measure the net lift with the grocer's scales."

That test was more satisfactory, but it suggested that the glider would need more speed to lift John's weight. Then he remembered Wilbur Wright's quip about Davey's weight. "Davey, how would you like to try it?"

"Show me how, Poppa." Davey was wide-eyed with anticipation,

They returned the glider once again to the small rise. While Ned and Juan held the lower wing to the ground, Davey lay face down between the wings and let John strap him to the glider. Before trying flight, he experimented with the wing-warping pedals. Then he stretched his arms to grasp the levers to the canard wing to his front. "I wish those levers were a little longer, Poppa. But I think I can do it."

"OK, men," John announced finally, satisfied that Davey was firmly strapped in. "Ned, you and I can run it down the hill and release the ropes a little bit to give it some room for lift. Y'ready?"

In the next ten seconds, Davey experienced real flight for the first time. While his father and Ned slowly released the ropes, Davey gently tried the pedals at John's command. He made the wing tips tilt up and down. He learned how to alter the angle of the canard wing to dip and rise slightly. A half-hour passed like a second for him as he felt the glory of controlled flight, the magic of lift pressing the wing against his chest. He screamed, "It's wonderful, Poppa. Let the rope out some more... let it out all the way."

Ned finally called out, "We better not let him go any higher. He must be fifty feet in the air now. If it crashes, the boy might be badly injured."

John nodded. "OK, let's pull him down." His heart swelled with the sheer glee of his success. For the next two hours, he repeated Davey's flight while measuring different lift values. He couldn't wait to take his data home and recalculate the power that his engine would require to lift a grown man.

With each test, Davey became more confident. Perhaps his illusions of flight with birds and eagles had armed him for the real thing. Instead of confused apprehension, he felt increasingly comfortable. By his fourth test, he felt like he was an integral part of the airframe. It seemed natural for the wing tips to dip and lift with slight movements of his feet. His right hand seemed welded to the lever to operate the canard wing. He tried simultaneous movements of pedals and lever to see if he could dip to right or left. He found himself so totally engrossed in the glider's responsiveness that he lost all sense of time. Each rest period made him disappointed to be pulled to earth.

"John, can he turn the kite?" Ned asked during one of the rest periods.

"No, that's something we haven't figured out yet."

"I wish I had a rudder, Poppa," Davey cried. "Up there, it feels a little like a boat. I bet a rudder would turn it. I could control it better if you changed the controls, too." With those words, Davey began to play a role that would bond father and son as nothing else ever had before. Because John would soon trust only Davey to test technical ideas, he soon treated Davey's hunches and suggestions with respect, whether they came from logic or imagination. Davey's proposal for a rudder also revealed what would become his lifelong passion for pilot safety and control of an aircraft. Through the next ten years, that single issue would generate shouting matches between father and son, the older man obsessed with structural efficiency and balance, the son focused on the human dimension of flight.

But for now, John could only stare at Davey with delight. *Of course! I'll install a vertical rudder on the canard wing. I'll run a lever back to the pilot for direct control. Then he'll have all three movements in his feet and hands: yaw, pitch and roll.*

By three o'clock in the afternoon, everyone was exhausted and exhilarated. They disassembled the glider, stacked the wings in the wagon, hooked up the horses and started their descent. Exuberant, Ned saw that the successful tests had lifted John's sagging spirit, validating his earlier tests and calculations and reviving his sense of self-confidence. *Thank God,* Ned thought. *For a while at least, we've postponed failure and whatever pathology that might afflict on poor John.* "So now you have to install the engine. How do you rate your progress compared to Manly, John?"

A smile of satisfaction across his face, John said, "In his last letter, he said he teased sixteen horses out of his new stationary version in early September. But several flaws still need fixin': tighter valves and valve springs, permanent water jackets that don't fill with oil, better carburetor and a different crankshaft. Their electrical system is still drivin' him crazy. De Dion's spark coil was too weak; so they have to wait for a new one from Paris. Their sparkplugs are totally unreliable. And, like we did already, Charlie must redesign the valve system; thinks an improved engine might deliver twenty horses by January."

"So we're way ahead!" Ned grinned at the thought. "Old man Langley must be chewing nails."

"Right as rain!" The smile suddenly disappeared from John's face. "Before he died, Jerry Ashley said Monk Eastman's thugs might sabotage Langley's great aerodrome. From Manly's letters, it may already have started."

"How so?"

"Parts disappear ever' day from the Smithsonian shop. Wires cut with pliers; acid eatin' through rolls of linen. I would be damned furious if it were me."

"How about Will Wright's engine?"

"Hell, Will isn't worried. His focus is still control of a balanced airframe. He figures he'll get an adequate engine off the shelf."

By five o'clock, they had returned the horses to the stable, the wings to the barn and the boys to the kitchen. Before locking up the barn for the day, John obtained a solemn pledge from both boys and Ned that Davey's role in the tests that day must remain a special secret. He warned them that if Maggie found out about Davey's daring exploits, there would be hell to pay. He might have to stop all tests just to keep the peace. Certainly he would have to bar Davey from any further rides on the glider. Just to reinforce their conspiracy, he promised little Juan that he too could be a pilot soon.

John could not know that his strict admonitions to Davey would have the effect of doubling the boy's burden of secrets. Maggie had already advised Davey to say nothing more to his father about his psychic skills. Maggie's journal on her son's gifts had become an astonishing record of extra-sensory phenomena, most of which she could not explain. She had also begged Ned to withhold those stories from John lest he explode in protest against Maggie's "corruption" of his son. Unwittingly, the parents thus encouraged their son to mask his knowledge as well as his emotions. He must not allow himself to blurt out his joy at either a new game of telepathy with Mei-yin or a new discovery about flight with his father. Thus did small deceptions breed a habit of taciturn self-discipline that would serve him well in later years.

John savored his glorious victory through the rest of the afternoon and into supper, when his gentle teasing echoed Maggie's evident good humor.

She explained that she had been out on her rounds with political supporters of William McKinley and Teddy Roosevelt. Still stimulated by a rousing reception to her several public appearances, she was feeling a tolerance for the masses that even included her husband. At first jittery, she had learned how to calm her nerves and had become a star attraction on the lecture circuit. It had been a good day, enhanced by Mei-yin's obvious adulation. For a moment, the parents could remember how much they had once loved each other.

PART VII

THE AEROPLANE

"I charge thee, fling away ambition;
By that sin fell the angels."

WILLIAM SHAKESPEARE, KING HENRY VIII

CHAPTER FORTY-FOUR

CARMEL, CALIFORNIA
NOVEMBER, 1900

"You did it, Maggie!" John exclaimed the night after the election. He raised a glass of champagne and even permitted the children to have a sip. "Here's to the fairest activist in Monterey county; may she long seduce the voters."

Maggie was in high good humor. As their truce had continued to November, John and Maggie had discussed politics every evening to a point where even the children understood that their parents shared a stake in the election.

"So, why does Poppa like him?" Davey asked, thinking that John's political views were not like Maggie's.

"Your father's a cowboy, isn't he?" Maggie replied.

"Yes."

"Well, cowboys always stick together. Finally, your father knows Roosevelt. They ran up San Juan Hill together. Maybe someday he'll be able to help us. So now's the time for us to help him."

As a general rule, John was indifferent to either politicians' promises or their critics. In a normal election, he would have taken no notice of McKinley's campaign manager, Senator Mark Hanna, who had observed acidly that there was only one life between that madman (Roosevelt) and the Presidency. Nor would John have cared about Maggie's view that Teddy Roosevelt was just an overgrown little boy bent on repeatedly proving himself by physical and athletic exuberance. But this election was different. Roosevelt personified John's values. Vigorous, optimistic, bright, courageous, articulate, the new Vice-President seemed larger than life, a role model for Davey and all red-blooded young Americans who yearned for something glorious.

"Will Mr. Roosevelt come to see us when he gets to be President next year, Momma?"

John chuckled. "So much for understanding our political system, Maggie." He turned to Davey and tried to explain. "Son, he can't even run for President until 1904. How could he possibly get the job less than a year from now?"

"I don't know, Poppa." Davey suddenly decided to keep quiet. How explain a flash of a scene, a clear picture of the other, fat man lying dead? If he tried to explain, his father would get mad and Momma would look sad. Better to dodge the whole thing. "I guess I'm too young to understand."

Maggie stared at Davey with a question in her eyes. Had he had a vision? If so, she was pleased that he had censored it. She would press for explanation later. She felt no guilt at encouraging her son to deceive his father about his continuing psychic experiences. Indeed, scarcely a week passed that Davey didn't share with his mother a new Davey Drea, a telepathic experience (usually with Mei-yin) or pre-cognition. Maggie's reasoning was sound, she thought. Why test John's patience and tolerance—or their marriage—with stories that only evidenced Davey's persistent "second sight"? She couldn't know that John already respected his son's insights because they had proved so creative and valuable for the emerging aeroplane.

Maggie thought of Julie Simmons as she savored Roosevelt's victory and sipped the champagne. What a wonderful friend she had been. Almost from the moment she met Davey, she had seen his potential for selfless leadership.

It made Maggie proud when Julie told her that he seemed to know who needed attention. One by one, the children had recognized his readiness to help them. Perhaps more important, the brighter children took their cue from Davey. Instead of competition for Julie's attention and for good grades, a spirit of cooperation had slowly pervaded the class.

Maggie was especially pleased that Davey reserved a special place in his heart for the children of the ranch. He had grown up with them, had played with them around the river and the corrals, knew their parents as "Aunts" and "Uncles" and felt a bonding which was neither proprietary nor patronizing but simply the imperative of friendship. As the school year progressed, Maggie often found Davey in the library at home with one or another of his friends, reading aloud to each other or writing on the library blackboard. And so the library had become a kind of school after school, where learning was fun and was occasionally rewarded with Ah Ying's cocoa and cookies.

Their blooming friendship inspired Maggie and Julie to try an experiment with the ranch children. They began producing skits in which the children would practice their lines and perform for proud parents on an occasional Saturday evening. Maggie and Julie reasoned that many benefits would flow from their collaboration: a community spirit among the parents and the children, improved reading skills, increased social presence among the children; and a discovery of the joy of learning. By the election, the youthful "troupes" had performed eight short skits, each reminding Maggie of another grievance against John, who had missed every skit because Saturday night was sanctified by poker tradition.

Everyone was surprised at Juan Cisneros' astonishing skill as a mimic. He could imitate anyone with such accuracy that the children would roll on the floor with laughter. Two years ahead of Davey and Mei-yin, he gratefully welcomed Julie's gifts of poetry and plays, which he devoured as if he had starved for them. As Julie taught Davey and Mei-yin to paint, so she continued to teach Juan to read and appreciate poetry. Through their hours together, she began to sense a rage beneath the surface of Juan's mask of deference and polite restraint. Finally, one day she asked him if he were having trouble at home. His ready answer in the negative only nurtured her curiosity. By early November, she discovered his secret: jealousy of David Harrison. Why should David receive so much attention and praise? Wasn't he older and smarter than David? Was he ignored because he was only a foreman's son? Must he have a big house like the Harrisons?

Emboldened by his new trust in Julie, Juan showed her a list of those who had offended him. Resentment for being treated as if he were a shadow presence fed that list. Of course he loved his rides with Davey and Mei-yin, and the glider fascinated him. But his dissatisfaction would sometimes send overpowering waves of anger crashing against his ego. In frustration, he would have to clinch his little fists and turn away from Davey's thoughtless generosity. Through Juan's increasingly warped perceptions, such an act was merely patronizing, a crumb of reward to the little Mexican tag-along.

While she solicited Juan's revelations, Julie's friendship with Maggie blossomed. Little by little, Maggie discovered depths in Julie that she had not expected. She had a keen eye for the dramatic moment, for the beauty of form and action, for subtle differences in texture and color of children's costumes. She became more than just a new friend. In Lily's absence, she became Maggie's closest friend, her confidante. Maggie thought they shared a deep mutual understanding. It was Julie who most empathized with Maggie's terror when word of the Boxer uprising appeared in San Francisco newspapers.

As China struggled through a chaos of anti-foreign violence, any friends of foreigners were fair game for the marauding Boxers. Between her arrival in Shanghai in February and this November election, Lily's letters had traced the acceleration of both her fear and Boxer brutality. In early August, a small foreign force under British Vice-Admiral Seymour had failed in an attempt to relieve the besieged foreign legations in Peking. The allied powers then had seized control of Tientsin and dispatched a 20,000-man multi-national army to the relief of Peking's foreign community, who welcomed the victorious arrival of the force on August 15. In September, Lily had written proudly of the critical role her father and Lin T'ai-chi had played in negotiations between Count Waldersee, the Allied Commander-in-Chief, and Li Hung-chang, the Chinese negotiator. The resulting protocol had provided for a severe limitation on the power of China's central government to make war on foreign powers and promised a period of relative stability.

Now, in addition to celebrating the victory of the McKinley-Roosevelt ticket, Maggie thought the Harrison family should also celebrate the stabilizing role of a young army commander named Yuan Shih-k'ai. Blessed with the confidence of the Court and Jung Lu, the commander in chief of the Army and the Dowager Empress' lover, General Yuan had dared to drive the Boxers out of Shantung province. His firm stand against anti-foreign sentiment seemed to promise a new era of peace—and safety for Lily.

CHAPTER FORTY-FIVE

CARMEL, CALIFORNIA
NOVEMBER, 1900–JUNE, 1901

As the holiday season approached, unusually heavy rain and fog enveloped the Monterey Peninsula that year. The foul weather forced John Harrison to postpone further gliding tests on the updrafts of Los Laureles. Instead, he tinkered with instruments and controls to facilitate pilot convenience, corresponded with Whitehead, Wilbur Wright and Charles Manly, coped with relentless engine breakdowns in his Monterey shop and impatiently waited for the weather to break.

The redesign of the pilot's "cockpit" proved especially rewarding because it occasioned an exchange of letters with Wilbur Wright about simplification of levers and control systems. Davey turned out to be a silent voice in that correspondence. John reasoned that if Davey could manage the controls, any grown man would also be able to do so. Accordingly, he placed a single lever to the prone pilot's left front to control the forward canard elevator.

"Explain all these instruments, Poppa," Davey said one weekend in late February while rain pounded on the barn roof and a wood-burning stove kept everyone warm.

"This is a French Richard anemometer near the base of the front strut. It will measure wind speed. It will also tell you how far the machine has travelled in meters. Above it is a stopwatch to time each flight."

"Why does the pilot need them?"

"After a flight, I'll combine distance and duration of the flight to get our average airspeed."

"What's this round thing on the table?"

"It's a Veedor revolution counter. When we mount the engine, I'll use it next to the crankshaft to measure engine revolutions per minute: RPM.

The pilot can turn off each instrument at will. Or he can stop the engine with this horizontal lever next to his right hand."

Davey frowned at the arrangement for a moment. "Poppa, can you fix a lever that turns off everything at the same time?"

John thought the idea made sense. Why burden the pilot with too many things to do when he would be busy enough trying to keep the glider in stable flight? And so it went... John made changes, then explained them to Davey, whose grasp of every innovation entered his mind as naturally as breathing. Often, Ned Ambler would drop by to get a report. He would invariably find Davey and John engaged in a dialogue of seemingly equal partnership. John treated his son as if he was capable of understanding any reason for any change in either the structure of the aircraft or the arrangement of components. Like Maggie had done with philosophy, he used Davey as a verbal backboard to clarify his own ideas to himself and to debate the pros and cons of alternative structural concepts suggested by Wilbur Wright.

Will's focus on structural flexibility and endurance found a sympathetic ear in John. In March, Will wrote,

The only way to learn how to build an effective glider is to do it and test it over and over, hundreds—thousands of times. From what you have told me about Gus Whitehead, that seems to be his process to a fault. You better listen to him. You won't really get the hang of it until you get in the air next summer. Davey sounds like a smart youngster to me; but if you let him do all the flying, you will never learn about the minute adjustments that make the world of difference in lift.

For example, too many people believe that rigid machines are the answer. Look at Hiram Maxim's monstrosity. I hear that even Sam Langley's "great aerodrome" is too rigid, overbuilt and therefore too heavy. It has no give, no resilience. To achieve that, we're going to cover our wings on the bias to give strength. As I told you once before, we'll let them float loosely in their cocoon of fabric to facilitate our wing warping while being able to readjust easily to stresses from wind and rough landings.

I also advise against high, daring glides. Keep them low so that you minimize risk either to the glider or the pilot. Your purpose should be to teach yourself to manage your controls intuitively, by instinct. From what you have told me about Davey, he is close to that goal already. We envy you for having such a bright, willing partner. If he keeps up, he may be a fine pilot some day.

We like your idea of a vertical rudder and may build one on our second glider, currently under construction. Your success with your first glider reassures me that this one will not be too big or too heavy, even if it will be larger than Lilienthal's 151-square foot glider or Chanute's two-winged glider of 134 square feet. Indeed, it will about duplicate yours, except for our camber: 1:12. (Back to Lilienthal). We think camber is so important that we will build our ribs with a variable camber so we can make changes at Kitty Hawk.

Of greatest concern to John were the many malfunctions that afflicted his engine through the winter. The promise of early success had suddenly waned. Vibration loomed as an unforgiving enemy. Water connections broke; water pumps proved unreliable; water jackets failed; valves cracked, permitting oil to enter cylinders; and power dropped far below the horsepower targets necessary to fly the glider. To increase power, John and Roger Macon hit on the idea of increasing compression. Quite aware of the time-consuming complexity of the task, John told Roger to bore new cylinders, design new valve and water systems and search for more efficient electrical components. The nightmare that had confronted Charles Manly and that John had hoped to avoid was soon a daunting reality, for which there were no easy solutions as winter turned to spring. Fortunately, Manly persuaded John to build lighter pistons and to shift to high tension ignition.

As the days flew by and April flowers began to spread across the Car-

mel hillsides, John's sense of urgency became a palpable, stifling fear that
he was falling behind. Although he offered Gus Whitehead every innovation that the others mentioned, he began to wonder if he had been too
generous. Optimistic letters from Gus invariably warned him that "the
Bird," as Gus called his monoplane, Machine Number 21, was entering final construction.

One day in late May, John received a photograph of the Bird.
Compared to the primitive structure of his glider, the Bird's beauty and
sophistication staggered him. It reminded him of Leonardo da Vinci's concept of an aircraft, its wings of light steel and bamboo arching away from
the body like bird wings with a wingspan of thirty-five feet. The boat-like
body was sixteen feet long. Wings and steel-framed body required 450
square feet of silk fabric. John had warned Gus that a vertical rudder could
control yaw, but Gus believed he could govern yaw by running one propeller faster than the other. Gus boasted that his version of John's 20hp dou-
ble-compound engine weighed only 75 pounds.

John tried to accept the credit from Gus for advances which would
have been impossible without John's advice and money, but he knew that
Gus had been responsible for almost the entire structure. While Gus was
already planning first flight tests for June, John felt that Balzer's damned
engine had become his nemesis. His frustration would sometimes plunge
him into such a black mood that he would mount a horse and ride aimlessly
into deep fog hanging over Los Laureles.

Ned Ambler watched those symptoms of depression with concern. He
prayed that they would disappear when the weather cleared and glider
testing resumed. But privately, he thought John was behaving like an addict deprived of his drug. John's drug was first flight.

For Davey, during those months, the weekend hours with his father
and Roger Macon offered the major meaning in his life. School was no challenge since he was already well beyond Julie Simmons' reading and arith-
metic goals. He could sometimes help Mei-yin and others in his class, but
Julie soon discovered his inattention when she found his many sketches of

gliders tucked into his notebook.

To Julie's credit, instead of criticizing him, she captured his loyalty and affection by complimenting his artistic sense. By the end of school, she considered herself almost a member of the Harrison family. Only she was acutely aware of the fact that she had never met John Harrison. She had seen him often as he trotted by the schoolhouse on the way to Monterey. She had thrilled to newspaper accounts of his fight with Jerry Ashley. His mysterious work with gliders fascinated her. As she became more intimately involved in the lives of Maggie, Davey and Mei-yin, meeting him became an obsession that gnawed at her dreams. Her opportunity came unexpectedly with an invitation to Davey's sixth birthday on June 1.

It was an outdoor affair with exciting horse racing for adults, primarily young vaqueros, potato races for children, two barber shop quartets and a feast for over a hundred people. Julie was quite aware of hungry glances from the young cowboys, but she remained cool and calm as she stayed close to Maggie and Davey. She wore a flaring, colorful Mexican skirt and a white ruffled blouse with short sleeves, a simple ensemble that accented her dark, flashing eyes and her shining black hair.

She was complimenting Maggie on the whole affair when she turned to find John Harrison across the table, his eyes fastened on her full bosom. She smiled, extended her hand and said, "I'm Julie Simmons; you must be Davey's father. And you must be very proud of him."

John had just come from winning a horse race. Sweaty and flushed, he quietly downed a mug of beer while he collected his thoughts. As soon as he saw Julie, he wondered how he had missed seeing such a beautiful woman for the past year? And then he felt a profound sense of deja vu, a haunting memory. What is it? Her perfume? The tilt of her eyes? That... luscious body? "Nice to meet you finally, Miss Simmons. Heard lots of good things about you from ever'one in my family. They really enjoy your house on the beach."

"You must come visit sometime," Julie said with a challenge in her eyes. "A huge cypress guards the house. You can't miss it."

For the next few minutes, their conversation masked an exchange of energy, signals of questions and answers that soon excited both of them with the promise of something, sometime. And then John flushed bright red with memories of Marie and Mathilde. Lest he reveal his aroused libido, he abruptly nodded goodbye and turned to manage the potato race. But in that brief exchange, he turned a corner in his life. He could not know that his initial encounter with Julie marked the beginning of the end of any peace of mind that he had enjoyed in his marriage.

He left behind a young woman whose eyes sparkled with visions of another conquest. Julie could hardly pay attention to her minimal responsibilities with Mei-yin and Davey as she fantasized about some coming tryst with the latest target for her affections, a man she now considered the very personification of the Western bravado, slender, bronzed, strong—and apparently willing.

CHAPTER FORTY-SIX

CARMEL VALLEY
JUNE–AUGUST, 1901

"Ned, there's no time to waste!" John opened the door of the shed they had built near some oaks at the edge of the Jack's Peak meadow. During that first month of summer gliding, the small hangar had saved them hours of time and energy. No longer did they have to dismantle and rebuild the glider for each day of testing or drive horses up the steep incline of Los Laureles at risk of life, limb and the glider. But John still behaved as if time were his enemy.

That worried Ned. John's sense of extreme urgency robbed the daily flight testing of most of the fun. John thought nothing of wolfing down a sunrise breakfast with the boys, then quickly saddling horses for the ride to Jack's Peak, checking wind speed, checking the glider for possible flaws from the previous day's gliding, then resuming a test series. Ned thought John was taking excessive risks. If he, Ned, had not insisted on scrutinizing wires and struts with care, several serious accidents might have happened with God-knows-what damage to Davey, who had become the principal pilot. "You've got to slow down, John," Ned replied. "You're treating Davey like a piece of equipment. Is winning so important that you'd risk his life for it ?"

"You don't understand, Ned. The wings still need the best lift-to-drag ratio I can get. We could win this summer even if the motor is still misbehavin'."

That reply astonished Ned, who could already feel the July heat burning into his shirt. He yearned to take off his tie and relax. "What good will a perfect airframe do you if the engine isn't ready?"

"Accordin' to my calc'lations, we only need ten horsepower. I get twenty horses out of the engine most of the time. So our engine is overpowered. But if it will behave only *one* day when the glider is ready, we'll win the race!"

Ned wondered what he would do if Davey was injured badly? Was friendship with John so vital that he should risk that youngster's life with his silence? He took a gulp of water from a large flask and wondered how John had stood the heat in Cuba. He envied the boys in their shorts and open shirts. Davey was as tanned as Juan Cisneros. "So what are we testing today?"

"Optimum angle of attack. I want the wings to be almost level in flight; but last week, remember how the glider would suddenly dive for no reason?"

"I remember, worried the hell out of me." Ned remembered the panic on Davey's face when that had happened. John had shouted confused warnings while Davey had barely corrected the dive by altering the angle of attack of the canard elevator. That single experience had told Ned that John was taking dangerous shortcuts before adequate testing.

"I'm worried about that reversal. Bafflin'. I want Davey to lift the nose up to a point where it begins to stall. I...."

"Now just a minute, John. You don't mean in free flight, do you?" In the past few days, Davey had achieved extraordinary glides of 400 feet, staying aloft for 14 seconds of free flight.

"Doesn't matter much. Nothin' we can do with the guy ropes if it falls off on one wing."

"And you're not worried about injuring the boy?"

"Aw, hell, Ned. He'll be strapped in; anyway, we won't let it go above fifty feet." John bustled around the glider and mumbled his catechism, "No time to waste; no time to waste."

My God, Ned thought, *he's lost all sense of perspective*. "What's the big rush, John? Can you explain it to me?"

"I don't have many facts, Ned, mostly just a hunch."

"How about the Wright brothers. Are they ahead?"

"Probably not. They still haven't adopted a rudder. Next week, they'll leave for Kitty Hawk for their second trip. They don't have an engine yet although they've just hired a machinist full time, name of Charlie Taylor. In his last letter, Will said they'll build a shed just like ours. I s'pose Huffaker could help them make a breakthrough."

"Who's Huffaker?"

"He worked for Sam Langley one time. Now he's usin' paper rolls to make a five-wing contraption for Chanute. What'll they think of next?" John busily tested guy wires and strut connections while he talked. "Anyway, he's goin' to Kitty Hawk with the Wrights to test his monstrosity."

"Doesn't sound like the Wrights are much of a threat now."

"To tell the truth, I think Gus Whitehead has an ace up his sleeve. You know how much I admire the man. But I'd still like to beat him."

By ten o'clock in the morning, everything was ready. Davey was strapped in, and a twenty mile-per-hour wind was blowing steadily across the meadow. John and Ned grasped ropes attached to each lower wing tip and started to pull. In a moment, the glider lifted off and the two men began to pay out rope to permit the glider to climb. Under shouted instruction from his father, Davey experimented with the canard elevator. He had become so familiar with the glider that he merely had to think of a maneuver and his feet and hands would make the right moves to alter the wings, the canard elevator or the new rudder which perched on the canard structure. He yearned to be cast free and to soar higher and higher. But he knew the big test was coming, the test to see if he could turn the glider in a circle.

By now, even John could see that Davey's coordination of feet and hands was so instinctive that he automatically corrected any erratic behavior by the glider. His confidence impressed John, who felt that, after lunch, it would be safe to try turning in free flight.

At one o'clock, wind speed had increased to twenty-five miles per hour and towering cumulus clouds soared upward. In free flight, Davey began banking around the lowered left wing. To his right, he could see Monterey Bay to the north. Then he felt a faint memory of being here before. He was so riveted by that memory that he became confused when the glider suddenly reversed direction and began to turn around the higher right wing. This astonishing shift and his feeling that he was trapped in a dream so disoriented Davey that the light craft crashed into an oak tree.

While John, Ned and Juan raced to the tree, John's mind was a tumult of mixed emotions, dominated by his fear that his son had been hurt. He could breathe again when he found Davey apparently uninjured, still firmly strapped to the lower wing, which was wedged between limbs about ten feet off the ground. The top wing had broken away from its struts and lay in a heap of sateen and spruce ribs twenty feet from the oak.

"I'm mighty sorry, Poppa," Davey moaned. "I forgot the front elevator when it suddenly turned around the higher wingtip. Isn't it supposed to turn around the lower tip?"

"It sure is, son." John carefully unstrapped Davey and lifted him down from the wreckage. "Take a good look at him, Doc, and tell me he's OK."

Ned Ambler gently examined Davey carefully, asked him to turn his head from side to side, thumped his chest, checked his vision and flexed his knees and feet. "Seems fine, John. A lot finer than the miserable glider."

"Don't worry about it. We can always rebuild the glider. But for god's sake, Davey, don't tell your mother about the accident."

After numerous calculations of different aspect ratios and cambers, John built three new sets of wings. As long as he and Ned had control over ropes, he could afford to be fearless. But the accident became a beacon of doubt in his mind whenever he released Davey in free flight. He felt trapped by his own success; Davey had become so skilled as a pilot that John didn't want to waste time learning for himself. Yet he didn't need Ned to remind him of the risks involved every time Davey went aloft. Nevertheless, for the next month into early August, he sent Davey aloft for over a hundred free flights in search of the reason for the glider's strange performance.

As they discussed the situation over a picnic lunch on August 10, Davey suddenly said, "We better try to fly with the motor tomorrow, Poppa."

Through the months of model building and gliding, John had become tolerantly familiar with such outbursts from his son. Indeed, the boy's sometimes startling insights had guided John to many innovations in the design of wings, airframe and controls. So he replied to Davey, "Why tomorrow, son?"

"'Cause somebody else is gonna fly this week."

John and Ned exchanged shocked glances. "You had the same hunch, John," Ned reminded him. "Are you sure, Davey?"

"Yessir. I saw it in a dream last night. I read the newspaper headlines. He used your motor, Poppa."

"Gus Whitehead!" John and Ned exclaimed simultaneously.

It had to be Gus because, two days earlier, a letter from Will Wright had dramatized the Wright's deliberate style of progress. Reaching Kitty Hawk in the second week of July, they had spent a week constructing a shed for their glider. Then a week of rains and high winds had grounded them. Complaining that they weren't ready for flight testing until late July, Will described glider behavior that mimicked the baffling reversals of John's glider. Will thought that their 1901 glider performed worse than their first one! He tested the new one to see if the porous covering of "Pride of the West" muslin should be sealed. He concluded that, sealed or unsealed, the unsatisfactory lift values didn't change much. He was feeling frustrated and depressed when Octave Chanute arrived on August 4 to see the paper rolls of his five-wing design dissolve in the rain. Then Will had an accident almost identical to Davey's accident with a difference—Will emerged bruised and shaken. He ended his letter on a note of wry self-criticism.

When we return from Kitty Hawk soon, we may have to drop out of the flying game entirely for a while. Too many imponderables; too many risks. And too much family stress. Katherine says that we can't utter a civilized word without arguing aerodynamics. And we need to sell some bicycles. Orville agrees that we rushed to full-scale tests too soon. We must return to our models and mathematics before we design our third glider. We will devise new tests for both Smeaton's coefficient and Lilienthal's table of lift and drag. Only then will we be able to design sensible controls for a sensible glider.

The next and final paragraph was ominous because it threatened the very thing that Octave Chanute and others had fostered for so many years—shared knowledge.

We believe that we know more about the realities of flight than almost anyone else now. It has taken us this long to ar-

rive at that conclusion and to agree with your early concern
for secrecy. In future, we will not be so generous with our
hard-earned theories and structural techniques. We have neglected our bicycle business so much that, for the next few
months, we must severely limit our attention to flying.

On the day after receiving that letter, John heard from Whitehead that
he had built John's design of a four-cylinder engine powering two propellers. His gas tank held two gallons and fed fuel into the engine by gravity
feed. "Machine 21," weighing 800 pounds, built with Shelby steel tubing,
pine, spruce and bamboo, was ready to fly.

"What the hell, Ned," John exclaimed, heedless of Will Wright's warning against a premature leap into full-scale flight. "Let's try it. The engine
has yielded a consistent twenty horses for a week without malfunction."

"And Davey seems to have mastered the controls in straight flight,"
Ned added, his enthusiasm displacing his normal caution. "If we give it a
try tomorrow, we'd better get Roy Emerson up here as a witness. He'll
plaster the story all over his *Monterey Cypress.*"

"Are you game, Davey?" John asked.

"Sure, Poppa. Everything will be fine."

Later, John would not admit to anyone, least of all Maggie, that
Davey's tone of confidence had tipped the balance in favor of attempting a
powered flight. Stimulated by his son's readiness to fly and his warning
about Whitehead, John felt a power in his loins. Like a deep river, the energy coursed upward until his heart pounded with excitement. "Then let's
do it. We'll knock off for today. I'll tell Roger Macon to have the engine
here tomorrow mornin'. Ned, I'll trust you to persuade Roy Emerson to
show up. Not a word to Maggie, boys. I want this to be a big surprise for
her."

CHAPTER FORTY-SEVEN

JACK'S PEAK
AUGUST 14, 1901

Before sunrise, John Harrison awakened from a restless sleep, which had been hounded by a sense of guilt for deceiving Maggie. Not only would she be angry for his risking Davey's life, she would probably be hurt for being excluded from this great experiment. Yet of all the risks, he feared most her reaction to his possible failure. He wanted to hedge against humiliation. If he didn't make it, he could probably keep Roy Emerson from printing a story. But then that would merely postpone the inevitable. Sooner or later the glider would fly. And Roy would print a story. And Maggie would fly off the handle. So his dreams had been filled with confrontation.

He quietly slipped out of bed, put on his Stetson, dressed in jeans and boots and wandered into Davey's room to awaken him. Together, they washed up in the kitchen where Ah Ying had already cooked flapjacks and coffee. He marveled that Davey seemed at peace with the world. Could he be oblivious to the momentous import of this day's work? Or did he simply have every six-year old's conviction that the world belonged to him?

By sunrise, John, Davey and Juan Cisneros were already mounted on horses, trotting west on the valley road. John decided to approach Jack's Peak from the Monterey-Carmel road instead of the Los Laureles ridge. He was glad to see no fog along the valley. By the time they reached Jack's Peak, sunlight had dried the dew off their four-hundred yard meadow where waving grass warned of a slight breeze. When they reached the hangar, John was especially pleased to see Ned Ambler and Roger Macon and a wagon loaded with the radial engine. "Where's Roy Emerson?" John asked.

"I told him not to come until noon," Ned said. "Roger said it may take all morning to mount the engine and test it. No point in boring Roy with the same noise he's endured for the past six months."

"What's in those bottles next to the hangar?"

"Champagne." Ned grinned. "It's customary to drink champagne after you've done something glorious."

"I wish I were as confident as you and Davey. Look at him. Already talkin' to Roger about mountin' the engine. You'd think he was on a lark."

"Why John, he is," Ned said. "He told me yesterday that Mr. Lin said you would win a great race. He thinks the whole thing is in the bag."

For the next four hours, Roger Macon and two workmen gently positioned the engine on its mountings and tested it for vibration before fitting the propeller. They finished just as Roy Emerson arrived.

"Well, gentlemen," Roy said, "what the hell's going on here? You don't mean to fly this thing do you, John?"

"No Roy, I don't. I'm too big a coward. So I've persuaded my son to fly her."

Startled, Roy stared at John in disbelief. "You're trusting a six-year old to fly that contraption? List just one qualification, beside his weight, so you can plead not guilty to murder."

"In the first place, Davey is no ordinary six-year old," Ned said heatedly.

"What makes him so special?" Roy held his pencil and notebook ready, suddenly aware of the human interest angle even if the machine never budged.

Ned and John glanced nervously at each other, silently agreed that Davey's psychic gifts should remain their secret. "He has a gift for machinery," John said. "Ever since I got back from Cuba two years ago, he's worked with me on the engine in the shop. You know the way kids learn things, by guess and by gosh."

Scribbling furiously, Roy nodded. His own six-year old revealed astonishing insights and skills at unexpected moments. "But what about this… aeroplane? Where did he learn about that?"

"In my barn," John replied. "He and Ned and young Juan there have helped me test every spar and rib of the machine. Last October, he started riding our glider just to test for the best drag to lift ratio. Now he understands the controls better than any of us."

"So you've been working on this rig for some time?"

"Nearly two years." John briefly described the process by which historical forces had finally drawn a handful of inventors into the now urgent race for first flight. He underscored the many possible prizes for winning, including nation-wide recognition to the newspaper that first broke the story. While Ned and John wove a net of plausibility around Roy's mind, Roger Macon, Davey and the crew completed final adjustments on the engine. Finally the scene, the story and the historic moment captured Roy's imagination and convinced him that Davey was uniquely qualified to be the pilot. "Does Maggie know about this?" he asked almost as an afterthought.

"No," John replied ruefully. "And I'll be grateful if you keep the whole thing under your hat for a while. We've been testin' the glider all summer. But this is our first trial with power. If Davey flies, he'll be the first human in history to do it. So this may be an historic occasion, Mr. Editor."

"Well, what are we waiting for now?" Roy asked. "Are you ready, son?"

"Yessir. Mr. Macon has taught me how to adjust power by this one lever. So I'm ready whenever Poppa is."

His heart pounding, John silently strapped Davey to the lower wing in front of the engine. When he was satisfied that the boy was secure, the thought struck him that if the engine bolts failed or tore loose from the struts, Davey might be crushed. That thought bred ten other potential disasters that suddenly threatened John's will. But once again, the quiet confidence in Davey's eyes dissuaded John from heeding his worst fears. He promised himself and God that never again would he place his son in harm's way.

"Now remember, Davey. Do nothing radical. Just get her off the ground and fly a few feet. We'll hold down the wingtips with guy ropes until we can't restrain her any longer. Then Ned and I will run along side until you're in the air. And son..."

"Yes, Poppa."

"God be with you."

Roger Macon started the engine, which purred steadily while Roger once again instructed Davey on the simple throttle. Satisfied finally, Roger stepped away as John and Ned took their places at the lower wing tips. Taking a deep breath, John nodded to Davey to rev up the engine.

Davey slowly shoved the throttle forward. As the power increased, he could feel the machine straining to break away from John and Ned. Finally,

John signaled to let the machine move. Conscious of their distant presence, Davey waited for the familiar feeling of lift-off after they cast free their ropes. When that moment came, he felt the immediate difference between past glides under wind-power and this new experience. For the first time he felt the pull of torque from the propeller, a pull that forced him to counteract the twisting motion. By the time he had stabilized the machine, he was twenty feet off the ground and a hundred feet upwind. Ten seconds later, the forest at the western edge of Jack's Peak loomed. He was tempted to try a turn; but John had warned him to do nothing radical. So he pulled the throttle all the way back, felt the immediate loss of power and listened to silence. He glided to a smooth landing and rolled to a halt fifty yards from the trees. Matter-of-factly, he unstrapped himself and stood up to wait for the men, all running and shouting like madmen.

John hoisted Davey to his shoulders and shouted, "We did it! *You* did it! You just made history, son. I'm… well, I'm mighty proud of you."

"I wouldn't have believed it if I hadn't seen it," Roy said. "How far did he fly, John?"

"We'll have to measure it to the inch," Ned said. "But I figure he was in the air for over five hundred feet. Do you have any doubt that it was a flight and not a glide, Roy?"

"No doubt whatsoever!" Roy exclaimed. "I'll devote an entire issue of the paper to this."

"Uh… you better take it easy, Roy," John cautioned. "Do some research first. Put this flight in context. I'll give you the whole history of this engine and the aeroplane. Otherwise, most folks will think you're blowin' smoke."

"You think they wouldn't take my word for it?" Roy sounded outraged at the possibility.

"Well, Roy," Ned said ruefully, "remember the airship craze four years ago. Most folks still think it was just a big hoax to sell newspapers. John's right. Write up your notes on this little flight. But prepare your readers for several issues before you reveal what's happened here today."

"Maybe you're right," Roy said thoughtfully. "I'll build up the suspense for a week, cover the history with your help…."

"I'll give you plenty of background on the engine." John hoped a delay in the story would give him time both to repeat the flight and to prepare

Maggie for the shock of Davey's role. "In fact, you might link this with that scoop you had on the shoot-out in my shop. If you do it right, you may sell your story to one of the big newspapers."

"How did it feel, Davey?" Roy asked.

"I didn't expect the machine to start rolling almost as soon as it took off."

"Rolling?" John asked. "It started to roll?"

"Yes, Poppa. It felt like it wanted to roll and turn at the same time. I had to warp the wings and turn the rudder a little bit to keep it steady."

John hit himself on the forehead. "Of course. I never thought of that. The propeller rotation must start an opposite reaction in the aeroplane. I'll have to warn Will about that."

CHAPTER FORTY-EIGHT

CARMEL, CALIFORNIA
SEPTEMBER, 1901

But he didn't warn Wilbur Wright. Something told him that he should say nothing to Will or Gus Whitehead or even Charlie Manly about his success. Maybe it had been a fluke. He wanted more successful flights on the record before he went public. The patent question also teased him. Why give anything to his competitors before he had firm ownership of his own innovations? And finally, he feared Maggie's reaction when she learned how he had used Davey. So he savored the secrecy for another nine days.

During that period, the *Monterey Cypress* ran a series on flight. To save the best for last and by agreement, Roy Emerson offered no hint of John Harrison's success on August 14. But almost daily, he observed Davey's short powered flights on Jack's Peak, proving that the first flight was no fluke. Roy knew he had seen something of national importance and filled his notebook with descriptions of the machine (a birdcage), the engine's size and shape (small, radial), power (20 hp) and sound (noisy and raucous), Davey's attitude (nonchalant) and skill (divine) and the significance of the flight (truly a testament to John's genius and his debt to hundreds of other inventors). Finally, on the afternoon of August 23, he announced, "I'm gonna spill the beans tomorrow, John. Are you ready for the mob?"

"Who knows?" John answered. He hoped the telegraph would spread word of his success across the world. He hungered for the adulation which he surely deserved. He could see the headlines: HISTORIC FIRST: CALIFORNIA ENGINE DESIGNER AND MANUFACTURER CONQUERS THE AIR. Goaded by such paeans of praise, surely Maggie would finally pay *her* respects to his genius, accepting even Davey's role in the great victory.

John would forever remember Friday, August 24,, as one of the darkest days of his life. The morning gave no warning of the convergence of shocks that would engulf him. Maggie spent the morning in Monterey with county politicians. John spent the day on Jack's Peak, tinkering with his engine. The day was sunny and mild, offering no ominous signs and portents. The flood tide of unpleasant news and crises began with a visit by Ned Ambler around noon.

"John," Ned cried as he entered the shed, "Look at this *New York Herald* of August 19. Gus Whitehead has done it!"

"Done what?"

"Claimed first flight!" Ned simply bustled, quivered and trembled with suppressed excitement. "On August 14, he also flew nearly a mile."

John forced himself to stay calm. "May I see the article?"

The headline read, **"Inventors in Partnership to Solve Problem of Aerial Navigation—Gustave Whitehead Travels Half a Mile in Flying Machine Operated by A New Acetylene Chemical Pressure Motor."**

John read, "Mr. Whitehead last Tuesday night, with two assistants, took his machine to a long field back of Fairfield, and the inventor for the first time flew in his machine for a half-mile. It worked perfectly and the operator found no difficulty in handling it. Mr. Whitehead's machine is equipped with two engines, one to propel it on the ground on wheels, and the other to make the wings or propellors work. In order to fly, the machine is speeded to a sufficient momentum on the ground by the lower engine; and then the engine running the propellors is started, which raises the machine in the air at an angle of six degrees."

John scanned the article for any reference to his own contribution. He felt an instant of gratification to read, "The inventor stated that he could never have achieved the flight without the technical skill and support of Mr. John Harrison of Carmel, California, one of the foremost machinists of the age." Well, that was something anyway. But why did he feel so disappointed?

"I wonder if he had any witnesses?"

"Read on," Ned said. "Richard Howell, the editor of the Bridgeport *Sunday Herald*, saw the whole thing and wrote an article about it in the

Sunday papers. He said Whitehead flew a half-mile at an altitude of over fifty feet."

"Ned, I feel... empty, deflated. I feel like I was a big balloon and Gus Whitehead has just stuck a pin in it. No wonder I felt some urgency two weeks ago. The rascal was winning while I was risking Davey's life."

"You could look at it another way, John," Ned said gently. "There were two flights that day. Even with time differences, Davey probably flew first."

"You're right, of course." John seemed confused as he picked up a letter from a workbench. "Have you read Roy's article on our flight?"

"Yeah. Roy said Davey made his historic flight at four o'clock, EST, several hours before Whitehead's flight. Let's get Roy to play up that difference."

"I don't know, Ned. Here's a letter from Tom Baldwin. He finally left his jealous wife and is livin' in San Francisco now. He wants me to build an engine for a giant airship, *Old Glory*, which he wants to launch in November. Maybe I should do it and stop competin' with the Eastern crowd."

"Is it possible that Whitehead was just lucky?" Ned asked while he scanned Baldwin's letter. "I mean, does he understand how he's done it."

"What are you sayin', Ned?"

"Look at it this way. A lot of your ideas are built into his engine. The newspaper article says that, even though Gus is known as a master engine builder, he needed your help. Do you think he knows all there is to know about aspect ratio, camber, lift-to-drag ratio and so forth?"

"Hard to say. I know he used my ideas from Will Wright and Charlie Manly to fiddle with 'the Bird' all last spring: changin' the center of gravity; shiftin' the wings and the rudder; replacin' wooden wheels with bicycle wheels; testin' the engine.... Then he tested the whole shebang all summer."

"But does he really understand the scientific principles at stake?"

"What difference does it make?" John's expression of disgust revealed his own essential disrespect for pure science. "Scientists like Sam Langley will study that stuff for the next fifty years. The point is that Gus and I used the trial and error approach to put it all together for the first powered flight in history. Maybe they'll stop callin' him 'Crazy Whitehead' now."

"You sound as if you blame science somehow."

"Yeah, I reckon I do feel stupid for lettin' my curiosity about science divert me from winnin' the race a week or a month earlier. I spent too much time searchin' for theoretical relationships among lift and drag and camber and... well you know how we wasted our time."

Wasting time? The man had been a demon possessed, Ned thought as he poured himself a glass of cold tea and added a healthy dollop of sugar. "What did you expect from winning, John?"

"Recognition, especially from Maggie! That's what I wanted. I wanted the world to beat a path to my shop in Monterey. I wanted ever'one to say, 'That's John Harrison; he was the first man to fly.'"

"And you think no one will take notice of your work now?"

John thought about that. Ned's questions made him realize how romantic his expectations had been. He knew that public opinion was quite whimsical and that the press wrote stories to sell newspapers, not to give an accurate account of the news. "You think I should team up with Tom and stick to engines?"

"Not entirely." While Ned sipped his tea, he searched for a diplomatic way to console John and encourage him to focus on his strengths. "There's no reason why you should abandon your own design of a better aeroplane. I can't imagine that Whitehead's achievement will dissuade either Langley or Will Wright from their own experiments. Neither should you. Your work with Balzer and Manly has already won an international reputation for you in light engines. Now your first flight should only add gloss to that reputation."

John brightened. "You're right, Ned! I wasn't thinkin' straight. Charlie Manly wrote recently that Langley gave him permission to build an entirely new, bigger engine. The old one displaced 380 cubic inches; the new one will displace 540 cubic inches. Since he got new piston castings, he's assemblin' all the larger accessories. He'll braze water jackets to cylinders this month."

"So there you have it!" Ned said eagerly. "With your experience, you shouldn't limit yourself at all. Improve your own aeroplanes; help Manly build his larger engine; help Baldwin launch the old *Ciudad de Mexico*. Is Baldwin a good businessman?"

John told Ned about Tom's great success with his balloons and his popular entertainment park in Quincy, Illinois. "He says the Army will buy a dirigible *before* it ever buys an aeroplane. So he's buildin' a factory in San Francisco."

"That sounds like an important project, John," Ned enthused. "And sincere congratulations for first flight. I hope you'll celebrate with Maggie tonight."

Ending his therapy session with John on that up-beat note, Ned said his goodbyes and pointed his buggy west. He happened to pass Maggie on her way home at three o'clock. He lifted his hat and smiled. But Maggie ignored him, her face such a grim picture of anger and determination that Ned was almost glad she hadn't seen him. He wondered what could be tormenting her. He hoped she wouldn't confront John, who just might bite her head off.

Maggie wheeled the buggy up the driveway and jerked the horses to a stop at the entrance. She hurled open the front door, her whip still in hand, and strode into the library where she found John reviewing his files on Tom Baldwin. Without warning, she brought her whip down on John's shoulders. "Damn your soul, John Harrison. I read the newspaper story an hour ago. You deceived me! You ignored all my warnings and risked my son's life all summer in your damfool contraptions. I... I hate you!"

John seized her whip, threw it into the fireplace and stared at her with an icy surface calm that belied the tumult in his heart. Before she pranced in puffed up with her damned accusations and complaints, he had almost recovered from the shock of Whitehead's victory. Now he felt the resurgent power of his disappointment and frustration transmuted into rage, a rage in search of a scapegoat. Maggie was suddenly the ideal candidate to blame for all his self-recriminations and doubts. Memories of his many conflicts with her drove any desire for peace from his mind: her attitude of pseudo-intellectual superiority, armed with her goddam high-toned culture and her dry-as-dust philosophers; her relentless complaints about the cultural desert of Carmel Valley; her assertive self-confidence in *her* way, the *only* way, to rear Davey, guaran- damn-teed to prepare him for a life of mystical indolence and self-pity; and her indifference to her marital duties in bed. "You're a sad excuse for a woman, Maggie! Now get your hysteria out of my library and go scream Chinese aphorisms at Ah Ying; or better yet, go dunk your head in the Carmel River. I've no time for your whining complaints tonight."

"No time *tonight?* You never have any time for the things that count."

"What's that supposed to mean? Some profound spiritual ideal? Some philosopher's stone? Forgive me, Maggie; I guess I'm too mortal for your taste."

"Not too mortal, John; just too childish. You always have plenty of time for your silly hobbies, making models, flying kites. I could tolerate that in a grown man if you didn't risk my son's life. But it would be too much to expect you to remember your duty to your son."

John recalled his pledge to his dead parents to prepare Davey for manhood. In this moment of self-inflicted failure, her accusation struck him where he felt most vulnerable. "My obligations to Davey? If you had your way, he'd be half blind and totally confused from studyin' a lot of useless nonsense about extra sensory gifts and spiritual guides. At least what I've done is to put him on a path in *this* world. Ask anyone. I've done right well with Davey." John glared at her for a moment, then continued. "Right now, barely six years old, he knows more about carpentry and engines than any youngster in California. He knows more about flyin' an aeroplane than anyone in the country."

Maggie snorted. "And that's your measure of achievement? Who will ever need such skills?" She shook her head impatiently. "Never mind; the point is that you lied to me, John. Your promises to me have proved no more reliable than your pledges to your parents. I wouldn't trust your word now about anything; and that's a terrible thing for a wife to have to say to her husband."

"My son and I have finally done something glorious. In all of human history we're the first to fly an aeroplane under its own power and control. Doesn't that mean anythin' to you?"

"Not a thing. It means nothing to me or most people, John. I'm warning you now. If I hear of you risking my son's life again on one of your stupid toys, I'll kidnap Davey. You'll never see him again."

"Don't ever threaten me with somethin' like that! You start throwin' such threats around and I'll have to banish you from the ranch."

Maggie thrust her face within an inch of John and whispered, "And who would occupy your bed and endure your pitiful fumblings that you call love? Maybe one of Mama Rosa's *putas?*"

The suggestion rendered John speechless—a condition to which his fights with her usually reduced him. Her insight struck at the foundation of a charade to which he had disciplined himself ever since his return from New York. His frustrated sexuality had become a ghost, haunting him at unexpected moments, driving him to unreasonable excesses of fear and anger and fierce physical activity. He had even wondered if his zeal for flight might be a substitute for his unfulfilled hunger for a loving, giving woman. He suddenly felt a sense of stifled, tongue-tied incompetence, the usual climax to an argument with Maggie. He couldn't answer her question, but he could get astride his favorite stallion and run for several miles. Maybe that would have its usual cathartic effect, taking him back to the Rockies, cleaning out some of the confusion and pain in his mind, centering him in his best nature, releasing him from a self-image of ineffectual inferiority.

He brushed past Maggie and raced through the front door to the stables, saddled his horse and, at five o'clock in the afternoon, dug his spurs into the poor animal's flanks for a long run westward into heavy fog. His mind seethed with a yearning to punish someone, anyone. But he couldn't identify the best candidate on whom to vent his fury. For no reason at all, he drove his horse at a punishing speed westward toward the beach at Carmel.

Scarcely an hour later, he found himself in Julie Simmons' yard. Impulsively, he jumped from the saddle and pounded on her door. When she opened the door, her appearance was hardly the schoolteacher he had first met three months earlier. She was so provocative that John had to fight a desire to seize her in his arms. He restrained himself although he also felt a stirring tension between them. For an instant, he had thought he was looking at Marie or her sister, Mathilde, his two New York instructors in sex as art.

Julie had tied her long hair back in a pony-tail and had smeared paint on her brow. Her blouse was loosely opened against the heat from a roaring fire.

Her feet apart, she stood with hands on hips—challenging, alluring, beautifully feminine—as if annoyed at the interruption from a tradesman.

"John!" she cried, "What an unexpected pleasure. I've just come back from school; getting ready for a school year always exhausts me. What brings you here?"

The question seemed to bewilder John. Why *had* he come here? "I guess..." he began lamely. "I just... wanted to see you."

Julie felt a tremor, a small earthquake race through her body. *He needs me!* The insight stunned her and made her heart pound. She could feel herself respond to the power of his need with a glow of pure lust that she had not experienced for a long time.

"Why, how very nice." She smiled, held open the door, seized his arm and led him into the house. "Would you like to see my work?"

In the next moment, John found himself directly behind Julie, who stood before her seascape and waited for his comment. In the midst of his stumbling critique, Julie leaned backwards and all but forced John to cradle her breasts in his hands. Without hesitation, she turned, reached around his neck and kissed him boldly on the mouth. The pressure of her firm breasts against his chest was a sudden, irresistible promise.

Astonished, he held her at arm's length. "How did you know I wanted to do that?"

"Because *I* did," she answered, flushed and wide-eyed. "I've wanted to hold you in my arms since the moment I first met you at Davey's birthday party. I can't help it. What can we do about this?"

"I don't have a quick answer," he said breathlessly, his mind alive to the possibilities. "Could we practice that kiss again?"

On familiar ground and ready for any move that John might make, Julie pressed against him and offered her lips. John felt an embarrassing stiffening in his groin as a passion seized control of his senses. Her mouth glued to his, her eyes closed, Julie reached inside his trousers and grasped his erection firmly. He gasped, hesitating for only a second. Then he banished restraints and warnings from his mind. Here was the uncritical reassurance and warm acceptance that he had needed all day—all year—all wrapped up in willing, faintly perfumed flesh, flashing eyes and a sweet mouth.

Mindlessly, he unbuckled his trousers and let them drop to the floor. Smiling and humming, she began to unbutton his shirt. Then, while she tried to breathe, she unhooked her skirt and stepped out of her underwear. John carried her into her bedroom, where he soon discovered that she was as practiced as Mathilde and Marie had been.

After barely ten minutes of play, Julie whispered, "I can't wait much longer, John. Please take me! Please! Please!"

In the next few minutes, their passion became a form of warfare, as if each wished to consume the other. Their lust finally spent, they lay in each other's arms for a few seconds, speechless, reluctant to tilt the delicate balance of competing emotions with banal words.

Julie finally broke the silence with a soft chuckle. "I didn't know you could be so decisive. When I asked you what we should do, this was the last thing I expected. I feel more alive than I've felt in years! Are you all right?"

"I'm more than all right, honey. But I don't think I can talk about it. I just want to hold you in my arms and breathe your hair and touch you here... and here... and even here."

In a moment, this experimental touching reheated the fires of their need. This time, their rhythm of urgency was replaced by a controlled pace in which John deliberately set out to give Julie pleasure, just the way Marie had taught him. As soon as she realized that he knew something about the art of love-making, Julie forced herself to surrender first and then to cooperate in nurturing a slow-burning flame that gradually consumed both of them. When this more prolonged exploration of selfless giving and receiving ended, they were satiated, each astonished that such a considerate and practiced partner had been found.

At six o'clock, withholding promises about tomorrows, John dressed, held Julie in a final strong embrace, then turned and mounted his horse for the hour's ride to the ranch. He had much to think about. But he felt a greater sense of peace than he had experienced since he had returned from New York. For the first time in two years, he was alive with power and possibilities. He refused to face the implications of that afternoon. He only wanted to savor the experience. His mind reeled at a dream fulfilled—Marie and Mathilde had come to Carmel!

CHAPTER FORTY-NINE

CARMEL VALLEY
SEPTEMBER, 1901–JANUARY, 1902

"You sure you can't persuade Maggie to let Davey fly again?" Roy Emerson slouched in a chair and gazed forlornly out the window at street traffic.

John Harrison regarded Roy's office with distaste. A shabby carpet separated his stuffed leather couch from the cluttered desk. Old yellowing papers were stacked waist high along a side wall. All wall space was covered with framed front pages, headlines proclaiming notable events such as the recent assassination of President McKinley. "Impossible," John said sadly. "It would cost me my marriage if I risked Davey's life again."

"But John," Roy remonstrated, "my correspondents around the country are accusing us of fraud. It's put up or shut up now. Can't you fly it yourself?"

"I s'pose I could try. But I'd have to recalc'late a lot of things and rebuild. My guess is I'd need a bigger machine, maybe a bigger engine. Until that was finished, I couldn't even practice gliding."

"Shit! You've boxed all of us into a royal pickle. With my own eyes I've seen a miracle. But without Davey, we look like a bunch of conspirators."

John burned with resentment and frustration as he left Roy's office. Two years of intense work and a lifetime of ambition were being held hostage by one person, the very person whom he had most wanted to impress: Maggie. It was brutally ironic that she should have become his principal obstacle to public recognition. While he rode around the coast to Carmel, he pondered his alternatives. Defy Maggie? Hardly worth it. That was a formula for more than a fight. It would probably lead to a noisy public brawl that would demean everyone, divert attention from his very real achievement and probably end in divorce. Build another larger machine? Possible. But it would take months, maybe years because a larger engine would be necessary. Gripped by a nagging sense of helplessness, he sought solace from Julie.

Over the next four months, he visited her several times a week, usually in the late afternoon after she returned from school and he had spent the day in his Monterey shop. Their signal was an American flag, flying high above Julie's house. If John saw it waving around four o'clock, he knew that no visitors were camped on Julie's doorstep. During those months, he explored her body as if he were examining a machine for its innermost secrets. He knew he was treading on dangerous ground, but his need was unrelenting. As long as Maggie thwarted aeroplane tests, he could at least assert himself with Julie. When he asked himself why he continued on such an insane path, the only answer he would allow himself to hear was, "Because I need her!"

Through the darkness of his growing infatuation, he sometimes glimpsed flashes of light. Some part of his mind hoped that his single-minded lust was merely an escape from his persistent frustrations about his aeroplane. Julie's body became an addiction, her lust his solace, and her unquestioning approval his measure of self-worth. Like any addict, he assured himself that he could break it off any time. In the interim, he built a wall of healthy rationalizations. Wouldn't this trivial caper benefit his family by releasing his tensions? Wasn't he a more tolerant husband and father? Thus did he rationalize his deception of Maggie, which slowly isolated him from his ranch and his family.

Wisely, Julie placed no demands on him but simply accepted what he could give to their emerging relationship. As far as she was concerned, her life was now complete. She enjoyed her work with the children; loved her painting when John was not there; and she gloried in the hungry strength in John's body each time they met.

At the ranch, the hostility between Maggie and John remained a ghost that permeated everything in their lives. Maggie tried to surround the children with the colorful rituals and excitement of childhood: Halloween, Thanksgiving, Christmas and New Year's Eve. But she feared that their future was still a hostage to John's whimsy. Her distrust of his demons filled each day with a premonition of disaster, all the more disturbing because it couldn't be named or defined. Despite her normal tolerance of ambiguity, she began to feel the effects of her gnawing doubts—lost weight, inattention to any task while a part of her mind waited for some unseen enemy to assail her, ragged nerves, eyes aching with sleepiness even at the moment of waking, and then brimming with tears for no obvious reason.

Her resentment of John's apparent indifference to her condition only fed—and fed on—all her symptoms. It did not help that John was gone most of each day in Monterey. While he seemed to thrive on his new schedule and his new partnership with Tom Baldwin, she wondered why he frequently stayed away so late, often returning home long after supper without explanation. But she wouldn't give him the satisfaction of questions about his long absences. All the unspoken rules of their alienation enforced her silence lest it appear that she still cared about him or anything else except Davey and Mei-yin. Even politics lost its allure. She therefore rarely went out except to see Julie Simmons, whose behavior sometimes seemed unaccountably cool. She felt like she had become a prisoner in her own home. At the age of twenty-nine, she was more thoroughly miserable than she had ever been before.

For Davey, the family battlefield was especially painful because he could feel both his mother's anguish and his father's roller-coaster mood-swings. In his experience, nothing could account for either. Night after night, during his roundup, his voice offered no response to questions about his parents except, "They have hard lessons to learn." Did that mean his parents were going to school also? Did that mean they were getting bad grades from God? Was that why Momma was so sad, why Poppa never played much with him any more, silently gone early in the morning to Monterey and home often after bedtime for him and Mei-yin? Was Poppa studying hard when he spent so many weekends away, maybe at the shop, maybe with Mr. Baldwin? He regretted that he was no longer allowed to fly the glider. He had begged Momma, but she had stared through him, and had said, "Absolutely not." He consoled himself with another kind of flight that no one could prohibit. In his mind he could still fly with the birds.

For five years, Davey's inner voice and Momma's support had guided him to a sense of mastery over minor crises because of his parents. He had never doubted their love for him or their membership in his magical universe of metaphors, images, signs and portents. Indeed, although he sometimes heard his father and mother in argument, they had seemed to reward him the more he behaved like a natural boy, filled with curiosity and limitless energy.

But by Christmas, 1901, he had discovered the virtues of discreet silence. Thanks to his many conversations with Mei-yin, he was learning how to navigate his own path through the tortuous maze of his parents' domestic battle. That the heart of their battle concerned many of his own choices and views made him feel guilty. By Christmas, approaching the age of seven, he could barely remember the idyllic first few years of his life, when everything had seemed to be a seamless web of love. Now it was fenced and cross-fenced into safe and unsafe areas, booby-trapped with warnings: don't mention psychic games to Poppa; don't talk to Momma about anything he might share with Poppa, especially anything dangerous like gliding; always tell Miss Simmons everything with total honesty so that she could help him decide what to do; don't show that he could read better or knew more than Juan Cisneros lest *he* become enraged. Some things were clear. He could get Poppa's approval only if he acted tough and didn't talk about his strange experiences; Momma was more likely to reward him if he *didn't* act tough and *did* talk a lot about his visions. He sometimes wished he could be as good an actor as Juan, then it might not be so hard to keep his various roles neatly separated.

On the Saturday after Christmas, Davey met Tom Baldwin for the first time in the Monterey shop. The boy was entranced by the big man, whose stories about parachuting and ballooning seemed to be endlessly varied and exciting.

"Well, John, we launched *Old Glory* near the corner of Eleventh and Market Streets in early November; carried nine passengers."

John chuckled. "I heard about it, Tom. She lost her ropes and went on a little free-flight trip, didn't she?"

"Yep. The best free advertising we could have asked for." Tom smoked a cigar and held the employees in thrall. Forty-seven and tending to portly, he still retained a youthful vitality. His round, florid, open face conveyed an impression of vigorous self-confidence. "Sailed over San Mateo, Menlo Park, La Honda, San Jose and finally landed near Santa Cruz around six o'clock. The press published every detail."

"You think there's money in these flights, Tom?" Roger Macon asked.

"Only if your new motor can drive them." Tom examined his cigar as if to find some secret insight in its glowing embers. "Frankly, I'm short of the ready; if I don't get an engine soon, I may have to find an *honest* business."

Everyone chuckled, sharing well-known Tom's disdain for venal politicians and ignorant army procurement agents. But John protested, "You won't put anything past a West Pointer, Tom. I served under them in Cuba and I found them brave, smart and utterly honest: finest men I've ever met as a group."

Davey listened to his father's familiar litany of praise. Poppa never tired of describing the thrilling exploits of the young West Pointers whose gallantry in Cuba seemed exalted. The boy wondered if he might ever be lucky enough to be a West Pointer, a speculation that John had warned him not to mention to his mother at risk of a beheading.

"All the better for our plans, John," Tom said. "I'll bet we'll have a powered balloon in the air before any West Pointer sees a reliable aeroplane."

Roger glanced furtively at John to see how he might handle the very sore subject of powered flight. "Well, Tom, in August we won the race for first flight. A few hours after we flew, a fella named Whitehead flew nearly half a mile using John's engine. But the Wright brothers and Sam Langley are still plugging their way. How are the Wrights doing, John?"

"I give 'em all credit, Roger. I heard recently from Chanute that Will's speech in mid-September was a hit with the Western Society of Engineers. He and Orv are now the unquestioned authorities on the theory of flight."

Tom Baldwin frowned. "You think they know more than you do, John?"

"About *theory*, yes. They made a wind tunnel recently, and they're testin' over two hundred airfoils to find a new Smeaton's coefficient and a different set of lift and drag tables for different angles of attack. I rate them the foremost scientists in the field today. Why, Will said they don't even use Lilienthal's tables any more. It's too bad they've got to stop work for a while."

"Why, what happened?" Roger asked.

"They have to make bicycles to make a livin', just like us, Roger. So they're quittin' research until next spring. It may give Sam Langley a chance to beat 'em—maybe next year sometime."

"But no one's motor is as good as yours; isn't that right, John?" Tom asked.

"That's true." John chuckled. "Poor Manly. They've spent over five thousand dollars so far and all they have is an engine that leaks. When I wrote to Charlie about Gus Whitehead, he wanted to know the dimensions of Gus' glider. So I told him to go to Atlantic City and see it on display."

"It's amazing that Will Wright still keeps in touch if he's so far ahead of the pack," Tom said. "You'd think they'd be a little more secretive. If I knew what *they* know, I wouldn't give it away for free."

"They'll be more tight-fisted now, Tom. Will said a lawyer is nosing around with offers of patents. Their third glider will probably fly like a bird. They think they've discovered the most favorable lift-to-drag ratio, the best camber...." John turned to Davey sitting in the corner and said with a smile, "Twenty to one, Davey, the same as we used on our glider!"

That evening, Tom went home with John and Davey for the first of many suppers with Maggie, who welcomed his worldly urbanity like a breath of fresh air. "I must compliment you, Maggie," Tom said at supper. "I've been on several world tours and I attend many soirees in San Francisco where ladies are usually overdressed with their plumed hats, their bustles, their corsets, their chokers and their jewelry. You would put them all to shame in that lovely gown. Is it your own design? It looks as if you adapted ancient Roman fashion to your taste. It's Shantung silk isn't it?"

While Maggie answered, Tom had a chance to examine her. *Too thin for my taste, he thought. But still an extraordinarily beautiful young woman. Maybe five feet seven inches tall; rich, shoulder-length, heavy auburn hair, glowing in the fire-*

light; small, slightly turned up nose; delicate eyebrows; troubled gray-green eyes; high cheek-bones; lovely oval planes on a slender face; sweet generous mouth; firm jaw; small ears; an inner light that conveys both softness and strength; something hidden, restrained. My God, this woman is carrying a terrible sadness! I wonder....

Maggie smiled at Tom's unprecedented gallantry. "Thank you, Tom; I see you have an eye for line. It is indeed Shantung silk. Out here in the country I hope we're not too informal for your taste."

"I feel warmly welcomed, Maggie."

"Maggie is very well acquainted with fashion, Tom," John said. "While she was at Mills College she attended many parties at the Sherman house. In fact, I bought this piano at the Sherman music emporium."

"I *once* met people like Lillian Russell and Enrico Caruso," Maggie said wistfully, implying that that life had happened so long ago that she could barely remember it. "Now, stuck here in this cultural backwater, I rarely meet anyone with your vast experience, Mister Baldwin."

Tom could hear the repressed pain in Maggie's voice. After his own recent experience with Carrie, he wondered if John's marriage was also in trouble.

"Anyway, I can't stand leg-o'-mutton sleeves or the upswept bird's-nest coiffure," Maggie said quietly. "I think Charles Dana Gibson's sketches are caricatures of *La Belle Epoque*."

Tom seemed to agree. "Last year in Paris, I met a man named Paul Poiret whose designs are just the thing for you. He wants to liberate women from the corset. Paul is an assistant to Jacques Doucet, the current the favorite of more daring Parisiennes and *grandes cocottes*."

"I know of Poiret." Maggie was impressed. In the last seven years, how many men had John brought home who knew a bustle from a stay? "His ideas about the liberation of fashion echo a liberating trend for women all over Europe."

The talk of fashion and liberation irritated John. He was also apprehensive that Maggie was about to launch into her customary plea for the rise of the common citizen—and women. But her next words were reassuring. "When Paul's gowns become popular, there will be no steel structures radiating from the waist. He gathers the material just beneath the bosom and allows it to flow naturally to the floor. I *have* been experimenting. Do you really like it?"

"Indeed I do. I like especially its simplicity; and the peach color is mighty pretty." Tom thought, *What a surprise! I had no idea I would find such a cosmopolitan world traveller hiding in the Carmel Valley.*

Now genuinely interested in Captain Tom Baldwin, Maggie asked, "What kind of enterprise are you starting with my husband, Tom?"

"I'm interested in airships as a means of commercial transportation. I believe that someday, people will be able to travel across the entire country in an airship. I would certainly like to make some money, but I really have a fascination with the technology of flight. No, it's almost an obsession."

"What do you mean by the techno… technology of flight?" Davey asked.

Tom was tempted to talk down to the boy. But he suddenly wanted to reach out to Maggie, capture her respect and maybe her friendship. If he could get the boy's support, maybe the mother would follow. "Son, we're right at the dawning of the age of flight. In this century I believe mankind will conquer the air. We're bursting at the seams already with all kinds of new inventions: the auto; the telephone; the steamship; electricity; medical gadgetry…."

"What do they have to do with airships and flying?" Maggie asked idly, careful to mask her weariness with the threatening subject of flight.

"I believe we'll take the best of each of those inventions and pour that best into huge airships—dirigibles. I don't want to sound like a preacher, but I dare you to imagine what such machines might do for civilization."

"Make a lot of noise?" teased John.

Tom joined the laughter with a smile. "Once we start the process of development, all technologies and all fields of science will be forced to learn more and design better equipment to keep the pace of improvements accelerating. I tell you, it is going to be something glorious!"

Maggie, whose chief entertainment was watching Davey, suddenly felt a cold fist at her heart as she watched the tears bright in Davey's eyes. She had told him, "tears are the diamonds of truth; never be afraid to let them flow from the heart." She could see that Davey believed he was hearing Truth. Would they never escape from John's glider?

CHAPTER FIFTY

CARMEL VALLEY
1902

On a cold morning in early February, John Harrison sat in front of a fire in the kitchen and sorted through mail that had accumulated for several days. He was nursing a slight hangover from a late night with Julie Simmons and was in a foul humor. Sipping his coffee, he looked forlornly through blood-shot eyes at the dun-colored hills, dotted with green oaks and brown cattle. The coffee made him feel somewhat better, but his memories soured him on his life in Carmel Valley. He turned to stare into the fire and reflected on the past eight years. "Failure" was a self-judgment that seemed inescapable. Failure—or at least waning interest—as a rancher, a state of mind that he wouldn't have believed possible before he married Maggie. Failure—or at least diversion—of his zeal for bicycles. Failure—or at least postponement—of his plan to build a motorcycle. Failure to win national recognition for either his radial engine or first flight. And that reminded him that he was almost a total flop as a husband. It all added up to one huge bust, a grand failure to fulfill his potential back in college. He idly opened a letter postmarked Hammondsport, New York.

January 31, 1902

Dear John,

In my last letter, I told you that Jim Smellie finally turned over his whole bicycle business to me last June. Through the summer and autumn, I closed out the inventory: Stearns, Columbias, Clevelands, Nationals and Racycles. Why? Because I decided to make my own brand. I also decided to build my own motorcycle. It was your idea. You may not remember that you told Teddy Roosevelt about the idea five years ago. Anyway, pedaling a bicycle isn't fast enough for me. I have a yearning, maybe a sickness, to push my speed up to the edge of self-destruction.

The engine has been my big problem. I started with castings from the E.R. Thomas Company, whose 1900 Auto-Bi was probably the first motorcycle in history. I designed my own carburetor; applied power to the rear wheel with my own design of a V-shaped leather belt; borrowed a spark coil from Doc Alden; and mounted the whole rig on my first bike, the "Happy Hooligan." But that first engine wasn't powerful enough. So I ordered the largest set of castings available from Thomas. The final motor weighed 180 pounds. It was a noisy, unreliable volcano that drank gasoline. It wouldn't suit. But since it was the best that Thomas could offer, I decided to build my own.

That brings me to the point of this letter. I'm no engine designer; I know just enough to be dangerous. Kirkham is a fair-to-middlin' machinist and his foundry is adequate. But we need a partner who knows engines from A to Z. You have told me about your work with Samuel Langley, Charles Manly and Gustave Whitehead. Congratulations on winning first flight! You've made an enviable reputation for yourself since we first met nearly three years ago. You seemed to like us here in Hammondsport. I can tell you that Lena and I and all the "Hammondsport Boys" liked you a lot.

So how about coming here to design the finest small engines in the world?

Bring your family; let your son grow up to love the Finger Lakes like I do. I think we could make a go of it. Young bucks around here are crazy for motorcycle racing. But if it didn't work out, what would you have lost? At least you would have had an adventure and a change of scenery.

If you can't come now, would you consider designing a good one-cylinder motor for me as soon as possible? My formula is maximum power for minimal weight—the same as yours, I bet. Please say yes.

Your friend in need,
Glenn Curtiss

While John toyed with his breakfast, his hand fell on a thick package from Gus Whitehead. Together with his heartfelt thanks, Gus had sent every article he could find about his August flight. What was new were articles about his recent flight over Long Island Sound on January 17. He had flown Machine Number 22, an improved version of Number 21. Flying at a height of 200 feet, Gus had actually turned his machine by altering propeller speeds. After an extended third flight of over seven miles, he landed safely on the water.

Bitterly, John wondered why the world hadn't taken notice of his glorious achievement? Was Wall Street censoring the story? Or did Gus have no eye witnesses? John thought he must get to the bottom of that story someday. Then it occurred to him that Tom Baldwin might be making money in Los Angeles. He'd been down there long enough with *Old Glory*. Maybe he'd make a name for himself with old Thaddeus Lowe's scheme to catch high altitude air currents and sail from Colorado to New York.

John turned next to a letter from Wilbur Wright. Without naming Whitehead, he wrote,

The newspapers are full of accounts of flying machines which have been built in cellars, garrets, stables and other secret places. They all have the problem "completely solved," but usually there is some significant detail yet to be decided, such as whether to use steam, electricity, or a water motor to drive it. Mule power might give greater ascensional force if properly used; but I fear it would be too dangerous unless the mule wore pneumatic shoes. Some of these reports would disgust me if they were not so ludicrous.

John felt grateful that he hadn't boasted about *his* first flight to Will. Would his report have disgusted Will also?

Until last month, we labored over the design of our third glider, which must capture all that we have learned with the wind tunnel. Now we are convinced that an aspect ratio of 6:1 is best. With a wingspan of 32 feet and a chord of 4 feet, 9

inches, we'll have 305 square feet of lift. We'll use a
sliver of a camber of 1:28, which should give us such an optimum lift-to-drag ratio that it will "kite" at a very low
angle of attack.

We think we've found the reason for the strange reversal
of turn which you and I encountered last summer. If you think
of wingtips as racing against each other when a left turn begins, the lower wingtip must turn through a smaller arc than
the higher wingtip. That means the higher wingtip has to outrace the lower one. We think reversal happens because in-
duced drag slows down the higher tip at a certain point in a
turn.

We think your rudder idea will solve that problem. We'll
put it in the rear. It should counteract the tendency of the
lower tip to outrace the higher tip.

Our only remaining problem is how to handle our dear
friend, Gustave Chanute. He has been a wonderful sounding
board for our ideas, but he is no longer of much value as far
as the science of flight goes. He persists in exploring ideas
that we know to be dead ends. Now he wants us to supervise the
construction of two of his gliders, including a multiple
wing horror. To do this would delay our own work. If we can
persuade him to use his own experts, we may still have to endure their presence at Kitty Hawk next summer. We could not
tolerate Huffaker again.

Furthermore, we want to preserve the secrecy of our work
from prying eyes now that Wall Street friends have expressed
their interest in our patent rights. For all legal intents
and purposes, we believe that we have truly invented the airplane, especially the best aspect ratio, cambers, coefficients of lift and drag and the pilot's control of roll, yaw
and pitch.

We think Sam Langley's "Great Aerodrome" will fly only if
lady luck finally smiles on him. Even though he hasn't done
the research that we have, we hear that he hopes to keep his
progress secret by not mowing the grass around the Smithso-

nian shop where it is being assembled. Ludicrous!

Will's determination to keep going after Whitehead's public victory should have inspired John; but he was annoyed by the letter's tone of superiority, which judged Whitehead's flights as mere lucky flukes, almost unworthy of scientific attention. John disliked the letter so much that he decided to support Charlie Manly and Sam Langley. He wondered if they were as conscious of potential sabotage of their work as they ought to be. Mike Coyle had written earlier, warning that Zeke Harner had recently moved to Washington to insure that the Smithsonian project either failed or proceeded at a snail's pace.

Within another week, John sent his drawings for a one-cylinder motor to Glenn Curtiss. Over the next four months, John and Roger Macon worked on that engine and a two-cylinder version in comparative calm while warm weather and the promise of summer vacation tantalized the children.

For the first time in years, John had time on his hands. It was a time for healing. He derived hesitant satisfaction from his progress with a small, powerful four-cylinder engine for *Old Glory*. Letters from Glenn Curtiss nurtured his confidence by reporting that John's one-cylinder engine on Glenn's motorcycle was selling like hotcakes. Julie Simmons also fostered his fragile sense of self-worth by agreeing to a routine of visits that enveloped their passion in a cloud of normalcy—if not legitimacy.

Only two things haunted him. He regretted that he could think of nothing to heal his marriage; Maggie seemed more unapproachable than ever. What bothered him the most was a sense that Davey was drifting away from him. As the boy grew older, he seemed to be drawing into himself, unable to share his problems and his ideas with his father. John recalled that his own lifelong sense of isolation had started with a similar estrangement from his father.

Through his first two years of school, David Harrison had perceived his formal education as an extension of his life on the ranch. While his parents had competed for his trust, he had shifted it to Julie Simmons and Mei-yin. It had never occurred to him that Julie Simmons might have ulterior motives for drowning him in affection, compliments and responsibilities that affirmed his privileged status as teacher's pet and class leader. Indeed, Julie's affection and art instruction offered Davey more security and reassurance than he could find at home, where he was forced to compartmentalize his loyalties and affections. Whether in class or at her seaside cottage, Julie encouraged the kind of freedom of expression that he had enjoyed for several years before he started school. As he continued to study charcoal sketching with her into the summer, he came to feel a strong desire to please her.

Mei-yin's primary loyalty lay with Maggie, whose interest in political action and public speaking had inspired what would be Mei-yin's lifelong passion for the drama of speeches from a soapbox. She often felt annoyed to see Davey race to a cuddle with Julie, who would close her eyes blissfully as she pressed Davey's head against her soft breasts. If anyone had accused Mei-yin of jealousy, she would have giggled at the absurdity of such an idea, for she felt firmly secure in her alliance with her "brother."

Thanks to his confidence in Mei-yin's discretion, Davey had told her everything about his eidetic memory, his precognition, his flights with the birds, his perception of a life force which escaped like smoke whenever a living plant or animal died, his conversations with a pair of mythic children and, most secret of all, his nightly dialogue with his Voice when he had his roundup. But their alliance found its most satisfying expression in their ability to communicate telepathically. What Mei-yin found especially delicious was the secrecy of their psychic bond. They agreed that John Harrison must be excluded from the privileged circle of initiates; Juan might be semi-excluded; and Maggie might be included only to the extent of occasional stories about their transmission and receipt of messages.

Davey spent most of the summer of 1902 with Mei-yin, roaming the ranch, swimming in quiet pools down hidden valleys, giving and taking dares to test their courage, singing favorite folk songs from China, Mexico, Ireland and Scotland, watching the stars through his telescope on a warm summer night, playing the new game of ping pong and behaving like inseparable twins who shared such a unity of perception and opinion that their exclusive use of Chinese seemed perfectly normal as only another way to exclude all criticism from their intimate world. Wiry and tough, Davey often used his strength to make the way easier for Mei-yin, who came to think of her brother as her protector and personal knight. Although she empowered Davey to experiment with his psychic gifts, the more he shared with her, the less inclined he was to reveal them to others.

As the bond between Davey and Mei-yin deepened, Juan Cisneros felt deliberately excluded. Worse, if they didn't do it deliberately, then they were doing it thoughtlessly, which meant he was beneath their attention or respect. On too many mornings of the summer, he would arrive at the kitchen door of the house only to discover that they had already left on an adventure. It didn't matter that they had promised nothing, planned nothing. It was outrageous that they hadn't even thought of him. His friendship must mean nothing to them. His resentment began to tilt Juan's mind toward hatred. Somehow, he must make them pay for their indifference. It made matters worse that he loved not only Julie Simmons but also Mei-yin, whose pixie beauty was a growing torment to nine-year old Juan. Unable to join them psychically, he began to follow his older brother, Jaime, who boasted of his sexual prowess at Mama Rosa's and his exalted horsemanship at the races.

And then one day in August, Davey heard Juan play the guitar, Jaime's one gift to Juan that would bring him friendship and recognition and moments of peace. "Would you like to learn, *hijo*?" Juan asked in Spanish. He wasn't all that good yet; but he saw the spark of interest in Davey's eyes and hoped for a revival of friendship.

"Of course. Poppa never has time to teach me. Isn't it hard?"

"Not at all. Here, let me show you a few chords."

And so music rekindled their friendship as they spent time in the barn's cool hayloft, a haven from the heat of the day and an ideal place of learning. For a while, as Juan taught Davey the lyrics of popular Mexican songs and correct fingering for standard chords, Juan forgot his fears and resentments. Their nasal wail drove the birds from the rafters and never quite achieved more than a caricature of accomplished guitarists on the ranch. But they rediscovered each other while the rest of the family, including Mei-yin listened indulgently to Davey plink, plunk and hum his own version of "Jalisco." His passion for the instrument soon rubbed his fingers raw. Mei-yin gently spread salve on the wounds and taped them so that the practice could continue. Stubbornly, Davey reached for a level of expertise that would match Juan, a goal that was not too hard since Juan brought nothing like Davey's dedication to the art. By the time school began in September, Davey had a feel for the instrument.

Then, Juan's resentment revived in December because Julie selected Davey to accompany the class in Christmas carols. It was always Davey who received the recognition, the acclaim and especially Julie's compliments.

Neither Juan nor Davey could know that Julie's vaunted independence had also fallen victim to something more powerful than lust. Julie could scarcely credit her own heart. She had fallen in love with John Harrison. As her attitude toward John shifted from lust to love, she began to imagine herself as the mistress of the great ranch house. She found increasing fault with Maggie's appearance, her treatment of the children, her candid stories about John's stony insensitivity, his rough ways, his immaturity. Julie could pretend great empathy for Maggie's plight with her unhappy marriage. But each story of alienation between John and Maggie only encouraged Julie to hope for a final separation between them. In her fantasy, Maggie would go to San Francisco, pursue her career in music and disappear forever from their lives. Julie would marry John, teach school, rear these two beautiful children and finally find the tranquillity that life had denied her so far. By New Year's, she thought of Davey as her own son and, almost as a ritual price for her most energetic love-making, urged John to do something about his unhappy marriage. Her impatience and jealousy of Maggie began to consume her.

CHAPTER FIFTY-ONE

CARMEL VALLEY
JANUARY–JUNE, 1903

"Well, Ned, it looks like my investment in Glenn Curtiss will pay off." John thoughtfully exhaled a cloud of smoke from his cigar and considered the unseasonable March rainstorm outside the barn.

"That's good news, John." Ned had been hoping that something would pay off for John. After a year of many disappointments, Ned wondered how much longer his friend could tolerate his relentless run of thwarted goals. Even Tom Baldwin's *Old Glory* had been caught in a fierce storm east of the Rockies in September and had barely gone a hundred miles before landing near Denver. That had ended all plans for profitable ballooning for the winter. "What has Curtiss done now?"

"After I sent him a design for a single-cylinder engine last summer, he built it and installed it on his 'Hercules' motorcycle last August. On Labor Day, he entered a big race in Brooklyn."

"So he won?" Ned smiled his congratulations. "That should boost his business."

"No; he didn't win. But the Hercules impressed so many people, includin' the *New York Herald*, that a lot of folks placed orders. When he started lookin' for investors, I sent him a thousand dollars. That helped him get into the automobile b'iness. He represents several companies now. He went to the big automobile show in New York two months ago. I think he's on his way."

"How about the two-cylinder engine? Are you going to have one for him?"

"That's the best news. I sent my final drawin's before last Christmas. He's right pleased; figures it will get five horsepower. Says he's gonna put it on all his new motorcycles, includin' the model he plans to race in the

New York Motorcycle Club race at Riverdale in May."

Ned nodded equally and looked out the window. "Now that's a beautiful rainbow, John, sittin' on top of Los Laureles." The rain clouds were moving swiftly eastward, giving way to the bright rays of a westering sun .

"Maybe it's symbolic of a change in my luck." John drew on his cigar and blew a perfect smoke ring. "Do you think we have a destiny in life, Ned?"

Ned thought it was a strange question for John. Could some of Maggie's philosophy be rubbing off? "Yes, I do. That doesn't mean I reject the idea of free will; I think we can avoid our destiny as long as we can stand the pain."

"So we'll find contentment only after we align life with a God-given plan?"

"Something like that. I believe in a divine plan; and I think each of us has a specific role to play." Ned stubbed out his cigar. He thought the view from John's barn was one of the most thrilling dramas that nature could offer. "Why do you ask?"

"I don't know. I guess I've wondered why all my projects have fallen short of something glorious. I suppose I could have tried to force the world to give me credit for first flight. I remember that you even urged me to pursue all my interests: the engine; the aeroplane and even Tom Baldwin's airship. But it's only since I've been workin' on small engines for Curtiss and Baldwin that... ever'thin' feels 'on track' again. Does that make sense?"

"If it makes sense to you, it makes sense to me, John. Are you saying that you enjoy working with metal and engine production?"

"Darn tootin'! Of all the times of day when I feel... at home, I feel most secure and confident when I can smell that acrid aroma in my metal shop, those lathes buzzin' their music, the men wearin' their goggles, those close tolerances fittin' two pieces of clean steel together...."

John's enthusiasm for engine production astonished Ned, who reminded himself that everything in the world must be a song, if the right person knew how to sing it. "Sounds like you're where you belong. How's Whitehead doing?"

John chuckled. "Last summer, Gus flew Number Twenty-three until he had ironed out some kinks. It was so heavy that even a forty-horsepower engine wouldn't lift it at first; but he finally got it off the ground last August. Stanley Beach, the editor of the *Scientific American*, believed in Gus so much that he financed him for a while."

"You did too, didn't you?"

"Yep; a good investment. He's finally received well-deserved recognition, too. Last December, the *Aeronautical World* reported on his flights and described his Number Twenty-four, which he finished about a month ago."

"Any change from his old monoplane?"

"Lots of changes. Number Twenty-four is a triplane with a set of small wings in a canard mode. A forty-horsepower engine drives two propellers, which are adjustable for turning. I'm real proud of ole Gus; he beat 'em all."

Ned thought that John's apparent escape from any sense of his own loss was healthy. At least he had helped Gus win and could take some satisfaction in his own focus: aircraft engines. "How about the Langley team? Have they finally built their engine?"

John shook his head sadly. "I swear, Ned; they've had all kinds of bad luck. You'd almost think *their* destiny doesn't include flight. Charlie Manly wrote in the autumn that the *engine* was ready last July. Vibration was still a problem but they had reduced it to the tolerable. In July, they damaged a cylinder; in August they damaged a propeller; even though the engine was workin' fine by mid-August, the propellers and propeller shafts were too weak on into November. Those props forced a delay of their plan to move the Great Aerodrome on down the Potomac River on a barge. I got a letter last month from Charlie sayin' that ever'thin' is finally ready. Sam Langley says Manly's forty-five-horsepower engine is the finest small engine in the world. But Charlie still isn't sure the carburetors will supply gas evenly."

"How about the structure of the Great Aerodrome? Do you trust it?"

"Not really. Compared to the way the Wright brothers have calculated ever' inch of their so-called Flyer, I'd say the Great Aerodrome is unworthy of Charlie's engine."

"Has Will Wright kept you abreast of their progress?

John nodded, then stubbed out his cigar, stood up and walked to the great north window to savor the beauty of the hills. "A little bit. They had to rebuild their shack and work on their glider for a couple of weeks before they could begin testin'. But once they started, they went like blazes: fifty glides in a single day; seventy-five one day in late September when it crashed from cross winds, dug a well with the wings, as he put it."

"That must have dented their spirits. Did they have to go home?"

"Not at all! Will said their glides proved they had mastered the science of aerodynamics He said they were in glorious high spirits right up to early October, when they had three glides of over five hundred feet. Then they ran into a strange thing, what we might call a spin, when they lost all control of the glider."

"What did they do?"

"Same thing that we did: made the rudder movable. They finished that job in the first week of October, when Chanute and a flock of visitors arrived to test their own gliders. They all left by the end of the month when it was plain that only Will and Orv knew what they were doin'."

"It's too bad they aren't working with Sam Langley," Ned mused. "What a powerful team that would make."

"Funny that you should mention that. Will said Langley invited them to come to Washington last month. By then they had become very involved in secrecy and patent applications. They decided to decline Sam's invitation."

"So what's their next step? Are they still game?"

"More than game! They've put everthin' they earned from their wind tunnel into their final Flyer. It'll have five hundred square feet of lifting surface, a forty-foot wingspan, and a weight of three hundred pounds. They'll use our old camber of 1:20."

"How about their engine?" Ned hoped it wasn't a sensitive subject for John.

"That's the ace up their sleeve, Ned. Based on their calculated estimate of a required velocity of twenty-three miles per hour, they need only an eight horsepower engine to lift the whole rig! What do you think of them apples?"

"I don't believe it! You're telling me that Langley has spent a small fortune to design a fifty-horsepower engine—a masterpiece—while the Wrights have concluded that eight horses will be enough?"

"Isn't that a joke? They tried to find a manufacturer last December. When no one could meet their specs, they asked their own machinist, Taylor, to make one for them. Now get this; he finished it in *two* months!"

Ned was speechless. He knew that John and Balzer and Manly had spent more than three years wrestling with their rotary/radial design, which had cost one life, several reputations and long delays in the race for first flight. Rather than seek the best engine in the world, the Wrights had focused on a goal of integral unity of glider, pilot and engine in a smooth process that could only be reckoned as masterful. "Amazing! Will that engine work?"

"Absolutely. Moreover, they're designin' the most efficient propeller and a chain-drive transmission system right now, usin' their wind tunnel data."

"Bully, as our esteemed President would say. You have to admire them, John. Even if you and Whitehead won first flight by trail and error, the brothers really know what they're doing, don't they?"

"They sure do." John frowned and gazed again out the north window. "I owe them an apology, Ned."

"Why?"

"I blamed them for a lot of Langley's problems. I thought they were in cahoots with the Wall Street crowd and Monk Eastman. But I realize now they're just fine scientists. And I'm gonna write and say so."

"Do you think Langley might still beat them?"

"Possible. The Wrights haven't quite finished their Flyer. Manly says the Great Aerodrome is ready. I wish Jim Smellie were here."

"Who is Jim Smellie?"

"A friend of Glenn Curtiss. Jim will bet on anythin' from the time of sunrise to time to smoke a cigarette. I wonder what odds he'd give the Wrights?"

"Whatever the odds, it sounds like at least one of 'em will fly this year."

CHAPTER FIFTY-TWO

CARMEL VALLEY
SUMMER, 1903

Since Tom Baldwin had first come to supper after Christmas, 1901, Maggie had enjoyed a succession of evenings with him before he had gone to Los Angeles to fly *Old Glory* and try to raise money. She had felt disappointment when he announced his plan to stay south for perhaps a year since people there seemed willing to support their interest in ballooning with their wallets. That she should feel so comfortable with Tom and even some affection for him surprised her and raised a question in her mind. Did she prefer older men in their late forties like Tom? Her best male friend was Ned Ambler, only two or three years younger than Tom. Who did she most enjoy working with, the younger ranch hands or feisty members of the school board? Obviously, she thoroughly enjoyed the older politicians.

Even John had once remarked that something subtle happened to her when an older man entered her sphere of influence. She softened and bloomed and reached out as if to invite his attention and approval. Never before had she given much thought to this facet of her personality. But her pleasure around politicians and Ned and Tom inspired her to scrutinize herself more carefully.

In the spring of 1902, when she brought her question to Julie Simmons, she had been surprised at Julie's enthusiastic agreement with the idea that older men were much more interesting and more appreciative than younger bucks, full of self-importance and immature self-testing. Julie regaled Maggie with stories of her liaisons with wealthy men in Philadelphia, the gifts that they had lavished on her and the power that they had given to her without the whining confrontations she had come to expect from her younger swains.

As to why she felt such an attraction to older men, Maggie didn't dare explore the subject with Ned Ambler. She preferred to leave their relationship where it seemed to have settled—mutual respect without flirtation. However, by the summer of 1902, her reading of William James had persuaded her that Lily was right. Maggie wanted something from older men that her father had denied her: attention. So now she must be looking for someone wise and gentle and tolerant who adored her without conditions.

In the summer of 1902, she had worked almost every day with the politicians to select their candidates for the forthcoming Congressional elections. It thrilled her to receive their unstinting approval of her public speeches, her flair for jokes and snappy answers to questions from her audience and, above all, the beauty of face and form that she brought to local bandstands. It also amused her to manipulate them. The fact that women didn't have the vote made her appearances all the more significant. From her viewpoint, they gave her a chance to protest a law that effectively banished women from political action. Local politicians had discovered that the promise of her presence at a fund-raising or a speech would attract a substantial audience, especially middle-aged men who would endure the heat and the lemonade and the boredom of candidate speeches if only to see a wind curl Maggie's skirt around her long legs and listen to her silver voice raised in satirical jibes at her opponents. By the time of the election in November, her name had become so well-known among both the pros and the electorate that many people, men and women, urged her to run for office.

The more politicians she met, the more she understood that campaigning fascinated them much more than victory; personalities persuaded them more than debate over the issues. When she realized that politicians liked vote-gathering and king-making more than ideals, she lost hope for their redemption of the laboring classes, for whose benefit she had first been attracted to the game. Thus her experience with the hurly-burly disorderly process of campaigning reinforced her belief in the essential hypocrisy of professional players, among whom she considered Teddy Roosevelt neither better nor worse than any run-of-the-mill pol. That John had met and served under Roosevelt, that Ned Ambler had gone to Harvard with him, that she had worked for his election with Mc-

Kinley in 1900, and that he had been President since McKinley's assassination in 1901, had not altered her disdain for his opportunism.

And then something extraordinary happened. In February, 1902, Roosevelt ordered his Attorney General to proceed against J.P. Morgan's Northern Securities Company for violating the Sherman Antitrust Act. For the next eighteen months, Maggie—and the rest of the country—followed the confrontation between "the interests" and the White House with a renewal of hope that maybe the common citizen had finally found a spokesman for *their* rights against big business.

It would take years before the Supreme Court would find against the Northern Securities Company, which would be dissolved. In the meanwhile, Maggie chortled with delight at what the press derided as Wall Street's outrage "that a President of the United States would sink so low as to try to enforce the law." By October, 1902, Roosevelt had settled the great coal strike on terms that were favorable to 140,000 mine workers. For Maggie, Roosevelt's quiet determination to "speak softly and carry a big stick" on behalf of the general public was a convergence of two elements of her nature: her affinity for influential older men and her zeal to save the underdog.

Suddenly, the possibility that the political process might save America diverted her attention from rage against John and her own loneliness at the ranch. Through the spring of 1903, she zealously collected and devoured books and magazine articles by reformers, "muckrakers" as Roosevelt called them: Lincoln Steffens' article in the October, 1902, *McClure's* against Boss Tweed in St. Louis; Ida Tarbell's exposure of Standard Oil in the November issue of the same magazine; Lawson's biting dissection of Amalgamated Copper; Hendrick's ruthless investigation of the insurance industry; Russell's diatribe against the beef trust.... She wrote letters of praise to Governor Bob La Follette in Wisconsin in support of his radical efforts to return political control to the electorate. His proposals excited her: the "initiative" to let the people craft their own legislation; the "referendum" to let them throw out bad laws; the "recall" to fire corrupt officials; "direct primaries" to give the choice of candidates back to the common man. As she had with her music, then her philosophy and Davey's paranormal abilities, so she now poured her energies into politics and the reform movement.

One evening in early June, 1903, when John announced that the President would be coming to Monterey for a visit, Maggie's enthusiasm startled the family. "Oh, John, do you think he would come to supper? Would you just try?"

They could not know that the President's visit would be a first tentative step toward the healing of their marriage. John hoped that Maggie's verve and knowledge and sparkling wit might entrance Roosevelt. Then maybe his old boss would leave Monterey with greater respect for Lieutenant Harrison, who had a humdinger of a wife. Their tour of Seventeen-Mile Drive laid the foundation for such an opinion when Roosevelt learned that Maggie was one of his most dedicated supporters.

"Did you read the January issue of *McClure's* magazine?" Maggie asked.

"I may have missed it." Roosevelt was delighted to meet an attractive, intelligent woman who loved politics. "Anything interesting?"

"The war between labor and capital in this country has reached unbearable limits! Ray Stannard Baker's article is called "The Right to Work." Lincoln Steffens has another article called "The Shame of Minneapolis." And in the same issue Ida Tarbell has her third installment of her report on the Standard Oil Company."

"Do you believe what they've written?" The eyes of Roosevelt, the naturalist, drank in the haunting beauty of the Monterey Peninsula while his mind soaked up Maggie's ideas.

"Absolutely! The coal strike in the Pennsylvania anthracite mines was just the tip of the iceberg. John Mitchell and his United Mine Workers' demands were very simple: recognition of the union and an eight-hour day. The way you used the big stick of government to help those people was admirable."

"Is that what the articles are about?"

"No, the articles in *McClure's* go way beyond a single strike. They document an attitude in this country, especially among the most powerful businessmen, the trusts, the municipal bosses and everyone that depends upon them."

"You mean their greed and disdain for the law?" Roosevelt pounded the side of the carriage with a fist as if to vent his frustration.

"Yessir. I fear lawless unions as much as lawless corporations. Don't you think we're really facing a state of armed conflict?"

Roosevelt stared at Maggie for a moment, his mind's eye reaching forward into the future. "The trouble is that it's spreading. People like Big Bill Haywood of the Western Federation of Miners and that damned academic, Dan DeLeon, who founded the Socialist Labor Party, and Gene Debs and Mother Jones and Father Tom Hagerty, who organized the Mexican railroad workers, have gathered in Chicago to launch a Marxist-Socialist labor party."

He's afraid of the Wobblies, Maggie reflected. "You're right. The issue is reaching into every household in America. Not a single day passes in my house that I don't read about another case of exploitation of workers or immigrants or farmers."

"The fact is, I'm on their side," Roosevelt replied. "But I feel helpless in so many ways, confused in others. What am I to think of a fine lawyer like Clarence Darrow, who represented the Mine Workers?"

"What's wrong with that, Mr. President?" John asked.

"In principle, nothing." Roosevelt frowned at the complexity of the issue. "Trouble is that he had the support of idealists, Fabians, radical Socialists, trade unionists and an army of capitalism's enemies."

"Don't you think they won a good decision in March?"

"Yes, I do; but not because the miners won concessions from management. That decision established the principle that the federal government has a stake in all large strikes. It means that I can stick my nose in where it wasn't accepted before. That's why I created a Department of Commerce and Labor with wide powers to investigate these malefactors of capitalism."

"What else can you do?"

"I'm going to encourage muckrakers to tar every trust with its wrong doings." Roosevelt was thoroughly enjoying the afternoon of fresh air, scented pines and eucalyptus and talk about his most annoying problems. "It's time the people were awakened."

Maggie was so impressed with the President and his heartfelt support for the little fellow that she resolved to fight for his re-election in 1904. Their ride around the Peninsula confirmed her status as a devout Progressive Republican. She arranged for the President to give a brief speech to ranch hands later that afternoon. Then, at her supper that evening at a glittering table, Ned and Amy Ambler and Julie Simmons sustained a sparkling conversation that ranged from politics to aviation; from art to medicine.

The evening charmed the President with informal western hospitality in a setting that reminded him of by-gone days on his own ranch. He was especially grateful to meet the Ambler and Harrison children. "How old are you, son?" he asked Davey. "And how are you spending your summer?"

"He just turned eight on the first of this month," Maggie interrupted. She glanced gratefully at Julie Simmons. "For several years, Julie has been teaching him to sketch; would you like to see some of his work?"

This was familiar ground to the President. A compliment to a child often captured the whole household. But he had not expected what Davey laid before him after supper. Imaginative monoplanes, biplanes and triplanes soared into the sky. As Roosevelt leafed through the pages, he could trace the flowering of a talent in increasingly sophisticated perspective and detail. "I'd love to take one of these home, Davey. May I have one?"

Expecting to see pride in John's eyes, Maggie was startled to see him and Julie exchange a glance of approval—no, adoration. For an instant, Maggie lost track of the conversation while she tried to digest the implications of the expression on John's face. *Is something going on here? Impossible! She would never betray our friendship; or would she?*

To everyone's surprise, Davey turned to the back of the portfolio and said, "You're welcome to any that you like, sir; but I like these the best."

Roosevelt found himself staring at beautiful three-dimensional sketches of engines. He glanced at John and remarked, "Looks like the boy has your passion for machinery, John. Has anyone built one of these motors?"

"Yessir. In May, a man named Glenn Curtiss, the best motorcycle builder in the world, used my design and these sketches to build an engine. He mounted it on his motorcycle and won two major races last Memorial Day."

"Why, John, I remember that you mentioned that idea in the Rockies six years ago. Bully for you for making your dream come true! I've heard about Curtiss. They call him the fastest man in the world now." Roosevelt turned to Davey and said with bubbling enthusiasm, "You should be very proud of your father and yourself, Davey. What books do you like to read these days."

Davey thought for a moment. "I liked Mister Conrad's *Lord Jim* and Jack London's *The Call of the Wild*. I just started reading Rudyard Kipling's *Kim*."

"I caught him last week tryin' to read a Smithsonian treatise on flight," John said with a grin. "It was heavy goin' for him; but he worked his way through one of Sam Langley's technical papers."

"Did you know that I started Langley on that whole project when I was Assistant Secretary of the Navy?" Roosevelt looked wistful for a moment. "I have been deeply disappointed at their delay."

"So have they, sir." John launched into a detailed analysis of the problems which had confronted him as well as Charles Manly. "But you should watch them closely now; Manly's engine developed fifty-two brake horsepower in March. There's no question that it's the finest small engine in the world today. They should launch the Great Aerodrome in late summer, I think."

"John made substantial contributions to that engine, Mr. President," Maggie said to John's pleased surprise. In a rush of proprietary pride, she wanted John to hear praise from his old boss. "He also designed the engine that carried Gustave Whitehead to victory in the race for first flight two years ago." Even as she spoke, she wondered if Roosevelt had the same effect on all such social gatherings. As the evening progressed, a spirit of ebullient pride and optimism had filled the room as the President lavished his famous smile and endless outbursts of "Bully! Bully for you!" on everyone.

"What about these Wright brothers?" Roosevelt asked. "Do you think they'll beat Langley?"

How does the man keep track of such matters? John wondered. *My dream of a motorcycle; Langley's progress. His memory must be encyclopedic.* John's answer echoed the spirit of good will that lifted everyone's mind that evening. "It may be close. The Great Aerodrome is finished, sittin' on its houseboat down the Potomac River. They're testin' the engine, makin' minor changes; the problem may be that they have too much engine for their needs."

"And the Wrights?" Roosevelt persisted. "What do you know about them?"

"He knows just about everything they know." Maggie said with a glowing smile in John's direction. "Tell him, Johnnie."

"I've corresponded with them from the beginning, sir. In my opinion, they are the most scientific students of flight in the world. Their research has been meticulous... exhaustive. They've just built their own engine and propellers and designed their fourth glider, called 'the Flyer,' which they're now buildin'." Through the President's persistent, probing questions and prompting from Ned and Maggie, he soon impressed Roosevelt with his knowledge of details: the meaning of camber and angle of attack and aspect ratio and coefficients of lift and drag; the way the wings were rigged with a slight droop at the tips to combat cross winds; the 1:20 camber of wing ribs with two strips of ash; a new layer of unsealed Pride-of-the-West muslin on the bottom of the wings as well as the top; improved struts with rounding of the leading edge to reduce drag; the arrangement of controls and the distribution of weight to reflect time-tested relationships between center of gravity and center of pressure. By the end of the evening, John was giddy, drowning in an unfamiliar sense of appreciation by his family, his friends and, perhaps most unexpected, the President of the United States. He couldn't explain Maggie's extraordinary generosity; but he felt such heart-warming gratitude that he hesitated to explore her state of mind or her reasons lest his own brief moment of self-esteem disappear. With praise from Roosevelt for his impressive knowledge of small engines still ringing in his ears, he wondered if he should accept Glenn Curtiss' persistent invitation to move to Hammondsport. A voice warned him that he still had unfinished business with Tom Baldwin.

CHAPTER FIFTY-THREE

CARMEL VALLEY
SEPTEMBER-DECEMBER, 1903

John Harrison enjoyed only a brief period of good will after Roosevelt departed for Washington. By mid-September, he awakened each morning with a clear mind for barely an instant. Then his problems would arrive from his subconscious, form up in close order and answer the roll call: Julie Simmons; Davey; Maggie; Tom Baldwin. Relationships; none of them new; all very familiar. In fact, he sometimes wondered if their very familiarity made them attractive. They were family, comfortable as old shoes. No need to search for new problems since they seemed to generate all the guilt and resentment and anger and indigestion he could handle day by day. Only their relative priority shifted, depending upon his latest sense of crisis. But their relentless demand for *some* attention helped validate his unique identity; no one else could muster a more varied or complex set of personal relationships, for which no final solutions seemed possible.

In early October, Julie Simmons finally unloaded her dreams and frustrations on him. Before Roosevelt's visit, she had been satisfied with guerrilla warfare: limited attacks and complaints across a wide spectrum of real and imagined faults. Her complaints had been tentative, delivered with a sigh of whimsy and transient regret ("How I wish we had met before you married Maggie." "I'll bet she isn't as innovative in bed as I am." "Wouldn't it be wonderful if we could be together all the time?" "I must see you more frequently, John; I miss you terribly." and then "Do you have any idea how much I hate being 'the other woman?'") John had never taken her seriously because he believed she was still the same fiercely independent woman who had first challenged, then had embraced him two years earlier. Also, she had never seemed to take *herself* very seriously.

After Roosevelt's visit, Julie acted as if she had suddenly discovered that she was a person of value, worthy of respect from anyone in society, including the President of the United States. Roosevelt's attention had uncovered a sense of dignity and self-worth that she had ignored, forgotten or banished during her wandering years. Now she wanted John to affirm privately and, God forbid, publicly, her new identity, which didn't fit her role as mistress. It might not have mattered if she had not fallen in love with him. But that overpowering new emotion now infected all her meetings with John. Indeed, her love for him—and herself—began to color her whole life.

Her behavior puzzled John like nothing else in his experience. He had never faced the demands of a jealous woman before. When the affair started, he had been grateful to find a playmate who offered so much for so little cost. She had given him brief escape from his other unsolvable problems at that time: Maggie, the engine and the aeroplane. Now, despite her ceaseless litany of complaints, her willing body was still the most pleasurable diversion he could find. But her possessiveness was raising questions that he had never before considered. He knew that mortality was, by definition, a guarantee of pain. But God's gift of choice must mean that he had the power to assign some meaningful order to his many sources of pain, perhaps even to balance one against the other. And so he began to measure and resent the increasing cost of pain that Julie was charging for her pleasure; he found himself comparing that with the relatively lower price that Maggie cost him.

It troubled John that Maggie seemed more distant than ever. Where there once had been anger, distrust or disrespect, and certainly confrontation over Davey's development, there was now cool indifference. John wondered if she had discovered his affair with Julie.

Certainly Maggie was so besotted with Roosevelt's election that she was rarely at home. Her days were full of meetings and speeches around Carmel and the Monterey Peninsula or lunches with politicians. Mei-yin was invariably at her side when the school year didn't interfere. From a period of self-exploration and almost excessive involvement with the ranch and family life, Maggie had shifted to energetic service to the community. Instead of fighting with John for power over his world, she had simply discovered a new world where victories and losses were much less personal and painful. Through the autumn of 1903, at supper table conversations she regaled the children with hilarious stories of political goals and stupid errors.

Even John loved her stories because they seemed to lift her spirits and immunize her against the pain of old grievances. He was pleased that politics had become Maggie's temporary anodyne. At least she didn't make demands on his time and energy the way Julie did. He wondered if he would ever find a comfortable balance between the two women. Then he realized that, in its essentials, his yearning for praise was the common thread among his relationships with Maggie, Julie and Tom Baldwin.

To keep Tom's respect, John merely had to design a light, powerful engine, something simpler than the Balzer radial. During the summer, John was grateful that Tom was diverted from motors while he built a new airship called the *Los Angeles,* and worked with Professor J.J. Montgomery in Santa Clara on propellers. However, in October, Tom resumed his plea for a better engine. After *Los Angeles* failed to fly with an air-cooled automobile engine, Tom demanded a proper engine from John—*immediately.*

"I can't give you a four-cylinder engine immediately," John said. Why don't you try Glenn Curtiss' *Hercules* motorcycle two-cylinder engine?"

"Did you design it?" Tom seemed to think that John's design was a guarantee of quality.

"Sure did. Just order one from Glenn."

Tom's agreement to use that engine temporarily removed the pressure on John to design a completely new engine. And so matters stood until months passed without word from Glenn. In exasperation, in early December, Tom finally announced that he intended to take a trip to Hammondsport in January or February. If there was a waiting list for fulfillment of orders, maybe a little personal pressure on Curtiss would reward him with the *Hercules.* John might have felt guilty about the delay; but two other events intervened to obliterate almost every feeling except John's old resentments. Langley's *Great Aerodrome* failed to fly and the Wright's *Flyer* flew.

The letter from Charles Manly told the sad story on December 16.

We tried and failed first on October 7. From the moment of launching, the aerodrome rattled and shook and barely escaped from the houseboat when it collapsed in the Potomac River in tangled wreckage. My pride took a wet dunking; but I was otherwise undamaged.

Was there some evidence of sabotage? I would swear that someone had been tinkering with the launching mechanism. After your warnings about Zeke Harner, we imposed very tight security around the aerodrome. But we obviously failed in that as in other things.

We recovered the engine from the river bed and found that it had suffered no damage. We rebuilt the aerodrome and tried our second great test on December 8. Another abysmal failure, deeply disappointing to Mr. Langley. Now we can only wait to see if the Wright brothers will do any better at Kitty Hawk. In the meanwhile, Mr. Langley must endure his public humiliation in the popular press.

On December 18, Roy Emerson ran the Associated Press' garbled account of the Wright flight of December 17. It was obviously "ghosted" by a stranger to aviation. It was not until the day after Christmas that Will Wright's letter provided credible details: how they had endured nearly six weeks of construction, testing and very stormy weather at Kitty Hawk before they felt confident to try a powered flight; how engine misfiring and excessive vibration had so badly twisted propeller shafts that replacements had to be ordered from Charlie Taylor in Dayton; how new ones had arrived on November 20 only to break again; how Orv had returned to Dayton to make new ones out of stronger steel; how he brought them back to Kitty Hawk on December 11; how their initial first try on December 14 resulted in a crash and further delays for repairs. Finally, how on the freezing morning of December 17, Orv flew for twelve seconds to cover 120 feet of powered flight. Will flew 175 feet; then Orv flew 200 feet. Finally Will flew 850 feet.

We owe some debt to Gustave Whitehead, whom we visited last summer, Will wrote. We are confident that we know more about the physics and theory of flight; but his natural genius deserves recognition. From crude raw materials he has fashioned solutions to problems that certainly delayed our progress. He flew seven miles; we only flew 850 feet! We salute him.

It warmed John's heart to hear such praise for Whitehead from as meticulous a scientist as Will Wright. By inference, he was also complimenting John because he knew of John's critical contribution to Whitehead's engine. But it rankled that even though Will credited Whitehead with first flight, there had been no national furor over the Whitehead victory, two years before the Wrights flew at Kitty Hawk. John wondered if the general public would give the Wrights any more credit than newspapers had given Gus Whitehead? In any case, he resolved to congratulate Will.

It was in that spirit of generosity and good will that John reflected on his most challenging relationship—Davey. Through Christmas Week, the house was aglow with decorations and the rich aroma of pine and hot buttered rum and festive meals for the pleasure of politicians and friends. John saw that Davey observed everyone and everything, but he seemed unusually quiet, to the point of reticence. Finally on the last day of the year, John asked him, "Son, you haven't seemed very happy for a Christmas boy. Is there anything on your mind that I might help?"

Davey hesitated. If he told Poppa what he *knew* was coming, he would have to explain *how* he knew. But John had mellowed in recent years. Davey's creative contributions to the engine and the aeroplane had somehow validated John's sense of the utility of his son's active imagination. In recent months instead of criticizing Davey for his visions, John had simply listened quietly. Tearfully, Davey replied, "We're gonna have to leave here, Poppa. I wish we didn't have to go."

"What are you talkin' about, Davey? Who said we would have to go somewhere?"

"I... I can't tell you more than what I've just said, Poppa. All I know is next Christmas will be our last one here."

John looked at his son quizzically. He was about to ask him to explain that prediction. But he suddenly felt as reluctant as Davey to pursue the subject. He was in such a fine mood of Christmas cheer and hope for the New Year that he didn't want any of Davey's visions to cloud the future.

PART VIII

DAVEY

"Courage is the price that life exacts for granting peace.
The soul that knows it not, knows not release
From little things;
Knows not the livid loneliness of fear,
Nor mountain heights where bitter joy can hear
The sound of wings."

AMELIA EARHART PUTNAM, COURAGE

CHAPTER FIFTY-FOUR

CARMEL VALLEY
JANUARY-JUNE, 1904

What event could drive the Harrison family from their home? Afflicted by that nameless apprehension, Davey began to search his past for reasons. Every night at his roundup, he asked his Voice, "Why must we leave here?" His Voice only answered, "Because you are ready for *new* lessons." That answer prompted a review of his life for *old* lessons.

Until he was three, since his parents never bothered him much, he had felt a sense of self-sufficiency while he focused his attention on his inner world. Momma, exploring philosophy, had been his defender, his apologist for his richly satisfying inner life.

But after Poppa went to war, she had forced him to pay more attention to the world if only to honor Poppa's interests. When Poppa had returned from the war, he had first discovered the notion of "safe" subjects. The lesson was that he must censor his speech if he wanted respect and rewards from both parents.

He remembered that, after he started school in September, 1900, Julie had taught him that his role in life must be to help others. From a childhood of introspection and detachment from others, everyone suddenly wanted him to shift his mind to other peoples' problems. The lesson seemed to be that he must make the world a better place for his family and friends. Although both parents had taught him ideals, their contradictory signals had also warned him that he could not always depend on either of them for consistent guidance. Momma wanted him to devote his life to a search for truth. Poppa believed that truth was science and wanted it used in some concrete way for something glorious. By his sixth birthday in 1901, he thought he had found a workable balance between the two views. As Poppa successfully applied some of Davey's ideas to both the engine and the glider, he seemed more tolerant of Davey's inner dialogue. For the next three years, Davey thought he had navigated brilliantly through conflicting parental and social pressures on his psyche. In brief, to mask the rich disorder of what he considered his real, private world, he adopted a social role that seemed very conventional: the *good* little boy who now believed in prevailing moral, ethical and religious values.

Through the spring of 1904, he assembled all necessary evidence from his life to redefine the social game as a drama, a stage set for pretense, role-playing. Under pressure to relate to other children, he conjured up formal patterns of defensive politeness that easily deflected scrutiny of his inner dialogue. He felt free only when he could pour himself into concrete skills like art, music and his work with hand and machine tools.

As summer and his ninth birthday approached, he might have sought solace for his lonely inner struggle from Mei-yin or Maggie. But the political campaign of 1904 had captured the interest and energies of both. Theirs was a life on the run. When she wasn't preparing a school assignment, Mei-yin could usually be found near Maggie and either a politician or a rostrum, behind which Maggie would be wheedling and cajoling the electorate. Julie Simmons? She remained his dedicated teacher; but something gnawed at her affections, something Davey could feel without understanding. She no longer seemed qualified to hear his most intimate doubts and fears.

His father might have been a fourth alternative for reassurance and support. But John's mood had turned sour after the popular press gave less attention to the Wright achievement than they had given to Gus Whitehead. *The New York Times* derided the Langley failure, observing that there was no hope for the development of a powered, heavier-than-air machine in the near future. The Associated Press was so unimpressed with Langley's efforts that it joined the stodgy *Times* in ignoring the Wright victory. John's fury at press indifference to the Wright brothers' December flight had scarcely waned in mid-January when a cryptic telegram—unsigned, but probably from Zeke Harner—arrived to rekindle his rage: "YOUR ENGINE DIDN'T HELP LANGLEY MUCH, DID IT?" For the next month, he railed against Zeke Harner and Wall Street and greedy businessmen who had surely sabotaged the Great Aerodrome.

John's tempestuous reaction to the whimsy of the popular press and the unsigned telegram had a curious impact on Davey, whose vivid imagination linked the idea of sabotage with the Wright brothers and their demonic agent, Zeke Harner. From that seed of childish suspicion he began to nurture a hatred for Wilbur and Orville Wright. He accused, judged and sentenced the Wrights without trial. In later years, he would discover that the words, "the Wright Brothers," could instantly evoke images of intrigue, fear and vengeance.

As if to divert energy from his own anger, John devoted himself with renewed vigor to an improved engine for Tom Baldwin, whose visit with Glenn Curtiss in January brought an explosion of correspondence from Glenn. He wrote that he had established a new motorcycle speed record at Ormond Beach, Florida, where he raced a ten-mile straightaway in less than nine minutes. Once again he urged John to come to Hammondsport to help build a new factory for motorcycle engines.

Tom wrote of his ambitious plans for the near future. Thanks to a small staff of volunteers in Oakland and to some investment capital in his new American Airship Company, Tom said he would build a factory in Oakland and start building a new airship immediately upon returning from Hammondsport. That letter galvanized John to action. After February, he took frequent weekend trips to Oakland to help prepare the great airship for its engine. His absence only reinforced Davey's sense of isolation, especially since Julie Simmons would often cancel her weekend class and disappear at the same time. It didn't occur to Davey that his father had taken Julie with him.

On rare occasions during that spring of 1904, a convergence of everyone's interests would transcend their separate boundaries. One afternoon in May, the family was gathered in the library before supper. John leafed through several of Davey's latest sketches of flying machines and engines, each one dated in Davey's tiny scrawl, thus permitting the reader to follow the progress of his visions. From dirigibles of different lengths, Davey had progressed to strange creations seen from every possible angle. He had a unique ability to see three-dimensional shapes in his mind as if he were looking at them in reality. He loved to twist and turn them mentally until he found what he called a "harmonious form," which he would then reduce with singular accuracy to a sheet of paper. His collection of sketches had grown almost daily, wings, tails and engines being shifted in every combination. He had tried monoplanes for several weeks, the engine shifting from rear to front to top to bottom. Then he added a lower wing for more lift after John talked to him about principles of aerodynamics.

John suddenly pointed to a sketch of an aircraft whose wings swept back like an eagle diving. "What's this, Davey?" he asked.

"Oh, that's what we would need if the plane had a rocket like the firecrackers we fire off on the Fourth of July. Someday, I'll bet all aeroplanes will look like that. If we had enough power, I'll bet we could ignore weight."

John simply shook his head in wonder. "I doubt that so much power could ever be mastered and clamped inside a streamlined pencil of a fuselage!"

"But Poppa," Davey replied, "they already used them in ancient Sumer!" He then showed John a picture of a Hittite glyph on which a rocket was clearly depicted against a background of stars.

"How could an ancient civilization know anything about rockets?" John shook his head. "That picture must be a figment of the imagination like your sketches."

"Now don't belittle his ideas, John," Maggie remonstrated. "You have no idea how much he has learned about ancient cultures since Ned Ambler first got us interested four years ago."

"I'm impressed." John looked at them both with new respect. You should listen to your mother, Davey; I hope you never lose your curiosity about mysteries and puzzles."

That comment surprised Maggie and gave her hope that John might be more open-minded than ten years of marriage had led her to believe. "Well, you fostered his fascination with engines and aircraft design. And I encouraged his interest in astronomy and ancient cultures. Now, almost every night before he goes to bed, he sits on the patio with Mei-yin and looks through his telescope at the stars over Los Laureles."

"Come on, Maggie, what does he know about the stars?"

"You surprise me, John. He knows a lot. He's familiar with major concepts of modern astronomy. He knows that the ecliptic is an imaginary plane which draws a line on the imaginary celestial sphere where the plane intersects the sphere. He understands the idea of the earth's precession and its impact on the shifting star patterns etched on the celestial sphere."

"Mei-yin and I have even memorized the names of lots of stars, Poppa," Davey interjected. "We feel... at home in the night sky."

John suddenly felt the familiar pain of guilt in the pit of his stomach. *Where have I been while he was learning these things? Is this what comes of "more important appointments" like Julie Simmons every other night? Like my correspondence with Will Wright and Charlie Manly? Like my studies of Smithsonian reports and Will's theories? While those things occupied my evenings, my boy has grown up, right under my nose!* He quickly consoled himself with the thought that astronomy and ancient cultures and music and art were of merely marginal value for entertainment; *his* work had taught Davey shopcraft and the ways of working men. But he reflected, *Maybe this summer, I should spend more time with Davey while Maggie plays her political games.*

That evening of lively conversation with both his parents was a rarity for Davey, who had grown accustomed to his father's absence and had come to think of supper as a time for discussion of art and music and other interests. Confronted by his parents' separate pursuit of their own lives, Davey had turned for support to Juan Cisneros, with whom he shared an active interest in the creative arts. Under Julie's affectionate tutelage, Juan had revealed precocious talents at poetry and plays. His skits at Del Monte Lodge were often subtle jibes at the prejudice of the adult world. But since Mexican children would often perform them in native costume, and since the adults never imagined that the author was only eleven years old, no one took the time to recognize the deep resentments energizing Juan.

Indeed, Juan's rage was fuelled by small slights and rejections that he had encountered as he progressed through school. His friendship with Davey might have mitigated his pain, but Juan had persuaded himself that he and Davey were competing for Julie Simmons' affections. He even referred to Julie as "our girl friend" on those rare occasions when he felt free to reveal his emotional state. As those fantasies accumulated, Juan nurtured an obsession, an overwhelming desire to humiliate Davey in Julie's eyes. In his creative mind, it only remained to find the right moment.

CHAPTER FIFTY-FIVE

OAKLAND, CALIFORNIA
SUMMER, 1904

Conversations through the rest of the summer helped foster a new sense of camaraderie between Davey and John. As the boy became increasingly familiar with engines, he learned how to measure fine tolerances with calipers, how to run a metal lathe, how to dissect a magneto and a carburetor, how to read blueprints and how to joke with adult mechanics, who seemed to look at life from a different perspective than vaqueros, especially Jaime Cisneros, Juan's brother and hero. The vaqueros respected a veneer of *machismo* with its roots in physical courage. The shop mechanics respected a man's skill with tools, especially his ability to create a piece of machinery that conformed precisely to a blueprint. The contrast between the two ways of looking at the world and measuring one's self was not lost on nine-year old Davey.

As Davey's familiarity with the shop increased, he discovered that he could talk to his father about everything. Like a dam that has held back the water for too long, he gushed with hundreds of questions. Surprised at such a display of interest, John was grateful that they could share a passion for the world of aviation. He confided to the boy that an urgency was building to complete the *California Arrow* because a grand prize was waiting in St. Louis, waiting for the winner of another race: the best airship in the world. The prize was a treasure of $100,000!

On April 30, President Roosevelt had opened the St. Louis World's Fair to celebrate the Louisiana Purchase. During the planning for the fair in the spring of 1902, interest in aeronautics had run high. The aeronautical planning committee had consisted of Sam Langley, a Brazilian named

Albert Santos-Dumont and Octave Chanute, who framed rules for competitions among balloons, airships and gliders. But the rules were so stringent that they both reflected the state of the art at that time and dissuaded all but the most daring to compete. Merely to enter, a competitor had to pay $250. Then he had to make three circuits of a ten-mile, L-shaped course at no less than 20 miles-per-hour. The grand prize would go to the fastest competitor. The competition would be held between June 1 and September 30, 1904.

By late summer of 1904, the Aeronautical Planning Committee knew they were in trouble. Chanute had gone to Europe to try to drum up some business in 1903. But all the most advanced thinkers of the age criticized the rules. The speed required was too great and the deck was stacked in favor of the only experienced European aeronaut with a chance to win: Santos-Dumont, who warned that no one—certainly no American—would be able to win the grand prize under prevailing rules.

"So two months ago," John told Davey in late July, "they changed the rules. We only have to travel twelve miles and hit fifteen miles per hour and we'll win fifty thousand dollars. If our average speed reaches eighteen miles per hour, they'll give us seventy-five thousand."

Davey couldn't imagine what fifty-thousand dollars would buy. But his father, Roger Macon and Tom Baldwin all seemed to be excited at the prospect. Davey shared their enthusiasm. "Can our engine make *California Arrow* beat Santos-Dumont Poppa?"

It pleased John the way Davey had adopted the shop and the engine and *California Arrow* with the frequent use of "we" and "our" in his questions.

"Only five airships have been entered in the contest, includin' ours. Late last month, someone nearly destroyed Santos-Dumont's airship in St. Louis. Some folks are accusin' him of doin' it himself, just to avoid the humiliation of losin'."

"What do you and Tom think?"

"We both think he's an honorable man, a great pioneer. But what we think doesn't matter. He went to New York after the incident; I saw in the papers yesterday that he told people in France he won't be comin' back."

For a moment John thought about the implications of Santos-Dumont's withdrawal from the race. "Tell you what, Davey, I'm goin' up to Oakland tomorrow to complete installation of our engine. Would you like to come with me and maybe see her first flight?"

The question excited the boy like nothing in recent memory. "Oh, Poppa, I'd love to go. Could we take Momma, Mei-yin and Juan, too?"

"Sure, we'll take the whole gang. They'll see somethin' glorious."

When Maggie took Davey, Mei-yin and Juan to see *California Arrow* on the afternoon of August 1, they were speechless at her size. Tom Baldwin listened to the children exclaim over the airship while it was being readied for transport from the factory to Idora Park. Maggie was almost as excited as the children. The pleasant trip from Monterey, an elegant supper with her old mentor, Leander Sherman, and an amusing performance of *The Gondoliers* had recaptured her sense of San Francisco. The prospect of seeing this great airship launched only added to her holiday mood.

John was understandably proud of their creation. "Two years ago," he said, "there was a long article in *The Scientific American* about the design of this airship." He pointed to each component as he spoke. "The bag has a capacity of eight thousand cubic feet. It should lift five hundred pounds. It's fifty-two feet long and seventeen feet wide at its widest diameter. Feel the Japanese silk... soft and smooth as velvet, isn't it? Note how we've used cotton netting draped around the bag to suspend the frame, which is made of laminated spruce."

Maggie felt apprehensive at the flimsy triangular frame that contained a narrow catwalk on which a pilot could move back and forth. John's engine, a two-cylinder, air-cooled, 7hp gasoline model built by Curtiss, was located about 12 feet from the bow. The propeller was mounted on the bow of the frame. "How will the pilot steer?"

"He controls pitch by shifting his weight and the center of gravity by walking back and forth along the frame; he controls yaw with the rudder. We don't think there's much chance of roll."

"It looks mighty flimsy, Tom," Maggie said. "Which do you think is more practical: the airship or the airplane?"

Tom and John stared at each other and broke into laughter. "Forgive us, Maggie," Tom said. "John and I have been arguing that question for several years. There is no final answer."

"I think the aeroplane will win out finally because it won't have to depend on weather like a dirigible does. But Tom thinks the airship is more practical in the short run. And so do the members of the Aeronautical Planning Committee at St. Louis. They didn't even include the aeroplane in the competition."

"Well, the subject has certainly captured public interest," Maggie said. "Ever since the alien airship craze of '97, people have been caught up in flying. You must be pleased with all the furor."

"I don't have to tell you about my love-hate relationship with the press." John recalled the airship over their house in April, 1897. "I sometimes wonder if Gus Whitehead ever flew when he said he did. He *told* me he did; and press clippings *said* he did; but I'm so skeptical about anythin' the press reports that I need to see it for myself. Even then, I sometimes don't believe my eyes."

"Speaking of the press, didn't Will Wright tell you recently that reporters have all but ignored them this past spring?" Tom asked.

"That's right. After the *New York Herald's* garbled front-page story about their flight in December, the Wrights had to correct all the misinformation in January."

Davey joined the group and heard John mention the Wright brothers. "Have they stolen something else, Poppa?"

"Stop that, Davey!" John warned. "They never stole anythin' from anyone. You gotta get that idea out of your head. They did *not* tell Zeke Harner to sabotage Sam Langley's Great Aerodrome."

Davey sulked, convinced that his father was being too generous. "So what's so great about their new Flyer?"

"It has a shallower camber and much greater structural strength. Otherwise, it's the same as their version last December. They've been testing her at a place called Huffman's Prairie. In May, a bunch of reporters watched some trial flights that were unimpressive. So even though they've been making flights well over a thousand feet under almost total pilot control, the local press has little confidence in the Wright *Flyer*."

"Most reporters don't know the difference between an aeroplane and an airship," Tom said. "All they care about is a story that sells newspapers."

The men spent the rest of the afternoon moving *Arrow* from the factory to Idora Park, where it was installed in a large shed near the baseball diamond. Maggie used the day to introduce the children to the delights of a seven-story department store: Emporium Capwell. Davey and Mei-yin agreed that cable cars to Golden Gate Park were the most fun. Next morning, August 2, Maggie complained when John noisily awakened everyone at four o'clock.

"Can't be helped, Maggie," he said. "The air is quietest in the early hours. We're gonna fly that beast in a few hours. If you want to see it, you better roll out of the hay."

She insisted on eggs, bacon and toast before they left their Oakland hotel for the park, where they found the Beachey brothers and others already tinkering with the dirigible. It promised to be a mild, clear day, still a little chilly when Tom stood in the frame at five-thirty and directed the ground crew to play out the anchor rope.

Although Tom Baldwin seemed imperturbable, the tension was high. Lincoln Beachey, obsessed with the idea of flight, scurried here and there to insure that no malfunctions might endanger either Tom or the *Arrow*. When Tom began his ascent, John kept up a running monologue. "He's reached about a hundred feet; hold her steady, boys. There's his signal! Let her go, boys. Now he's moved to the stern to point her up; she's doin' fine, no drift, no unsteadiness; engine sounds fine. By glory, now she must have reached five hundred feet! Here he comes for a landin'. Bully! Bully! He's done it!"

Tom was ecstatic and with good reason. At the age of 50, he was the first man in American history to complete a circular airship flight under power, both with and against the wind. Ever conscious of the value of public support, he immediately told a *San Francisco Examiner* reporter that he intended to take *Arrow* to St. Louis to compete. "This airship has exceeded my fondest hopes both for simplicity of construction and for easy handling."

The next day, *Arrow* repeated the performance, starting later in the morning because everyone stayed up half the night celebrating. Hung over and slightly let down, John was in no mood for trifling mistakes. Unfortunately, while others released anchor ropes at John's signal, Juan Cisneros held on too long and was almost lifted off the ground. Irritated and fearful for Juan's safety, John yelled, "Goddamit, Juan, why can't you tamales ever listen? Get your head out of your ass; let go of the damned rope!" It seemed a minor incident that shouldn't have marred the day. In fact, the dirigible sailed gracefully out of the park on a route parallel to Telegraph Avenue to a landing site near Bushrod Park where a small crowd cheered this second confirmation of Captain Tom's great achievement.

But Juan Cisneros fumed from the humiliation of the patrón's booming voice, a public denunciation that only ignited all the accumulated resentments in Juan's soul. Through the rest of the day and on the return trip to Monterey, he tortured himself with the memory of his disgrace. *He yelled at me! He called me a tamale! He thinks we're just… peons. Well, I'll get back at him… some day.*

CHAPTER FIFTY-SIX

CARMEL, CALIFORNIA
SEPTEMBER, 1904

Juan's opportunity came a week before school started. He and Davey had spent much of August on trail rides; so it didn't surprise Davey when Juan arrived after lunch one day and vowed to show him "something very interesting." Juan said their trip might require several hours. Ah Ying gave each boy an apple and a sandwich for a snack. Intrigued, Davey thought Juan was going to show him some discovery on the ranch. It was mid-afternoon when Davey realized their ride had brought them to Julie Simmons' cottage.

About a hundred yards from Julie's home, Juan dismounted and led his horse into the woods. He then selected a position from which he and Davey would be concealed while affording them a clear view of the approach to Julie's house. "We'll leave our horses here," Juan said. "We'll wait here for a little while and eat. Someone will be coming soon."

Davey felt some concern about skulking around Julie's cottage. If Juan had something to show Davey, why not let Julie show it to them?

After a half hour of munching on sandwiches and idle chatter, Juan suddenly pointed down the road to an approaching horseman. Davey soon recognized his father. Juan restrained Davey from emerging from their hiding place. "We must wait about thirty minutes. Then you will see something very exciting."

After a half-hour, Juan led Davey forward to a window that Davey knew to be Julie's bedroom. Juan warned Davey to be very quiet. In a moment, the boys positioned themselves so that they could look into the room. The scene was indeed exciting.

Completely nude, Julie was sitting on John, riding him vigorously, her full breasts swaying and bobbing with her exertions. Having never seen such a thing before, Davey thought at first they were fighting. But the two made love with exclamations of such pleasure and encouragement that he dismissed his first fear from his mind and slowly realized that they weren't wrestling; they weren't fighting; they were fucking.

Davey had listened to the men in the Monterey shop talk about fucking. Juan and Ramon had showed him a stallion servicing a mare. But he had never associated such an act with either one of his parents. In a rush of confusion, he suddenly felt shame, guilt and anger that Juan should have known in advance that this would happen and, worse, had lured him into Carmel to witness this scene.

He turned to Juan to protest and faced a leer of pure hatred on Juan's face. "So your proud father lies with the local *puta* and betrays your mother and his name. Is this the something glorious that he is always boasting about?"

"How many others know about this?" he whispered. A wave of nausea seized Davey, whose first reaction was to hurl himself at Juan for his insults. But something warned him to stay cool.

"So far, just you and me," Juan answered as they crawled away from the cottage.

"How did you know about this?" Did others know? Was this betrayal such public knowledge? Did his mother know?

"I come here sometime and... just watch our girl friend, the bitch. I saw them for the first time three months ago."

"But how did you know ahead of time?"

"'Cause she told me yesterday that I couldn't come for a poetry reading today. She said she expected a special friend. Now we know who the special friend is and what they do together. I think I'll tell every ranch hand. After everyone knows, maybe your father won't be so uppity. Maybe it's time for him to see what public humiliation can do to *his* pride."

It struck Davey that this little trip had been an act of pure vengeance for Juan. In the confusion of his own emotions and loyalties, he discerned his immediate goal as damage control. He must stop Juan from telling anyone until he could sort out his own thoughts and choose a reasonable course of action. "Juan, I'll give you anything you want if you'll say nothing about this for a while. I'll give you anything or do anything.... Just name it."

Blackmailing Davey or spreading the story of John's extra-marital athletics had never been Juan's intention. He knew that such an affair was not so uncommon among the vaqueros, who found their way to Mama Rosa's prostitutes in Monterey like clockwork on paydays. But Davey's offer was an unexpected opportunity to even old scores. As the boys rode back to the ranch, they negotiated the price of Juan's silence. In fact, it wasn't very expensive after Juan exacted a few trinkets from Davey's horde of small treasures.

But the price that Juan paid for his moment of triumph was far greater than its value. Its most immediate effect was to evict Juan from Davey's small circle of trust. Davey thought that never again would he be able to trust Juan Cisneros's protests of friendship.

More destructive was John's fall from grace in Davey's eyes, his reduction to mere man from his prior status of demi-god. Certainly such a fall might have come with the years. No son can avoid the experience of such a discovery—that his father is somewhat less than omniscient, a flawed mortal finally. But Davey was shattered by the discovery long before he could handle it.

If he had not loved his mother so deeply, it might have been easier. He might have seen his father's conquest of Julie Simmons as an achievement, worthy of his respect and small pride. He might even have boasted of his father's prowess with women. But his memory reinforced a sense of betrayal by both his father and Julie that haunted his dreams. Juan had known Davey too well and had sensed just how deeply Davey would be affected by his father's infidelity.

More devastating than the loss of Juan's friendship and the respect for his father was the return of Davey's terrible sense of isolation. More than ever before, he must be ever watchful lest some slip of his tongue reveal his guilty knowledge. From that moment at Julie's cottage, all of Davey's perceptions were forced into a contraction of mind around humans, especially his father and mother. Now he became a prisoner of a single scene, indelibly imprinted on his memory. With whom could he speak of this scene of his father and Julie, rutting and struggling like animals in heat? Some part of his mind warned him that he could turn to no one without damaging his family. Over the next few days, he couldn't bring himself to confront his father. He certainly couldn't discuss it with Maggie. Mei-yin? Probably not.

And so through the first day after the visit to Julie Simmons' cottage, he disappeared into the hills in search of consolation and perhaps some new perspective that might restore the sense of wholeness which he had recaptured briefly during this summer. And that was when he experienced the greatest shock. He couldn't find his way back to his unconscious! In answer to his yearning for the old, familiar sense of brotherhood with animals and birds; in response to his plea for his nightly dialogue with his Voice at Roundup; he heard... silence. His pathway to the glory of inner flight was suddenly blocked, perhaps destroyed. Even more than his father's betrayal and Juan's vengeance, that loss of his grounding was like being banished from God.

It was a trauma from which he fled to his only other consistently reliable source of security: music and art. Immediately after breakfast for the next six days, he disappeared into the barn with his guitar and sang sad songs to himself until lunch, when he showed his face briefly to Ah Ying. Through the afternoon, he sketched airplanes and airships against glorious cloudscapes and dreamed of liberation from earth's complexity.

Through that week, his apprehension of the fifth grade haunted him. How would he be able to listen to Julie as if he still respected her? Confide in her? Never again! From this life-changing event, it would be six years before Davey could come to terms with the memory of her nude body on top of his father. Until then, he would not be able to reassemble the millions of fragments into which his orderly world had been exploded. It would be much longer before he would bring himself to trust any woman.

CHAPTER FIFTY-SEVEN

CARMEL VALLEY
SEPTEMBER–DECEMBER, 1904

After the emotional upheaval of John's betrayal, Davey's entry into the fifth grade brought an aftershock from Julie Simmons. Perhaps the clash was inevitable. Contributing factors had been gestating for four years while Julie's deepening love for John Harrison endured frustration, impatience and envy. Anguished introspection had tormented her through the summer when she watched John entertain Maggie in San Francisco and Oakland. As if to compensate for her gnawing sense of powerlessness, she decided that she would force young Master Harrison to bend to her discipline and justice when the new school year started.

Whether to manipulate John's affections through his son, or to project her frustrations onto the boy, or simply to exploit his unique vulnerability, she decided to brand Davey's behavior in class as unacceptable. She couldn't complain about his class work; his grades were excellent. But she could "prove" that he was too self-assertive and independent. She could even rationalize her zeal with a spurious generosity. How might she help "poor John" with this wild little boy who could talk Chinese, understood engines, went into trances and communed with eagles? At first she consoled herself with the thought that he owed his desperate need for discipline to an absentee mother, besotted with politics. But the more she pondered the case, the more she was convinced that his headstrong behavior in her class was her own fault. She had simply been too lenient. People might even think she had given her authority away to a nine-year old. No matter how precocious he might be, how could John respect her if she were so indifferent to classroom discipline?

On the first day of class, Davey couldn't bring himself to look at Julie. He feared that a mere glance would reveal his knowledge of her secret. But he was bemused when Miss Julie interfered with his attempt to settle a simple dispute over class seating. Sensitive to her sudden break with precedent, Davey sat down when she said firmly, "Davey, be quiet; I will handle this."

Later, he knew something was wrong when she asked him to stay after class. Her tone of voice betrayed her impatience and controlled anger. He had no way of understanding that her emotions had been fuelled by a symphony of other frustrations. He was merely a convenient scapegoat.....

"Davey," she admonished, "I believe you take excessive liberties in my name. From now on, I will decide on most of the issues which you used to handle for me. Do you understand?"

"No," Davey replied.

Unexplainably, such an honest answer enraged Julie. "Don't be smart with me, young man," she almost shouted. "Just because you run wild on your ranch doesn't mean you can march in here and take charge. Now, for that back talk, you can sit here in silence for half an hour. You had better learn how to be more sensitive to discipline. And you had better stop trying to be 'Mister Popular' all the time. If any child asks for help from you, refer him to me. Do you understand me?"

Davey said nothing about this incident to his parents. He did discuss it with Mei-yin. Above all, he tried to put the incident in perspective during that night's Roundup; but his Voice remained as silent as it had been for the past week. Baffled and resentful, he felt compelled to avoid Julie Simmons. She made him feel as if he were guilty of some obscene act, some gross violation of well-accepted social norms. Her persistent coolness toward him was so confusing that he decided to focus his energies on good grades. Otherwise, he tried to avoid another confrontation.

His confusion was all the more dismaying because she insisted that he continue coming on weekends to her cottage for instruction in watercolors. Indeed, when they were alone, her veneer of authority fell away and she turned on the charm, playing the coquette one moment, the loving foster mother the next. In either role, she acted as if the mood of the classroom didn't exist. This alternation of peace and war reinforced Davey's new sense of distrust of her specifically, and women generally.

Davey found it curious that Juan Cisneros seemed to enjoy his trouble with Julie. He would have preferred a truce with Juan. Instead, Juan

ribbed him, called him teacher's pet and acted as if he deserved his fall
from grace. One Saturday evening, his skit at the ranch satirized Davey's
disagreement with Julie while carefully avoiding John's adultery. Davey
found himself blushing while everyone laughed—even his mother and father. It was humiliating; but he was most dismayed at the injustice of a
story of half-truths.

The next day after class, Juan went out of his way to bully Davey in
front of his classmates. Suddenly, Davey had had enough. He lowered his
head and butted Juan onto the ground. Furious, Juan started swinging.
Julie Simmons, overhearing childish shrieks from onlookers, rushed into
the school yard to break up the fight. She sent both boys home with a
warning note to parents.

When Maggie read the note, she was chagrined. But nothing she could
say would tease the story from Davey, who said, "We just had a disagreement."

It was John who finally wormed part of the story from Davey while
they were fiddling with an engine at the shop. John heard Davey's side of
the story—minus any reference to John's extra-marital adventures. John
felt mixed emotions—outrage at some unnamed injustice against his son,
yet pride in Davey's manful response to ridicule. "You may never get to the
bottom of this, Davey. Maybe you've been too rambunctious in class.
Maybe you did take some liberties. And maybe Juan shouldn't have teased
you about the situation. But maybe you've learned somethin', too."

"What's that, Poppa," Davey asked.

"Well, most of the time, fightin' doesn't solve anythin'. But sometimes it's the only way to stop someone from misbehavin'. Or maybe you'll
have to fight to catch their attention. Sometimes, that's all the other feller
wants: attention."

"Was I wrong to fight?"

"No, I think you did the right thing. But you should have done it away
from the schoolyard. If possible, always fight away from the public eye.
Then, if you're winnin', you can give the other feller a chance. If you're
losin', he may do the same for you. But when the crowd is screamin' for
blood, it won't be easy for either one of you to stop."

The fight did nothing to change Davey's status in Julie's eyes. To compensate for the difficult atmosphere in his classroom, he sought weekend solace at his father's shop in Monterey. After the tensions of school it was reassuring to work with the machine tools, talk with the craftsmen and express his growing practical skill with mechanical problems. Here at least, there was no double-talk, no confusion about his sense of responsibility. Nevertheless, Julie Simmons' little games with him and his father had the subtle effect of challenging his confidence about all of his relationships with adults, especially women. Once he tried to talk to Maggie about the problem, but she was too busy and, unaccountably, asked him to wait. It would be many years before Davey would give her a second chance....

Insensitive to his problems at school and with Juan, Maggie and Mei-yin could talk about nothing except the election. They swamped the house with political pamphlets, broadsides, magazines and newspapers, for which Maggie's respect had reached a new low. One night, she shrieked with laughter at an editorial comment in *The Evening Post* about William Randolph Hearst. "An agitator we can endure; an honest radical we can respect; a fanatic we can tolerate; but a low voluptuary trying to sting his jaded senses to a fresh thrill by turning from private to public corruption is a new horror in American politics."

As election day approached, they monopolized supper conversations with twisted analyses of the local political scene: who wanted power, who had it and how you could measure it. They would shift to paeans of praise for Teddy Roosevelt's dreams when it was clear that John and Davey seemed to lose interest in the local balance of power. "He wants abolition of child labor." Maggie said one evening in late October. "So do I. He wants the right for anyone to organize a union. So do I. He wants to control monopolies and legislate an eight-hour day. He wants the electorate to have the power of initiative, referendum and recall. I want all these things. He truly believes in the good sense of the common people."

In early November, after the returns were safely in, Maggie led the family in a celebration over Roosevelt's victory. She toasted, "To our good friend, Teddy, and his two million votes ahead of Parker. Now that he's the President in his own right, we'll see some reforms!"

Through the rest of the month to mid-December, demand for bicycles boomed so fervently that John had to lend a hand in the shop. He was grateful the locus of interest in flight seemed to have shifted east to St. Louis, where Tom Baldwin had taken *California Arrow* to the World's Fair in early September. By then, even press interest in the Wright brothers and Gus Whitehead seemed to have waned to a point of nonexistence. Then a week before Christmas, John received two letters that updated the world of aviation for him. He found Tom's letter most interesting.

Dear John,

You wouldn't believe the excitement at this fair. I haven't written before now because it seemed that I needed forty-eight hours of energy every day. And even with the pressure to prepare *Arrow* for the competition, it took us six weeks to get the dirigible ready for her first trial flight. I was embarrassed at first because *Arrow* seemed so primitive compared to Santos-Dumont's old "*Number 7.*" It was built like a fine Swiss watch; ours looked like it had been turned out with a butcher knife and a bucksaw. The first trial flight added humiliation to my embarrassment.

It happened on October 25. I stood on the frame, surrounded by a crowd. The engine ran fine; the bag was fully inflated with inferior St. Louis gas; but nothing happened. The whole rig simply shuddered. I was so mad that I took off my shoes and socks and even my shirt. The more I swore, the more people laughed. Frankly, I put on such a good show that I wondered if I should build an amusing malfunction into every flight. I wanted Horace Wild, who only weighs 110 pounds, to come to my rescue. But he had sprained an ankle and was on crutches.

Then a young fellow named Roy Knabenshue stepped out of the crowd and rescued me. My usual luck! He normally operated the fairground's captive balloon and took passengers for a ride for a dollar each. He stepped into the frame, bawled some instructions and, suddenly, *Arrow* was airborne. He

barely missed the high fence around the concourse, avoided
the Brazilian Building by feet and the Ferris wheel by
inches. He told me later that he had never learned how to do
something so fast; namely, pilot *Arrow*. When he was ready to
land, the engine died, converting *Arrow* into a free balloon.
Winds sailed her across the Mississippi to Cahokia, Illinois. I paid a carter ten dollars to haul the airship back to
the fair.

That single flight made our reputation. Roy was the hero
of the hour and everyone wanted to offer personal congratulations, especially assorted young women. I added Roy to my
crew and promised him a percentage of winnings. On his next
flight about a week later, he took the ship to 2000 feet and
covered over three miles in 28 minutes before returning *Arrow* to a spot less than a hundred feet from start point. He
repeatedly demonstrated his superb control. On November 1,
thousands cheered his exhibition. You would have been proud.

Then the engine began to protest. It died twice, forcing
us to try to walk the balloon back to the fairgrounds. But on
November 3, we lost it into the night. We finally recovered
it 16 miles west of St. Louis. It never flew again because,
even though we couldn't compete for the prize, the Aeronautical Committee refused to pay me anything for my previous
flights. That made me very angry because *Arrow* saved their
bacon. The other two dirigibles couldn't hold a candle to *Arrow*, which had won the good will of the crowd. The committee
even stole our ship for a day or two. It was an outrage when
you consider that, without *Arrow*, the crowd would have considered the whole aeronautical game a big bust, hardly as exciting as Barney Oldfield in the auto races or the Olympic
games or the appearance of Geronimo (a cutthroat if I've ever
seen one) or the introduction of something called an ice
cream cone. It's ice cream stuffed into a crisp cookie, hol-
low like a cornucopia! I walked around with it in my hand and
kept cool by licking it before it could melt.

I went to New York in mid-November to apply for patents on

our airship, especially its suspension system. While I was there, I had a chance to visit the offices of *The Scientific American*. I had thought a lot about arguments with you about the relative value of airships versus airplanes. I told them that I see the aeroplane as good only for sport; it has no real commercial value. I think the airship is the future of human flight.

You may note from the postmark on this letter that I'm now in Los Angeles. Roy Knabenshue and I intend to make a little money from demonstrations of *Arrow*. But sometime next year, I'll be back in the Bay area. We can talk then about your further interest in airships, airplanes and engines. I think you and Glenn Curtiss could have a near monopoly on fine small engines if you ever decided to join him.

John thought the tone of Will Wright's letter reinforced Tom Baldwin's pessimism about aeroplanes.

Dear John,

Please forgive the long silence. After all our creative work on our 1903 *Flyer*, we have felt a bit let down over the past several months. We didn't fly for as long as a full minute again until mid-September. Five days later, we finally made a circle of over 4000 feet under full control. So you could say that we have been perfecting our construction and control mechanics. However, these are mere refinements, not inventions. They're important to confirm most of the principles that we have discovered. But they don't give me the zest and lift and challenge of those days when we probed nature's mysteries for the secrets of flight.

Frankly, I'm not sure that we'll go much further with the aeroplane. We're thinking about forming a company to build them; but practical businessmen don't need to know the principles of flight to do that. I doubt if the aeroplane has a practical future of any commercial value….

Please drop me a line and tell me about your plans.

John wondered if the letters contained a special message for him. A faint trembling nudged at his spine as if to force him to pay attention. Thoughts played around the fringes of his consciousness, elusive but beckoning. He tried to focus on them, bring them to the light, but it was no use. He had important meetings, Christmas was coming, and there was no time for speculation about what the coming year might have in store for him.

CHAPTER FIFTY-EIGHT

CARMEL VALLEY
FEBRUARY, 1905

"I haven't seen Julie lately, John," Maggie said quietly one evening in February after the children were in bed. "Do you ever see her in Carmel?"

The question startled John because he had been torturing himself about next steps with Julie. He could not ignore her discrimination against Davey much longer; nor could he pretend that she still personified love and passion. Four years of the affair had about exhausted his illusions about her. Last night they had had a blistering argument about his delaying tactics. "You don't really love me! You're just using me! You'll never divorce Maggie." As usual, they had ended the argument in bed where they could dissolve their tensions in aggressive sex. All the way home he had wrestled with his options for extricating himself gracefully. Now he wondered guiltily if Maggie might have finally discovered his adultery. "No, I'm working pretty hard on a new engine design. Are you worried about her?"

"Why no, John. But when your clothes are so heavy with her perfume, like they were last night, I assume you've been *somewhere* in her vicinity."

John could feel the blush surging upwards. He knew he must face this crisis directly if he had any hope of keeping his self respect, not to mention Maggie's. He forced himself to look directly into Maggie's eyes. "So you know! What are we to do?"

Now that she had finally confirmed what she had only suspected two years earlier, Maggie resolved to maintain a veneer of cool detachment. "At least you don't try to lie about it anymore, Johnnie. And I'm pleased that you ask about us. I was afraid for a moment you might think decisions were your exclusive privilege."

John could feel his heart pounding like a sledge hammer as questions flooded his mind. How long had she known? How much did she know? What did he really want to do about this? He felt as if he were the accused and Maggie was the prosecuting attorney, the jury and the judge, all wrapped into one. He had to clear his throat before he could say, "So what do you want to do?"

"I'll tell you how I feel; then you can tell me how you feel; and then maybe we'll know what to do." It took all of Maggie's discipline to maintain a surface calm while her sense of betrayal and outrage roiled her stomach and every nerve in her body. She lifted a glass of cognac to her lips and welcomed its liquid fire. As her suspicions had grown, she had practiced this conversation over and over in her mind until she had worked out all her strengths and all John's weaknesses. She probably would not have chosen this particular evening to launch her attack, nevertheless it was time to clarify their future.

John waited, his shock scribing lines of tension across his face. "How long have you been aware of my... relationship with Julie?"

"I suspected it when Teddy Roosevelt came here for supper. I was shocked at the way the two of you behaved like love-sick children, fawning all over each other. I can only hope the President didn't catch on to your infatuation."

Since the summer of 1903! More than eighteen months! John quickly tried to recall all his lies and meetings with Julie since that fateful summer. It was hopeless. He could only work backward from last night. He felt fleeting gratitude that she had missed the first two years of the affair. "We were that obvious, huh? It must have made you very angry," he said regretfully.

I didn't know enough to be angry—just suspicious. I suppose I was too stupid—or fearful—to investigate. Or maybe my years in China prepared me for your behavior."

"What do you mean?"

"Sex—and betrayal—are taken for granted there. Like a storm or breathing."

"You mean you *expected* me to betray you?"

Maggie paused. She wasn't sure how to continue. She knew she was in dangerous territory. In the emotionally supercharged silence, the old Seth Thomas clock sounded like a noisy heartbeat, ticking away the seconds. "Trouble is, I forgot the *Yi-ch'ing.*"

"Chinese philosophy at a time like this!" John exploded. "My God, what does the *Yi Ch'ing* have to do with us?"

"I know you aren't impressed with Chinese philosophy and mysticism. But they are my roots, John, especially the *Yi Ch'ing,* the Book of Changes. It's much more important to me than the Bible.... It is especially relevant to us."

John waited for Maggie to clarify herself. The wait was killing him. He could feel his finger nails digging into his palms, his shirt drenched with nervous perspiration.

Maggie lifted her cognac again and sipped slowly. She could not, *would* not indulge herself with a screaming fit. She intended to torture John to the bitter end of the conversation. But she needed more information before she could choose among her options. General abstractions from the *Yi Ch'ing* were a fine way to frustrate what she knew must be his impatience for answers. "The central lesson of the *Yi Ch'ing* is that we had better not become too smug about the way our lives are going, when they're going well or when they're going badly. Because they'll change; nothing stays the same."

Miserable, John complained, "I don't think I can stand this cool analysis of our emotions, Maggie. Let's face it. I've betrayed you; I admit it. Now where do we go from here?"

Maggie studied John quietly, her eyes unblinking, her face immobile. "Why did you do this, Johnnie?"

"Who the hell knows! I can speculate about it; but nothing I say can excuse it."

At least he's remorseful about being caught—if not about his infidelity. Maggie's expression softened. "Maybe I'll understand. Tell me...."

He couldn't admit—even to himself, much less to Maggie—that lust was an insatiable mistress to whom he had pledged his soul after she had been awakened in the arms of a pair of French prostitutes in New York City.

Instead, he tried to mask his addiction with confession. "I didn't think. I just fell into it. Maybe I put the whole affair in a special box in my mind."

"Did you go to Julie because you felt so alienated from me?"

"Maybe." John remembered that first year after his return from the

East coast. He recalled how distant he had felt from Maggie and Davey, excluded from their intimacy, which they expressed in the Chinese language, in "the Game," in their love of myth and the stars and ancient cities. "I guess I was depressed about our differences about rearin' Davey. As I watched Davey grow up, I began to think my role was unimportant. Maybe I thought Julie would help me get even. Childish—stupid!"

Thanks to her exploration of philosophy, Maggie was much clearer than John about the awesome dimensions of their battle for Davey's allegiance. To Maggie, the goal had been peace of mind—understanding it and learning how to attain it. She knew that one's approach to such a goal must be informed by a vision, a sense of a reality unbounded by either space or time. Such a vision had been her goal for Davey. That had been the purpose of her study and her search for possible explanations for Davey's startling psychic gifts.

John's goal of "something glorious" Maggie had seen ever more clearly as egocentric and fatefully destined at least for disillusionment if not failure and tragedy. In her view, something glorious meant the bubble reputation, prostituting one's soul for recognition. She thought that search for tawdry notoriety had almost shattered their marriage.

To John, Maggie's goal for Davey had been and was still ephemeral if not unattainable. He had feared that the price for its achievement would be sacrifice of everything he believed in: hard work; the rewards of pride of name and status and solid standing in the community.

Maggie knew her decision must finally turn on these issues. If compromise wasn't possible between them, then the marriage might have to end. But first she must explore the process by which John had abandoned even his own values. "Surely your sense of alienation hasn't lasted five years?"

"Absolutely not!" John protested, perhaps too quickly. "By the time Davey first flew in August, Ought One, I had come to respect his insights and his imagination." He didn't dare remind her that the affair had started in protest against her refusal to allow Davey to continue testing the aeroplane. He felt instinctively that she might forgive him for an eighteen-month affair while a four-year liaison must be unforgivable.

"So what drove you into Julie's arms?"

"I thought I had failed in everthin' I touched." John knew his answer would excite Maggie's disdain. But he saw no hope for retrieving her trust if he tried to blame her in any way. Better to admit guilt for everything.

"Why did you see yourself as a failure? Weren't your bicycles popular?"

"Maybe," John answered ruefully. "But even before I went to Cuba, I had lost interest in the ranch and bicycles."

"So you thought Cuba was a new chance to do something glorious?"

"I reckon." John felt miserable not only because he could feel his marriage slipping away but especially because he hated the kind of introspection to which this confessional was subjecting him. "But I didn't do much in Cuba, except to stay alive. I almost didn't do that."

"You thought your battlefield commission was also a failure?"

"In your eyes it seemed to be nothing. Don't tell me you were impressed."

"You were wrong. I was astonished and mighty impressed. But then you refused to come home. Instead you abandoned your family for the lure of an engine in Washington and New York. It seemed to me that you no longer cared about your family at all. Were you still hunting for a cause while you were recovering from Yellow Jack on Long Island?"

"I was desperate, Maggie. The Langley Aerodrome sounded like a golden opportunity when I heard about it. If I built an engine for the first flight in history, I thought maybe I would finally recapture my own self-respect."

Maggie nodded, increasingly satisfied that her diagnosis of John's shallow goals had been the root of the trouble. "And after you came home, after you saw what Davey could do, why did you treat him like some kind of freak?"

"I didn't feel like I could talk to you about Davey. You were always a lot smarter than me; you and your philosophy and such. Frankly, I thought you should have married someone like Ned."

Maggie shook her head in dismay and sadness. Her sense of empowerment had rewarded her with fulfilling satisfaction as she managed the ranch and guided Davey's development and explored great ideas with Ned Ambler. Her hunger for authority had blinded her to John's sense of disempowerment. No wonder he had searched for compensations. "But you did design Whitehead's engine. You helped design Langley's engine. And your son actually flew first. Wasn't that glorious enough for you?"

"Not good enough." John reviewed his failures with ruthless self-criticism. "No one knows that my son flew first." *And your anger prevented him from flying again*, he almost said. But something warned him to bite his tongue.

"What about *California Arrow*? Without your engine, Tom Baldwin would not have been the first man in American history to fly a powered airship."

"Maybe it was *my* engine; but Glenn Curtiss built it. And Tom flew the airship." John refused to be consoled. Nor did he want to be diverted from the main point. "Of course, Julie proves that my biggest failure is our marriage."

"So you convinced yourself that you were a failure as a rancher, an engineer, a soldier, an inventor and a father. Did you decide to complete the picture with Julie to prove your final failure as a husband?"

"Or to compensate. Crazy, isn't it? Maybe I needed to get the self-loathing out of my system. So how do you feel? Do you want a divorce?"

"I've given this a lot of thought. I was furious at your obvious affection for Julie when Roosevelt came. I'm not made of stone. But soon after that initial shock, I felt a curious detachment. In fact, I was disturbed—and saddened—that I didn't care more. That told me something about my real feelings for you and our marriage. If I didn't care, why should I expect you to? I felt as if I had been play-acting, pretending. Like you, I hated myself for drifting away from my own convictions."

"I don't think I understand, Maggie."

Maggie drifted into a reverie, almost as if John were not there. "All my life, I've been attracted to power. I've wanted it so much that it frightened me. Maybe I felt that way because I saw so much injustice and stupidity in China when I was young and idealistic. I blamed men for that because men run China—mostly for their own benefit. So I married you to give me security against such stupidity, to insulate me. But even at our wedding, I couldn't control my resentment at some of your friends."

John remembered how his friends had felt sorry for him because he had married a woman with opinions. "Are you sayin' that Davey stimulated your old demon, your attraction to power?"

"Not at first. When I first came here, I was offended at the way the ranch was being managed and our primitive school system and everyone's smug acceptance of poverty in our society. When you went to war, it gave me a chance to experiment with all kinds of ideas. I was very proud of myself until you came home in '99. Then poor Davey became our battlefield."

"But we haven't fought over Davey for a long time...."

"That's true; but maybe we haven't fought because we haven't talked. You went your way and I went mine. Mei-yin fascinated me first; then, after Teddy Roosevelt's visit and my discovery of your affair with Julie, I found my true calling. My whole nature cries out to help people; and politics is my way. You became infatuated with Julie; I became obsessed with politics, which even diverted me from the one thing that gives my life meaning—Davey."

She is really a cool customer, John thought. He remembered that she had continued to arrange skits at the ranch with the children until the late summer of 1903. Now he understood why she had shifted them to the school at that time. She had continued visiting Julie frequently to talk about ideas, fashion, politics and art. And she had continued to extend love to him and Julie as if they were slightly flawed children, worthy of her compassion and her support until they came to their senses. Where had this woman gained such inner strength? "You mean you wanted to minimize damage to him if you could confirm my... infidelity?"

"Something like that. My initial reaction was childish, possessive. Now, I feel less betrayed than betraying. It is I who have failed you, I think."

"Is that attitude some more of your Chinese mysticism?" John could not hide his disbelief and suspicion. "If it is, I don't think it's very amusin'."

"I'm not trying to amuse you. That you should need to turn to Julie for your passion tells me that I may not be a fit companion for you any longer. Perhaps we're now supposed to separate. Or perhaps we're supposed to stay together while you lust after other women. But I don't think I could stand that."

John started to object to this statement. But Maggie raised her hand to quiet him and allow her to proceed. John had never been able to understand Maggie's use of words like "supposed to." He knew she believed in a divine plan. And she would sometimes mention her "guidance," as if she were actually trying to march to a distant drummer. No wonder Davey listened to an inner voice. More baffling, Davey seemed to have total confidence in his voice. Miserable, he asked, "Does that mean you want a divorce?"

Maggie regarded John over the rim of her glass. *Sorry, Johnnie; no quick answers. You must wait and wait.* "I don't know. Perhaps I still love you very deeply. But it's no longer romantic love, what my Presbyterian parents called 'Profane Love.' I don't regret your destruction of that as much as I thought I would. The whole experience has taught me that childish romance is built on self-indulgence. Your infidelity has burnt out my capacity or desire for it."

"So why are you still so angry... and cold?"

"Because you treated me like an idiot. Your blatant weekends in Oakland and your late nights with Julie revealed how blind you thought I was. I can do without romance, John. But I can't live with your disrespect."

But you want me to live with yours? John almost shouted. He bowed his head and stared at his boots. He felt as if he were falling into a deep pit of despair. He felt so guilty and lost that he couldn't think. "I'm deeply sorry, Maggie. Can I do anythin' to restore your confidence?"

"I don't know. I'm not sure I'll ever be able to trust you again to foster harmony for everyone under your care, especially Davey. You've made me realize how terribly selfish you can be." She paused, took another sip of cognac and stared at John as if she might be evaluating a dead fish.

John's face was a mask of self-disgust and confusion. "I'm a fool, a great stupid fool! Don't you have any deadlines or conditions?"

"Deadlines? You can't put a deadline on trust. I don't think it will return soon because I don't know who you are anymore. You aren't the man I married. I'm willing to wait for a while to see if I want to stay with whoever you may become. Conditions? The most important condition is your decision. Do you want to be with Julie or with me? You can't be with us both. I only ask that you stop trying to deceive me. It doesn't become you. Besides, you're really not very good at it."

"So I'm on a kind of probation. Where would you go if we break up?"

"I'm not sure. If we decide to end our marriage, I will not tolerate Davey in that woman's hands. I've been thinking of taking him out of her classroom. But with only three months of school left, I'll accept the situation only if you break off your affair. If you can't or won't, I'll use Lily's money and all the legal power in this state to be sure he stays with me. Anyway, I can't take more deceptions. I can't pretend anymore; my patience has run out."

CHAPTER FIFTY-NINE

CARMEL VALLEY
FEBRUARY, 1905

Early the next morning, John saddled a roan and rode east into the rugged wilderness of the Carmel Valley. He finally reached his goal, a quiet pool where he and Maggie had spent many joyous hours in that first idyllic summer after their wedding. Dismounting and dropping the reins, he sat down, leaned against a gnarled oak and waited for the beauty of the place to spread its balm across his troubled mind.

The choice seemed clear: Maggie or Julie. But before he could make a choice with conviction, he needed to sweep away several obstacles to clarity. First, he had to convince himself that a choice was really necessary. He had enjoyed the charm and grace and foibles of two women so long that he couldn't easily imagine his life without one of them. But Maggie's threat to gain sole custody of Davey banished that fantasy. So he must choose.

Were they both equally important to him? For an hour he reflected on their differences. Where Julie reveled in her high-spirited gusto with life's crises and surprises, Maggie's cool detachment offered the illusion of order to life. Julie's youth, bubbling with generosity and mindless of its transient vitality, invariably galvanized John to dreams of glory, astounding achievements. When he was with Julie, anything seemed worth a dare. For she was a child of vibrant nature, as lusty and irresistible as river rapids. In contrast, Maggie seemed to be a visitor from a world of abstraction.

They were as different as earth from sky, body from mind, emotion from reason. Which, he wondered, could he do without most easily? His heart told him that Julie was most like himself, met him with the same love of color and dash that ranch life had bred into his very soul. But his mind quietly argued that Julie's similarities accentuated his own flaws. Grudgingly, he began to feel resentful at Julie for echoing and approving of his prolonged childishness.

If Julie promised a life of playful irresponsibility, Maggie promised growth into something that he could barely imagine, something permanent.

But could he live under the cloud of her suspicion and distrust? For a moment, Julie's adulation revived his doubts as he thought of the battle that he must still fight to retrieve Maggie's respect. Then he remembered the pledge he had made to his parents on behalf of Davey. Was it possible that the court could award Maggie with sole custody? And did he dare risk losing his son for the sake of Julie's alluring charms? The more he thought about such a loss, plus the social ostracism that would certainly result, the more he drifted toward a conviction that he really had no choice. Now he understood what Ned Ambler had meant when he once said, "The more choices you make early, the fewer you'll have to make later." He had made a big choice when he chose Maggie in 1894. Davey's birth only a year later had reinforced that choice. Now they must be the foundation for any life of meaning and significance that still remained open to him.

He spent another half-hour reviewing the logic of his decision. As he went through that process, he felt a familiar rush of confidence, a lightness of self that had always validated an important decision with a sense of liberation from doubts and obstacles. That feeling was all he needed to steel himself for the confrontation with Julie Simmons. He considered further delay until the weekend in order to prepare himself for the ordeal. Furthermore, he hoped to devise a strategy to let Julie down lightly. But the more he thought about that, the more a postponement seemed unkind, if not dangerous—unkind to Julie and dangerous to himself and his future with Maggie. He waited until school was over, then walked into Julie's classroom after all students had left.

Tired from her long day, Julie's heart lifted at the sight of John. She was always stirred by something in him: his rugged good looks, his gait, his carriage, memories of their love-making. "Hello, stranger," she said breezily. "To what do I owe this unexpected pleasure?"

"You owe it to bad news, I'm afraid, Julie." At the sight of her, John could feel his resolution wilting. Even after a day with rowdy kids, she was still the sexiest thing he had ever seen.

"Bad news? Do you have time to sit down and talk about it?" Julie swept her papers into a drawer. "Would you like some tea?"

John hesitated. Should he start this cordially only to watch it dissolve into recriminations? "I'm afraid this news won't wait."

"Well, for heaven's sake, John; at least take a seat."

John felt suddenly that even that concession to friendship would undermine his determination; he must stand, his arms folded across his chest. He forced himself to look at Julie. "I'd rather not, thanks. There's no easy way to tell you; so I'll say it straight out. We can't see each other any more. I've decided I don't want to divorce Maggie and marry you. Besides hurting her, I think my procrastination has turned your anger against Davey. So we've gotta end this affair here and now."

Julie's face fell and she became very still while she tried to digest the depths of John's conviction. His words were less important to her than the language of his body, the expression on his face, his tone of voice and his eyes. Was he really determined? Had he made a decision or was he only pleading for more time? She decided to stall. "Why, John, you shouldn't take my complaints so seriously. Maybe I *have* been too hard on Davey; but I can change that easily. Let's not do anything that we would regret later. I'll try to curb my tongue and my impatience. Come on home with me and let's talk in comfort."

John felt sorely tempted. Surely one last time in Julie's bed wouldn't do any more harm. And she gave him such a fine sense of control and dominance. Hard and soft; taking and giving; back and forth. But a small voice warned him against the slightest concession to his weakness. "Sorry, Julie. I've made up my mind; there's no wishy-washy indecision about it. I just hope you won't take it out on Davey."

My God, he really means it! Julie felt a pool of acid anger build in her stomach, rise to her esophagus and choke speech for an instant. Her face changed from a tired loveliness to a scarlet flame around eyes through which she poured bitter resentment. "Do you honestly think you can prance in here and break off our affair without warning? What do you take me for, your doxy, your "other woman" that you can cast aside at your pleasure? *I* will decide when this affair ends, not you." For a moment, she turned away from John and stared out the window at the dusty road past the schoolhouse. Her failure suddenly overwhelmed her. "What happened? Did Mommy find out and threaten to kick you out? Did you crawl?

That would be your style; there isn't much man left in you, is there?"

John was grateful that she was so vehement, so outraged. It made it easier for him to watch the fireworks in silence. The least he could do was to allow her to vent her anger on him. While she raged, he cooly compared her style with Maggie's and drew some comfort from the difference. Maggie would never have demeaned herself by cursing and shrieking like a fishmonger. When she became angry, she turned into an iceberg, freezing her adversary with chilling silence. Julie became a tidal wave, hoping to drown her enemy with a fiery torrent of abuse. John thought heat was easier to handle.

When Julie finally exhausted herself, John said, "I'm sorry you've taken this so hard. If you had taken it differently, I might have felt obligated to explain myself. But I can see that no explanations will suit you. So I might as well leave."

"Are you taking Davey out of school?"

"We thought of it. But I can't believe you'd take vengeance on my son. If you tried somethin' like that... well, I'd have to crush you and drive you out of this town, Julie." He turned to walk out and then paused in the doorway. "I'll never forget you. You'll never know how important your love and affection have been for me. You taught Davey a lot of things; but I think you taught me a lot more, mostly about myself. After some time passes, maybe you won't hate me—or yourself—so much."

Defeated and despairing, Julie couldn't move after John left. She couldn't think. She wallowed in a confusion of emotions, denouncing herself for her childish dreams and pretensions. Men! How could she have forgotten that they're all selfish, pleasure-seeking brutes. And John Harrison was fully qualified to lead the pack. Well, she would show them all. One day, her chance would come. And in the short run, she *would* make life hell for his brat. Maybe she could make life hell for Maggie as well, and drive *them* out of Carmel. As she drove her carriage into Carmel, she began to lay plans for adequate vengeance, one that might redeem her self-respect and vindicate her renewed condemnation of men.

CHAPTER SIXTY

CARMEL VALLEY
FEBRUARY-MAY, 1905

From that day until school ended in late May, Julie besieged Davey with reprisals. She gave him special assignments and called on him for long recitations of homework, which she interrupted with frequent sarcastic questions. His achievements she ignored or belittled; his small mistakes she interpreted as deliberate challenges to her authority resulting in hours after school and even the occasional official ostracism—the lonely vigil in a corner with his back to the class. She didn't have to tell him that his art classes after school or in her cottage were finished.

Once they were released from class each day, Mei-yin could review the day's injustice with him while they walked home. She was curious—and grateful—that Julie focused her hatefulness on him alone. In support, she dropped her classes with Julie also. As baffled as Davey about the reason for Julie's abusive attacks, she offered imaginative flights of fancy, which only revealed the extent to which Maggie's instruction and example had lured Mei-yin away from the wisdom of her own cultural tradition. In China, even children knew that nothing happens without a personal reason. In contrast, Maggie's stories were grounded in credible political, rather than personal, vengeance. ("Julie is a Democrat, a flaming liberal. Poppa and Momma are Progressive Republicans. I bet Julie is mad because Teddy Roosevelt won the election.") In response to speculation among other children about the reasons for Davey's torment, she could only reply, "I don't know the reason why she's so mean to him; but it's unfair and you should be glad that he's taking her punishment for all of us. Who would she pick on if Davey weren't there to take it?" At least Mei-yin understood the role of a scapegoat in all cultures....

Most of the children, except a gloating Juan Cisneros, agreed with her judgment and waited each day for recess to offer Davey small consolation. They came to see him as a kind of hero, unjustly accused but manfully accepting his fate on their behalf. After the final school bell rang to end class each day, everyone was glad to escape from class lest Julie turn her venom on one of them.

Maggie also tried to console Davey. But since she couldn't be honest with him without revealing John's infidelity, her efforts at sympathy were mere band-aids of shallow comfort, suitable perhaps for a minor psychic scratch but inappropriate for the raw wound that Julie persisted in aggravating until it festered and itched and irritated him throughout his day. Under normal circumstances, Maggie would have confronted Julie with protests about her blatant discrimination against her son. These were not normal circumstances.

First, the extra work imposed on Davey was not so excessive as to justify a formal complaint to the school board. Second, although Julie might be found guilty of disliking Davey, it would not be reasonable for Maggie to try to mandate a change in her attitude. No teacher could be told whom she must like or dislike. Even if she had been warned by a sympathetic member of the board, she had too many subtle weapons of intimidation at her disposal. And anyway, third, there was no doubt that Davey's personality could be abrasive and exasperating. When he wanted to, his eyes, silently accusing, could make any adult squirm with indignation. If he were confronted by questions that he chose not to answer, he could fall behind a mask of infuriating politeness. ("Yes ma'am; no ma'am; I'm sorry ma'am; I don't *have* a reason ma'am.") Maggie herself had endured those tactics when she had forced Davey to choose between an outright lie and silence. His mastery of the role of polite, dutiful son sometimes seemed an arrogant parody of prevailing social custom. ("A child should be seen but not heard.") Julie's handling of the boy might thus be seen as a reasonable application of the popular aphorism, "Spare the rod, spoil the child." Indeed, Julie never touched him physically. But fourth and finally, Maggie could not bring herself to confront her husband's former mistress in some brawl that Julie would almost certainly reduce to the gutter level. Maggie didn't want to give the harlot the satisfaction of seeing her pain, even if her silence only added to that pain. Her very essence, her natural passion for the underdog, cried out for equity. Paralyzed by conflicting emotions and impulses, the burden of her silence, even with John, and her powerlessness exacerbated her misery and her sense of alienation from him, Carmel polite society and even ranch families.

Also, her doubts about her own responsibility eroded her self-confidence. Her experience with Chinese peasants and her Chinese teachers had taught her that no crisis was a one-way street, especially in marriage. She spent hours alone in the library in a review of her own contribution to the crisis of her marriage. At the head of her list of personal flaws were her inordinate expectations of John, their marriage, Davey and herself. In order to freeze the stage set and the characters in the theatrical production of her life, she had waged a life-long battle against her need for complete control of everyone and everything around her. If anyone failed to fulfill an assigned role, Maggie unconsciously—self-righteously—judged such a failure as a *deliberate* betrayal. Now she reminded herself that even Lin T'ai-chi had warned her that the path of her soul's salvation would be littered with disillusionments, including those ambitions that she had satisfied only to see them breed new yearnings and new betrayals. That John had fallen into the same trap did not permit her to ignore her own flaws and warped priorities. Now Davey, among others, was paying the price for her selfish obsession with philosophy and ESP and paranormal phenomena and, most recently, the sweet success of politics.

Her sense of outrage and victimization was mollified somewhat when John promptly ended his affair with Julie. But she couldn't be sure that the public display of fidelity didn't mask the affair conducted underground. She suspected that behind her back, people smirked at her past innocence and gullibility and her present discomfort. Only Ned Ambler paid no attention to gossip and rumor. Instead, he became a rock of sanity offering neither consolation nor advice. And so she waited for something to point the way through what seemed to be a very cloudy future.

John could offer Davey no more satisfying solace than could Maggie. Even when he helped with Davey's homework, John felt more tongue-tied than usual. He was frustrated and baffled at his powerlessness against

Julie and Maggie. Nor would his pride permit him to seek help from friends like Ned Ambler, who might have played friendly mediator. Like Maggie, he sought no haven among friends, whose suspicions, speculations and jokes he preferred to avoid. Confounded by his own doubts and demons of failure, he felt blocked by a sense of paralysis. His only tactic, usually on Saturday, was to invite Davey into Monterey to the literal and figurative warmth of his mechanics' jocular raillery and fellowship.

As the months passed and May brought the promise of an ending to his torment at school, Davey's sense of isolation and rejection guided him inexorably to two life-shaping conclusions. First, as he had concluded after his fight with Juan Cisneros, he could easily learn and abide by most social rules, but sex was a dark cave full of mortal dangers. Second, he could no longer depend upon his parents to guide his decisions.

One lesson was clear. The obvious reason for all the misery at school and even at home was physical intimacy with a woman: sex. He didn't understand why it must cause so much pain for everyone. It wasn't reasonable. From what Jaime and Juan Cisneros had told him, it was supposed to be pleasant. But it seemed that ever since he had seen his father in bed with Julie, he had endured nothing but misery from Julie, antagonism from Juan and confusing signals from his parents, whose relationship was still so baffling and so complex as to defy easy explanation. As he approached his tenth birthday, he came to the inescapable conclusion that it was very risky to get too close to most girls or women. In general, they were flighty, prickly, hateful and vindictive if crossed, and much too demanding if you wanted their affection. The very thought of sex with one of them made him shiver with apprehension. That would require more daring than he imagined he could ever muster.

More important for the immediate future was his disappointment with his parents. For several years, they had disagreed on how he should behave for their approval. Their recent dithering on his behalf with Julie belied all their brave words about moral and physical daring. Their explanations for their inaction and their silence were so shallow that either they had never understood him or, more likely, they were terrified. When his discussions with Mei-yin failed to craft a story that would explain their terror, he had to conclude that he must never again rely on them to define his best interests. A tough-minded self-sufficiency within a chaos of confusing family and social rules must be his goal.

To be safe from the kind of trauma that he had endured lately, he would have to be skeptical of other people's motives. Society was clearly insane with whimsy. No rules of behavior or public opinion were guarantees of personal peace of mind. Even Momma and Poppa could get lost. So he must seek anchors for his identity and action in something else, perhaps his Voice—if it would ever come back. In the meanwhile, he must reserve to himself the right to define and interpret prevailing social codes according to his own priorities. No one else could be relied upon. That meant that, lest society or even his parents interfere, he must "go along to get along." If he could persuade everyone that he was loyal to social protocol, he might avoid confrontation and be permitted to pursue his own interests, especially his skills with tools, music and art. If that philosophy only reinforced his commitment to pretense and even deception about the real world, well, "All the world's a stage...."

To Davey's surprise, Juan begged his forgiveness. "It was a stupid thing I did," Juan said. "But... well, you're my best friend and... it's no fun to be... alone." They began to do their homework together in the barn, sometimes in the loft where bundles of hay served as desks for their papers and sometimes in the carpenter shop, where model gliders and long work tables reminded them of their bygone days in the air. By late May, Juan had persuaded Davey to experiment with smoking, a skill that no one had warned him against and seemed to be the mark of manhood, which Davey believed had been thrust upon him before he was quite ready for it. Maybe skill with a cigarette would validate his maturity some day when his parents and friends least expected it. In any case, smoking with Juan would satisfy his curiosity and confirm their new friendship. Thus did Juan set the stage for a fateful convergence of forces that would overwhelm the Harrison family in early summer.

CHAPTER SIXTY-ONE

CARMEL VALLEY
JUNE, 1905

At around eight o'clock in the morning on June 4, three days after Davey's tenth birthday, Juan Cisneros led Davey to the barn to discuss possible adventures for the day. They climbed a ladder, pushed through a trap door and settled down on a bale of hay to enjoy their first illicit smoke of a day that promised to be a well-deserved celebration. School was over! Lazy summer beckoned. And Davey felt an unfamiliar sense of peace in a world which the adults had certainly brought to confusion and disarray.

"Carajo!" Juan exclaimed when he failed to budge the doors that normally opened on the second floor of the barn to permit the lifting of hay bales from a wagon into the hayloft. "I think Jaime closed these doors yesterday to keep the hay from getting wet. He must have wedged a stick into the outside hasps. Should I get a ladder outside and open them?"

"Why bother?" Davey replied. "It's not very hot now. Later we can move down to the carpenter shop if it gets warm."

Juan brought out his cigarettes and idly struck a match. He lit one for Davey, lit his own and, mindlessly, tossed the match away. Davey experimented with the gestures, language and ritual of a smoke. He still couldn't inhale without violent coughing. As usual, he chose to defer that trial and test until he could muster the necessary courage to endure Juan's invariable laughter. Fifteen minutes passed before he noticed the fire that was already burning merrily. "The hay's on fire!" he cried while he stripped off his shirt and tried to snuff it out.

Even after Juan followed his lead, their gestures only seemed to fan the flames. When it became obvious that they must get help, Juan raced to the trapdoor. It wouldn't budge. He screamed, "Help me, Davey; if we can't get this open, we're trapped."

Unfortunately the inset handle of the door could accommodate only one hand. In sudden shock, the two boys realized that they could be roasted alive if they failed to attract attention from some farmhand. They raced to the upper story doors and began to scream through the cracks for help.

John slept late that morning. There were few chores facing him and he too could review his priorities for the day—for the whole summer. Uppermost in his mind was his desire to please Maggie. He reached a hand across the bed to find that she had already risen. He closed his eyes and prayed silently for God's help to save his marriage. He had been doing a lot of praying lately; for the first time in his life he was giving serious thought to the fragility of his strength and his will. The last few years had eroded his life-long belief that he was indomitable. So many failures and so much disaster could not be random accidents. He hoped that a dialogue with God might clarify their meaning. He swung his feet out of bed, went into the bathroom and stared at himself in the mirror. Nothing missing; same bronzed face, sad eyes. After he shaved, he wandered into the kitchen where he found Maggie conversing with Ah Ying.

"*Ni hau ma?*" Ah Ying asked with a smile. Sipping coffee, Maggie looked up and offered him a tentative smile of greeting.

"And a good mornin' to all. Where's Davey this mornin'?" he asked.

"My goodness," Maggie replied. "Davey and Juan disappeared more than an hour ago into the barn to plot their day."

John cast a glance out the west window toward the barn and froze in horror. "My God, Maggie, the barn's on fire!"

Maggie rushed to the window to see that a halo of fire encircled the top of the barn while slender shoots of flame were working their way down the western edges threatening to envelop the workshop. Smoke poured from the cracks and crevices of the structure. She turned pale at the thought that her son might be trapped somewhere in that oven. "John, it looks... it *feels* like... like it's bulging..., like it's under pressure from the inside. Oh God, what can we do if the boys are in there? Could it explode?"

John was already racing out of the kitchen as he cried, "Sure it could; depends on how hot the air is. Get Ramon; he'll know what to do." He had seen barns burn before. He knew that the greatest danger came from superheated air, primed for a trigger of fresh oxygen. As he ran the hundred yards to the barn, his mind raced. *The wind is rising from the west. If this thing gets out of hand, it could threaten the house. I'm glad we moved all the horses out when I converted half into the workshop. I hope to God the boys aren't in there. I'll have to get in…. But how? If I open those upper doors, it'll feed oxygen into the fire. The whole hayloft may blow up in my face. I'll try the trapdoor first.*

But the heat had expanded the wood so much that the interior already felt like an oven. The trap door wouldn't budge. He could hear pieces of roof joists crashing down on the floor above. He sensed an expansive thrusting outward as if only a few minutes remained before the pressure of heat and smoke might explode the structure into kindling. He raced past empty stalls to the outside and found a ladder. Out of the corner of his eye, he was glad to see other men mobilizing a water brigade. Until that moment, he wasn't sure that the boys were still in the barn. He almost backed away to let the barn destroy itself while he supervised a backfire between the barn and the house. But then he heard the faint cries of their voices near the upper doors. He climbed the ladder and yelled, "Davey, get away from these doors. When I open them, no tellin' what will happen. Get down low and stay away from the doors!"

Taking a deep breath, John took off his shirt and draped it around his head. Then he slipped the wedge out of the hasps. The doors opened outward with such explosive force that one struck him in the face and almost hurled him to the ground. That might have been a blessing compared to the ball of fire that enveloped his head and shoulders. He slapped down the flames licking at his hair and yelled, "Where are you boys?" Through the smoke and burning hay, he could see nothing; nor could he hear the voice that had called to him only a minute before. Were the boys hidden behind a wall of burning hay? Were they so terrified that they couldn't answer? Or did the noise of crashing timbers and crackling fire drown out their cries?

It took only a moment for John to see that the roof was about to cave in. In a matter of seconds, the entire upper floor would be engulfed in flame. Then he saw the boys huddled near a bale that was already ringed in fire. He surged forward, seized the nearest, Juan, and carried him to the open doors where Ramon waited to take him down the ladder to safety.

"The roof is about to crash, patrón!" Ramon cried. "You can't go back. You must come out now."

Maggie, standing at a distance, could see that John had rescued Juan. But where was Davey? *I couldn't live if he died,* she thought despairingly. *Oh Lord, give John the strength and the courage to go back in there!* Mindlessly she noted that the workshop had just caught fire. *All of John's work, his models, his precious plans, his tools and... his dreams—gone. A terrible loss. But nothing if he leaves our son to burn to death.* "John," she screamed, "Get Davey!" "Get Davey!"

"I'm going after him!" John yelled. He cleared his lungs with a deep inhalation, then plunged back into the thick smoke. He raced to the bale of hay, rimmed with fire, and seized Davey's legs. Just as he gathered his limp body into his arms, the wall of hay bales dissolved into flame and set that section of the floor on fire. Hunched over to protect Davey from falling embers and shingles, he carried the boy a few steps when he suddenly felt the floor begin to give way behind him. *I'm not gonna make it!* he realized as he watched Ramon stretch his arms out for the boy. Instinctively, he heaved Davey to Ramon even as he felt himself falling under a fiery rain of flooring, roofing, shingles, joists and hay. When he struck the ground, it felt like he'd been thrown from a horse.

Heedless of searing pain on his back, he shook off burning debris and began to crawl under a fiery beam toward the main doors of the barn. Hot nails and wood splinters hammered at his back while he crawled through a wall of fire. Twice, heavy wood wounded his back, which felt as if someone used it as an ironing board. Instinctively fearful of hot smoke, he held his breath until he reached the main entrance to the barn, where the shock to his system finally overwhelmed him. As he slid into unconsciousness, Ramon and others gently wrapped his burning body in blankets and carried him away from a fire that had destroyed the workshop and was spreading across the dry grass to the western wing of the house.

Sputtering and gasping, Davey soon recovered and tried to wiggle out of his mother's tight embrace. But she wouldn't permit him to move lest he endanger himself once again. She watched in horror while the westerly wind blew the fire to the northwest corner of the house almost as if an unseen hand was determined to invade the library. The fire brigade finally halted its progress, but not before it burned a wall of books. She closed her eyes and squeezed herself as if to withdraw into herself, perhaps to banish the image of so much destruction. She turned back to Davey with a keen awareness of gratitude. *What matters is what has been saved: my son. Let me never forget again; nothing else matters.* Then she saw Ned Ambler kneeling over John.

"Poppa saved me, Momma; he saved my life. Is he all right? Is Juan all right?"

"Juan is fine, Davey. But... I think your Poppa has been severely burned. Let's go take a look." They reached John's side at the same instant that Ned Ambler was gently removing the blankets around John's body. "Why Ned, how did you get here so fast? What a blessing!"

"I was on my way home from delivering a new baby when I saw the flames." As if he were in a cathedral, Ned talked quietly. "I've seen a lot of courage in my life, Maggie. But this man...." His eyes brimmed with tears and, for an instant, he couldn't continue speaking. "You can have no idea what love he must have felt for Davey to overcome his lifelong fear of fire."

"Why Ned, he never told me that!" *Fu t'ang tan huo* popped into her mind, a sudden regression to her childhood. *He really walked on fire and risked his life for me.*

"John doesn't *talk* a good game about courage or strength or much of anything, Maggie. But I think he's the most courageous human I've ever met. I arrived just as you yelled at him to save Davey. I saw the expression of terror on his face. But he willingly offered his life for the boy, certainly because of his love for him, maybe because of his love for you. Remember that in future years when you think about him, accuse him of his many flaws. Today, he redeemed all of himself."

"I'm glad you told me, Ned," Maggie said with tears in her eyes. "Will he be all right?"

At first glance, Ned was reassured. John had somehow defended his face from the flame. Aside from singed hair, he looked fine. However, as Ned unwrapped blankets, the horror of his burns revealed themselves. While he had crawled, fiery hay and shingles had burnt the back of both legs. Before Ramon had put out the fire with blankets, John's shirt and back had been scorched. "My God, Maggie; he must have collapsed from intense pain. He has suffered at least second degree burns across his entire back. We must move him out of the sun into the house immediately."

They lifted him onto a stretcher and carried him into the bedroom. Then Ned closed the bedroom door and excluded even Maggie, who had to wait in the same hallway where John had waited for Davey's birth ten years before. Once John moaned, "Hurts like hell, Doc." Ned replied, "Good! That means your nerve endings are still alive and screaming. If there were no pain at all, you probably wouldn't have long to live. Now shut up and sleep." He cursed his primitive knowledge of the skin and the best treatment of fire burns while he examined John's back and legs. He had just bought Doctor MacLeod's Handbook of the *Pathology of the Skin*. But a cursory glance at it had not rewarded him with much more than a shallow knowledge of the horror on John's livid body. Large areas of the back and legs festered with small blisters. In a few places, the skin had been burned crisp with pieces of skin hanging loose over angry red, black and yellow discoloration. Once he had completed his examination, he concluded that John's lungs were the first order of business.

"Maggie, I'll make no bones about it," he said as he exited the room and closed the door. "John faces a fight for his life. I don't dare move him to the hospital in Monterey now. He's gonna have to make his fight here. Are you up to it? Will you help?"

"Of course, Ned. How badly is he burned?"

"We're lucky; his lungs appear to be fine, God knows how or why. But his burns are bad second degree and some few third degree. He collapsed from unimaginable pain. My first concern is shock."

Despite a knot of guilt that contracted her stomach, Maggie tried to be clinical. "What are some of the symptoms and consequences?"

"He has all the symptoms of traumatic dehydration: pallor; cold feet and hands; dilated pupils; weak, rapid pulse; low blood pressure. That fire sucked him dry and reduced the efficiency of his circulatory and metabolic processes. You better expect sluggish mental reactions when he awakens."

"What can I do? Feed him whisky?"

"No, no stimulants. Quiet and rest are paramount. He's gonna feel very cold even though he may be seized by severe fevers. You gotta keep him warm; but the problem is that you can't cover his back with anything that might infect those blisters. I'd prescribe a light blanket on top of a clean sheet."

"What about melted butter or grease or lard? I seem to recall that's what my mother used once in China."

"Lord love you. Maggie; we've advanced a little since then...," Ned said with a smile, "but not much. Those things would only threaten infection, our biggest enemy after shock. He needs a tremendous replenishment of liquids. Before I leave, I'll inject him with a normal saline solution with six percent gum acacia. As soon as you can, you should make him drink all the water and orange juice he can drink."

"Should I bathe him frequently?"

"With any luck, you won't be able to move him for two or three days. He'll do a lot of healing in his sleep. Until he awakens, a damp sheet spread lightly over his legs and back will be all he could take. Your biggest problem will be to replace the sheet every two or three hours to be sure it doesn't dry out and stick to his skin. You can't do this alone; get Ana and Ah-ying to help."

"What should we do after he can stand?"

"Plunge him into tepid baths. Make him sleep on his stomach. And talk to him; read to him; bore him to death so that sleep is preferable. In cases like this, I believe in a lot of sleep."

"What about pain? Won't the pain keep him awake?"

"Maybe. That's why I'll also give him morphine now. That'll reduce his awareness of pain and the saline solution will help his body retain its fluids."

"How long will it be before..." She almost said, "before I'll know if he's going to live." But she continued, "before he recovers?"

"My rule is that for every percent of area of the body burned, he'll need a day to recover. Maybe twenty percent of his body has been burned. If as little as a third of his body had been burned, he would certainly die, regardless of the degree of burn. He'll need at least three weeks, probably four, before he's out of the woods."

"When will he be recovered from shock?"

"In two days, at most. Then fever and infection will threaten him for perhaps two weeks. Our big problem then will be complications like bronchitis, pneumonia, meningitis, pleurisy, maybe even ulceration of the duodenum. After *that*, he'll need at least a week or two to recover." He thought for a moment about the burden he was inflicting on her. "If this gets too hard for you, we should probably move him to the hospital."

"Never, Ned!" she answered with a ferocity that startled him. "I won't send him away to strangers. He offered his life for Juan; for Davey... and for me." She choked on a powerful emotion that suddenly seized her, then added in a whisper, "Now it's my turn. I'll mobilize everyone and everything here to help him. Thank you, Ned, for being here, for being our friend, for being... my teacher."

CHAPTER SIXTY-TWO

CARMEL VALLEY
JUNE–AUGUST, 1905

John's recovery proceeded almost exactly as Ned Ambler had forecast. During the first forty-eight hours after the fire, he was delirious. But morphine helped quiet him and symptoms of shock began to disappear as his color returned, his shivering stopped and warm extremities evidenced a revived circulatory system. Maggie wondered at his meaning when, from a deep sleep, he said morosely, " I don't *want* to go back!"

For the next five days, morphine could not completely banish the constant pain that tortured his back and legs. Maggie mopped his brow, dried his blistered skin with towels, fed him orange juice, water and chicken soup, exercised his legs daily and forced herself to let nature take its course. She slept peacefully for the first time only after she knew that his fever had broken. At the end of the first week, he awakened, quiet, thoughtful and very hungry. That's when she began to read to him while he lay on his stomach and stared at the floor. She felt increasingly concerned about his apparent depression until she read a letter from Tom Baldwin.

July 20, 1905

Dear John,

Lots of things have happened since my last letter. In late January, Roy Knabenshue piloted California *Arrow* for forty-five minutes in Los Angeles. In mid-February, Roy raced *Arrow* against a Colonel Hancock in a fast auto from Chutes Park to the golf course at the Raymond Hotel in Pasadena. Roy beat Hancock by only two minutes. About a month later, I sold *Arrow* to some eastern toffs; but a fellow named

Stevens has flown it until recently. He told me that he's going to give it to the Aero Club of America when the club finally gets organized some time this autumn.

You should take an interest in that club. Its list of August members includes some of your old cronies in New York:
Harry Payne Whitney, John Jacob Astor and William K.
Vanderbilt, Jr. They're planning their first public show and
exhibition for next January. They'll hang *Arrow* from the
rafters of the 69th Regiment Armory in New York. Glenn
Curtiss will display several of the engines that you designed for him. Sam Langley, Octave Chanute, Alexander Graham Bell and the Wright brothers will attend. I expect you'll
receive an invitation soon.

You should also receive another plea from Glenn to move to
Hammondsport. His business is busting out all over, now that
he has built a factory building there. But he sure needs your
engineering talent. You should know that your name is spoken
in hushed whispers around his house. He and the Hammondsport
Boys seem to idolize you. Last November, I tried to convince
them that you are just as mortal as they are, but they trace
their success in the motorcycle game to your fateful bicycle
race when you and Glenn beat them all.

Maggie paused at that paragraph and smiled at John. "You never told
me that Glenn Curtiss wants you to go to Hammondsport. We'll have to
talk about that." She couldn't decipher the dull, placid expression on
John's face. Was it the morphine? Or was he even listening? Where *was* he?

You may have heard that your neighbor, John Montgomery,
has sued me for $100,000. I think he's really mad because I
lost interest in him last year. He alleges that I promised
him a lot of money and half interest in *Arrow* in return for
teaching me aerial navigation. Isn't that a laugh? What he
knows about aerial navigation you could fit into a thimble.
Most interesting is the fact that in April this year, he applied for a patent on his monoplane design and his system of
flight control, including wing-warping. But the Wright

brothers had already beat him to the punch. Chanute told me
that Will Wright knows about Montgomery's work but doesn't
respect it much because it's "unscientific." Incidentally,
Will thinks I'm just a "profit-seeking showman." I'm not
complaining.

I expect the court to throw out Montgomery's case, which
is full of hot air. But the interest in aviation up there
persuades me to come back North. I'd ask you to join me; but I
think you really belong in Hammondsport in charge of building the best small engines in the world. If I have one of your
engines in a dirigible, I can feel confident that it won't
quit on me. You should move this summer and stop wasting your
days on bicycles for elderly matrons.

"Now tell me about this business with Glenn Curtiss," Maggie said as
she laid the letter aside.

"Glenn's been after me for three years. Last November, Tom Baldwin
visited him and persuaded him to improve his engine for a series of '*California Arrows.*' During their discussion, as they warmed up to each other,
Tom raved about my design skills so much that Glenn urged me once
again to come to Hammondsport."

"Johnnie, would you like to move?"

"Come sit on the floor so I can look at your eyes." John looked at Maggie for a clue to her own thinking. Since the fire, his priorities had endured
a revolutionary shift in favor of his marriage and his family. "Tom's letter
makes a good case. I'd go if you would. The air age may seem to be just a
tiny stream now; Whitehead and the Wright brothers are just a trickle. If I
join Glenn now, maybe I could help make it a powerful river. I'd love that
challenge." He liked how she didn't seem to disagree: no frown; no glassy
stare; no tension. "And maybe all of us could use a change of scene."

Privately, Maggie agreed with that assessment. After seeing Julie
Simmons' treatment of Davey in the Fifth Grade, she could easily imagine
a repetition of her vindictive discrimination in the Sixth. Also, the destruction of her books and John's models symbolized an ending to a life
that had turned sour. For five years John had been spoon-feeding his most
compelling addiction: the romance of flight. Maybe it was better to en-

courage that passion than to waste any more energy on Julie....That John had turned a corner and had retrieved some of his vitality thrilled Maggie. But she wanted to be sure that the move made sense. "Why Hammondsport and Glenn Curtiss?"

"I think the key to commercial flight is gonna be a light, powerful, reliable engine. Glenn Curtiss is buildin' my designs right now. I think I can improve them. I think Tom's ready to join Glenn, too." John thought, *Enough of explanations. I can't stand all this talk anymore. I've got to know if she's made up her mind. If I lose her and Davey, then nothing's worth a plugged nickel.* "Is it possible to put my betrayal behind us?"

Maggie's Chinese upbringing now came to John's assistance. In the hands of her Chinese teachers, she had learned that no crisis could ever be a one-way street, especially in a marriage. If she wanted to preserve her marriage, it was time to meet John half-way. "Johnnie, don't think your adultery is something I can forget in an instant! Remember, I've been living with it for two years. I'll need more time for it to fade into history."

John thought, *Well, what the hell. What more can I expect, even from her. That's the bad news. I wonder if there's some good news as well?*

Maggie leaned against the bedside table and smiled sadly at John. "Your experience underscores the idea that lust and elegant things and social status and rank and achievements and other such false gods don't guarantee inner peace."

John nodded. "So you think serenity comes from treatin' wealth and fame like... like trifles?"

Maggie smiled her gratitude for his insight. "I believe Julie Simmons was your answer to a long list of failed expectations of yourself. But you're much more than an engine designer. If that's all you think you are, that's the way you'll behave; and you'll put everything else at a lower priority than your engine."

"You say I'm much more than an engine designer. And you've tried to teach Davey the same idea—or he taught you." His eyes brimming suddenly, John turned his head to look out the window. "I wonder if I discovered who I really am during the fire?"

"What do you mean?"

"It's hard to explain—just a fantasy, maybe. There was a moment when I was lyin' on the ground; but I wasn't *really* on the ground." He frowned in confusion, wanting to make Maggie understand and perhaps explain the whole thing from her reading in philosophy. "Anyway, I found myself lookin' down on my body, on Ned Ambler, on you and Davey. I was... up in the air watchin' ever'thin'."

"How did it feel, Johnnie?"

"Detached... no connection with my body... no pain...."

"What happened then?"

"I walked into a tunnel full of light. I saw my father—only he was a young man—at the other end of the tunnel, smilin' and ready to greet me. We..., we talked; or maybe I should say that I listened. He said it wasn't my time yet; said I should go back...."

"And you said, 'I don't *want* to go back.'"

"I sure did; how'd *you* know?"

"You spoke in your delirium."

"Can you explain all that?"

"No. I've read about such things in *Borderlands*. And Mr. F.W.H. Myers' recent book on the survival of personality after death mentions such things. But I don't understand them. I'm glad you told me about your experience. It just reinforces my answer to your question about our marriage."

While she paused to collect her thoughts, John thought he couldn't bear the suspense. This was a moment that would change their lives.

"A lot of things have changed in my mind since the fire," Maggie said with a quiet smile. "You revealed something in you that I had forgotten, that even *you* had forgotten: your courage. Especially your courage to love. As long as you love Davey the way you did in that fire, I'll follow you wherever you want to go." Her heart turned over at the expression of joy that came over John's face then. *Maybe it's really going to be all right. And a move may be just what we need for a new start.* "As to Glenn's proposal, I think we should consult the children. Lily has written that she's returning with her father next month to New York City, where she plans to teach Chinese brush painting and make her home. Perhaps it's time for Mei-yin to join her."

"You've given me new heart with your answer, honey. I swear I'll try to see myself and our lives from a different angle."

"We both need to be more alert to people and ideas and things that divert us." Maggie smiled wistfully at the thought of the price they had both paid to satisfy their narcissistic needs. "I think we both tend to invest ourselves too deeply in our causes. If we embark on a new adventure at Hammondsport, once again it will be tempting to hurl ourselves into that community."

"Like letting the job with Glenn Curtiss warp my sense of priorities?"

"Yes. We're lucky because we can always come back to Carmel. We don't have to worry about where the next dollar is coming from. You don't need this job for money. But you seem to think you need it for a clearer sense of your own self-respect."

"The fact is, Maggie, I want *your* respect. When I thought I lost it five years ago, I went nuts."

"Johnnie, I never loved you because of either your money or your reputation. Society may be impressed with such things. I'm not."

"What does impress you in another human?" he asked.

"I'm impressed with another person's ability to forgive people for their fear-driven behavior. Fearful people who rise above it impress me most." *Like the way you overcame your fear of fire to save Davey's life*, she thought.

"That's why you've tried to teach Davey to be fear-less?"

"Yes. I think that's true strength in a person. When I see someone who can look past anger, petulance, jealousy, envy, greed, ambition and many, many other expressions of fear, and extend love instead of confrontation, I'm deeply impressed. It's the way I tried to feel about you and Julie. If our son can learn how to be that way, I'll know we were successful parents."

"But there's a dilemma, isn't there?" John stared out the bedroom window and thought about his life. "Society *wants* us to compete for status and rewards."

"That's true," Maggie said. "But if we soon weary of that game and wish for a deeper meaning in our lives, society isn't much help. Only I can be the judge of the deepest meaning of my life!"

John nodded. All his life he had rebelled against the hypocrisies of polite society. "Then what do we tell our son? He's only ten years old. We still have some time…. How do we help him choose?"

"I don't think we can substitute for his own experience. We can't guard him against life. He has to discover and conquer his own false gods like money, power and privilege. Only through his own personal experience can he hope to learn his own lessons."

"Yeah. Like the rest of us, he'll follow his own path. He'll make mistakes. He'll get lost occasionally. But I trust Davey's instincts. I think he'll pull through childhood in spite of our disagreements and confusion!"

"I agree. I think our battle for Davey's loyalty has had one positive effect."

"What's that?"

"I've noticed in the past year that he has become very self-sufficient in his decisions. Oh, I know he wants our approval and support. but he thinks things through for himself now. He marches to his own drum. Do you know the single quality I would hope that Davey may retain from his childhood?"

John waited.

"I want him to be compassionate and thoughtful. I want him to be generous and forgiving. But above all, I want him to have your daring! I want him to discover what Lin T'ai-chi saw in him five years ago. I want the warrior in him to be empowered. I pray that his youth may not imprison him in fear. So far, I'm simply overjoyed with his willingness to explore the farthest reaches of his mental and physical limits. I think we should be very proud of our son. Of all the things we've done in the last decade, I think *he* is truly something glorious."

CHAPTER SIXTY-THREE

CARMEL VALLEY
AUGUST, 1905

Early in August Davey told Juan Cisneros that the Harrison family might soon leave Carmel. "What makes you think you'll leave?" Juan asked.

"Oh. It's just a hunch." Davey didn't want to share with Juan the thrill he had felt two nights before when his Voice had returned and had told him what was coming. In clear thought-forms, it had warned him of the impending move. He had been so grateful to hear it that he had wept with joy.

Juan's reaction was curious. His expression seemed to be in conflict between a certain sadness and a smile of expectation. Davey's intuition told him that Juan was glad he was going. He was determined to draw the truth out of Juan before he left. "Juan, I think you'll be glad to see me leave. Why?"

At first Juan was tempted to mask his pleasure at Davey's departure. But he decided that Davey deserved to know the truth. "I hate how your family owns everything here. The only thing I own is my poetry and my plays."

"Is that why you fought with me?"

"I guess so. I know you don't think you're better than me. But I'm still hot under the collar about it."

"But what will change when I leave?"

"While you're away, my father will be in charge here. Maybe then I'll feel better. I know it's stupid. But I hate to see you win all the time."

"I think I understand, for the first time," David said softly. "What do you want to do with your life, Juan?"

"I'm going to be a great writer," Juan replied with deep conviction. "I love to hear people speaking my words. It's like... I bring them to life.

Someday, the whole world will read my poems and my plays. Then maybe I'll stop feeling so small when I think of you and your family."

At breakfast the next morning, John confirmed Davey's hunch that they would not spend Christmas of 1905 in Carmel. "Ramon could run the ranch while we're gone. He's running it now anyway. I can return periodically to review things. What do you think?"

Davey waited for Mei-yin's reaction. Now a slender, lovely ten-year-old, blessed with a lively mind, an impish sense of humor and a keen instinct for political manipulation, she was tempted to be funny. Instead, she turned to Davey, who understood that he could speak for both of them. Since the fire, he had been surprised and delighted at the sea change in the family mood. Maggie's tenderness toward John had blessed everyone. John's question made this day special not only because he had consulted the children but especially because it confirmed the reliability of Davey's Voice. Now he could barely restrain his enthusiasm. "I think we oughta go."

"Won't you miss your friends here?" Maggie asked.

"Sure." Davey searched for the right words to express his feelings. Besides his intuitive approval of the move, he felt revulsion at the idea of enduring a sixth year with Julie Simmons. He knew that his freedom from her weighed more heavily in his decision than all the good things about his life on the ranch. "But I don't own my friends and they don't own me. Anyway, they're so clear in my mind that I can always talk to them."

"Won't you miss the shop?" John asked. "You may not be welcome in the shop there."

"I've been reading some of Mr. Langley's papers; I've looked at his designs of his aerodrome. I think it was... clumsy; but I've run out of ideas for sketches. Maybe Mr. Curtiss will have some people there who could help me think about such things. Anyway... I think... I think we've gotta go!"

Later that afternoon he rode to a high hill from which he could survey the valley, the Carmel River, the ranch house with its charred west wing, the Pacific Ocean up valley and a sky so clear and blue and vast that it seemed to enfold him with love. Swooping over his head as if to catch his attention, an eagle caught an updraft and gracefully climbed higher and higher. Watching the eagle soar effortlessly into the sky, Davey glimpsed a memory of another time— another eagle, the image so faint that he wasn't sure whether he had seen it or merely imagined it. But *this* magnificent bird's maneuvers were so hypnotic that Davey thought wistfully, *I wish Poppa and Momma would love each other. I wish they could be high flyers like that eagle. I wish I could be up there right now.*

And then the magic of Becoming happened again. Davey felt a sudden shift of his senses. Instead of looking across the Carmel Valley, he now looked *down* on the ranch and the Aguajito Range between Monterey and Carmel. The wonder of it! More startling than that grand view was his eyes' power of magnification. There a rabbit! There a snake! There a mouse scurrying into his hole! Instead of the former heat of the leather saddle, he felt the fresh caress of the cool moist updraft. He felt the bold strength of his outstretched wings lifting him, holding a long glide, dipping slightly for a better view of the earth below. He felt such exaltation that he prayed it would never end.

A sense of awkwardness suddenly warned that he no longer could control his arms. He turned to see that his eagle's wings had been transformed into rigid, muslin-covered wings stretching away to right and left. What had been a joy of silence became the sound of a very powerful engine roaring behind him. On both flanks he saw other machines that resembled the Wright *Flyer* and yet... they were clearly bigger, more advanced. When a pilot waved to him, he realized that he too was in control of an aeroplane, his feet against pedals, his hands on a wheel and his shoulders in a crude harness.

A strange sense of confidence replaced what had been his mood of confusion and doubt on the ground. He felt... older, almost as if he had grown taller, stronger. Was this a dream? Was it real? What mattered was that all his problems had disappeared, replaced by the joy of such a seamless unity with sky and earth that he felt complete and at peace. When the flight ended as suddenly as it had started and he could feel his pony, Su Su, tremble, the shape and rhythm and feel of his life rested lightly on his mind for the first time in two years. His very essence seemed to be imbued with a new clarity of vision.

To most people, a frail structure made of wooden sticks and wires and muslin might seem ugly. A loud, dirty engine might seem the antithesis of beauty. But he knew that the power and mystery of his vision must some-day transform frail gliders and sputtering little engines into something glo-rious. His lenses were tinted now by that romantic dream, a conviction that hovered behind his every thought.

After that epiphany on the hill the core of his vision became his inner island of sanity—the central meaning of his life—transcending family ties and more important than intimate friendships. As an article of faith he *knew* he had been born for flight....